The Alpha's Kitten

Vera Foxx

Table of Contents

Dedication

I'd like to dedicate this book to my Bergie followers. Without the constant push from you all, none of this would be possible.

Chapter 1
Charlotte

The click of my heels against the dull, New York concrete was quick and precise. The hours of practicing each night at home had finally paid off to the point where I could wear tall heels in public. The one thing I did not account for was the ever-present grates throughout the city. I watched the ground periodically for the ever-boding danger of a quick slip and fall to the ground. My phone began to ring annoyingly, distracting me from focusing on looming grates.

With a huff, I buried my hand inside my trench coat, which elegantly flowed down far enough to reach my mid-calf and began to rummage through the coat pocket. Quickly picking up the ancient, old flip phone, I looked at the number, only to see I did not recognize the number. With a quick sigh, I opened the phone to click the accept button. "Good evening, this is Charlie Crawford from After Hours Computer Care; how may I help you?" I said with the utmost professionalism I could muster.

"Yes, we need service on one of our company computers. Are you available this evening to travel to the Royal Ebony?" the voice asked annoyingly on the line. I glanced at my watch to see it was only 8 p.m., meaning that I should have enough time to make a quick service call before attending my friend's birthday party—at one of her favorite clubs. "Of course, sir, please text me your room number, and I will head that way now. I should be there in 15 minutes."

He said, "Thank you," rather shortly, and then proceeded to cut the call.

1

With a good eye roll, I changed direction and started to stomp my way back to where I had been let off by the taxi only ten minutes prior. I had only just passed the hotel a few minutes ago, so it was a blessing in some ways. I would be able to keep my promise to Ashley and join her at some point in the night and also earn a few bucks to help pay for the expensive taxi ride deeper into the city.

The lighting of the streets began to brighten, and the hotel came into view. It was a massive hotel, one for only the wealthy and money-hungry people. There were no substandard rooms here. All were suites and meant for big CEOs visiting the city or hosting out-of-town guests. There were many times I'd stopped in to drop off business cards at the concierge desk for them to recommend my services.

CEOs and businessmen alike always needed their computers serviced, and it didn't matter what time of day they wanted it. Most large computer businesses had regular business hours. At the same time, I took it upon myself to have a small business on the side instead of my usual 9 to 5 job. It helped pay the extra bills and student loans from piling up. No scholarships here, I had to remain under the radar and a smart kid earned the extra stares.

"Good evening, Thomas," I spoke with a smile to the hotel's doorman. Thomas was in his late 20's but carried the aura of an old soul. He had said once he has worked here for years. It was only a year ago that I met him and took a liking to him immediately. He was the father figure I never had in some ways, always making sure to take care of me. The first night coming to the hotel, he was worried I was some poor child lost in the big city. It was the first time I had to explain to anyone that I was just a computer freak who liked to help people with computer software to earn extra cash.

Thomas didn't like that I went into these prominent businessmen's suites alone to work on their computers, so he started following me and standing outside the door. He always scolded me that I would get in trouble one day, but it has never happened so far. I am always sure to keep room doors open while present and keep my trusty mase with me.

"Well, hello Charlotte! It is good to see you again. Job this evening?" he chided.

"Yes, thank goodness. Things have been rather slow recently, and my bills do need to be paid. You wouldn't have had anything to do with that, would you?" I gave him the side-eye. It was Thomas's job to get to know the hotel patrons. Often, they needed help with computers after hours and would always slip them my business card.

"Oh me? Never." Thomas winked.

"Well, thank you, nonetheless. I'm on the top floor tonight. Don't worry about coming with me." I waved my hand in dismissal.

"Wouldn't dream of it; the man that needs it fixed is a good guy." With his quick nod, I headed to the hotel's golden elevators.

The hotel was grand; the cream of the crop, you could say. Chandeliers, large staircases, and a lot of classical art either hung or sat on tables. Fresh flowers were sitting on every end table, and many maids scurried across every floor.

I made it to the top floor, and I was able to step out with a ding. I wasn't planning on having to walk so much in heels, so I knew my feet were going to be painfully sore in the morning—or even before I had the chance to get to the club. Walking softly to room number 2350, I gently knocked on the door, waiting for the customer to answer the door.

Within seconds the door flew open to show a very disheveled man in his mid-twenties. His hair was a dark brown, along with his eyes. The man was massive, standing at least 6 foot 5 with muscles through his body. There was a light stubble to his face, and his lips were in a slight frown.

"Who are you? We don't do prostitutes here; we also aren't into child trafficking!" he yelled. As he was about to slam the door, I stuck my foot into the door, which I instantly regretted.

"Ouch!" I screamed. "I am not a prostitute; I'm Charlie Crawford, here to work on your computer," I said in slight annoyance. "I know I look young, but I graduated top of my class. I graduated very early from college, so of course, I look young!" I squinted my eyes directly at him as he contemplated my words.

"Your attire doesn't seem appropriate." He spoke with skepticism as he folded his arms across his chest.

"I was on my way to a colleagues' birthday party; your phone call just happened to be intercepted while I was on my way." I tightened my coat tighter around my body. "I usually have different attire," speaking with conviction. "If you have questions about my intentions, you could speak with the hotel's doorman or the manager. I could also leave and let you figure out your computer problem yourself." I turned around, ready to walk back to the elevator when he grabbed my arm.

"Listen, I'm sorry. People are trying to find any dirt on the president of the company, and the last thing I need is some underage person coming into his hotel room." He wiped his forehead with a handkerchief and motioned me back toward the room.

"That's understandable," I said. "If you could, please leave the door open. That would be for the best since the doorman is busy at the moment to accompany me." I walked inside the giant suite; it was bigger than the ones on other floors, and lavish was just a tiny word to describe how it looked.

"My name is Evan," he held out his hand as he walked with me to the large desk at the back of the main room of the suite. There was a laptop with several papers spread across the desk. The room was messy and in shambles. He was most likely dealing his frustration out on documents, small pens and pencils, and maybe a paperweight or two.

"Charlotte Crawford," I spoke. One eyebrow raised in question, and I quickly added, "Sorry, I go by Charlie while doing this job. Most men find women working on their computers either intimidating or a joke," I said with a laugh. With a nod of understanding, he pulled the chair out for me. "So, tell me, what seems to be the problem."

After a brief explanation of the problem and Evan's theories of what it might be, I got to work. Lucky for him, I was able to hack into my computer at home using his laptop to use my own software to scan. I usually bring along my laptop to these things, but I wasn't about to go all the way home for it—and then back again to drop it off.

After a few minutes of scanning, probing, and searching, I realized this wasn't a virus as Evan had predicted. It was something more than that. His computer was in the process of being hacked by an unknown location, and it was doing it so securely that I almost missed it myself. This wasn't going to be a brief virus ridding session, but a full-blown defense and possibly offense job.

"Evan," I sputtered. "How many confidential files do you have on this computer?" Evan looked at me quickly with his mouth agape.

"Everything about the company is on this computer or has access to other computers in the network that could get information," he said quickly.

"We have a problem then, you are currently being hacked, and they are trying to disguise it as a virus. I need your permission to be able to have access to your confidential files before I pursue this. I'll be able to tell you what information they have as well as retrieve it and secure your network." I said while typing on the laptop.

Evan sat and thought for a moment. "I need to know now, Evan. You and your CEO's company are at stake of losing valuable information," I pressed.

"Take care of it." He growled while grabbing a notebook and slung it at me.

"What's this?"

"Passwords you may need to access the files." He said pointedly.

"That won't be necessary; I've already cracked them." I continued my assault on the keyboard while I felt eyes bare into the side of my face. I'm sure he felt threatened now; some young girl had the entire company at her fingertips while trying to fight off an unknown assailant. He's either in awe of my ability or pissed off. I'll take the former.

I grabbed my off-brand AirPods and stuck them in my ear while I turned on music from my home computer to listen to. Linkin' Park was my go-to when dealing with an active hacker. Halfway through the battle, my phone began to buzz from my trench coat. Rolling my eyes and ripped the headset from my ears, and saw it was Ashley. She was going to be pissed.

"Charlie Crawford," I answered, annoyed.

"Where are you, Charlotte? You said you were coming!" she whined.

"I got a last-minute job; give me an hour and I'll be there," I said quickly as I scrolled through the data on the screen.

"You'd better, your quarterly obligation of clubbing is well overdue. You can't skip out on this. Plus, this is for my birthday!"

"I'll be there, gotta go." I quickly hung up the call and stuck the headphones back in my ears.

Evan was pacing across the floor in front of me. His hands were behind his back like he was waiting for his wife to pop out a baby and was awaiting the gender. Every time I made a noise of annoyance or sighed, he would stop and stare. It was funny, and if I wasn't concentrating so hard, I would have thrown some funny comments his way.

I had finally put the defenses up on the network, successfully changing all passwords and even putting up a firewall—designed by yours truly of course; I was now on my last step. Finding the hacker's IP number of the computer as well as a nice picture. My smile must have started to look manic as Evan came towards the desk. He tapped the desk three times with his index finger. I quickly looked up to realize there wasn't just Evan but also another man.

This man had dirty blonde hair, pulled back into a man bun. His face was chiseled to perfection with his striking green eyes. I could almost get lost in his forest of green eyes as he bore into my hazel ones. He was breathing hard, looking at me pointedly as if he was holding back his anger or some sort of inner beast within him. My eyes furrowed, wondering what this god-like of a man was thinking. Possibly upset that I could hack his very own corporate system within a matter of minutes. Go me.

I pulled the headphones from my ears quickly and tried to speak but couldn't. Evan finally cleared his throat, and I was knocked out of my longing daze into this man's eyes.

"Are you finished?" Evan taunted. I cleared my throat.

"Um, yes, actually. I'm working on getting a picture of your hacker. In fact, here you are..." The computer loaded the webcam as you could see a man on the other side. I slid the laptop so both men could see. His skin was white while his eyes looked almost red. His features were sharp, and his lips were in a frown. Obviously aware that I'd captured his face. I quickly hit the "print screen" button to capture the man's face so they could hunt the man down. The webcam was then covered by his hand, and I disconnected his connection to all of the networks.

The printer's noise broke the unusual tension in the room, and I reached for the paper, slinging it onto the desk. I wrote down the IP address and to which the computer belonged, which was Roman Vanderveen. *No, it couldn't be*, I thought. The lump in my throat was slowly swallowed as I pushed it forcefully down my throat. There had to be more than one Roman and *his* last name was Smith.

"Here is all the information you will need to press charges." Quickly logging off the computer, so my home computer was now safe from their prying eyes, I stood up. I fluffed the collar on my jacket, preparing myself for the wind outside.

"I also put on some of my virus and hacker software to help you build a better firewall until you are able to buy something more suitable for your needs. You will also need to reset all of your passwords to be sure this doesn't happen again." I grabbed my phone and earbuds from the desk and put them in my coat pocket, trying to ignore the stare from the blonde god in front of me.

When my eyes lifted, Evan had his hand on the blonde's shoulder. I paused for a moment, not sure what they wanted me to do. "Is there something wrong?" I spoke slowly.

"Where did you learn how to do all that?" Evan spoke. "How could you do all of that in under an hour?" The blonde had both hands on the desk, leaning forward, breathing in deeply. Evan was awaiting my answer, but I couldn't help staring at the man beside him. With a clearing of Evan's throat again, I shook my head to reply.

"Like you said earlier, I'm young-looking because I am. I graduated high school at 14 and continued my computer and software education in college. I'm currently finishing my master's and working as an IT Tech during the day." I started walking around the desk and walked with them to the door. "Just trying to make ends meet." I finished.

"Well, it is quite impressive," Evan spoke with certainty. "I've never seen someone work so quickly and effectively. How much do I owe you?"

"$350," I said flatly. I knew I didn't charge as much as I should with these high-paying CEOs, but the work I did was easy to me, so I shouldn't charge an arm and a leg. I was doing what I like, the thrill of finding a problem and solving it as quickly and effectively as possible.

"That's all? You aren't going to charge me thousands of dollars for a house call? You also did more than remove a virus but saved an entire company. Other people would have become greedy and charged more, especially for Hale Incorporated." Evan reached to his wallet to pull out the money while my eyes widened. Hale Inc.? One of the top physical security consulting companies in the nation. I should have been paying attention to some of the company name headings.

"I'm sorry, I wasn't aware of what company I was working for; I came here to do a job and I treat every one of my clients fairly." I smiled and held out my hand to accept the cash. While we conversed, the blonde was still staring at me. However, it didn't make me feel uncomfortable, just more curious about the man. I wasn't that attractive. The only thing appealing about me was probably the black strappy heels on my feet under my trench coat failed to cover.

"That's honorable of you; hard to find that in the business world." Evan looked at the blonde. My phone started ringing, and I let out another one of my infamous sighs. I held onto the phone tightly while still in my coat to silence it. It was probably Ashley wondering where I was; I still had 15 minutes to get to her drunken birthday party.

"Thank you, it was nice to meet you," I paused, "both... By the way, I didn't get your name, Mr....?" I held out my hand to the blonde, who still had not let me out of his sight since he arrived in the room.

He held out his hand and took a giant breath as he grabbed hold of my hand. Tiny tingles erupted on my hand as I took his in mine. It wasn't a lot but enough to be noticeable. "I'm Wesley, Wesley Hale." His voice was rough, smooth, and gentle. It was enough to calm my nerves. His voice spread over my entire body that gave me a slight shiver. Wesley was better looking than any other man I had ever seen. Instead of a CEO, he could pass for a movie star or model. I'm sure he could have any woman he desires, and they would just be putty in his hands.

Shaking the thought, I quickly shook his hand and pocketed the $350 in cash. "Well, thank you both. I appreciate the opportunity to have worked with you." I then turned to walk out the door. The door gently clicked behind me, and I continued to walk to the elevator in silence. I turned around as I entered the elevator only to see Wesley Hale standing outside of his closed hotel room door, watching me as the elevator doors closed.

Vera Foxx

8

Chapter 2

Charlotte

The walk to the club only took me 25 minutes; these shoes were the only thing slowing me down. I don't know why I had ever agreed to come out; going to large public places with a ton of people was not my style. I could sit at home and not have to socialize with anyone in particular which I would have been just fine with. It was the whole reason why I went into computers.

One of those annoying recruiting companies had actually gotten me to work in the big city to help with IT issues within a pretty sizeable real estate office. When I first moved to this city, Ashley was one of the first people I met. She was one of the best real estate sellers in the company but always had issues with her computer. To her, the print button in a Word document had simply ceased to exist.

I never realized how stupid and annoying people could be when it came to this job. People really did not understand the concept of restarting a computer before calling the on-call IT worker. That's why I had to keep my skills up, do my little side job, and reap the benefits of paying off my mountain of student loans.

I walked up to the club and skipped the line, and after hearing a ton of groans and whines, I tapped on the bouncer's shoulder. "Ashley Brush's party?" I quickly said. The bouncer nodded his head and let me in. As soon as I walked in, I headed to the coat rack and deposited my coat there, and grabbed my clutch that had my credit card, ID, cash, and phone in it.

My dress was a tight pink mauve color that exposed my neck and hugged my entire body. Only small spaghetti straps held up the dress, but with it

9

being so tight, I doubt it would slide down any time soon. I kept a small, cropped cardigan wrapped around my shoulders, covering my back. The length of the dress went down to my knees to cover up my thighs. To say I was uncomfortable was a complete understatement. I hugged my body tightly as I walked through the club and headed straight for the VIP section upstairs.

Ashley's cousin owned the club and let her rent out part of the area for her 21st birthday party. I could already see a lot of people from the office and many people I didn't know. Every hand had a drink, and almost everyone had a date or dance partner with them. I told Ashley I didn't have anyone to bring, but she still forced me to come.

"Charlotte! You made it!" Ashley tried to scream above the music. Her martini sloshing around as she stumbled closer. She was already drunk and ready to party, I guess. I grabbed onto her to steady her in her 6-inch stiletto heels.

"Looks like you are ready to go?!" I laughed.

"Of course not; I'm just getting started. Here, what would you like to drink? I know you aren't much of a drinker, but you have to try something!" She grabbed my arm and took me to the private bar. Several couples were making out, and some sitting on their dates' laps.

"Ashley, this is definitely one of your wilder parties," I spoke with conviction.
"My out-of-town family and friends decided to surprise me; they are heavy on the PDA. Don't worry about it; they will leave you alone." I side-eyed her and her friends and continued to look at the drink menu. "Give me something fruity, and just one." Ashley laughed and held my hand as I sat with her at her booth. I held up my finger and held my head lower to show her my 'in all seriousness' look. She giggled and got me something called an Appletini. It tasted like a liquid Jolly Rancher which only made me squeal and drink it a little too fast.

"Everyone, this is Charlotte!" she shouted, holding my hand closely. "We need to be good to her; she only comes out once every couple of months to appease my clubbing addiction." Some of them chuckled, and I was forced into the booth.

Her friends were amicable, which helped my social anxiety. I was never one to go out to clubs or any place with a lot of people. After my childhood, I stayed to myself. I quickly learned never to trust anyone and telling anyone your secrets was definitely a no-go. People are only out to use others, but I always showed kindness, not being overly bitter about my belief. Do unto others, one of those golden rules I liked to live by.

As I was listening to her male cousin's 5th dumb blonde joke, which I didn't appreciate too much since I was, in fact, blonde, I started to zone out. This happens from time to time when I start to feel overwhelmed. I end up reliving my past while others around me continue in their conversations and banter.

The dark nights with large groups of people in my childhood home flooded my memory. The late nights of people drinking, dancing, and socializing in the tiny, run-down place I used to call home gave me shivers. Never feeling safe, never feeling secure, and never feeling the love of real parents. The foster parents that took me in only gave me the bare minimum and took the state's checks to help raise me for beer and drugs. I bounced around until I landed with my last foster parent, Roman. I was knocked out of my haze by Ashley tapping my shoulder.

"Are you alright there, Charlie?" I blinked a few times and looked up at Ashley, she seemed completely sober, and the look of concern flooded her eyes.

"Oh, of course. I'm good." I drank the last sip of my Appletini and put it down. "In fact, let's go dance." Ashley's eyes widened in shock, and she quickly nodded and took both my hands. Ashley always wanted me to dance with her, and I would always decline. The fear of some man rubbing his body parts on me, people staring at me, and feeling overall uncomfortable was not something I wanted to experience.

I would like to think I was a good dancer; I spent a lot of Friday nights dancing in my room to music videos and watching clubs live from my small apartment while other people danced. I wasn't completely innocent in the ways of those arts. With a few skips and almost tumbles, we reached the middle of the dance floor, and Ashley started to sway along with the music.

It took me a few minutes of learning to let go of my arms and finally feel the music. The dress Ashley made me wear was going to be the death of me. I already felt prying eyes in all directions. As the lights flickered and the room became darker, I began to listen to my body as the music played.

Swaying back and forth, moving my hips and my arms to the beat of the music, I began to get comfortable. I let go of the worry, stress, and anxiety in the middle of the dance floor with so many bodies. Being thankful and grateful, I felt as if a small bubble was around me. No guy had come up to dance with me yet, and I was ecstatic about it. As karma had read my mind, I felt a hand slip around my waist from behind me.

Tiny tingles erupt over my hip as another hand slipped to the other side of my waist. The hand was large, calloused and the thought of repulsion slipped my mind. The alcohol must had fuzzed my worry, I held no fear. Keeping my back turned, I put my hands on top of his as I continued to sway to the erotic beat.

His arms pulled my back to his chest. He was tall, muscular, like a wall behind me. I didn't mind it, not like I should. Our bodies molded together, and I could feel him lowering his head into the crook of neck. His lips graced my exposed skin, and I couldn't help letting a small whimper escape but my lips. His touch felt good, too good especially as his kisses turned into small bites right along my shoulder. Whoever this was, had captured my body in ways I couldn't comprehend.

One of my hands stayed on top of his that sat tightly around my waist while my other arm lifted upwards. My fingers slinked behind me gripping his thick hair wanting those lips to press harder into my skin. I had no clue where I got this sudden urge to be so bold, but I felt comfortable, erotic, with this feeling inside I felt. Giving the pull to his hair, I felt a smile and growl from his lips on my shoulder. Tiny chills erupted across my arms letting me know I was a goner.

Soft little hums left my lips as he continued his assault on my neck. He slowly started to kiss up my neck, and little trails of warmth and tingles went along with it. We were in our own bubble, and I didn't even take notice of anyone around us.

A loud scream over by the bar that snapped me back to reality. I quickly put my hands down and step forward to get out of the man's arms. I gazed over at the bar only to see Ashley laughing and squealing as a man was drinking a shot from her navel. I turned around with a quick laugh, wanting to know where this mysteriously handsy man went, only to see that he was no longer behind me. He could have been anyone, so with a slight huff, I head back to my seat to grab my clutch and go wish the birthday girl a goodbye. I paid my quarterly dues to her and stayed past the well-respected time I usually do.

"Please don't leave! It looked like you were having so much fun!" She winked. "I knew that dress would catch you a man, and such a handsome one too!" she continued to squeal.

"Did you see him?" I asked excitedly. "I didn't see his face. Do you know who he is?" I grabbed her arm quickly, pulling her close to me so I could hear.

"Oh, does dear Charlotte care about a man now?" Ashley cooed while putting both hands to cup my face. I smacked her hands away and stuck my tongue out at her while she hooted hysterically.

"Forget it, you are right," I smiled at her while blowing a kiss goodbye.

"Sure, you won't stay longer? The night is still young!" she yelled while cupping her hand to her mouth.

"I'm sure. Midnight is my limit! See you Monday!" With that, I left the club, both confused yet intrigued by the night.

Chapter 3
Charlotte

After the long trek home with an expensive Uber, I rolled up to my shabby apartment in the edge of the city. It was ten stories high and probably one of the oldest buildings on the block. The foundation was slowly crumbling, and the safety of this side of town was definitely iffy at best.

With my taser in hand, I shuffle through my pockets to grab my keys and open the main entrance to the apartment building. After climbing six stories and jumping three or four broken stairs, I finally reached my door. It was the newest-looking door out of the whole building; I naturally replaced the doors and locks once I moved in just a year ago.

Once inside, I threw my keys to the table at the entrance of the hallway. I bolted the seven locks I had on the door and walked into my tiny studio apartment. My cat, Macaroni, padded up to me with her judgmental look. The only separate room was the bathroom, but even that didn't have a door, just a curtain to divide the living room and bedroom to the toilet and shower. It was alright, though, since I never had anyone over anyways.

I let out a groan and headed to her water and food bowl, filling it with her food and a few treats. Macaroni had been with me since I was 10 years old, dealing with my abusive foster parent. She kept me sane and a reason for living. Macaroni began to make her warrior cry for food and rub her body up against my legs before she dove headfirst into the food bowl.

My small desk with my computer sat near the window that was boarded shut. Windows were a great luxury but also a target for those who wanted to break in. Safety from the outside world was what I craved. I had boarded up my window the second day I arrived here to keep any intruders out. I decided I would just burn up inside the apartment if a fire broke out and called it a done deal. There were only a few cracks between the boards to let me know how the weather was outside.

This was supposed to be my safe place, and I would keep it as safe as possible. Having your guard up constantly was utterly exhausting.

Stripping out of my attire, I head to the shower to rinse off the smell of smoke and alcohol from the club. Hot showers were rare, and since it was in the middle of the night, I knew I would get the bulk of the hot water in the building. With the hot water cascading down my achy legs and feet, I let out a small sigh. I forgot how good hot water really felt.

While getting dressed, I thought of how strange how Mr. Hale looked at me and rarely spoke. His business partner or assistant was doing the bulk of talking while I fixed his computer. Maybe he was one of those men that didn't like to talk to people lesser than him? He was ridiculously handsome and mysterious at the same time. It is the perfect combination for a hot romance novel or for any woman in the city to let their inner sex goddess out.

I checked my computer for any email messages from my professors; it was hard to believe this was my last day as a master's student. I would be officially free from all my education, except for the occasional refresher courses because technology never slows down.

My thesis was nearly finished, and I planned on sending in the final draft in the morning after I proofread it at the local coffee shop, I attend every Saturday. That was my treat for the week since I rarely spend any money and all towards my loans.

With an over-exaggerated yawn, I sat my butt on the rickety bed and laid down. For some reason, my thoughts consumed only the mysterious Mr. Hale and the hot dance I encountered at the club. The tingly touches were the same. He couldn't have possibly been there too, could he? Even though I am totally opposed to any relationships, especially romantic ones, I let my mind wonder of what could have been if I wasn't so broken and messed up myself. I could have been happy in some other lifetime but as far as this one, I knew for sure; I'd be alone.

My alarm woke me from my deep just 7 hours later, and Macaroni hopped on my chest. Smacking the alarm off the table, I threw my arm over my eyes. Macaroni took it upon herself to turn around and stick her butt hole in my face. She knows I hate that, the dumb calico cat. "Good morning to you too," I whispered with a huff.

Again, I got her cat food out, filling the bowl to help satisfy her needs for the day. The cat had a bottomless pit of a stomach and was ridiculously huge. The vet said that was just how her body was built, and she wasn't unhealthy, just big boned. Sure, I'll go with that as long as I don't have to pay more vet bills.

Since I had a shower the night before and wasn't really wanting a cold one this morning, I put on my skinny black jeans, baby blue t-shirt, and a black cardigan. The weather was trying to turn off cold, so layers were a must in the morning. After brushing my teeth, a little bit of foundation, mascara, and lip-gloss, I head out the door and lock the multiple locks on the door.

I take the ten-block walk from my apartment to La' Petite Cafe and order my usual ice vanilla latte with my computer in hand. Scanning through my thesis one more time, I opted to finally hit "send" and hope for the best. I have worked hard to get to where I am, especially after all the obstacles I've had to go through. With this final degree, I could pay off my loans quicker with a better paying self-employed job and hopefully have a tiny house in the country somewhere and never have to be bothered by people again.

I sound like a complete lunatic. I really do not have a fear of people; in fact, I do like people. Unfortunately, they don't like me. Every single relationship I have had, which have all been friendships, ended up in ruins because of my foster parents' unwillingness to keep me, thus sending me away or end up with an abusive man that made me think he cared about me.

I've never had a best friend; I have not confided in people in a long time. Ashley has probably been the closest friend I've had in my entire life, and I've only known her a year at my current job. She still doesn't know a thing about me, and I've been trying to keep it that way; it is best not to get attached to people; it only leads to heartache in the end. If you get too close and form relationships, people get to know you. They find out your past and start putting pieces of the puzzle together. They will realize how broken you really are and don't know whether to give you pity or throw you off the friendship wagon because they just can't deal. Heartache. You only get heartache with these supposed friends. Your heart can only be broken so many times before it can be repaired again.

With one click of the send button, I was free. A genuine smile finally graced my face, the first one in a long time. I was about to reward myself with one of the fresh muffins that just came out of the back of the cafe' when my phone started to ring.

Ashley.

That girl had to be hungover; it was only 9am.

"Charlie!!!" *Dang, she is peppy this morning.* "What are you up to?!" she screeched into the phone.

"How are you not hungover, Ash? You drank a ton and left the club way after me, I'm sure," I joked.

"I had been practicing my entire life for that moment. I'm completely fine!" she chuckled. "Did you send your thesis in? Where are you? What are you doing?"

"Easy there, tiger, I'm at the cafe." I took a big sip of my latte.

"Oh, I'm not far from there; I'll meet you!" With that, she hung up the phone. Ashley had always been the peppy one, and she was indeed lovely. She made my life bearable at the real estate office. The only reason we were that great of friends was because of her constant need for help with her computer. She couldn't even open a PowerPoint without my help. Where did this woman grow up where she didn't learn basic computer skills?

There were weekends I would spend at her place just to teach her basic computer knowledge. She said she was such an outdoor girl that she spent most of her time outside playing and camping in the woods as a child. She didn't have time for computers. Plus, she was homeschooled, and her parents didn't see a need for it.

I enjoyed helping her, however. She could make me laugh, and I loved hearing stories about her family and home. She grew up with a large family, and they all lived relatively close to each other. They were only two hours away from the big city, so she visited almost every weekend.

I had just bought my muffin and sat back down when Ashley burst through the door. She came up and gave me a giant hug from behind, and I couldn't help but stiffen with the sudden contact. "Calm down, Charlie; it is just me." She whispered. Letting my body relax, she grabbed her black coffee and sat in the booth with me.

"So, did you dream of your mystery dancer last night?" She took a big sip and gave me an over-exaggerated wink. I rolled my eyes at the thought.

"No, slept like a baby." I lied. I had, in fact, dreamed of dancing but more so to the mysterious Mr. Hale that couldn't leave my mind. It was like he infiltrated my dreams, and I knew he wasn't going to leave anytime soon. A girl can dream as long as I don't act.

"Hmm, sure." She hummed. "I want you to meet someone."

"If they are anything like your male cousin of yours that kept telling me blonde jokes, I'll pass." I rolled my eyes. Ashley had been trying to hook me up with a lot of her friends from work, but I always instantly denied it. She said it isn't healthy being alone without some sort of romance or at least getting laid. If only she knew how broken I was.

"I don't need a man, and I don't need a lot of friends. I just have to pay off my loans, and then I'll move somewhere outside the city and work from home."

"That sounds utterly depressing." She rolled her eyes. "Why would you want to do that? Don't give me, 'it's a long story' deal either. You have to open up to someone; you keep things to yourself way too much. I'm an open book, yet you tell me nothing about yourself. It isn't healthy."

"It may not be mentally healthy, but it keeps me physically healthy," I mumbled quietly. The way Ashley's eyes softened told me she heard me. "Ashley, you are the closest thing to a best friend I've ever had. I do trust you, but things about me are better left unsaid." I took a small sip from my latte and grabbed her hand across the table. "One day, I hope to tell you." Ashley smiled and squeezed my hand.

I honestly hoped that Ashley would continue to be my friend; it was the first time in a long time someone actually fought to be my friend and ignored my brutal attempts to stay away. Even though she was a partier, she did have a good heart that I had seen so far.

"I'm glad you feel that way, Charlie. Now, about this friend," she continued. I rolled my eyes and shoved a large portion of the chocolate chip muffin in my mouth. I gave out a muffled, "no."

"Come on, he is on his way!" Ashley said in a sing-song voice. Here I am stuffing my face with a muffin, and some guy is on his way. I started shaking my head furiously while forcing the muffin down my throat. With a giant gulp, I washed it down with the rest of my latte.

"Ashley, you can't spring this on me," I seethed.

"You would have never agreed to it! Besides, you have met him before. You met him yesterday."

"Please don't make me do this right now; cancel it!" I could feel my eyes starting to tear up; a full-blown panic attack was in my wake. Ashley had only seen me like this a few times when I had to do a presentation to show people how to put together a PowerPoint in front of her entire floor. That was a tremendous mess.

"OK, OK, chill there. I'll cancel it. I didn't mean to freak you out." Ashley came to my side of the table and gave me a side hug. "I just thought you would get along with him really well. Maybe some other time, alright?"

"Thank you," I whispered. While Ashley was texting on her phone, I got a phone call. Bringing out my old flip phone, I saw a familiar yet unsaved number, so I knew I had to answer professionally.

"This is Charlie Crawford."

"Yes, this is Evan, how are you?" I let out a breath.

"I'm great, Evan. How are you, is there a problem with the firewall?" As I was speaking, I could see Ashley smirking into the phone and looking at me. I gave her a quick eyebrow raise to ask what was going on, and she mouthed, "nothing," and hung up the phone.

"Well, we have a new problem entirely. The hotel's IT guy isn't in the building, and we are having issues connecting our computer with the projector. We were wondering if you could come to help us set it up."

"Sure thing," I glanced at my watch. "I can be there in twenty minutes."

"Great, see you then, Charlie."

"What was that?" Ashley smiled mischievously. "Just a client I worked with last night before your party. They need some help with a projector that won't connect with their computer." I grabbed my bag and took my empty plate to the trash. Ashley smiled and sashayed to the garbage to throw out her coffee.

"You won't have to work too much longer to pay off those loans," she said, giggling. "What are you up to, Ash?" I questioned.

"Nothing, nothing. I'll see you Monday, yeah?"

"Yeah, see you then, I guess." I waved and walked out of the café.

Chapter 4
Charlotte

The walk over didn't take me long since I was on the nicer side of town. The occasional breeze would wind my hair to the back of my neck and then around my side. I didn't mind the cold as much since I started to learn the whole layering process regarding the switch of seasons.

The barely-there tip-tap of my shoes reached the revolving doors to the hotel, and I saw Thomas on the other side. "Good morning, Sunshine. What brings you here on a Saturday morning?"

"Well, why would I be here? I've got a job again!" I smiled and waved.

"You are not here to see me, just because?" He patted his chest. "I've hurt Charlie, I'm hurt!" I giggled at his expense. I pulled out the cookie wrapped in plastic wrap from my computer case and handed it to him.

"Here, how about a truce then. Your favorite snickerdoodle from La Petite." I handed it to him with a smile.

"Charlie, you didn't have to do that. You are too nice for your own good, you know."

"A simple thank you would suffice, Thomas." I waved him off. "Just do unto others," I spoke over my shoulder.

I tiptoed over to the conference room to not be seen by the weekend manager. She hated me with a fiery passion, and I had no clue why. The night managers and the day managers of the hotel appreciated my services to their clients. They didn't even hesitate to take my cards and put them all over the hotel. It was one less expense they had to deal with about keeping an on-call IT person over the nights and weekends.

Not Tammy though, she was a monster. If she saw me come in the door, she demanded to know what room I was going in, what client, and how long I would be working on their computers. Like I could tell her that anyway, everything depended on what needed to be fixed.

As I snuck past the manager's desk and walked down the long corridor to the conference rooms. Evan texted me the conference room number, and I knocked as soon as I rounded the corner. A quick "come in" was spoken, but it didn't sound like Evan.

In all his glory, Mr. Wesley Hale sat in front of the computer at the head of the long conference room table next to the projector. The scowl on his face still made him look drool worthy. It was serious, mysterious, and I couldn't help but let my eyes wander on his tense jawline. I'm starting to think his furrowed brows were permanently creased since I've never seen his face any other way.

His dirty blonde hair was still in a neat bun, and the scruffiness of his beard was still apparent. His jaw was bitten tightly as he continued to click various icons on the screen. As I approached the table, I pulled out the chair and laid my computer case beside me, just across from him. He quickly looked up, and low and behold, he smiled. Damn, his smile looked good. Perfectly straight teeth and the crooked smile were now embedded within my heart.

"Good to see you again, Ms. Crawford." He held out his hand to shake mine. The tingles that I felt last night telling him goodbye were there but definitely stronger. My neck tilted to the side, not really knowing what to think or say about it. Does he feel it too?

A hum almost left my lips when our hands dropped. "Please call me Charlotte, or Charlie, whichever you prefer."

"Likewise, Wesley, of course." He smiled that million-dollar smile. We looked at each other for what could have been hours, but I'm sure it was just a few seconds.

"What seems to be the problem, Wesley?" Wesley swiveled his computer and slid it across the table.

"I can't get it to connect to the projector." He said, frustrated. I looked over his computer, checking for his Bluetooth and Wi-Fi to be connected correctly, only to find the projector couldn't be recognized. I looked at the computer and then glanced at the projector. I couldn't help but start giggling. This was a basic fix, and usually, I get so irritated when people miss such a simple mistake. I found it utterly adorable that the dominant CEO of some big company couldn't realize the problem.

When he glanced at his phone and sent a text message, I pulled the projector towards me and flipped the "on" button after plugging it in the wall. Once it was switched on, the computer screen was automatically flung up onto the wall screen. I made a small smile and looked over at Wesley, who was staring at me with a look of amusement on his face. I quickly hid my smile and pushed his laptop to his side of the table.

"What was the problem?" He smirked.

"Just a little hardware problem; it's fixed now." I almost snorted. He sighed and looked at the screen on the wall and let out a huff.

"I bet I look like a real idiot right now." He put his hand to his eyes and trailed it down his jawline.

"Not at all; it happens to everyone, really." I stood up and collected my things. "I am not even going to charge you; I didn't do anything anyway. You would have figured it out in time." I smiled. What was with me? Usually, I would at least charge for the house call. There was something about him, though. I'm sure he gets whatever he wants with his good looks, and stupid me was falling for him, and I didn't even know him from Adam himself.

"Nonsense, you came all the way here." He started to pull his wallet out of his back pocket.

"No, no, sir. I won't take it. I was just a block away at a cafe. I'm on this side of town a lot." I smiled. "I was just walking out of the cafe when Evan called, so it didn't bother my time at all." I started to head to the doorway when he grabbed my hand. That was fast; he walked all around the table just to catch me?

"Then, at least let me take you out to dinner." I looked at him confusingly. Me dinner? He had to be joking; a guy like him doesn't just ask a girl of my caliber out on a date. I gave a little scoff and laughed. "No, really, it's alright." His hand gripped a little tighter and came a little closer. I continued to back up against the wall. Wesley was just a foot away from my body, and my heart pounded in my chest. What is this guy doing to me? Usually, I would push a guy away.

"It is just a dinner, Charlotte. Just as a thank you, nothing more." He said huskily. I nodded my head; I mean, how could I not with a hot invitation like that?

This is going against everything I have stood for so long. Not getting too involved with people. Ashley and Thomas were the only ones I've let through, and it hasn't been too terrible. One night with the CEO hottie, and he will be going back to where he came from. It is just dinner and nothing more. I'll do it, it's settled, and I'll do it.

"Is that a, yes?" he whispered in my ear. This was so wrong, but right now, maybe I do want to be wrong.

"Y-yes." I stuttered. Wow, that was really smooth, Charlie.

"Great, I'll pick you up at 7." He backed off like he wasn't just inches from my body. I'm pretty sure he would have to bend down to even get close to my ear. That was too hot, way too hot. I quickly opened the door and made quick steps through the lobby, only to be caught by the one and only Tammy Bermgardner. Dang, it.

"Miss Crawford!" She said in a sing-song voice. "What do you think you are doing?" Tammy demanded and put her hands on her hips. I turned around quickly and tucked a stray hair behind my ear.

"I just came from a client; I'm just now leaving." I started strongly. I won't show I'm weak around her. A clipboard came from behind her back and pulled a pen from her ear. Where did that come from, and what is up with the clipboard?

"The other managers and I have decided to have a sign-in and sign-out sheet for you from now on. It is for the safety of the facility when outside services are being provided. You know, for the safety of the customers and those who work here." She snubbed.

I quickly raised my eyebrow, walked towards her to sign the stupid clipboard, and gave her the exact time I was in the building today. As I signed my last initial to sign me out, she took it from me and asked, "Who exactly were you helping this morning, Miss Crawford?" Her middle-aged, middle of the forehead wrinkle line started to twitch. Meaning she was about to get pissy real soon.

"Mr. Hale from-" I was quickly interrupted by the banshee in front of me.

"THE Hale!! You are not allowed to be associated with him or any of his colleagues, they are owners of this hotel, and I swear, if you mess anything up, it would be MY HEAD." Tammy whispered screamed into my face.

"Then who will take care of their computer needs? You don't have an on-call IT computer specialist?" I spoke. "Forget it, that is fine. I'll let them know next time they try and contact me." This was not the time for me to argue. I don't work for her, and I don't work for this hotel. My sanity didn't need this.

Sensing my distress, Thomas came over and held out his arm to grab my elbow. "Is there a problem, Charlotte?" He glanced over at a fuming Tammy fanning herself with the clipboard. "Oh, just someone on a power trip. I'll be fine." I gave a small smile and walked to the door. Hoping for an easy escape, my joy was easily broken because Wesley Hale made his presence known when he entered the main lobby seeing me a bit flustered with Thomas trying to console me as I walked out.

"Charlotte? I forgot to give you this." He held out his hand that had his business card in it. His eyes scanned the scene, and he saw an angry Tammy automatically soften her facial features and walk towards Wesley. "Sir, you won't need to contact her; we will be sure to provide a better service provider for you." Tammy reached out and touched his arm.

Thomas gave a little chuckle, and I looked in between the 3 of them. Something was going on that I wasn't aware of. "Listen here, Tammy, I don't need anyone else. Charlotte will handle all my computer problems. You just go back behind your desk where you belong." Wesley said pointedly with a no-nonsense attitude. Tammy's mouth opened and closed a bit and turned to me, giving me a scowl. She trotted off in her fake Prada shoes and gave me one last glare as she left.

My eyes widened as Wesley got closer to me and handed me his card. "Here is my number if you need anything. I'll be at your place at 7 to pick you up." Before I had a chance to tell him, I could just meet him at the restaurant, he had already walked off, and Evan joined him from the couch in the main lobby. When did he get there?

"Wow, impressive, Charlie. You just bagged the most eligible bachelor." Thomas chuckled as he walked me out. "Don't even think about it, Thomas. Men like that don't go for girls like me except for trying to get an easy lay, and that won't happen." I said meaningfully. Thomas frowned at that statement.

You know he isn't a man that goes on dates, Charlie. He's a really great guy. I honestly think you should give him a chance." I looked at him. Thomas had never steered me wrong before, and here he is defending this handsome man. "How well do you know him, Thomas? Can I trust him?" Thomas knew my trust issues with people; he knew I don't just lightly be friends. It took me a good few months to feel comfortable with him.

"With my life. I promise you that." He said with absolute certainty. "Alright, I'll give it a try. It is just a thank you dinner anyway." As I walked away, I could have sworn I heard, "whatever you want to think it is."

Chapter 5

Charlotte

I stood outside the hotel. Thomas had just had to make that silly comment. I looked up to the sky, and I sighed out the phrase, "Why me?" This is only going to complicate things. I had just gotten my life into a comfortable routine. My thesis turned in; I was on my way to start paying off my loans more effectively and move somewhere outside the city, and then this "thank you date" happened.

I don't even have anything to wear! I'm stuck with either business attire, clothes for work, or very casual clothing that is not anything worth for date. Calling for backup will have to happen, and the only person for that job is none other than Ashley.

Grabbing my phone, I flipped the old thing open and dialed her number. The phone barely gives out a full ring, and Ashley was already answering. "BAAAABE!" she screeched into my now damaged ear. "I heard all about it! Get your skinny ass to my apartment now!"

"What? You heard about what?" I asked confused.

"Thomas texted me!" I kept forgetting that those two are friends and that she likes to keep tabs on me. There are too many connections here; this is why I need to leave.

***

After twenty minutes of walking, I find myself at Ashley's apartment building. It was pretty fancy; it had a doorman as well as a receptionist on the main floor. I had only been to Ashley's apartment a handful of times though, so I knew she wouldn't remember me. "Good afternoon; I'm here to see Ashley Brush." The receptionist looked down from her high desk to scout me out. She gave me a quick nod. "Name please?" "Charlotte Crawford," I said quickly. With another quick nod, she led me to the elevators and pressed her floor number and let me carry on my way. I would kill to have some security like this around my place. I am pretty sure the devil himself could waltz right into my apartment building and burn the whole thing down, and no one would even bat an eye.

Once the elevator let me off, I walked on my tiptoes to the end of the hall where her apartment was. I had gotten in this horrible habit of tiptoeing everywhere. It made me silent so people couldn't hear me, and it just became a force of habit from my earlier years. Before I could even knock on the door, Ashley threw the door open, grabbed my arm, and slung me into the apartment.

Gripping my crossbody computer bag tightly, I saw we weren't alone in the apartment. Several guys as well as girls sitting around watching TV and rummaging through the fridge. They must be friends from out of town for the party. "Hey, guys! This is Charlotte!" I gave a small wave, and everyone's ears perked up and glanced over my way. Most of them dropped what they were doing to come to say hello, and I couldn't help but back up a little.

My social meter was at an all-time high after last night at the club, and this was definitely going to break it. "Easy guys, she's a shy one. Go back to gaming, eating, or whatever," Ashley waved them off and dragged me to her room. I turned around and watched how they kept their eyes on me the entire time as Ashley quickly shut the door behind her.

"What was that all about?" I asked.

"They find you interesting, that's all." Ashley went to her closet to rummage through her clothes.

"I still have your dress; I'll get it cleaned and bring it back to you this week," I said while putting my bag on her bed and looking through her pictures on the walls. Ashley was so flirty and bubbly; she had tons of pictures of her and her friends from back home. Most of the photos were in the woods around large bonfires, and it looks like they always did lots of drinking. No wonder she never has a hangover; she really has been prepping all her life.

I glanced over to one picture that caught my eye. She was standing between two giant Wolves—Wolves so large they were practically as big as cars. Did they live near a nuclear plant?

"Hey, Ash, what is up with these Wolves? They are freakin' huge!" Ashley rushed across the room to see which picture I was talking about. "Oh, those? Wolves get that big where I'm from. They are pretty tame actually," she said, clearly a bit nervous. Her demeanor changed almost immediately though, perhaps to gloss over the subject entirely.

"Now, let's play makeover!" She jumped excitedly.

"No, no… this is just a 'thank you' dinner. So, nothing fancy at all. I just need an outfit that doesn't scream, 'I'm obscenely poor.'" I laughed. "You know my budget is limited; I just needed a little something to borrow, that's all.

"Well, you are getting an outfit but a makeover as well. You have never let me work my magic, and I'm famous for it back at home," Ashley bragged. With a heavy sigh, I agreed as she squealed; she shoved me into the bathroom and pulled out her waxing products.

"HELL NO, WE AIN'T DOING THIS!" I scream bloody murder. Ashley's evil laugh echoed throughout the bathroom, and big hairy men came barging in.

"The fuck Ashley, what are you doing to her?" A man growled into the room… growled?

"I'm getting her nice and waxed for her big date with Mr. Hale!" Ashley giggled excessively. With that, she gave me a large tug and ripped my leg hair that was embedded into my soul.

"OH MY GOSH, PLEASE HELP ME!" I screamed to the man outside. I didn't care who he was, I needed someone to save my poor legs.

The man barged in; he had honey brown hair with deep brown eyes; he was muscular and kind of intimidating. Ashley laughed maniacally while the man gave her a look. "Hi, Charlotte, I'm Ryder. One of Ashley's friends from home." I nodded, and he grabbed Ashley's arm. "Ashley, let's step away from the wax for now. Baby steps with her. Baby steps." Ryder led Ashley out of the bathroom, and I followed, putting a towel around my waist. How she was able to rip my skinny black jeans off my body that fast I'll never know. I went to grab my jeans to put them back on.

"Please, Charlie, don't leave," Ashley pleaded. She took my hand in hers and pulled me into a hug.

"You never trust people and, this guy, I know he is a good guy. I want to see you happy. You are such a good person and deserve it." Those words, it made me want to cry. I've always wanted happiness and to be around people, but I had been taken away, lied to, and broken. Would one more time be OK for me to try and trust someone?

"No waxing, Ashley, or I swear to all that is holy I will kill you and leave." Ashley's eyes lit up, and she squealed. "Ryder has to stand outside the door, so he will help me if you go crazy, though." Ryder laughed and nodded his head as he left the room.

Four long hours later, which included pampering, two movies, music, food, and talking with Ashley's friends and relatives, I was finally finished getting ready. The last thing I really needed to do was get dressed. I didn't realize how close Ashley was to all her friends. It almost made me wonder why she would even come to the city in the first place. Why leave all that family for the cold city? People in the town were mean and only looked out for themselves.

Thirty minutes before my date, a knock was heard at the door. Ashley came back to her bedroom with a white box with a black ribbon around it. It was almost too pretty to unwrap, and it was addressed to me. I'd never gotten a present delivered before. I kept asking if she was sure, it was for me.

"Of course, it's for you silly; it has your name on it." I looked up at her with tears threatening to fall from my eyes. I don't want to cry in front of her, but I couldn't ask for a better day after today with her friends being so kind to me. A present for me was just icing on the cake. "Charlie, what's wrong? Why are you about to cry?" her voice broke.

"I've never gotten a present before," I whispered as I traced the ribbon with my finger. How pathetic was I? Never receiving a present at such an age. Parents and friends were supposed to give you gifts as you grew up, but I never had the chance to. With a gentle tug, I pulled the ribbon to open the box. With a small gasp, I saw the dress. It was a royal blue spaghetti strap dress that flared at the bottom. Small black beading was around the bodice of the dress and the hems. On top of the dress was a small box as I opened it. It was a beautiful red heart single-solitaire necklace. It was small, and it was so perfect. I felt like a princess in a movie.

The small gasp left my lips, and Ashley came and hugged me from behind. "I told you he would be a keeper." She smiled into my neck. "I can't accept this; this is too much. I just fixed his computer; that's all I did," I whispered quietly.

"Well, maybe you fixed something else?" she chided. With a slight chuckle leaving my lips, I picked up the dress. "How did he know I was here?" I turned around to question.

"I've been texting Thomas," she said. I hummed, still too stunned at the beauty of the dress. "Let's go put it on." I walked into the bathroom and closed the door. Looking at the dress, it was beautiful. It was more skin than I was used to show, and I was becoming more afraid to wear it. What if my scars showed? I guess there was only one way to find out.

I took off my clothes and pulled the dress up from my toes to my shoulders. The zipper zipped on the side, giving it a perfectly snug fit. The dress was beautiful, but my scars were not. I silently started to cry, ruining my perfectly placed mascara. The knock at the door had me trying to push the tears away.

"Charlie, what's wrong? Why are you crying?" Ashley asked worriedly. I couldn't even form words to make a sentence. "Let me in, Charlie, open the door." Her voice was panicked. I didn't want her to see me like this. I put a towel around my body to hide the scars and unlocked the door.

The dress that I had borrowed for her party and the club's darkness hid my scars well, but this dress had more of an open back, and it was something I wasn't going to be able to hide. Especially since we would be in a restaurant where lights would be prominent. Nowhere to hide.

"What's happened? Why do you have a towel on?" Ashley's mouth frowned. Should I show her? Should I open up to her? Maybe she could help me hide them? My heart just ached. I didn't want this beautiful dress to go to waste, and here I am crying over my first present I don't feel pretty enough to use.

"Ashley, I'll show you." I sniffed. "It is part of my past, and I've never shown it to anyone on purpose. I need you to help to hide it, make me feel pretty. Can you do that and not tell anyone what you see?"

Ashley nodded, "Of course, Charlie. I would never betray you." She grabbed my hand and held it close to her heart. I want to believe her; I want to know that she won't run away from me. With a slow turn and her to my back, I dropped the towel.

"Oh, my goddess!"

Chapter 6

Wesley

I stormed into my hotel and pulled at my tie. The humans around this city are filthy. Always grumbling about money and how many women they want to take to bed with them. I can't say that all Werewolves are any different in their desires, but it was just sickening to me.

On top of everything else I have to deal with in this city, my Beta, Evan, informs me of an active hacker trying to infiltrate our network. Fucking perfect. Our business typically just handles security on the physical level, such as bodyguards, but lately, we have been trying to get into the technical side. It has been proven difficult just because Werewolves are more physical beings instead of cyber. It will be a great business adventure once we get it off the ground.

I headed towards the elevator, and I caught a whiff of something insanely delicious. I could almost taste the vanilla and cinnamon on my tongue. I rushed past Thomas that was holding open the doors for me. In my crazed state, I didn't even tell him hello.

Taking long strides after exiting the elevator, I only realized the smell grew stronger the closer I got to my suite. I knew Evan was in there; I could smell him too. My Wolf huffed with violence. He better not have touched anything of mine. This smell was too appetizing, and I was almost sure my mate was in the other room.

Barging in the door, I see Evan pacing back and forth in the living room, marching right up to him, grabbing him by the neck, and leading him to the sitting room. "Are you fucking someone in here?" I demanded. My breath, uneven, and my nostrils flared. This wasn't like me; I was a fearless leader but one of the more level-headed alphas in the country. Losing my head over this was going to create some waves.

"No, no, Alpha!" Evan waved his hands and putting them on my wrists. "There is a computer techie taking care of a hacker that is trying to get into the system. I didn't touch her, I swear!" I grunted and put him down.

"Sorry, Remus is on edge, and I'm having trouble controlling him," I growled out.

"Alpha, have you seen her? Is she your mate?" he asked excitedly. "It's a she? The person working in the next room?" I question excitedly. I had been looking for my mate for years; I was a bit older, in fact, a lot older. Werewolves weren't immortal but continue to live until we are killed or die when our mate passes. I was 145 and still had not found my mate.

"Yes, her name is Charlotte Crawford; she does an after-hours computer tech business. She's in there right now trying to find the hacker.

"Shit!" I whispered and walked into the other room. "She is human?"

"Yes, Alpha."

There she was, under the light of the desk lamp, my mate hunched over a computer screen with her light reflecting glasses. The thick-rimmed glasses reflected the computer screen, so I couldn't get a great look into her eyes. I could hear the Linkin' Park in her earbuds as she continued to type away on the computer.

Her hair was strawberry blonde and curled at the ends, giving her an innocent and appealing look. The trench coat she was wearing let me know she wasn't planning on coming here, and the shoes she wore made me think she was going to a party. As she was biting her plump lip between her teeth, her phone rang.

Not being aware that I was staring at her, she quickly picked up a phone I hadn't seen in ages. A flip phone. "Charlie Crawford," she spoke softly with a firm notion in her voice. Her voice sounded like honey dripping from her mouth, so sweet and heady. "Yes Ashley, I will be there. Give me an hour tops," she replied, annoyed. I knew Ashley; I could recognize her voice on the other side of the call. Charlotte has more Werewolf friends than she realizes. She hung up the call and began to chew on her bottom lip again as she pounded the keyboard with her fingers.

Her fingers were so delicate as she touched each key swiftly and effectively. I couldn't help but come closer to her, like an actual wolf stalking its prey. I reached the desk, and she still didn't notice my presence, but I could feel Evan just beside me. Remus must be trying to take over because Evan put his hand on my shoulder and shook his head gently. I was getting impatient; I wanted to see my dear mate's face.

I tapped on the desk a few times, causing her to come out of her daze. She looked up at me with her large doe eyes as she took off her glasses. Her headphones quickly taken out of her ears, and she looked deep into my eyes. It felt like an eternity having her look at me. I tried to memorize every little freckle on her tiny face. I knew she could feel something, but she quickly pulled away when she heard Evan clear his throat. What a dick.

"How is it coming, Charlie?" Evan spoke. With a few more taps of the computer, she quickly slung the laptop around and showed she had not only stopped the hacking but found the name and picture of the guy who was trying to get into our account. We knew it was him all along—well as soon as we knew we were being hacked—but having the physical evidence was all the sweeter.

I couldn't keep my eyes off her, and I knew I was making her uncomfortable, but I couldn't help it. It took all the restraint I could to not touch her and make her mine just in the other room. Her scent wafted into the air as she flipped her collar out and handed me the picture from the printer of the hacker's face. Her sweet smile would forever be embedded into my heart.

What surprised me the most was how she charged so little to take down such a high-profile hacker. Alex Ruffo was a skilled Vampire who helped create computer code when computers were first becoming a thing, and she smacked his screen like he was a bug. She's a fighter and a humble one, and I craved to know more about her. Though the one thing that struck me as odd was that even though the face in the picture was Alex Ruffo, the IP Address to a man named Roman. Strange.

Charlotte was closed off; she doesn't show her emotions. Not to brag, but I have women throwing themselves at me all the time, and she didn't even falter at my glance. She never looked too long or batted her eyelashes at me once. It made me want to chase her and chase her I would.

"I just charge for what I do, I came to fix it, and I did. No worries. I would suggest you get a better firewall, though. I put a temporary one on there until you can hire some better security," she stated as she turned to open the door. Her little walk already had me in a trance. Little does she know she is going to be the one that is the head of security for our pack. Not only is she my mate, but she will help protect the whole pack with her genius. The goddess truly blessed me with her presence.

I went to shake her hand and immediately felt the sparks across my fingertips. She gave me a quick look and took her hand away, and with a small smile, she left the room. My mate was going to provide me with a chase, and I would enjoy the hunting. The little game of cat and mouse has begun, and I will have her no matter how long it takes.

After she left, I quickly called Ashley; she was a part of my pack who had decided to look in the big city for her mate. She was getting older; she was

45 but still looked at and acted like 21, which was the age she decided to settle on when she moved here. The city was a more neutral place, and many of our other pack members moved here to settle for jobs but were always welcome back at the packhouse; in fact, many came home for the weekends.

"Evan, find everything out about Charlotte. I'm going to give a call to Ashley," I walked back into my office and through my jacket across the desk, opening up my computer that she just had her hands on. The room smelled of her and calmed my beast down to a gentle purr. With a quick dial to Ashley, she picked up the second ring. "Alpha, a pleasure to hear from you. What do I owe the call?" I don't usually call pack members, typically I just use the mind-link, but knowing she was in public and at a club, I thought this was best.

"You know Charlotte Crawford, don't you?" I spoke.

"Yes, Alpha, I'm one of her only friends. May I ask why?"

"I need to know more about her, I–" before I could finish my statement, she was squealing in my ear. This girl had a set of pipes.

"Is she your MATE!?!" I could practically hear her jumping up and down in the club.

"That she is," I smiled. "I take it she is different than others, so I need a quick rundown of what she's like personality-wise. I'd like to have the upper hand," I joked.

"Well, she is going to give you a little trouble, Alpha. She's a secretive one. As I said, I am one of her only friends, and she has never spoken about her past. Hell, I don't even know where she lives. She comes to my apartment sometimes, though." She said out of breath.

"Is she going out with you for your birthday? I saw she had heels on?"

"That she is, Alpha. You were already invited, but I'm guessing you are coming now, right?"

"But of course, I wouldn't miss it." I smiled at the phone. "I'll see you then."

"Wait, Alpha," Ashley said quickly. "She's a shy one. Charlotte hardly ever goes out to clubs and places with a lot of people. She's doing this for me. Charlie is really sweet, just overly cautious as all. Be gentle with her," Ashley urged with concern.

"I will always be gentle with my mate," I said, comforting her with a giant grin on my face. "Happy birthday, see you there." I then cut the call.

"I take it we are going clubbin' then?" Evan walks out in his dark wash jeans and his black dress-down shirt. The idiot likes the party scene, especially when his mate tags along. She was already at the club. "Yeah, yeah, let's go. We'll take the Porsche." Throwing me the keys, we head to the valet and get in the car to head to the club.

After we arrived, I stayed behind the scenes and just watched my mate. You could tell she was nervous by the way her body moved. She always had her arms wrapped around herself and kept to the sidelines, only allowing herself to sit with a group of Ashley's friends when she was forced. She made small talk and gave little laughs here and there, but you could tell she was very reserved.

Her eyes never sparkled, and she continued to keep her arms wrapped around her delicate frame. Her arms left her only to drink her Appletini, which seemed to be a favorite. After sitting and rolling her eyes at Grant, the sexist douche of the group, she got up to go dance with Ashley. At first, she looked uncomfortable but finally let the beat of the music take over her body. Once she got over her fear, I thought it was time to make my move.

Her eyes were closed as she swayed back and forth, and I gently put my hand on her hip, still keeping my distance from her. Tingles erupted over my hands, immediately making me pull her closer to me. She didn't reject the touch and even leaned back into my torso to feel the wall behind her. Charlotte was already feeling comfortable with me, and my Wolf was howling. I wanted to see how far I could go with her before she turned around or told me to stop.

Nibbling on her shoulder made my lips hot and puffy. I continued to kiss and suck up to her neck, and I could hear quiet moans drifting from her pouty mouth. She was enjoying this just as much as I was. I smiled into her neck when I felt her pull at the back of my head with her hand. She tugged on my hair, making me groan. This woman was going to be the death of me, and she didn't even know who I was. I was about to turn her around until I heard Ashley's scream fill the bar. Charlotte was out of her trance, so I immediately stepped away, not wanting to scare her off.

I backed away and headed back to my group of friends, to which all were staring in shock. "Damn, Alpha, she's hot!" Eric said lustfully under his breath. I heard it using my Werewolf hearing, and with one swift movement, I pushed him back against the wall. "That is your future Luna, I suggest you watch your tone!" With that, all the Werewolves around us spun their heads so fast they could have fallen off their bodies.

No one thought I would find my Luna, especially not now. It had been so many years I think everyone had begun to lose hope. Our pack of 3000 members was always rooting for me, and now that my queen was here, they knew I would never let her go. I just hope I don't scare her off.

Vera Foxx

Chapter 7

Wesley

"Think she will like it?" I said to Evan while I was putting on my royal blue tie to match Charlotte's dress. I've always had trouble putting on ties, no matter how often I wear them.

"Sure, she will, Alpha. Chicks are into that sort of shit," he laughed. "It is cheesy as fuck I will admit, but I'm sure she will like it." He pats me on the back of the shoulder as I am looking at myself in the mirror, still trying to get the damn thing on.

I've never been nervous about going out on a date, but I am a train wreck waiting to happen this time. I've made Ashley give me updates on Charlotte throughout their make-over session. I wanted her to feel beautiful like she was. A hard-working woman like herself needed it, and Ashley was the woman to take care of her.

Once Remus sensed Charlotte, I knew I was screwed. She was beautiful, her strawberry blonde hair matched her lightly tanned skin tone and those eyes, fuck I could drown in those hazel eyes. I felt Remus's purring reverberate in my head.

I'm just hoping Charlotte will like the dress I sent over to Ashley's; I still have not heard back if Charlotte even wanted the dress. I fisted at my tie, still trying to get the damn thing straight.

An old Alpha like me needs their mate. I was becoming restless, angered easily, and hostile, something that my pack wasn't used to. We as a pack tend to be more peaceful, but we are strong and fearless if there is a threat.

Being the stalker I was, I had Ashley pull her file from the real estate office she works at to get her sizes. They supplied her with a uniform when she first arrived, and I went off of those measurements. I also found out that Charlotte lives in a shitty apartment building entirely run down on the wrong side of town. No wonder she doesn't want anyone to come over; she probably feels embarrassed or thinks people will think less of her. She won't be living in that shit hole for much longer; she's going to be living at the packhouse where it is safer.

I haven't wholly dug into her past because I want her to be the one to tell me about it. I want to earn her trust and have her tell me how she grew up. It will be a process to get to know her, but I'm willing to wait another 100 years to have her.

As I finally finished tying my tie, I could hear Ashley trying to contact me through the link.

"Alpha," Ashley said.

"Yes, Ashley. Did she like the dress?" I smiled, thinking about her opening the box. I hand-picked the dress; royal blue was our pack color, and thinking about it going against her smooth, creamy skin gave me joy and longing of her wearing it. She would be wearing her pack colors.

"She loves the dress, Alpha; she cried and said it was the first present she's ever received," Ashley said solemnly. I sighed; how could a girl like her never receive a present? Remus was angry that our mate had probably been treated harshly, and that was why she didn't let people in. *"Alpha, the dress fits but..."* she trailed off.

"But what, Ashley?" I asked flustered. Assholes possibly raised my mate, and now there is something else?

"I promised I wouldn't tell anyone; I don't want to betray her trust. However, she will be wearing a black cardigan over the back of the dress, if that is alright with you, Alpha. I don't think you should ask her to take it off." From Ashley's voice, this was very difficult for her to ask of me. Pack members typically do not make requests of their Alpha when it comes to their mate and well-being. Remus was pacing in my mind wanting to know what was wrong. I could command her to tell me.

"Is she in any sort of pain, Ashley?" I asked, gritting my teeth.

"Not physically, Alpha. She is upset, it brought back memories for her, and she doesn't want anyone to see what is on her back."

I gripped the desk beside me. This was going to be difficult. Knowing my mate has a bad history is going to rip me into shreds. I could feel my Remus pacing wanting to comfort our mate, but this was going to take time; I couldn't go to her and tell her I was going to protect her and keep her from any harm. Jumping to conclusions wasn't going to help my case. Ashley hasn't even told me anything but, of course, I'm going to think the worst.

"Ashley, I need to know," I stated harshly.

"Please, Alpha..." she began to beg. *"It isn't my story to tell, and I–"*

I interrupted her, *"Do I need to use a command on you, Wolf? She is my mate, and her safety is important."* I shouted through the link. I could feel her submission pouring off of her. Remus wasn't going to have any of these secrets. If our mate was hurt or a possibility of her being injured in the future, we needed to know. I calmed my Wolf and took back over to speak with Ashley.

"Just tell me what is on her back," I said calmly.

"Scars and branding, Alpha. It looks like she had been cut on her back with whips or knives, and there's a branding scar in the middle of her back," Ashley sputtered.

"WHAT!" I screamed out loud. My mate had gone through something unthinkable, ruining her trust in people and possibly me if I didn't take my time with her. What sort of monster would hurt such a precious woman?

I slung the desk lamp to the wall, and it broke into pieces. Papers flying off the desk, and I continued my assault on the room. Nightstands were turned over, my suit coat had ripped, and the bedpost was on the floor. Evan came running in after hearing all of the commotion.

"The fuck, man?" I darted my head to him quickly while in my offensive stance. He promptly showed submission by muttering, "Alpha." He knew my Wolf was pissed, something he didn't show often. He wanted blood. "Alpha, what is wrong?"

"Mate was hurt, mate was tortured." Remus growled through my teeth. My breath was heaving, and my nostrils were flaring as I went to the window, looking out over the skyline. My anger and emotions were getting the best of me. I would have to be near her to calm down, but I can't let her see me like this. So long without a mate, and now that I've found her, it would be even more difficult to win her trust and make her entirely mine.

"What? Was she tortured? How?" Evan was shocked. "Whipped, cut, and branded. That is all I know; I'm not even sure long ago this happened. Pull the car around; we need to pick her up," I said in a clipped tone.

Grabbing the keys and throwing them to Evan, I stormed out of the room. As we reached the lobby, I went to the front desk to see Tammy filing her nails like the materialistic bitch she was. I was glad I didn't have to deal with her on pack lands while she usually stayed in the city. "Get someone to clean up the mess in my room," I stated and barged out the door, not giving her a second glance.

Evan opened the limo door for me, and I got in. I ran my hands through my hair and quickly grabbed a whisky through the small compartment underneath my seat. I don't usually drink, especially not whiskey because it doesn't help Werewolves get drunk, but the burn feels nice. Laying my head back in the seat, trying to calm myself, I tried to contact Ashley again.

"Ashley, is she alright?"

"Yes, Alpha. She's wearing a cardigan; she isn't crying anymore. I think the date will be good for you both."

39

"I'll be there in 10 minutes."
How the fuck am I going to control my anger now?

Charlotte

"Oh, my Goddess!" Ashley screamed.

"Shh, not so loud," I said with a quiet sob.

"Charlie, what the hell happened?" she asked in a whispered tone.

"I was a foster kid; it happens to some of us. Not all; there are some nice foster parents out there, from what I'm told. I just got a bit unlucky." I spoke sadly. I wiped a few tears from my face, trying to make sure I didn't smear the mascara.

"Did you not ask for help? How? It looks like they burned you! Is it on more of your body?"

"Yeah, but it is mostly covered. He didn't want to get caught," I chuckled lightly. I took the towel off and went into Ashley's closet, not caring about the invasion of privacy on her things. I found a black, fancy cardigan with some black beading that looked like it would go with the dress. Ashley looked like she was in deep thought; her eyes were glazed over. I tried to wave my hand in front of her face, only for her to be startled when I finally said her name.

"It's fine, really. I'm doing okay now." I gave a small smile. "I'm just sensitive to trusting people because all my foster parents lied to me a lot as a kid. It is all I know—people lying, giving you up, and false promises." I put the cardigan on and looked at myself in the mirror. I was straightening the dress. I had never worn anything like this. I didn't deserve to wear such a beautiful thing. Not with these scars.

Sensing my thoughts, Ashley came up behind me, put her arms around my shoulders, and gave a squeeze. "You look beautiful, Charlie. I promise. If you don't believe me, I'll tell you hundreds of times." A small tear fell from her face as she looked into my eyes through the reflection. Putting my hand up to comfort her, I sighed.

"It feels good to tell someone about it, honestly. I haven't told anyone in a long time. I would get punished when I did." With a deep breath and a burden almost feeling lifted, letting part of my heart out, I heard a knock at the door.

"That's your date," Ashley whispered in my ear as she grabbed my hand and led me to the door. Her friends all looked at me as I walked across the living room. The girls present gave me a thumbs up and the men just stared at me in awe. The dress is stunning, no denying that.

Before she opened the door, Ashley took both hands in mine and got close to me as she spoke. "You have been through a lot, Charlie. Just know," she paused, "that this man would never hurt you. He's a good friend of my family back home, and he protects those he cares about." I tilted my head in confusion, and she quickly opened the door.

Mr. Wesley Hale, in all his glory, walked into the apartment. He was wearing a black Armani suit that fit to his body like a glove. He was tall, delectably gorgeous. You could see the muscles underneath his suit as he adjusted the sleeve of his shirt with his large hands. Everyone in the room froze as he entered. Many bowed their head at the dominating aura that this man oozed from his body. Even Ashley gave the nod as he approached us.

"Miss Crawford," he said in a smooth velvety tone. "Are you ready?" His eyes met mine after I had become drunk off of his exceedingly god-like looks.

"Y-yes," was all I could mutter as he took his large hand in mine. The roughness of his hand let me know he wasn't just a white-collar worker behind a desk but a man that liked to work manual labor. I found comfort in that he wasn't afraid to leave the luxurious ways of life. He knew how to work hard.

I smiled gently at him and let him guide me out of the apartment. As the door shut, there were rounds of hoots and hollers from inside the door. My eyebrow lifted in confusion, and he started to laugh. "I'm sorry, we are all old friends; they like to tease me," he said. He had such a wonderful laugh; it made my heart skip a beat, even though it shouldn't.

"By the way, thank you for this dress," I whispered quietly. Yet, he still heard me.

"You are most welcome." He guided me downstairs by placing his hand on the small of my back.

Evan was waiting in the car downstairs and opened the door for me. I nodded a thank you, and we drove off to the restaurant for our "thank you dinner". As we reached the restaurant, Peril Mio Amore, I bounced my leg up and down in nervousness. The extent of my restaurant experience had been limited. I usually did fast food or the once in a blue moon I'd allow myself some takeout from TGI Fridays. Looking out the window at the crowd of people waiting to in, Wesley put his enormous hand on my knee.

Such big hands.

"This is my favorite restaurant; I hope you like Italian." I nodded in agreement because, in all honesty, I didn't know if I liked Italian or not. The closest thing to Italian was Domino's pizza.

The hostess took us up to the restaurant's second floor, where all the tables were booths and more secluded from the rest of the patrons. My eyes wandered the restaurant looking at the bright colors, the artwork, and more importantly, Wesley. I couldn't help but stare at him; something was telling me to stay near him. It was a feeling I was never used to, to feel safe. Ashley told me I should feel safe with him, and she knew him, so that made it OK? Right?

I would still be cautious, because I'd been lied to so many times before. I couldn't fully trust anyone.

"So, Wesley?" I started. He looked up at me with that million-dollar smile. I couldn't help but blush, and I'm sure his ego shot through the roof. "Do you travel here to the city often?"

"Usually once a month, which makes it surprising that I haven't seen you around. People at the hotel seem to know you." He took a sip of his wine while I drank some of my water.

"Well, I guess you didn't need any work done on your computer then." I laid my drink back on the table. "I try to be discrete, in and out."

"I see, so do you often go on dates with your customers?" I started choking on my water; I took the napkin to my lips and tried to pat the water from my chin. Wesley laughed uncontrollably while my face continued to turn red.

"I am just messing with you, Charlotte. It took a lot of begging to get you out here. I just wanted to see your beautiful face turn pink." The toothy grin of his was going to be the death of me. As soon as my face calmed down, I gave a small smile. This was honestly the most I've smiled in a while.

"I guess I should turn the question back to you then. Do you go out on dates with those who fix anything of yours?"

He chuckled, "I can honestly say that I haven't." Wesley had to have been out on millions of dates, his body and face just demand it.

"I do have to say, though, I didn't just want to take you out for a 'thank you dinner." He spoke as he twirled his wine in his hand. "In fact, I want to offer you a job." My eyes widened a bit. I couldn't read this man, I was starting to think it was a date, but a job would be for the best anyway. I smiled and nodded, asking him to continue.

"As you witnessed firsthand, we have had hackers try to infiltrate our network. I own several companies and invest in several properties, and right now, I need excellent security within those systems. I want to be able to have the ease of checking on several companies and do some home security. Now, with this, it would be imperative that you work closely with me, and we would see each other every day. I'll need reports, honest reports of what my employees are doing on said networks." I nodded as I gripped my napkins nervously.

"Now, saying that. I would need you to move into my mansion with me."

My eyes grew wide, and I began to shake my head. What the hell is this? I am not moving in with some random man.

"Slow down there, just hear me out," he started to butter his bread and acted like this was a normal conversation. "The mansion I live in, many other people live there that work for me. This includes maids, butlers, security personnel, family members, and friends of the family. You should think of it more like a big hotel, really, than my house." He popped the bread in his mouth. I squinted my eyes at him and crossed my arms. Rich guy? People living in his house? This dude is in the mafia.

"Are you in the mafia?" I said in a monotone voice. He began choking on his bread and banging on his big muscular chest.

"No! No, no, no! We are into security. If a bodyguard needs to protect someone, then there could be someone shot, but we are not actively trying to kill people." Wesley's voice panicked.

I laughed, feeling a bit more at ease. "Just checking!" I said in a singsong voice. He wiped his brow as if he had some sweat on it.

The entire menu was in Italian, so I couldn't order for myself; I asked him to do it for me and whatever he picked was divine. That was the first time I felt fully satisfied after a meal that I may not have to eat breakfast the next day. As I scraped the last bit off my plate, he spoke again.

"What do you think? Would you be interested in working for me?" I tried to let any dirty thoughts about him leave my mind and really think about this. Would I feel comfortable living in someone else's house? I'm going to need to have some questions answered.

"It isn't a no, but I have a few questions I want to be answered first," I said as he nodded. "Can I have my own lock on the door to my room where no one else can get in or out except for me?" I looked at him thoughtfully. He looked at me for a moment trying to understand my question. "I like my privacy; I just want to feel safe at night."

"Of course, anything you need," he said with a restrained voice. "You will be in the safest place being in my home, trust me. However, if you feel more comfortable with locks within your room, I am happy to make that happen." I nodded and continued.

"What is the pay?"

"What type of payment are you wanting?" I sat there for a moment, figuring out how much a computer tech with a master's in cyber security degree should make. After a few minutes of tapping my finger on my lips, I just shot out a number. "$150,000 a year?" I questioned. He looked at me, studying my face. Was that too high?

"Done," he said. "Oh, you will not be paying rent, food, or utilities, you have your own wardrobe allowance, and your student loans are paid off." My mouth hanging open in shock.

"I'm sorry?" I whispered.

"That is how it is going to be. When you work for me, you are rewarded handsomely." He smirked.

"You cannot do that; that is too much! I don't deserve all that." I waved my hands around.

"You deserve that and more, Charlotte." He whispered as he touched my cheek. After blushing profusely, he led me back to the car. As Evan drove, Wesley turned to me, "I will give you until tomorrow to pack up your things, and we will head out of the city back to my community. We like to stay secluded. I think you will like it there." He adjusted his tie.

We pulled up to my apartment complex, and I was horrified. How did Wesley know where I lived? The shock on my face was evident, and they looked at me with sympathy. "You will never live like this ever again. I've got guards standing outside the complex if you need help for tonight and tomorrow. I'll pick you up in the evening."

Everything was happening so fast; I didn't know if I was making the right decision. I hadn't even let my current boss know I was no longer an employee. He was going to be pretty pissed. Evan opened the door for me without saying a word, and Wesley followed me up the stairs. I skipped a few knowing, letting him know not to step in certain places. Wesley's foot would have fallen straight through the rickety steps.

His face was stoic as he walked me to my apartment door. I rattled the keys and harshly pushed the door open. Macaroni was instantly at my feet screaming, "I'm hungry," cry while Wesley looked at the poor scruffy cat. "I'm sorry, I have a cat. I can always have her stay in my room. She's all I have for a family." *Please let me keep her*, I prayed to any higher power.

Wesley just smiled and nodded. "Anything for you, Charlotte." I smiled, looking up at him. This guy would be my boss, so I couldn't have any warm fuzzy feelings toward him. I took out my hand for a handshake, but he quickly disregarded it and gave me a gentle hug. This was nice. So warm.

This was the first hug from a male I've ever received. I should be repulsed by it, but I'm not. We stood there a few moments until he let go. "We will load your stuff tomorrow and pick you up at six."

"Thanks," I mumbled as he walked out the door. After leaving, I locked all seven locks and slid down the door.

What had I just gotten myself into?

Chapter 8

Charlotte

After quickly gathering myself from the intense stare-down from Mr. Hale, I walked over to the kitchen cabinet and quickly fed Macaroni. I remember finding her when I was ten years old in a dumpster behind an old restaurant where I washed dishes. The poor thing was meowing, half-starved, and had only looked like it was a few weeks old. Being the young girl I was, the only thing I could feed it was some macaroni. I could not go out to buy food for her because I had no money. So, the calico cat's name was then dubbed Macaroni. She kept quiet in the house and only meowed when I could lock myself in my room.

Washing dishes with my then foster father was brutal. The dishwasher was always broken at the old restaurant slash bar, so he took it upon himself to use the foster child for some manual labor. The checks from the state weren't enough, so why not use me instead of hiring the evening dishwasher.

After feeding Macaroni regular cat food, I pulled out the one suitcase I had and started packing the few clothes I owned. I often wore the one tech uniform I was given at the Real Estate office and on occasion wore a pencil skirt with a nice white blouse. It honestly didn't take me long to pack; I didn't have much. Even the furniture in the apartment was left by the previous owners. It was all trash, really, but I kept it, so I didn't have to buy anything new.

Walking to the window, I had my fake succulent plants that gave what little life and color the apartment. I placed them gently into a bag so I could carry them safely wherever we were going. I knew it wasn't too far, but still, what little possessions I had I was going to protect.

It was nearing midnight. Only a few hours ago, I was told I would move the next day to a new life. Even though he said it was ultimately up to me, I didn't feel like it was a choice. I was getting paid 4 times the amount that I was receiving now, plus my student loans would be paid off. It all seemed too good to be true. It probably was. Nothing good ever lasts. It all crashes down when you think things are going to get better.

I quickly sighed and rushed through my nightly routine. I set the gorgeous dress on top of my suitcase and laid down on the squeaky bed. As I was trying to close my eyes, I heard a *ping* by the nightstand. Looking around, I couldn't figure out where the noise came from. It didn't sound familiar in my crappy apartment.

Ping

There it was again. I glanced over to my make-shift nightstand table that consisted of an overturned trash can with a book on top. An unfamiliar phone plugged into the cracked outlet. I picked it up, unplugging it and stared. The case was a bright pink and a heavy-duty one at that. If I dropped the thing, I'm sure the phone wouldn't realize it.

I tapped on the home button and found several messages ready to be read. Looking around the apartment, I opened the messages to the touch phone. They were from my new boss.

Wesley Hale: You are going to need this. Consider it part of your welcome to the job. I expect you to always keep it with you.

Wesley Hale: You will also find several people on the contact list who are trustworthy to me, and you can call them at any time if you cannot get a hold of me. Sweet Dreams Charlotte.

I quickly looked in the contacts and there were only a few names. My friends Ashley was at the top, then there was Evan and Thomas. Wow, my whole life's friend list.

I didn't even respond to his text messages. How would I react to that? How did this phone even get in here? It was late, and I didn't want to think anymore. His company was security; I'm sure he had the entire room scouted before he brought me up here.

Walking up to the kitchen cabinet, I grabbed a few herbal sleeping pills and downed three. Hoping that would keep the nightmares away and keep me sleeping until I had to get up in a few hours. Cuddling into the bed, Macaroni sat on my chest like she always did to help me feel safe. Her purring lulled me to sleep.

***

The following day, I woke up slightly refreshed. I didn't have any nightmares because I never got the deep sleep that I really needed. My mind kept drifting in and out of consciousness, waiting for someone to break down the door.

After a thrillingly cold shower, which was not of my choice, I put on my uniform for my last day of work. This was going to be complicated. Andrew was my supervisor, and he was not going to be happy that I was leaving. Grabbing my laptop and my keys, I bid farewell to Macaroni, and she gave a long yawn as I shut the door.

Once I reached the bottom of the stairs, a man in a suit and aviator sunglasses greeted me. "Miss Crawford?" his voice was thunderous and resounding. It had scared me to no end, and I could feel my body begin to shake. "Miss Crawford, I'm Mr. Hale's bodyguard; I'm here to escort you wherever you need to go today." I looked up at him, still shaking as I held my laptop to my chest. I didn't move.

The sudden ringing in my bag broke the awkward silence that was standing between us. I grabbed it, not letting my eyes leave the man, afraid he would do something I didn't like. "H-hello?" I answered, not even bothering to look at the caller ID. "Charlotte, are you alright?" I could tell from his husky voice who it was.

"I-I…" I couldn't get the words out. The freakishly tall man gently took the phone from my hand and spoke to Wesley on the phone. "Sir, it's me. I think she is afraid of me." The man in the suit finally took off his glasses, and I could see the concern in his eyes. Not seeing someone's eyes could be frightening to me; like they said, eyes are the windows to the soul. Upon seeing his eyes, my tension finally started to loosen.

"Yes, sir, she's alright now." There was some yelling coming from the other side of the line, and the man in the suit was bowing his head. I had finally stopped shaking, and the phone was handed back to me. I held it up to my ear. "I will make sure the bodyguards take their glasses off, alright? I'm sorry they scared you, Kitten." He cooed. I was still so shocked that I didn't realize the pet name he'd just given me.

"It's alright. I was just surprised."

"I have to get going now; just let them know if you need anything. I'll see you tonight, Kitten."

There it was again. It almost made my heart flutter. Wesley was my boss, and I wasn't going to think anything of it, even if he was the only one that had made me feel safe in a long time. We said our goodbyes, and the bodyguard smiled. "I'm Tony, by the way." I shook his hand, and he led me out the door to a black SUV.

Along the way, Tony told me that he also lives in the small community along with Wesley and his family. He would also be staying in the same home as me. He was starting to grow on me, even though we'd only known each other for the duration of the short drive to the office. He had a peppier attitude as the drive went on, I'm sure Wesley had something to do with that.

Once we arrived, he let me out of the car and walked into the building with me. He let me know that Mr. Hale demanded that Tony stays with me through my last day on the ride over. Something about being a protocol, I didn't question it because what was my old boss going to do? Fire me? Pushing the doors open to the floor where my office was, I saw Ashley sitting on my desk. "Well, look who it is! I didn't get a text or a call after your date!"

"It was a thank-you dinner which came with a job offer." I smiled at her as I put my bag on the desk. Tony took the liberty to stay at the entrance of the floor to give me privacy.

"Really now? Are you moving to his estate?" Her smile grew wide and mischievous. I gave her a quick smirk.

"It appears so. My loans will all be paid off, and I won't have a leaky roof over my head." Ashley frowned. She still didn't know where I lived. Quickly brushing it off, I looked at the corner of my desk with a big box of photos and plants. "What is that?" I questioned Ashley.

"Oh, my things. I'm moving back home. Since you will be there, I figured you might need someone to show you around." She grabbed a nail file from her purse and started shaping her nails.

"What? Are you serious? How did you know?"

"I told you, Thomas knows Wesley. I know Wesley... we are all from the same community," she babbled.

I sat in my chair and gave a huff. How does everyone know each other? "Small world, isn't it, sweet cheeks." She came up and gave me a squeeze on my cheek. I swatted her hand away. "Yeah, too small." I rubbed my cheek gently.

"CHARLIE!" I jumped quickly out of my seat, holding my hand to my heart. It was Andrew and his screechy annoying voice. I groaned. He probably couldn't open an attachment in his email again, the dumb grump. "Yes, Mr. Andrew?"

"In my office!" he screamed through the phone intercom. I took a big sigh and looked at Ashley. Her eyes were squinting in anger as she folded her arms. She knew how badly I was treated, but I made her swear not to say anything because I needed the job. "I'll be back at my place around 3 to finish packing. I'm sure you are probably doing the same?"

"Yeah, I'll be riding with you to the estate. Good luck, sweets." I nodded as she left, and I walked out of my office down the hall to Mr. Andrew. I could feel the overwhelming shadow behind me, now known as Tony. I looked around, and he gave me a smile, and I could help but giggle. I've been doing a lot of that lately, smiling and laughing. It was a strange, new thing but I was growing to enjoy feeling happy.

"You wanted to see me, sir?" I knocked on Andrew's open door. He was scowling, something he started doing immediately after I signed up for employment papers. Andrew was charming when he wanted to be, especially when he wanted something. I remember being reluctant to start work in such a large office, and he reassured me it would be a good fit. It hasn't been. He was a dictator on this floor, and the fear of quitting and not having a good reference in my field kept me here.

"Who the fuck is that?" Andrew said, pointing to Tony. By Tony's look, he didn't like it.

"My bodyguard?" I said in question. Why would he care?

"Get him the fuck out of the office; I need to speak with *you*!" he yelled. Before I could say anything, Tony stepped forward.

"Wherever she goes, I go. Orders of her new employer." I cringed. I was going to tell him gently, but that was out the window.

"Your. What?" Andrew spaced out his words.

"I am leaving the company; I have a new job," I said meekly.

Andrew stood up and walked around the desk. I looked at him in bewilderment. His frown turned to a sinister smile as he crossed his arms over his chest. "You can't, you signed a contract." I signed that I would not work any IT during the daylight hours but not a contract to stay here.

"No, no, I didn't! It said nothing about me having to stay here!"

"Learn to read the fine print, Charlie. For the next 5 years, you are all mine." He threw his head back and laughed. "You also signed a payment freeze, so there will be no raises for you either."

I could feel the tears well up in my eyes. This was so not fair, I knew once things got good, they would come crashing down. Another lie. Lies have surrounded me from day one. I try and trust people, only to be disappointed, now twice by this man. Sensing my defeat, Tony stepped up only a foot away from Andrew. Andrew shook but tried to contain his composure as he glared up at Tony.

Tony bent down to get into his face. "Wesley Hale sends his regards." There was a silent conversation going between the two. Neither of them said a word, but the more time passed, the more Andrews began to shake. Honestly, it felt so good to see such a douchebag shake in fear. If he peed his pants, it would make my day.

Once the staring contest was over, Andrew stood up and straightened his tie. "Thank you for your hard work, Charlotte. You may pack your things and go. I'll be sure to mail your check. I'm sorry for how I acted; I hope we can part on good terms," he backed away from Tony.

My mouth dropped, and I looked at Tony. He gave me a smirk and nudged my arm to leave. I didn't say another word to Andrew and went to gather my things. I was finally free.

Vera Foxx

Chapter 9

Charlotte

Finally, back at my apartment, I decided to clean up what little there was to clean. Tony was able to help me carry my belongings back to the black SUV from the office, and he had a smug look on his face. Being so large and showing your power to some jerk can give you that bragging right, I guess.

Macaroni was eating the last bite of her food when I heard a knock at the door. I still had an hour before Wesley arrived, and I was a bit hesitant to open it. Looking through the peephole, I saw that it was Ashley. I'm sure Wesley told Ashley where I lived, how embarrassing.

Groaning in embarrassment, I unlocked all the locks and opened the door. Ashley's eyebrows furrowed. "Shit girl, think you think you have enough locks?"

"I could fit one more at the bottom if I wanted," I laughed. "Let me guess, Wesley sent you?" Ashley nodded, and I squinted my eyes at her.

"Come on, Charlie, he just wanted me to make sure you had help if you needed it. It looks like you are already packed, though." She sighed and sat at the edge of the squeaky bed. "Why didn't you tell me, Charlie. I would have let you be my roommate; this is too much. You don't need to be here. The walls are basically falling down." Ashley waved her hands to the walls. The paper was peeling, and plaster was slowly crumbling. I did my best to sweep every day and patch the best I could, but what could I do? The rent was cheap.

"I've been fine. This is one of the better places I've stayed at anyway." Her grimace turned into a scowl. I rolled my bag to the door and came back to sit on the bed with her while Macaroni hopped up to be petted. "I'm glad you are getting out of here. You are so damn stubborn I didn't think you would accept the job."

"You know I'm independent. I can't rely on people; I'm used to it being that way." I began to pet Macaroni, who instantly started purred.

"That's it, the one bag?" She pointed. I nodded and picked up Macaroni to put her in her carrier.

"I wish you would have told me, Charlie. Some people are good. Do you at least trust me?" Her voice was soft, almost to where I couldn't hear her.

"I do trust you, Ashley, I really do. I think you are the first person I've been able to trust. Plus, something is telling me to trust Wesley, but I'm still a bit leery of everyone. One day I'll tell you the whole story, I promise." Ashley nodded, and we heard another knock at the door.

Ashley noticed my straight posture when I heard the knock. She put her hand on my shoulder and walked to the door opening it to reveal Tony and Wesley. Both were so tall. Wesley, being taller, but something about him didn't make me feel scared.

Tony and Wesley looked around, I'm guessing they wanted to see more boxes or suitcases, but I stood up with the cat carrier and laptop case in hand. "I only have one suitcase." I pointed.

"Only one? Where are the rest of your things?" Wesley asked. I bit my bottom lip, unsure what he was thinking.

"This is it. I know it's not much. It's all I needed." I smiled.

Wesley's hands became large fists, and he had a frown on his face. I put my head down in embarrassment, only to have it quickly lifted by Wesley's finger under my chin. "Never again will you go hungry or not have enough clothes. Do you understand?" All I could do was whisper a quiet yes, and we all headed downstairs and piled into the stretch limo SUV.

The car ride was tense. No one was saying anything. Wesley took the occasional business calls, but Tony and Ashley kept quiet. I was sitting beside the window and watching the trees go by. I wasn't going to miss the city at all; I was excited to be out in nature, and the further away we got, the more light-hearted I felt. The tension was slowly falling away as I continued to sit in the silence.

I felt a burning on the backside of my head as if someone was staring, and of course, someone was. Turning my head, I could see Wesley watching me look out the window with curiosity. He gave me a pleasant smile and ran his hands through his hair. He wasn't sporting the man bun today, and his stubble had grown since yesterday. I couldn't lie to myself; he was sexy as hell, and his white collared shirt rolled up his forearms were really attractive.

I gave him a quick smile and tried to break the silence in the car. "So, what is this community called exactly?" I tried to speak confidently, but I came out with a raspy voice from not talking the past hour.

"It's called the 'Black Claw,' it may sound scary, but it really isn't. It's been around for a few hundred years, passed down from my descendants. Everyone that lives here is quite peaceful; we like to stay to ourselves and be closer to nature." Wesley said.

"We do have our parties, though!" Ashley chimed in. I laughed at her; of course, there would be parties.

There was light chatter about what I was moving into. The main house, called a "packhouse," that some members lived in, but mostly there were homes spread out throughout the property. Everyone was very close in the community and often found themselves at the packhouse playing games in the massive game room, watching movies, or just hanging out and being with others. In a way, it was like a giant hotel and community center. The more I sat and listened to everyone, the more comfortable I felt about the situation, but with more people in the house, it also meant more people could try and get through the door.

I was then suddenly dragged headfirst into a piercing memory of my unfortunate past.

"Knock, Knock, Lottie!" Came the sing-song voice through the door. "It's time to come out to play!" Boisterous laughing went through the door as they pounded until the wooden door splintered. Curling up under the bed, I waited for him to break it down. Only a few kicks and it would be off its hinges.

BAM

"Lottie, Lottie, come on out." I was pulled from under the bed with one quick grab as I let out a head-splitting scream. "Please no! I did what you asked! I cleaned the dishes!"

"Well, there was a spot on one, Lottie, so you know what happens!" The man dragged me down the stairs by foot, and my butt hit every single stair. The men and women in the room all began laughing as they continued with their drinks.

"Ah, who is this sweet thing?" one of the men snickered.

"Back off, Allard. She's still underage, won't taste as good."

"How old is she, Roman? Are you fostering again?"

"You could say that…" he mumbled with uncertainty.

"What are you up to, you old bat?" Roman ignored him and proceeded to drag me down to the basement.

"Charlie! Charlie!" Ashley waved her hand in front of my face.

"Sorry, Ash," I shook my head. "Started thinking about something and got a little lost." I laughed, trying to break the tension. How embarrassing. "Are we close?" I tried to change the subject.

"Yeah, we are pulling up on the gates now," Wesley spoke. His hand came over mine and gave it a tiny squeeze. It felt so nice; I wondered if he would keep holding it to calm my nerves.

I needed to stop this having these feelings. I'm just an employee. But why would a boss hold an employee's hand? No one has ever held my hand; it is kind of nice, kind of comforting.

We rolled up to the gate, where men without shirts began talking to the driver. Ashley had her forehead glued to the window staring intently at the men outside. The heat of her breath fogged the window. "Ashley you might want to close your mouth over there or drool might come pouring out." I laughed at her expense. She turned around and stuck her tongue out at me. The one she was staring at was a burly man, not as tall as the others. Tattoos covered his entire upper body, and he had a scruffy beard. He looked like a lumber jack, just missing the big ax and plaid red shirt.

"Did some new people move in?" she questioned Wesley. He nodded, and her eyes grew large, and a smile stretched across her face. Ashley practically jumped up and down in her seat until we finally pulled up to the front door.

"Welcome to the packhouse, Charlie! I have to go, but I'll catch up later, OK? OK! Bye!" Before I could say a word, she was running back out to the gates, but before she got too far, the lumber jack that had let us through the gate came barreling into her. They started hugging each other and whispering into each other's ears.

"Wesley, did you know she had a boyfriend? I didn't know that!" The two of continued to make out on the lawn. Butt and boob grabbing was going on, and I couldn't help but turn around and cover my eyes. "Oh, my poor eyes," I whispered. Tony and Wesley held their hands to their mouths, laughing hysterically and guided me into the house.

"Just so you know," Tony started, "There are couples here that are very open to PDA. Just a warning."

"Good gracious," I said, whispering. "They were practically doing it on the law." Wesley had a smirk on his face as he led me into the mansion.

With all the commotion outside, I didn't get a good look at the front of the house, but inside was something to behold. The walls were bright, light tans and whites adorned the main living area. A large fireplace that could easily fit two Santa Clauses with room to spare.

The chandelier in the middle of the foyer was extravagant; it didn't look like it belonged in this community in the middle of the woods. "Even though this house has been in my family for generations, we just recently upgraded," Wesley spoke up.

As we walked to the large stairway on the right side of the foyer, the cast iron railing led up to what seemed to be 3 open floors. Each floor we stepped on was long hallways with many rooms lit with elegant light fixtures. The rugs on the darkened floors were intricately designed with swirls of leaves on a beige background.

"What do you think so far?"

"It is beautiful. I've never seen anything like it," I said in amazement. His eyes twinkled as he continued to lead me.

Wesley held his hand close to my back, always trying to touch me in some way. I didn't find it weird or out of place; I really liked him being close. Feeling my face heat up, I had to remind myself still that he was my boss, and I couldn't have feelings for him. This community was just filled with a lot of people that were touchy and nothing more.

We rounded the stairs and headed up to the third floor. "*I'm going to be getting a real workout every day if I keep this up,*" I thought to myself. We walked down the hallway, which was not quite as long as the one on the 2nd floor. "My room is there," he pointed. It was right across the hall from another set of double doors. "This will be your room." My face red as I held my laptop close to my chest. Why would he have me so close to his room? I don't see many other rooms here on this floor.

Wesley opened the door; the room had stark white walls with a pale grey comforter on the king bed. Many decorative pillows were askew on the bed of greys and pinks. The carpet was thick and lush that was around the bed. The hardwood floor didn't even seem cold as I took off my shoes. I didn't want to dirty anything in this room; it seemed so pure.

My eyes widened as I looked at the other doors in the room. One was a bathroom and a closet; it was deep and filled with clothes from casual to fancy ballroom dresses. I turned to Wesley to give him a questioning look, and he just smiled at me. "W-why? I-I don't need all this?" My mind was blank; why would I need all this? "There are many functions around the estate as well as in the city. You will need a wide array of clothes for those activities. I told you I would take care of you." Wesley walked up to me and put a hand on my shoulder.

"Relax, kitten, you will be taken care of, I told you. We will be working," he bent closer to whisper in my ear, "*very* close to each other." His warm breath tickled my ear as I lightly gasped. My questioning looks faded while my blush went down to my toes. I have to keep reminding myself that nothing lasts forever, and I'm sure some unbending doom lurked around the corner; I nodded my head. It won't last; nothing good ever does. I may just be a toy.

Wesley put his hand down and turned around. "I'll let you get settled; everyone is going to be downstairs and having a late dinner and watch some movies. Would you like to join us?" His blonde hair that reached his shoulders swayed as he turned around to close the door. The sunset from the window graced his perfect jawline. His eyes showed a bit of mischief in them. Before I could speak a word, he laughed, like he knew something I didn't.

Realizing I had been staring for too long, I cleared my throat and put a hand to my beating heart. "Um, yes. That would be great. I'll be down in a few." He gave a quick wink and shut the door. Being close to the bed, I fell on my back and let out a sigh I didn't know I was holding.

This was going to be so hard. I was falling for my boss, and I hadn't even started working yet. He would never accept who I am; I was broken. I was trash. If he ever saw my tattered body, he'd run for the hills. A man like him deserved more.

I walked over to the full-length, elegantly adored framed mirror. I generally avoided mirrors; in fact, the only mirror in my old apartment was a compact to put on foundation in the morning. Pulling my shirt over my head, leaving me in just my plain bra, I winced. Just looking at the cuts, branding, cigarette burns, and the name of my foster parent of a father etched into my side made a single tear run down my face.

Right. Never going to be good enough.

"You dumb whore, no one will want you. You will just become mine when your blood is of age."

Chapter 10

Wesley

After leaving Charlotte in her room, I quickly changed into jeans and a black shirt and headed downstairs. The house was cleaned to perfection. Since finding out that Charlotte was my mate, I had made every pack member come deep clean every crevice of the house. Not that it was that dirty to begin with, but I wanted everything perfect for my mate's arrival. Wolves are very passionate about caring for what's theirs, and Charlotte was very much mine. This was to be her home, and if she didn't love it, I would rip it to pieces and build something else for her from the ground up.

Evan stood in the kitchen in his joggers and a band shirt. He had just gotten off the phone with the pack gate guards letting them know that a pizza delivery guy was on the way. We decided on something simple for dinner since I hadn't officially shown her the rest of the house like I'd wanted to do in the morning. "Is she getting settled, Alpha?" Evan asked as he put the phone back into his pocket.

"Yeah, she is." I smiled and took a bite of an apple from the fruit bowl. "I think a little overwhelmed, I'll have to take my time." Ashley and her mate, Beau, came into the room hand in hand. The significant mark on each of their shoulders was ever-present and only made me a bit jealous.

"Hello, everyone!" Ashley said in her usual energetic voice. "Beau is my mate!" She held one of his hands in both of hers, and you couldn't help but see the affection in his eyes towards her. He gave her a peck on the lips, she giggled when his beard scratched her face. Who knew the energetic personality would be mated with one of my newer serious warriors? Beau had just arrived a month ago after transferring packs because he hadn't found his mate and felt like he needed a change. The Goddess must have planted something in his mind that this was where he was supposed to go because he found what he was looking for. Werewolves would always find their mates. In what time was a different story.

"Congratulations to the both of you, I'm surprised you are here, actually. I thought you would be off continuing the mating," Evan said with a laugh. Ashley gave him a glare while Beau growled at him. He was never one for talking, so Ashley was going to be his soundboard.

"Well, we were. I told Beau we should take a break because my bestie is the Luna. Getting her comfortable here was a priority. Charlotte's first night here might be hard, so we will eat dinner and watch a movie with you guys until she goes to bed. After that, you are on your own, Alpha." She giggled into Beau's neck. I rolled my eyes. I was happy for Ashley, but my Wolf was insanely jealous we couldn't hold our mate like that.

Thinking back to the car, there was something off about Charlotte. I haven't spent enough time with Charlotte to know her habits, but when she looked out the window, there was a haze in her eyes that looked like she remembered something. A forgotten memory or one she was trying to f forget was evident as her eyes glassed over. Only Ashley, who realized that Charlotte was about to cry, helped her to snap out of it. Everyone in the car saw it, and it embarrassed her that her mind had taken her somewhere else. This only made me more curious about her past and wanted to protect her. Was something after her, or was it just bad memories?

I looked over to Bruce, who had just walked into the kitchen, "Bruce?"

"Yes, Alpha?"

"I want a full background check on Charlotte," I stated.

"What? Alpha, no, you shouldn't do that," Ashley interjected. There was silence from everyone, and Beau pulled Ashley behind him.

"Don't question me, Ashley. Know your place," I said sternly. One who questions an Alpha can get in some serious trouble, and she knew it.

"I'm sorry, Alpha," Ashley bowed her head as she spoke, "it is just, she has a lot of trust issues. If you go digging in her past and she finds out, will she really trust any of us?" Beau looked at his mate in understanding. I was looking at the bigger picture, one where I needed to know if she was hiding from someone. The numerous locks on the door and the way Charlotte shied away from most people made me think she was hiding rather than just being scared of people in general. Charlotte would go to work and hotels to fix computers but stayed away from most crowded places. Another piece of the puzzle was missing.

"No, end of discussion Ashley, Bruce gets started on it by tomorrow," I said.

I could hear the light tiptoeing of little feet coming down the stairs. Something else I noticed about my mate; she was quiet when she walked. As if not to bother or disturb anyone. I'm grateful for the better hearing Werewolves have. Otherwise, she could walk in on any given conversation without us knowing, and that would be disastrous right now.

"We're in the kitchen!" Ashley spoke up. The soft padding of her feet neared the door, and everyone waited for her to come in. She peeked her head in the door to see who all was in the kitchen and her eyes lit up once she came in. Inspecting everything she saw; I knew she thought it was huge. Hell, it was four times the size of her dingy apartment. As she was looked around, I noticed her attire, and hell it was gorgeous.

She had tight black biker shorts that went halfway down her thigh and knee-high white socks with an oversized baby pink hoodie. Her hair was in a messy bun that helped me see the rest of her gorgeous face. If you weren't looking for it, you might miss it, but she did have a few scars around the base of her neck and a few near the bottom of her shorts.

Others noticed and let out a low growl knowing that their Luna had been in distress before her time here. Charlotte quickly looked up with her eyes wide, "D-did you hear that?! It sounded like growling!" she whispered. I noticed that a lot, she whispered. It was precious and cute and made me want to pay attention even more, so I never missed a sound.

"There are a lot of animals around the area, Charlie. You are living in the middle of a forest now, you know," Ashley chirped.

"Right, but it just sounded so close." A brief shiver ran up her spine as she hugged herself. I hope it was my growl that gave her that.

"Ashley, I'm hurt. You haven't introduced me to your boyfriend?" Ashley looked at Beau, and they both gave each other the biggest smiles.

"This is Beau, Beau, this is Charlotte—or Charlie if you want to call her that."

"Nice to meet you," Beau's deep voice had me started. I think that is the first time I've heard a complete sentence from the guy.

"Nice to meet you too, Beau. How long have you guys been together? Must not be that long since you weren't at her birthday last week?"

Ashley butted it, "Uh, yes, just recently. I'm not trying to keep you in the dark, Charlie." Ashley nervously chuckled.

"Hey, it's your business, I'm just happy for you both!" Charlotte smiled happily.

The doorbell rang, knocking everyone out of their trance. "Pizza's here!" Evan yelled as he ran out the door. The dumb bastard is always hungry. "Shall we go?" I lead Charlotte to our large entertainment room. The couches were the biggest you could buy; it was like a giant bed in the way it wrapped around the room and with several ottomans placed in front so everyone could relax their feet. The pizzas were brought in, and everyone began to dig in. Charlotte sat and watched as everyone grabbed their plates.

After I filled a plate with three pieces of pizza and a coke, I handed it to her. She looked at me questioningly, and I gave her another nod for her to take it. "I got it for you, Kitten. It's alright."

Whispering a quiet 'thank you,' she began to eat, and I sat beside her. Our Wolves want to serve and provide for their mates. If any other male had handed her a plate, it would be an insult upon me not providing for her.

After everyone had their fill, we sat back to watch a movie everyone wanted a horror movie. "Charlotte? What would you like to watch?" I asked her. She thought for a moment, "A horror movie is fine, just not any with kids in it. I don't like it when kids are in it getting scared or being part of the scaring." She chuckled nervously.

Everyone nodded in agreement, and Evan put in the movie. Every couple in the room had a blanket to share. Ashley and Beau, Evan and Jenny, and Bruce and Anna curled up on the couch, snuggling together. I grabbed the last blanket and threw it over our legs as I sat beside her. This was too perfect.

Charlotte

The movie started, and I was really insecure. I honestly hated scary movies, I'd only watched two before, and both times it freaked me out for days. I stayed in my apartment shivering under the blankets at night when I was on my own. Living with my last foster dad, Roman, my entire life was a horror movie, so I didn't care to watch any more after that. Not that I was allowed to anyway.

Everyone had a blanket around them and was paired up with their partners while I was stuck on the couch beside my boss. He smelled so dang good, I must admit, and I couldn't do a thing about it. Not that I should, or wanted to, or... I wasn't really sure. The more time I spent with him, the stronger the feelings got, and it really scared me. He was so nice, I'm sure I'm just reading into him being so nice. My body just craved a gentle human touch that I have been denied most of my life. That's all that it was.

Wesley reached behind the couch and pulled out a large blanket. "There is only one left. Care to share?" He smirked while my face lit up like a stoplight.

"S-sure," I mumbled, hardly audible. I came a little closer as he put the blanket over our legs that were hanging onto the ottoman when ominous music began to play.

This brought me to pay attention to the movie instead of the flaming hot man beside me. As the music begun to fade and the intense scene arrived, I slid my knees up under my chin and held my legs close. I could feel Wesley's eyes burn into the side of my head. Between the movie and him staring, my heart was about to explode. As my body stiffened, a jump-scare scene popped up on the screen and all the girls, including myself, screamed like our asses were on fire. I jumped so high that I landed on the ottoman in a defensive stance, ready to run while everyone, including the girls, started laughing at me.

Laughter filled my lungs when I realized what I had done in front of people that have only shown me kindness from the start. My mind was already hardwired for the flight of fear instead of the fight. Even Wesley was laughing, then picked me up and set me back on the couch. He put me back under the blanket and scooted closer to me.

"Damn girl, I didn't know you could jump so high!" Evan belted while his mate continued to laugh. "That was quite impressive!"

Ashley and Beau had stopped laughing and continued to make out on the sofa, and soft moans and hums came from their lips. Their hands began roaming around each other's bodies, and I could have sworn Beau's hand went up to Ashley's shirt. "Ew, get a room, you two!" I squealed while everyone glanced in their direction.

"Don't mind if we do!" Beau said with a grunted strain under his breath. He carried Ashley with her legs around his waist and out of the room while she laughed contagiously. Beau was obviously aroused and only made my blush go all the way to my ears.

"What's wrong? See something you didn't like?" Evan whisper-yelled while his girlfriend smacked him in the chest. "What, I think it's hilarious. She got so red."

Both my hands went up to my face as I tried to hide. Wesley put his arm around me and pulled both my hands away from my face. "Don't hide that pretty face; Evan is just an ass," he chuckled and pulled his hands away. Me pretty? He was just so pretty. Can a guy be pretty?

After laughing and making a few more hard jokes about my impressive reflexes, the movie continued. I couldn't help but feel safe with Wesley. He was a giant wall of muscles and I felt nothing could hurt me with him around. He was like a magnet, and his pull was getting stronger. Halfway through the movie, he scooted his entire body right up next to mine and put an arm around back behind the couch as if to spread his body to become comfortable. A contented sigh left my mouth, and I found I was no longer scared of the demon-like creature trying to escape the TV. In fact, I was relaxed—strangely comfortable. Like I was meant to be here. I don't know that I'd ever felt that way about anywhere.

There had been so many sleepless nights, always having one eye open. The nightmares had made sure that I never got more than 2 hours of sleep at a time, and being just 20 years old, it was giving me wrinkles. As the movie progressed, my eyes begun to drift. This wasn't like me; falling asleep during a film or with any noise was next to impossible. It had to be completely quiet for me to sleep. Otherwise, I would think someone would come and grab me from my bed.

Taking one large blink of my eyes, or so I thought, the movie was over, and my head had tilted on Wesley's chest. I was curled up under his arm, my face buried into his side. Most of the couples were asleep from what I could see as I was batting my eyelashes. Looking up, I could see Wesley was passed out too. His steady breathing and the rhythm of his heart were sounds I would cherish.

My biggest decision right now was to stay and pretend to go back to sleep and enjoy this for as long as I could or get up and go to bed. My heart tells me one thing while my mind tells me another. I can't get close to anyone, what if my foster dad came back to get me? I've done so well hiding and coming out here really has helped me. He could never find me. Right?

But what if he did find me? He would ruin anyone and everyone I ever came in contact with. Do I want to put all those that I am starting to care about in danger? My heart was breaking, most of my body had been broken, but what about my soul? It was all I had left. If that died, there would be nothing left. I would genuinely be a hollow shell of a person. My decision was made, I had to get up. Being meticulously slow, I unwrapped his thick, muscular arm from around me and placed a pillow in my stead. The blanket that he had me wrapped in was now wrapped around his own body.

I winced at the loss of his warm body against me. I didn't realize how cold it was in this house. Satisfied with my work, I tiptoed up the stairs and retreated to my bed and curled up into the blankets. The soft pillow clouds engulfed me. Being warm was something I always craved, blankets in excess were heaven. However, I didn't feel the warmth I thought I would have. Instead, I felt a weight sitting on my chest at the loneliness I felt in my bed.

Chapter 11

Charlotte

I woke up to the loud beeping noise of my phone's alarm going off. I'm not sure exactly what time I went to bed last night, but I'm sure it was late. Macaroni was curled up next to me, purring on my chest. I couldn't take my herbal sleeping pills or ask about having a lock put on the door. Waking myself up every few hours to make sure I didn't go into a deep sleep and listen for any noises at the door was exhausting. With a giant yawn and feeling my back crack a few times, I went to shower.

This was the first time I had a good look at the bathroom. It was huge. The light colors in the room matched the rest of the house. Splashes of pink and grey decorated the counters with soap dispensers, towels, and loofas. The small green succulent plants lined the nearby shelving, giving it a relaxing spa feel. Stripping my clothes and trying my best to avoid the mirror, I hopped in the steam shower and let out the best lovely moan I could. My eyes were closed, and I could just feel the hot steam scorch my body. It felt so good! When I turned and opened my eyes, I saw the shower I was in was indeed glass, so I could see myself in the mirror. The ugly scars are fully on display.

Most had faded and were barely there, but the deeper ones were still a light shade of purple and blue, and that man's name was still visible on my ribcage under my right breast. "*No one will want you. I've ruined you.*" Holding back a sob, I continued my assault with the soap. I scrubbed until my body was beet red.

The smell of coconut and vanilla filled the shower as I shaved, washed, and cleaned every inch of me. The water seemed so pure here than in the city. City water always made me feel dry and flaky, this was heaven. Turning off the shower, I quickly dried off, lotioned my body, and put on my makeup to hide the bags under my eyes. Going bold, I put on mascara and cat eyeliner to make my eyes pop a bit. I'm pretty sure eye makeup has become my obsession now; I just could never afford it before. Every bit of money I had went to the credit card bills I racked up.

After finishing my hair, meaning straightening it to perfection, I headed to the closet. I felt like this was too much, I couldn't help but feel excited. A whole wardrobe, for me. I've only ever seen these many clothes in Ashley's closet or, better yet, in a store. There were shoes, dresses, workout clothes, shirts, and jeans. I'm sure I could wear a new outfit every day for a year.

Heading to the jeans, I put on a pair of dark wash denim with a few holes in the knees and a black band shirt. Looking at the shoes, I put on some cute red, low-top converse sneakers that would shape up my outfit nicely. Looking in the mirror, I couldn't help but admire it. Besides the royal blue dress at my "thank you" dinner, this was the first brand new outfit I've ever had to call mine. As a smile crept up my cheeks, I heard a knock at the door. "Come in!" I turned around to see those forest-green eyes and sandy blonde hair draped to his shoulders.

Wesley's eyes trailed my body from top to bottom, and instead of a smirk, he had a genuine smile. "Wow, you look beautiful," he said underneath his breath.

I blushed and looked down while rubbing my palms together. I let out a quiet, "Thank you."

"I've come to collect you for breakfast. Will you join me? I can show you around also if you'd like," he said with hope.

"I would like that, Wesley." I walked to him and took the arm that he held out for me. Such a gentleman. That is all it is, just a gentleman. *"He is your boss, that's all,"* I reminded myself.

Glancing back at Macaroni, she had become brave and sat his large butt on the end of my bed. Her judging eyes against Wesley had become soft while he finally curled up next to my pillow. She would be fine, we all both would be fine here.

Walking downstairs, he led me to the dining room with many tables and chairs, at least 30 people could sit at one rectangular table. "Sometimes we have more members come and eat meals with us, that is why we have such a large kitchen and dining room," Wesley said, answering my silent question. I nodded while everyone from our group last night sat down.

"How was your first night here, Charlie? Sleep well?" Ashley asked while holding Beau's hand on the table.

"Yes, it was great." I lied. I could see Wesley's jaw tighten after I said that. Is he upset that I left him on the couch?

"Today's the day you get the grand tour," Bruce spoke up. "I think Al— Wesley was wanting to show you around the estate." He smiled.

"Yeah, Ashley said there was a lot to do around here, even if it is in the middle of nowhere."

"Kitten, there is always something to do around here, from swimming to basketball, soccer, video games, movies, the game room." Wesley stuffed a mouth full of eggs into his mouth.

"Usually, I just like to fu-" Jenny smacked Evan before he could finish his sentence. "Do not talk like that at the table, or you won't do what you enjoy!" She glared. I held my hand over my mouth to cover my laugh, but the redness in my ears gave it away.

"I'm sure Ashley and Beau could agree," Evan pointed his fork over to the couple.

"It is kinda fun," Ashley giggled as she twirled Beau's long beard. My face was glowing. I'm sure I could help guide a plane to land on the estate property.

"Charlie, are you into any fun activities?" Evan wiggled his eyebrows, and Wesley let out a low growl from his throat. I glanced at him from my peripheral vision, and he began to cough.

"Come on, spit it out." Evan urged. Everyone was looking at me, waiting for an answer. How can they talk about this so carelessly at the table, during breakfast, with a coworker? Isn't this some form of sexual harassment?

"I-I uh, um no. I do not go around engaging in such activities." I tried to remain calm. While the sweat beaded up on my forehead.

"No, don't tell me." Evan boomed, "You're a virgin!?" I think I just died. I can't breathe. There is nothing more than I would like to do right now than to just faint to get out of this conversation.

Ashley spoke up, "Evan! That is enough! What the hell is wrong with you!? Leave the poor girl alone! Charlie, don't answer him, he's a dick." Evan's girlfriend, Jenny, was sending out daggers from her eyes. When Evan caught sight, he recoiled and turned to me. "I am so sorry," Evan begged. "That was out of line. Please forgive me."

"Um, it's a-alright," I whispered. I looked around the room. People still staring, I shuffled in my seat. Was I still supposed to answer the question? It is pretty obvious, I thought. "Y-yes, I am. I haven't really had time to have a relationship." Looking up at Wesley's face, he had the biggest shit-eating grin I had ever seen. His eyes sparkled. Great, he probably thinks I'm going to be a notch on his belt or bedpost—whatever.

Everyone began eating again, carrying on with their conversations, and I couldn't eat a single thing on my plate. I stood up and excused myself to put my dishes away. "Kitten?" Wesley's voice came from behind me. I felt the heat on my back as Wesley walked into the kitchen with me, but I sped up the pace.

"I'm sorry for what Evan said and put you on the spot like that. We are just so open around here, we are just a big family."

"If you want me to say it's OK, it isn't. That was embarrassing and not something I wanted to freely talk about my first full day here. It could easily count as sexual harassment in the workplace." I folded my arms across my chest in a huff. "Show me what you want me to do so I can get on with my job."

"Woah, hold on now." Wesley held his arms up in surrender. "Let me show you around first, introduce you to some people you will see a lot. I am really sorry about Evan, nothing like that will ever happen again, I can assure you." He rubbed my arms up and down. Unfortunately, it was calming me down when I really wanted to be angry.

"Ashley is right, Evan is a dick. We just put up with him, and he works really hard around here. You will come to find him the annoying older brother in time; he just has no filter. Besides," He paused, "I was kind of curious myself." Wesley gave a mischievous smirk as one finger traced my jawline.

"Mr. Hale," Wesley's facial features faltered, "the only relationship we are having is a professional one. Now, let's see the house." I walked out of the kitchen, trying my hardest not to turn around. I had to be strong, I could not be weak around this man.

Wesley showed me a game room that doubled as a panic room, I'm not sure why. We are out in the middle of nowhere, and everyone seems pretty nice. I brushed it off as if it was nothing and continued to follow Wesley around like a helpless puppy.

It was the most lavish house I had ever seen. There was a ballroom, indoor pool, outdoor pool, living room, guest parlor, study/library, offices, bedrooms, and a small medical clinic. Wesley was extra attentive and looked at me every time he showed me a new room. It was like he was waiting for me to disapprove. How could I disapprove of anything?

Walking outside, we saw other people walking down sidewalks. It was its own mini neighborhood. The roads were wide enough for cars to drive on, plus there were sidewalks for kids to ride their bikes and play. Many homes looked the same, but they all had their own unique charm from a different bush, tree, steppingstones, or windchimes.

We passed a small building with many children running around in the fenced-in yard as we walked. There were squeals of excitement as the children played tag with each other. "This is our daycare which doubles as the preschool. This way, they are close to their parents. Once they are older, they go to the school in the town over so that they can interact with people other than just us and enjoy sports and other recreational activities."

Walking up to the fence, I saw a woman holding a baby in her arms, rocking it to sleep. The baby looked disgruntled and tried to wrestle from her arms. "Do you want to hold him?" the older woman said as she held the baby out to me. I'd never held a baby before, I looked at her worriedly.

"Come now, he won't bite." She laughed a little too hard at her own joke, and I held out my arms to hold him. It was a little boy with his little blue hat and white onesie wrapped in a warm blanket. Having the baby close to my chest, the little one slowly calmed down and closed his eyes. The tiny thing went to sleep. A small little smile crept up my face, I just put this baby to sleep. The first time ever holding one, I put it to sleep.

"You are a natural, he has the hardest time going to sleep without his mother. I'm Emma," the woman that had held the baby told me with a smile. "Anytime you want to come by and rock babies, you are always welcome." Having him was so relaxing, I could just sit and rock babies, which seemed like an easy job to do in my free time.

"S-sure. I'll think about it." I chucked and handed the baby back, who decided to let out a wail as soon as my touch vanished from its body. I mouthed "Sorry," and we continued on our path back to the house.

This place was its own utopia. Everyone had their own home and family and were all provided for. It really was a tight group of people even though almost thousands of people were spread across the entire property. "What do you think?" Wesley held his hands behind his back as he leaned forward to see my reaction.

"It-It's amazing. I've never seen or heard of anything like this before. It's like its own little world." I stopped in my tracks and looked at him. "Oh my gosh, is this a cult? Are you some kind of supreme leader we worship or tell us to worship something else?" Wesley let out the biggest laugh causing other couples to join in from afar. My head jolted to the sight of three couples looking at us from a playground at least 100 yards away. Did they just hear us?

"Goddess, no. No one worships me, and I don't tell them to worship anyone else. We are just a small community of like-minded people. We just want to live out peacefully and take care of one another. You can come and go as you please, move in, move out. No one is forced to stay no one is forced to leave unless laws are broken." He chucked and wiped away a fake tear.

"Hmm, still, it seems like it is too good to be true," I mumbled. "I'm still waiting for something or someone to pop out and do something scary."

"Trust me, there is nothing scary about us or the property. In fact, it is very safe. With you here, it will be even safer. Tomorrow, I'll show you to your office, and you can start setting up. Right now, I've got scouts out putting up the hardware, the cameras and motion sensors, and such. I just need you to work in a small office working on the software for the estate and computer protection for the corporate offices."

"That sounds more like my speed." I grinned. "I can still have a lock on my door though, right? We did agree to that." Wesley's face fell, the look of disappointment or sadness was evident.

"Of course, if that is what you wish. I can promise you though, that nothing will happen here. I'm right across the hall from your room if anything were to happen, I would know." Wesley's hand grabbed mine and gave a quick kiss at the top of my hand. I didn't like seeing him disappointed it made my stomach churn in the weirdest way possible. The butterflies felt like stones weighing me down.

However, this guy was a major flirt. I shouldn't feel this way towards him. I shouldn't like the way he caresses my hand or how he pays attention to me. He probably does this to many other women, but I really liked it. The panty-dropping smile doesn't help either. He makes me feel wanted, and beautiful and makes my heart skip a beat. After all I have been through, I should feel repulsed by their touch with any man. With Wesley, I didn't.

"I-I'll think about it," I whispered. I did get through last night without the lock. I got the same amount of sleep I normally did. Wesley did say he would hear me if I needed help. Could I really trust him, though? Could I trust him with my life?

"Alpha, Alpha!" A little girl was screaming as she was running toward us. She quickly stopped running, but she was panting so harshly her little lungs couldn't take it.

"Amelia? What's wrong?" Wesley's voice laced with concern.

"I just wanted to see you!" Her little doe eyes looked up at him like he was the world. Amelia made grabby hands and looked up to Wesley. He picked her up and put her on his hip, the most natural thing in the world to him. I couldn't help but smile at her, she was so happy as she squealed at the height she was at. She was up high, Wesley was gigantic.

"Charlotte, this is Amelia, my cousin's daughter," he smiled at her. Amelia looked down at me and then right back to Wesley. Full of confusion, Amelia began speaking. "Alpha, who is this? She's important?" Wesley's voice cleared, and he started tapping Amelia's leg.

"Alpha? What is Alpha?" I questioned. "Is it like a boss or something? Alpha usually means like, dog or something, right?"

"Yeah, exactly," Wesley said. "We all call him Alpha," the little girl said. "It shows respect, he's the leader and takes care of everyone." Amelia looked at Wesley with pride as she gave him a quick peck on the cheek.

"So, who is this? Is she Luna?" Amelia pointed at me.

"Um, I'm Charlotte. I'm here to help with computer stuff." I explained the simplest way possible. Amelia's eyes were knitted in confusion. Wesley moved her hair behind her ear and whispered something I was unable to hear. Her eyes lit up like Christmas morning. With a quick peck on his cheek, she wiggled to be let down and ran away.

"What was that about?"

"She had to get home; her parents were waiting on her." Without thinking twice, he took my hand and led me back to the packhouse. I felt little tingles across my fingertips as they were laced between his fingers. This is not good. Why is he doing this? But it feels... just so good.

I'm having these feelings for my boss, but what if we broke up? What would other people think of the hired help dating the boss?

As soon as we entered the mansion, I tried to take my hand away from his, but he only gripped it tighter. "I've got some work to do in my office. If you need me, I'll be there. Feel free to settle in, tomorrow I'll show you your office." Wesley leaned down and gave me a kiss on my cheek and smirked as his muscular back walked away from me.

Chapter 12
Wesley

The quick kiss I gave Charlotte on the cheek went straight to my toes. I know she is feeling the mate bond. It takes humans longer to recognize the bond than supernaturals. Their little bodies just can't understand that kind of gift.

Once leaving her in the foyer, I headed upstairs, where Bruce was waiting for me. He had mind-linked me while I was showing Charlotte around, letting me know he'd gotten all her background information. As much as I wanted to stay with her and show her more, I knew I had to see what we might be dealing with. I needed to know what she was so afraid of instead of forcing her to talk to me.

I was intrigued by how much Charlotte liked our pack territory. She loved the idea of the packhouse. She was so inquisitive and upbeat about every detail. From the large community dinners, parties, childcare, and how we provide for each other. There were several rooms in the house that I didn't like personally, but she would give a big smile nodding her head warmly. Charlotte was still quiet around me, the only person she reacted well to was Ashley, but I had to keep Charlotte away from her mate for the next few days because she'd found her mate. Charlotte will just have to make do with me, which I'm happy about anyway.

When we headed to the library, I saw her eyes widen at the large bookshelves. It was impressive; we made sure we had the classic literature and Werewolf history in here. If she really wanted answers, she could hunt through the books and find answers.

Charlotte's hands brushed along the spines of the different books, and she looked in awe at how tall the room stood. The library was at the back of the house and was three stories tall. One could easily get lost or play hide and seek for hours.

"Do you like to read?" I asked.

"Very much, I spend a lot of time reading." She continued to walk down one side of the room, tracing her finger on each book as she went by.

"What are some of your favorites?" I said, walking closely behind her.

"Oh, the basics. *Great Gatsby, Jane Austin, Pride and Prejudice*, and maybe *Twilight*." Her face blushed red. "I'm a sucker for that one. Don't ask why," she laughed.

I started laughing. "Really? You didn't seem like a person who would like those books after everything else you just named off."

She shrugged. "I can't help it. I liked the Werewolf and Vampire stuff. After that series, I started looking into other books online with that kind of theme. It was just a…" she paused, "a good escape."

I put my arms around my back and held my hands. "Escape? Why would you need an escape?" I pried

She stiffened and paused, her finger on one of the spines of an extensive encyclopedia. "You know, teenagers always want an escape from the real world," she gave an uncomfortable laugh.

I pulled her arm so she could face me. Tears were lacing the corner of her eyes, trying her best not to let them fall. "Kitten, tell me, why would you need to escape?" Keeping my voice as tender as I could as I stroked the sides of her arms. Trembling of her lips had my Wolf whimpering. Charlotte took deep breaths and closed her eyes her heart raced.

"Kitten love, come back to me." Putting a hand on either side of her face, I chanted, "just breathe, in and out, alright?" After a few minutes, she calmed down, and she grabbed my hands with hers.

"Thank you. I'm sorry. I'd rather not talk about those things right now," she whispered. Knowing she wouldn't say anything more, I led her outside.

Who would have hurt my little mate? She is so tender and meek, just like the nickname I had for her. She had no malice towards anyone, someone took advantage of her, and I was going to find out who and rip them to shreds.

Once we were out of the packhouse, her mood changed dramatically. The sun looked beautiful on her porcelain skin and strawberry blonde hair. Her curls dangled around her face in the wind as she took giant sighs of contentment. Keeping my hand on the small of her back, I took her to one place my mother likes to go to, the preschool and nursery. Emma was holding one of the more irritable babies trying to get him to sleep, then Charlotte saw the baby. Her eyes widened, and a small smile came to her lips.

I mind-linked Emma and quickly, "*Emma, see if she will hold the baby.*" Emma and most pack members knew that Charlotte was coming and that she had no knowledge of Werewolves. Many stayed away to give space, but many members were still too damn obvious with their actions and words.

Charlotte held the baby like it was glass. Carefully wrapping the baby, snuggle into her chest. Charlotte traced the baby's face with her finger causing the little one to fall asleep. She was a natural and didn't even know it. Emma smiled at me and linked me, "*she's beautiful Alpha. A mother to the community already.*" I smiled with pride at the comment.

The older pack members can sense when there is a new Luna or powerful being around. Werewolves can live to be very old, and once you start to be more tune with your Wolf, and years of practice, you can sense things that younger Werewolves can't. Charlotte was lightly humming as she rocked the baby.

Charlotte was going to be a perfect Luna She may feel weak from whatever past befell upon her, but she will rise above it. Making this far is a feat unto itself. Once she gave back the baby, Bruce had linked me, telling me he had her background information.

Opening my office door, Bruce stood at the side of the desk flipping through several papers he presented. "Alright, show me what you found," I reached my hand for the documents.

"Are you sure, Alpha? She's a very private person, shouldn't you earn that trust?" I growled at him, and he quickly lowered his head. I know what is best for my mate, I will protect her in any way I can. Ripping the papers from his hand, I began to skim through.

Charlotte was an orphan dropped off at a local fire station only hours old. She jumped to different foster care homes until she was 7 and taken in by a single parent, Roman Vanderveen. Charlotte stayed until she was fourteen and then was reported missing as a runaway. Never found, and once she hit 18, she graduated from the foster system and is no longer being searched for.

I sat down at my desk and started to rub the temples. "Then how the hell did she go through so much schooling? Did she really graduate from high school and college, or was it all a farce?" I asked Bruce. Bruce shrugged his shoulders.

"How she was able to stay away and keep low is interesting. She's smart though, I don't think it was fake. She had to have finished school." Bruce rubbed his chin.

"Nowadays, it's hard to stay off the radar like that; everything is digital," I hummed in response.

"Maybe we should contact this Roman guy? Maybe he can shed some light on some things? She probably got hurt after she left."

"Or she was running from him..." Bruce paused. I didn't think of that one.

"Either way, I need to get more info, this isn't enough." I threw the papers on the desk as I leaned back in my chair. I can't protect her if I don't know what's going on."

"Then you need to talk to her, Alpha. Don't play games. She doesn't trust people. Earn her trust, don't just assume. She'll come out in her own time. We all know you suck at patience, but the Goddess is teaching it to you with your mate." I let out a scoff. Yeah, she would do that.

"Fine, I'll do it the old fashion way."

Charlotte

After regaining my senses from the kiss Wesley planted on my right cheek, I decided to find Ashley. Before even going near her bedroom door, I was going to text her. Who knows if she was doing the nasty with her new boy Beau?

> **Charlotte: Hey, what are you up to?**
> **Ashley: I'm in my room, want to come hang for a little?**
> **Charlotte: Taking a break from Beau?**
> **Ashley: He's rehydrating hehe :)**

Walking up to the second floor, where a lot of staff and other members of the estate stay, several doors were open. Walking down the hall, one door was blasting music that I was instantly falling in love with. Peeking in the door, a guy around my age was dancing and belting song lyrics at the top of his lungs. I started smiling watching his reenactment when he caught sight of me in the mirror. We both jumped scaring both of us. He ran to the stereo and turned down the music, and smiled at me, "hey there, I'm Zachary." I gave a small wave, diverting my eyes from his bright shiny ones.

"Hey, I'm Charlotte." Moving my eyes back towards his sparkling ones. "I'm sorry, I liked your music, I was trying to figure out what it was."

"Oh, this? It is from the greatest movie musicals, *The Greatest Showman*." I gave him a blank look. I didn't watch much TV, I always stuck my nose in books or computers because they were quiet.

"Goddess, you don't know that movie?" He dramatically screeched. I shook my head no, and a high pitch squeal left his lips. "WE HAVE TO WATCH IT TOGETHER!" I jumped back and held out my hands, trying to shield myself since he was prancing towards me.

"ZACHARY!" A voice from my left yelled. Thank you, cheeses; it was Ashley. I jumped behind her and whispered a quiet 'thank you.'

"You cannot freak her out like that. Small movements and voices, please, she is a jumpy little thing." Ashley scolded him like a child.

"Hey man, I'm sorry, I just get so upset that you haven't seen my all-time favorite movie! Have you seriously been living under a rock? In the dark? In a cold dark basement somewhere because there is no way you haven't heard of this movie!" Zachary rambled quickly.

I started chuckling at the irony of all that. "Sorry, I haven't, but I would love to watch." I laughed as he ran to his dresser picking up his TV remote. "What song were you listening to?"

"'*This is Me*' is one of my favorites, but the whole movie is fantastic! Wanna watch it with me? I think the theater room is taken. Ashley, wanna join?" Benjamin enthusiastically held the remote in both hands shaking with glee.

"For a little, bit. Let me tell Beau where I am." Ashley walked out, and I continued to look inside Zachary's room. The walls were a bright royal blue with white floating shelves filled with plants of succulents and flowers. The room was fresh and clean, the cleanest I'd ever seen a male's room.

"I'm kind of a neat freak, only because my mom would beat me if I didn't clean." He chuckled as I looked at him flustered.

"Are you serious? She beat you?" I asked, upset.

"She did, she was an alcoholic, now I have a fear of messy rooms. I moved here several years ago to get away from her. Best thing I ever did." Hearing that someone as happy as Zachary being beaten or hurt was devastating. His own mother did that to her child. "I'm not sure why I told you that," he chuckled quietly. "I just met you." He sniffed.

I moved over to the bed where he was now sitting and sat beside him. A small tear dropped from his eyes. Ashley was leaning against the door frame holding her phone. I glanced back at Zachary. "You aren't alone, Zachary." He looked up at me with his eyes glassy. "There are a lot of people that go through what you went through, having a parent, or foster parent, hurt them."

"You?" he whispered. I nodded and rubbed his back. "I feel like I can talk to you, Zachary. You kind of understand what it's like"

"I haven't really talked about my story to anyone," he said, face turning red. "Would you like to share?" I pursed my lips together, glancing at Ashely on the other side of the room. Giving a small smile, she nodded in confirmation I should.

"Me either," I whispered, "but seeing we have similarities, maybe we could help each other?" I haven't had the urge to share my story with anyone in such a long time. Not many would believe me and only a few adults that did would check on my home situation just to turn away like they had seen nothing. They couldn't find anything wrong. So, I stopped trying to get help. I stopped telling people because the more people I told and didn't get me out, it worse it got.

Zachary's own mother beat him. I thought your real parents couldn't hurt you, but here I am judging too quickly.

Maybe I was tired of keeping it inside. Having someone to hear my story could relieve some of the burdens. I wasn't alone. Someone else suffered too. My heart instantly lifted, deciding to share my story with Zachary.

I looked over at Ashley, who continued to watch my features. Ashley walked in and closed the door with bare feet and sat at the end of the bed. Her hands intertwined with both of ours as Zachary began his story.

Chapter 13

Charlotte

"You don't have to talk about it, Zachary. We just met. That is kind of a big step," I spoke cautiously. Zachary nodded and balled his fist on his leg. "I want to, I feel comfortable around you. You're almost like a mother figure… weird, right?" He gave a sad smile. "Like the good kind." I hummed at the comment.

"I was about 10 years old," Zachary began. "My parents and I lived in a pa—community like this one, except much smaller. We were all happy. Mom was actually pregnant with a set of twins, and we decided to go on a picnic. It was the perfect day, the sun was shining, and we headed to the lake. It took a good fifteen minutes to get there, and my job was to bring the blanket, Mom hated to sit on the grass." Zachary laughed for a moment, then his smile faded. "But I forgot the blanket, so my dad said he would go back and get it. At first, I said I would, it wasn't that far, and I knew the way. Dad insisted, though. Mom was pretty sore at me cutting into our family time, but aren't most parents when reminding you over and over when they want you to do something?" I rubbed Zachary's hand to continue.

Anyway, it hadn't been long, maybe ten minutes, when we heard a loud scream, it was dad. I ran into the forest while my mom tried to catch up as much as she could. She was far along with the twins, so running wasn't something she could easily do." Ashley curled up on the bed, holding one of Zachary's pillows to her stomach.

"In the middle of the path, my father just laid there not moving. Blood was, everywhere." Zachary sniffed as the tears began to flow. I pulled him into a hug tightly and didn't let go. "He... he was dead. An animal got him. He was dead before we even got there." A few tears escaped my eyes listening to Zachary. "We were so close, my dad was my best friend, and I felt like it was my fault. As soon as my mom got there, it only got worse. She screamed in pain and told me to run back and get help. By the time I got back, she was lying against his body, sobbing. Everyone gathered her and my dad and took them to the hospital."

Ashley sat rubbing Zachary's hand, and he gave her a small smile. I continued have my arms wrapped around him, his nose buried into my shoulder. "Mom lost the twins." I gasped, covering my mouth. "From heartbreak and stress."

"It isn't your fault," I grabbed his shoulders, pulling him away. It could have been you, Zachary, don't you dare take the blame. You are here for a reason; your dad would have wanted it this way." I sniffed. My own tears for Zachary dripping on his jeans. Zachary only nodded, wiping his nose with the back of his sleeve.

"My grandparents took care of me for a month or two to let my mom heal. Once I came back, she was different," he shook his head, his beautiful curly locks shaking in front of his face. "Cold, distant." He shivered. "At first, it was verbal threats of the whole thing being my fault, then it turned physical. She would hit me for the smallest things." Zachary's hands clenched.

"This went on for 5 years until I couldn't take it anymore. No one believed me, or they didn't want to believe me. I had scratches, and bruises and still, no one did anything. I reached out to Wesley in the neighboring pa— community, and he immediately requested a transfer and got me here. He's kept me safe; everyone has kept me safe. They make sure that she is nowhere near the area. I've been here for 3 years now, and I've never been happier." I gave him a nod of approval.

"You are really something, Zachary. Going through all that," I whispered. "You survived it, and I'm glad you came here because I got to meet you." I smiled warmly at him. "Do you have nightmares or flashbacks?"

"Not as much anymore. She would hit me, slap me, give me a couple of good bruises once or twice, and I got a few deep scratches, but it wasn't anything I couldn't handle. I don't think she would have killed me. I was all that she had left for a family," he said solemnly, holding Ashley's hand. I hummed in response." I couldn't really say the same for myself. "She was my mom, so I didn't have the heart to fight back."

Zachary looked up, "So what is your story? I know what 'emotionally damaged' looks like. We are all spilling secrets!" he said, trying to lighten the mood. Ashley looked at me, knowing I wasn't sure. I've kept it for so long, hiding in secret, running from a man that may not even be looking for me anymore. I rubbed my sweaty palms together. Should I come clean of everything? To everyone? Even Wesley? That way, he could go ahead and stop being overly friendly to get my hopes up. It would be so much easier if he stopped now than find out later, I was damaged goods. Who would want someone with some guy's name etched into their side?

"Well, I guess you could say I've been hiding from someone. Would I be protected here if I told Wesley?" Looking up from my lap, Ashley's brows went to a scowl while Zachary pulled me to his side.

"If you have someone that you think is still looking for you, Wesley will protect you, Charlie. You need to tell him so he can really put a security plan in place. With all your great ideas, this place will be a fortress, to keep you and everyone safe. If you feel comfortable, you should tell him." Ashley's eyes looked to the door, her jaw tightened.

I let out a heavy breath and looked anywhere and everywhere but the two friends in front of me. "Hey, Wesley will still like you," Ashley spoke softly. Zachary nodded his head quickly in reassurance.

"Ha, he doesn't like me. He is just touchy-feely. He hired me to work here and nothing more." I crossed my arms. Apart of me wish he did like me.

Zachary whistled, "Girl, you are bliiiiind. He is all up in this." He waved his index finger all over my body. "Have you seen the way he looks at you? Gets upset when others look at you? I was spying from the stairs watching you guys in the dining room. He's into you, trust me." He put his hand on his chest.

I let out a short laugh, "He won't be once he sees these scars, both physical and psychologically." I ran my hand through my long hair. "Come on, I'm done talking about this. Let's get it over with." Ashley took the lead and took us to the office on the second floor. You could hear yelling on the other side of the door and heavy objects falling to the floor. "Maybe this isn't a good time, I'll come back later." I turned around to walk away until Zachary picked me up and threw me over his shoulder.

"Hey!" I squeaked. "Put me down!"

"Nu-uh, you need to spill about this foster parent that hurt you. I'll protect you with my life, but we gotta know who we are dealing with."

"Ok, ok, just put me down." He let me down softly, and I straightened out my clothes, so I didn't look like a big mess. Ashley knocked on the doors a few times, and we heard a big gruff, "come in."

Walking in his office, you could feel the testosterone. Evan and Bruce sat on either side in front of the desk in massive leather chairs while papers were thrown across the floor. Heavy paperweights laid in ruin on opposite sides of the room. There was a deep scowl on Wesley's face, something I had never seen before. I was about to turn and run out until Zachary grabbed my arm and pulled me forward. I squeaked.

Wesley's head perked up and saw me, his eyes visibly softened. His scowl instantly retreated from his face, and he continued to stroll around the desk. "Kitten, what's wrong?" Wesley came over quickly and took my hand. I was not going to cry. I couldn't cry. There were too many people in this room for me to break down and see how fragile I was.

Ashley cleared her throat since Wesley, and I kept staring into each other's eyes. Wesley's eyes were so comforting. It breaks my heart to have to tell him this. Now he will know I'm ruined, that I'm something that cannot be fixed and should be left in the dust. Wesley was the epitome of a perfect man. Strong, fearless, and natural leader while I was just the pebble in someone's shoe. A nuisance, a pain in the butt, and a whiny baby.

"Charlie would like to talk to you about something," Ashley said softly as she reached for my hand to lead me to the couch in the room. Everyone was now sitting down, and Wesley made Ashley get up so he could sit beside me. There was warmth was radiating from his body, and I instantly felt comforted by it. I was going to miss him trying to get close to me.

"What do you want to say, Kitten?" Wesley soothingly rubbed my knee. I looked at my knee and then at his face. Laced with concern and curiosity, I decided to begin.

"I was brought up in the foster system," I began as I cleared my throat. Occasionally glancing at everyone in the room as I spoke. "I had an average life up until the age of seven, just bouncing around from home to home until I landed into a man named Roman's home." I choked back a sob. "He had a really nice house, was rich even. Better than anything I had ever seen in past foster care homes. He was really kind. I thought it was weird that he didn't have a wife or girlfriend with how nice he was. He gave me a nice room, a few toys. He took me to school, fed me, clothed me. It went great for two years. I was actually starting to trust him, thinking maybe he would adopt me." I laughed lightly as everyone stared at me.

"The foster care system came by a lot those first two years to check on me. They saw how happy I was, and I even told them I would be happy if he adopted me. They finally said they wouldn't come by much anymore because he seemed like a good guy. But that is when things went bad." I put my head in my hands and choked back a sob. Wesley rubbed my back, scooting me closer to his body.

"The moment they left, he had a mischievous on his face. It was so evil," I whispered. "I've never seen anything like it. His eyes almost glowed with how happy he was, I swear they were red. I was confused at the time, thinking he was playing a game, so I go to run to him and give him a hug. Until I felt a sharp sting in my cheek," I cupped my face in remembrance. "He had backhanded me. From that moment on, I dealt with his abuse. First, it was just hitting, slapping for not cleaning something right or just 'being in the way'." Wesley's fists ball up into his hands, and his knuckles cracked turning white. "Then we moved out of his nice house and into a rundown house. I had to clean it then go do manual labor at a dirty restaurant he owned and had no clue about." I sniffed, trying to control the tears. Looking at anyone right now would break me to see their sympathetic faces. "I would wash dishes as soon as I got home from school until the bar closed. My hands would be bloody by the end of the night." People in the room began to shuffle around, not wanting to stay in their seats, but I continued, I had to. Get rid of all the heaviness.

"Then the cutting started. When he would get drunk, he would bang on my bedroom door, which had been stripped of everything but a mattress and a box of clothes. He would drag me to the basement, cutting places here and there. He would take his finger and put it in the wound and then put it in his mouth telling me how sweet I was going to taste once I was properly aged." I shivered. Wesley rose from his seat, breathing heavily, grunting under his breath. I didn't want to go on, so I stopped and started to silently cry. Ashley came to my side, holding me tightly.

The males in the room gathered around Wesley, holding him in place as Wesley growling from his chest and swinging his arms. His perfect hair now messy as it fell into his eyes. He was acting fierce, savage as he pushed Bruce to the floor. To help soothe me, Ashley rubbed her hands up and down my arms as she sat with me. "Keep going, it's alright," she whispered.

"What else did he do?" Wesley's voice was deep, unrecognizable like he was another person. Whispers from Evan telling him to remain calm. I shook my head, not wanting to continue. "It's Okay," Ashley comforted me again, pulling my face to her chest. Her fingers entangled in my hair, pulling it away from my face.

"He branded me with a hot iron on my back as well as in between my, m—my chest." I heaved out a long sob. "I can't talk about this anymore." I stood up to leave the room as the tears rolled like giant waves into my hair. Before I could run out the door, Wesley picked up his entire desk and flipped it over. I was too shocked to move afraid he would come after my friends or me because when he turned around, his eyes turned the brightest yellow I had ever seen. They glowed, and I'm sure it could shine through the darkest of nights.

My breath hitched as he walked towards me. My heart rate picked up, and I could hear people talking, but it only sounded like I was underwater, too muffled to listen to their cries. Holding my arms up to my chest to get some protection, Wesley stopped in front of me. Pulling me into his chest, he engulfed me into his arms, and immediate relief came through my body.

I let out a dramatic sigh as the tears continued to flow. *"You are ruined; no one will want you."* Roman's words continued to Cyrene in my mind and a heavy cry left my throat. As I tried to back away, Wesley only held me tighter.

"You are strong, Kitten. So strong," Wesley continued to whisper in my ear and pet my hair. Everyone else in the room began filter out, some giving me an encouraging pat on the back as Wesley continued to hold me close.

He pulled me back to look into my eyes. I was a mess, I knew I was, yet he still looked at me like I mattered.

"I will protect you until my last breath. You are worth protecting, and you are worth everything to me, do you understand?" I nodded my head in agreement, and he put my head back to his chest, pulling my messy hair from my wet face. In one swoop, he put his arm under my legs and the other behind my back. My body, my mind too tired react just held onto his neck while he walked up the stairs where took me to his bedroom.

Sitting me on the plush bed, he laid me down and his body didn't leave mine. He was wrapped around my small body my back to his chest. His hand continued to pet my hair as he tried to lull me to sleep. Letting out a contented sigh, my eyelids felt heavy. I'd never felt so safe, so warm. "Sleep, Kitten. I'll keep you safe," he kissed the side of my head, and I drifted off to some of the best sleep I had ever encountered.

Chapter 14

Wesley

"Alpha, we found this Roman character," Bruce walked into my office.

"That was fast, thanks," I mumbled. I took the thumb drive and plugged it into my computer to pull up Charlotte's foster parent. Even though she had yet to disclose to me what her past was, I felt it was my duty to find out what she could be so scared and timid about. She hardly trusts anyone, and Ashley has known her for a year what the hell could she be hiding that she couldn't even tell one of her closest friends about it?

Ashley spoke about the scars on her back, it pissed me the fuck off. Why not ask for help or protection? There is so much more to the story that I don't know, and I want to take my time with Charlotte, but time might be something we don't have. Once you find your mate, you imprint on them before you mark them, wolves want to protect them at all costs, and my wolf didn't have a whole lot of the patience thing right now. Being an Alpha, it is even worse. She is my queen, the Luna of the pack. She will be the ultimate mother, the nurturer. It had been embedded into her soul since she was conceived in the womb, and if any part of her is broken, I had to fix it.

Scrolling a few pages down from the open file, I found that this Roman was a restaurant owner in the upper-middle class. Nice home, cars, boats, and even single, which is surprising. However, there was no record of Charlotte ever at the residence. This puzzled me because I could have sworn that she was a foster child when she was seven and had to jump into a new home. "Pull up the state's foster system page and find out when she was moved to Roman's home," I told Bruce.

Once Bruce had obtained the information, it showed she was indeed fostered by Roman but was recorded as a runaway at age 14. The case was closed a year later. No records of trying to find Charlotte at all. "This isn't protocol, is it? To just give up a search for a girl like that in the foster system?"

"I don't believe so. That's strange," Bruce says, rubbing his chin. "I'm sure she was abused awhile then, Ashley said some scars were still purple, meaning they were still healing. Scars fade on humans but that can take years to fully heal."

"Fucking shit." I threw my phone on the desk and ran my rough hands through my hair. Evan then barged through the door. "What do you want, Evan?" I sighed in exhaustion. The harder I dug through Charlotte's past, the more questions I had. This wasn't going anywhere, and Wolf was getting pissed. She must have been at this guy's house for quite some time; how did she escape?

"Alpha just wanted to let you know Luna is in Zachary's room." I perked my head up. Zachary had an abusive past with his mother. It makes me wonder if he could get Charlotte to talk. "I know what you are thinking, but I really think you should let this go. Just get to know Charlotte. In time, she will tell you." I put my hands over my face, rubbing it rough so my hands feel the prickle of my 3-day old scruff.

"I know; I just want to help her. She feels the bond. I know she does. Something is holding her back." I sigh exhaustedly.

"You know, humans and wolves feel the bond differently," Bruce commented. "She may be fighting it because she doesn't know what it is. If she knew, maybe she would accept it more." Bruce shrugged his shoulders as he reached for a peppermint candy on my desk and threw it in his mouth.

"Not yet!" I snarled as I stood up. "Look what she's been through, she's been through hell and back, and she's scared for her life. Going up to her and saying, 'hey there, yeah, I'm a wolf, and I'm your mate, and I'm going to spend the rest of my life with you,' are NOT good ways to start a relationship with a human!"

Just then, we heard a loud knock at the door, it was Ashley with a not-so-convincing- smile on her face as well as Zachary. Zachary turned around and grabbed Charlotte's hand, which she seemed apprehensive to take. He made a motion with his head for her to follow, and she accepted with hesitation. Something was bothering her, so I went around the desk to grab her hands. Instantly, her tense body relaxed when I gave her a small hug. "Kitten, what's wrong?" Did someone hurt her? I will fucking murder them. Looking into her eyes, I see a swirl of hurt and chaos melted with regret.

"Charlotte would like to tell you something," Ashley spoke. She then mind-linked at me. "*She heard of you protecting Zachary from his mother; she's hoping you could offer her protection too.*" This worked out in my favor, and I didn't have to order anyone to do it. Of course, I would offer her protection. What the hell is she thinking? I'd do anything for my mate, I'd walk through the depths of hell for her.

I kept my eyes on my mate and rubbed her cheek with the pad of my thumb. She was on the verge of tears, and there was nothing I could do to stop it. I led her to the couch and led her to sit beside me. Rubbing one of my hands on her back while holding her hand in the other, she told me her story.

With each word that spilled out of her sweet, plump lips, I felt anger searing through my veins. My heart clenched at the thought of someone as precious as her having bruises, cuts, scars, and branding to her body and being afraid to sleep at night. There were times I couldn't even look at her, not in disgust but in pure rage. The yellow eyes I usually have when I feel a strong emotion are seeing red. Red, screaming for the blood of her abuser, to feel the warmth of his tainted soul across my filthy hands.

Bruce, Evan, and even Zachary felt the pain that their Luna had felt. My rage was becoming the best of me, and the men had to physically restrain me as she continued. I waited, waited for her to say that he sexually assaulted her, but it never came. Once she brought up the branding, the fucking branding, she lost it. Charlotte couldn't go on, she couldn't tell me anymore, and I don't know if I could either. Tears came down in waves as her broken soul. Dear Goddess, was there more to tell?

Taking that glance at her being in so much emotional pain, my wolf came forward. He took over my body faster than I could ever control him. My eyes burned yellow, and I flipped the 100-year-old mahogany desk and cracked it down the middle. Everyone stood in surprise as I continued to breathe heavily. Trying to regain what little self-control I had left, which wasn't much, I turned to Charlotte, who was staring in shock, I'm sure she saw my eyes, but at this point, I didn't give two flying shits about it. I needed to touch her, I needed to comfort her, I needed her.

"You are a strong Kitten, so strong," I whispered into her ear as I held her tight against my body. I continued to tell her what an amazing woman she was, how strong, and how fierce. Charlotte may not think she is a warrior, but to put up with such emotional and physical torture at such a young age and still come out to be this beautiful and fascinating creature is the definition of a warrior.

Everyone filtered out of the room. At the same time, Charlotte continued to bury her face into my chest, probably fearing for anyone to see her pink face. I placed a small kiss on the top of her tiny head, feeling sparks and a contented sigh from her. Feeling the purr in my chest, I could feel her relax evermore. My wolf was howling in my head for making our mate feel better.

"I will protect you until my last breath. You are worth protecting, and you are worth everything to me, do you understand?" I whispered with the truth. Feeling her nod her head, I picked her up and held her close to my chest tightly, letting her know I wasn't going to let her go. I kicked the door into my bedroom open and walked to the bed. Not hearing any complaints, I laid her down, put her beside me, and draped the covers over our bodies, not even bothering to change our clothes. Holding her back against my chest, and my chin rested on her shoulder. She had not spoken one word, just silent tears of tiny raindrops chasing down her wet cheeks.

Smelling her hair calmed my wolf, I relaxed as I held her in my embrace. Her heart rate began to slow, and her breaths became even. "Sleep, Kitten, I'll keep you safe," I whispered into her ear as I nuzzled into her neck. Gently placing tiny kisses on her marking spot.

Soft snores escaped her lips, and my wolf danced in delight, being able to protect and keep our mate safe. Charlotte being comfortable to now sleeping in my bed with me had me elated. Maybe she did feel the bond, perhaps she won't fight it anymore and stay with me. The thought of her rejecting me after her being in my arms tonight will kill me inside. A soft snarl came from my lips at the thought.

Holding her tighter into my chest, I continued to kiss her head, her neck. I'm going to be a possessive bastard, but I've looked for her for ages, and I'm never letting her go. The pack has looked so long for their Luna. Hell, I've looked so long. I've traveled all over the world looking for her and come to find out she was in one of my hotels the whole time. The Goddess works in mysterious ways.

It is still early in the night, and I can see the moon rising from my window. The light trickles in and lands on her sweet face. The moon almost pauses before rising high in the sky as if it was giving her, it's a blessing. The moon has always been a werewolf's solace, the moon calms us, but it can awaken our beasts on a full moon. Wolves become possessive, upset quickly, and once they find their mate- they evolve to be overprotective. The full moon is approaching, and I'm not sure how I will handle this situation. I won't be able to stay away, my wolf won't allow it.

If she sleeps well tonight, I wonder if she will continue to stay. I don't want to force her, but my wolf will come out if she isn't here, which would be bad for both of us. I have two weeks to win her heart to trust me, stay with me without force, and let her know about werewolves. Such a short period, but since we know about her past, maybe this will help the future. I will be able to handle how I break the supernatural world to her.

"Evan, find the bastard Roman. Address, place of work, all that. Send some warrior scouts to kill him." I mind linked.

"Alright on it, Alpha."

Cutting off the link in my mind and I nuzzled even closer if it was even possible.

Chapter 15

Charlotte

It was so warm. I hadn't felt warm like this in a long time. I continued to snuggle into the bed, the scent of pine and cedar invaded my nose as I inhaled deeply. No thoughts of my past, no nightmares, and no pain. All I felt was comfort, solace, and for the first time, warmth. There were so many nights when I felt cold. Once Roman had drastically changed from a foster father to a malicious monster, I thought I would never love a hug from any man. This warmth I never want to let go of.

As much as I love this warmth, I wanted to know where it came from, or maybe I didn't. If I find out, would I run in fear? Or would I continue my comfort and stay in the nest that I made for myself last night in this embrace? Being the curious creature I seemed to be, I fluttered my eyes open to see myself pinned up against something hard. A thin material separated me from something that felt so warm it was as if there were a space heater was on the other side.

The wall moved, and my senses began to waken. Hearing breathing, soft breaths of inhaling and exhaling, and its feel on my neck piqued my interest even more. It was a person, their body laid up against me, and not one fragment of space was in between our bodies. Afraid to move my head to wake the sleeping person, I tried to remember the night before.

Right. Pretty sure I fell asleep in my boss's arms after telling him about some of my childhood. How embarrassing. I told so many people my story. What would they think of me now? Weak? A bother? Just another nuisance to this small town? They accepted Zachary so quickly, I just hope they could do the same for me.

Hearing a soft, purr-like sound, I gently moved my head up to see the green eyes staring down at me. "Morning," he said in his hoarse, raspy voice. It was velvety, it smoothed through his lips like butter on toast. It was the sexiest sound I ever heard.

Feeling the heat rise to my cheeks, I cleared my throat to whisper a "Good morning."

"Did you sleep well?" His curious face looked into mine.

"Y-yes, thank you," I stared back. We stared into each other's eyes and didn't move. I felt like looking in Wesley's soul with those eyes. I wanted to memorize every line and feature into my own thoughts and never let it leave. He was handsome, rugged, and held so much warmth in his eyes. A man like him, how could he not have a wife or a girlfriend and yet wanted to take me on a date? Take care of me last night? Who is he really?

"I hope it was alright, having you stay." He reached behind his head to scratch his neck. "I didn't want to let you go after hearing what you went through. You didn't deserve to be alone after that. You don't deserve to ever be alone." Wesley whispered the last part into my ear. Chills flowed through my body at the brief contact.

This man could do terribly good things to me if he really wanted.

"It's a-alright. Thank you, really." *What am I doing?* My body and mind continue to argue with themselves. "Best sleep I've gotten in a long time," I smiled back at him.

"How about I bring up some breakfast? We can eat in here away from everyone?" I nodded and watched him get up. We'd both slept in our clothes from yesterday, so he continued out the door as-is. Looking around his room, I didn't realize how massive it was. I sat on a prominent California king bed adorned with a cream comforter. He had a large white, fuzzy blanket that had us wrapped up in a giant burrito. A small desk in the corner with a computer and several books along with the shelving with large bookcases of personal favorites, I'm guessing.

The window in the room was from roof to floor and covered the entire side of the wall. A small sliding door was there to get on the balcony that also had a hot tub out on it. I couldn't help but think Wesley has had some women in there with him. The thought riled me up, and I crossed my arms across my chest in a huff. Why should I care? Why do I care?

There was a knock at the door, and Wesley came in with a tray full of fruits, juices, coffee, and pancakes. The smell of food made me forget about the hot tub, though, and I couldn't help but smile. He looked so domesticated, a big CEO and leader of a small community bringing some broken girl some food.

"I brought a little bit of everything, I hope you don't mind. I'm not sure what you like," Wesley said nervously. I laughed and nodded my head.

"I can eat anything. I've never said no to food." He smiled and set the tray on the bed so we could eat together. After a few minutes of silence, I decided to break the awkwardness. "Thank you again for taking care of me last night. That isn't something I'm used to. I mean, I'm sorry if I was a burden," I continued looking at my food as I continued to cut a pancake. Wesley quickly put his hand on mine.

"You are never a burden, and it was my honor to be able to help. I really enjoyed having you in here." Wesley continued to rub my knuckles with his thumb and smiled up at me. I think I just melted.

Clearing my throat, "I guess you could show me where I'm supposed to be working today? I need to start working on the security system for the community area and talk with your other IT personnel at your companies so I can integrate all security systems here," I said, popping a strawberry in my mouth.

"Only if you feel up to it, you can take a few days to settle in." He waved his hand in dismissal.

"Nonsense, that is why I am here, right?" I chuckled.

"Not the only reason," Wesley whispered under his breath. I don't think it was meant for me to hear, but I heard it, and I felt my heart start fluttering like a lovesick puppy.

After breakfast, I left Wesley and went to my office or the 'control room' explained to me yesterday. My desk had three computer monitors, while on the other side of the room held ten large flat-screen panels divided nine different ways, each mounted to the wall. A large desk laid at the bottom with computers and buttons across them. Needless to say, there were a lot of cameras up around the property.

"Good morning, Charlotte!" a new, unfamiliar, deep voice said as I walked into the room. "I'm Taylor, I'm your assistant, and these," Taylor waved around to three people looking at the monitors, "are your patrollers." Taylor was large, like most men here in the community. He had pale skin and bright red hair and beard. Once his beard was shaved, he probably had a cute baby face.

"Pleasure to meet you." I held out my hand to shake.

"Is this your first time in?" We walked together as he led me towards my desk.

"Wesley showed me around, I was able to glance in here briefly." I smiled and placed my cup of hot cocoa on the desk.

"Excellent. So here are the big screens that watch the community borders, we have the cameras up, and we just wanted you to run through the system for any bugs."

"I'll get on it, thanks Taylor."

I spent the next few hours going through all the cameras' diagnostics, making sure each camera could swivel, move, zoom in and out. The three people that sat in front of the TVs were vigilant. They never took their eyes away from any of the screens and took their jobs very seriously. The girl's name was Nene, she was shorter than the men with dark brown hair and hazel eyes. When she spoke, her eyes never left the screens, but she was sweet to me, nonetheless.

The other two men that sat with her never spoke, they were too busy clicking on different sections of the screen, zooming in at odd angles of the border area. The nods only let me know that they heard me.

The day dragged on, and I really wanted to see Wesley. I kept having this tugging feeling to at least go say hello or tell him how everything was going. I've been known to be fast in running my own computer software, but he told me only to concentrate on the security cameras today. Tapping my finger on the desk a few times, I decided to text him. He told me I could text him whenever I wanted, so why not try?

Charlotte: Wesley, all security cameras for the border are up and running. :)

I put my phone down, only to glance at it every few moments to see if he replied back. Back and forth, I looked. Nothing. I was stupid. Why did I put a smiley face? Maybe I shouldn't have texted at all. Now I'm overthinking; this is getting annoying.

Wesley: Great job, Kitten. That was fast. How about we celebrate? ;)

My heart jumped at his response, and his cheeky winky-face caught me off guard. Though I didn't hesitate to reply immediately.

Charlotte: What did you have in mind?

Wesley: Dinner with me. I'll meet you in the foyer at 6. x

"You must be having too much fun. You shouldn't be giggling at work." Zachary slapped his hand on the desk, causing me to jump.

"Zachary!" I whined. "Don't scare me like that!"

"Well, at least you didn't shit yourself like you normally do. Seems like that talk about you being safe here did you some good," Zachary sat in the chair next to me as I continued to scroll down the computer screen. I tilted my head towards him.

"You're right. I do feel better. First time in a while, actually," I said, fiddling with the mouse on my computer.

"That's because," he wiggled his eyebrows, "you also have the strongest male in the entire place fawning over you."

"What?" I blushed. "No, no. He is just being friendly." I waved my hand at him.

"No? Well, I just heard him on the phone talking to his driver wanting him to be ready at 6 so he could take a special girl out." My face felt hot, and I thought I saw stars.

"H-he's my boss! I can't get into a relationship with him. What would people think?" I whispered harshly.

"Trust me," Zachary looked around and leaned over to whisper, "people are rooting for you two. Wesley's been single for a long time." Zachary winked and got up from his chair. "I'll tell Ashley to be in your room at five to help you get dressed."

***

Five minutes to six, and my butterflies felt like full-blown eagles in my stomach again. I swore I could almost soar out the window. Wesley really liked me? A plain computer geek with a terrible past, and he still wanted to take me out on a date?

Ashley just left, and I brushed down the black fitted dress to my knees. It had lace from neck to wrists. People might see this as plain, but I really liked it and loved how it fit. To dress it up, I picked out gold strappy heels that wrap up to mid-cal. My strawberry blonde hair was curled and pinned to the right side of my head with slightly tousled, side-swept bangs. Picking up the small ruby solitaire necklace and putting it on, I gave one last quick glance. I felt pretty. I felt a little more confident.

After looking at the clock and seeing that it was now just one minute to six, I headed down the stairs. Putting my hand on the railing and slowly descending, looking down at my feet so I didn't fall, I heard a collective gasp. Down the stairs that veered off to the right, I saw Ashley, Zachary, and the man of the evening, Wesley. They kept looking at me, worried I had something on my face. I started to touch my face, look at my dress, and look behind me to make sure there wasn't any toilet paper on my shoe. Ashley continued to wave at me to come down, so I did cautiously.

Once I continued down, Wesley held out his hand once I was at the last step and kissed the back of my hand. He was wearing his black Armani suit with his matching all-black shirt and tie. It was crisp, just cleaned, and hugged his muscles. He looked delicious with his low, short ponytail in the back. I giggled how it reminded me of some princess movie. One particular movie with a beast and a massive library.

"What's so funny, Kitten?" his voice said hoarsely.

"You just remind me of someone," I smirked. "Story for another time." Giving my hand a light squeeze, he led me to the door.

"Shall we?" he said.

"We shall."

Chapter 16

Wesley

After the fiasco yesterday, bearing her soul and history of her past, I wanted to do something nice for her. Even having her wake up in my arms this morning, letting me nuzzle her, and not having a full-blown panic attack was a miracle in itself. Charlotte was starting to trust me, and the bond that we shared was helping with that.

Stepping out of the limo, I grabbed her hand so we could enter the restaurant. I wanted to shower her with things she had never acquired or experienced. She left home at just fourteen, and I have yet to hear the hardships she had to endure on her own. I hope that she will be able to tell me more tonight.

Putting her hand in the crook of my arm, we walked into the restaurant with all eyes on us. She continued to blush as people started taking pictures, I wasn't aware people knew we were coming to look at the CEO that never dates. Still, she's too beautiful to not take a picture of her. Soon, even in the human and supernatural in the world will know she's mine as I am hers.

Approaching the podium, the hostess takes no time to ask my name and grabs the menus as we walk to the back of the restaurant. Large chandeliers, white marble columns, and a soothing live band played in the background. Normally, I would walk quickly to the back of the restaurant, but Charlotte was taking it all in. Her mouth parted once we reached the back. I liked this restaurant because the back had VIP private tables where curtains could be drawn for complete privacy at our booth.

The golden curtains were lifted to each side as we both slid into the booth and sat closer to each other. Charlotte didn't seem to mind as I grabbed her hand under the table as we looked at our menus. Her nose liked to scrunch up while she thought and squint her eyes as she read the menu with such concentration.

"Wesley?" she said my name quietly.

"Yes, Kitten?" I glanced down at her. She was just so small, my giant hand engulfed hers so well.

"I'm not sure what to get. Will you order for me?" With those doe eyes, how could anyone say no?

"Of course, my love." Charlotte's eyes widened, and a blush appeared on her face. Does she really not think she couldn't be loved? I grabbed her face with one of my hands and lifted her head up until her gaze met mine. Her eyes were glassy, not about to cry but a look of longing.

"What are you thinking? What is going on in that mind of yours?"

"I, I don't know. It's silly." She laughed. I tilted my head to the side, begging her to continue. "You give me all these terms of endearment. I just like it, I suppose." Charlotte grinned happily while trying to hold in her blush.

"I will call you anything you want if you'd please stay by my side." I reached for her hand and caressed her knuckles. "Will you, Charlotte, stay by my side?" The waitress opened the curtain and brought a man to the table as she was about to speak. Charlotte's face paled, and fear was radiating off of her. I didn't even have to use my Wolf senses to know it.

"Pardon me, Mr. Hale, but this gentleman asked to speak with the young lady." These were private booths for a reason, for privacy. The woman looked robotic as she spoke of the man's intentions. His complexion was pale and dead. Vampire. The fucker was a Vampire, and he was using his compulsion.

I stood up quickly and buttoned my jacket. Charlotte's body shook, she knew who he was, and I had a sickening feeling that I might know who he was as well. "Can we help you? This is a private area. You shouldn't be back here."

The Vampire gave a grim smile and nodded toward Charlotte. She was now stark white, not a bit of color on her face. My Wolf was ready to spring forth in front of a bunch of humans. "Leave," I growled loudly. "Don't cause a scene. We both know we don't want that."

"I'm just here to get back what's mine," he picked up my glass of wine and took a sip. "Her branding will suffice as proof." Tears started were building in Charlotte's eyes as she clutched the table. This fucker had another thing coming.

"She isn't going anywhere. I suggest you leave." I walked up to the smell of rotting flesh and put my chest next to his. I was still inches taller than him, but I knew he had some brute strength through his Vampire capabilities.

"The branding is special. She is mine. Why don't you show him, dear?" His voice was calm, the calm before the storm that was stirring in his mind.

"I'm not yours," she whispered delicately. "Never was, never will be." Even though her voice swung in the air like a floating feather, any supernatural could hear it. She meant every word of it, and she wasn't going to change her mind. Charlotte may have been scared shitless, but she knew what she wanted.

Roman growled lowly in his throat, "And do pray tell, who takes ownership of you now?" Charlotte stopped shaking and stood up. Something about this mark that I heard of kept her in a submissive state while she was with him. Roman gripped his hands into fists, watching her defy his requests. Feeling the compulsion in the air that he was throwing at her, I watched as her eyes narrowed.

"No one owns me. I am my own person," she spoke in a monotone voice. A few moments went by again, and she glanced from me to Roman, shaking whatever compulsion he had on her. How she was able to get away from this Vampire is beyond me, human minds haven't been trained for mind trickery.

Within the blink of an eye, Roman lunged at Charlotte ripping her black lace dress from top to bottom, looking in between her breasts. A light scar that looked to be a brand laid there. Charlotte fell forward into the seat from his brute force. The rest of her body was littered with deep scars, gashes, and even Roman's name spelled out on the side of her ribcage as she tried to cover herself.

"Fuck!" he whispered and turned to me. My hands were already around his neck, trying to keep the demon from drawing any more attention. "You are her mate," he spat. "She's still mine, I marked her first! Her blood is MINE." Roman continued to lunge at me as I wrestled him to the floor. All hope to keep this under control was out the window.

Glasses and plates were shattering as people screamed around the restaurant in terror. People were running in all directions while my mate sat at the table, trying to cover herself. She was frozen in place, watching the two men fight. I prayed to the goddess she wouldn't find out what we truly were at this moment; I don't think her heart could take it.

The warriors stationed outside stormed in with a mighty fury, and Roman realized he was surrounded. Glancing between the warriors and Charlotte, he let out a snarl. His eyes glowed red. "I'll be back for her. I claimed her first, you filthy dog!" With that, he ran out of the restaurant before I could even get another claw into his neck. Picking myself up, I ran to a stunned Charlotte. Taking off my Jacket, I covered her body. The warriors began to pay the restaurant for the damages, and some scanned the area for more threats.

Scooping her up quickly, I carried her bridal style out of the car. So much for a nice date and getting to know one another.

I kept whispering to her as we walked out of the restaurant. "It will be alright, I've got you." Charlotte buried her face into my neck, and I could feel the wetness from her tears. Gripping her tighter, I sat in the SUV and drove back to the packhouse in silence. My grip on her tightened as I covered her with my arms to keep her safe.

Charlotte

He found me. After all these years, he'd finally found me. I had let my guard down, and he approached me even when Wesley sat beside me. Wesley was not slim and trim. He was muscular, you could see the rippling muscles underneath his dress shirts when he would simply run his hand through his hair.

I had never seen such a fight, Wesley fought with his jacket on, unable to remove it since Roman moved so fast. I've never seen Roman move so fast before, it was unearthly, he was something else that I had never seen, or maybe I never dared to see it. His strength felt the same, he ripped the front of my dress to shreds, and all my scars were out in the open for Wesley to see. Shame was all over me, my heart ached for him to see me like that. I tried to cover myself, but it was all in vain with a torn dress. A dress I had specifically picked out to cover my shame.

Wesley never said a word after he fought valiantly against Roman. He fought for me, no one has ever done that before. It made me feel like I could be safe. However, Roman will always be at the forefront of my mind until the day he's dead and cold in the grave.

Feeling Roman's rage from across the table was unfathomable. His aura, his being, was being outreached throughout the restaurant, and I was at the brunt of it. When he asked me who I belonged to, I usually told him that I belonged to him. However, this time I didn't which shocked me to the core. I always told him I belonged to him, but my mouth deceived me and told him I didn't. I would get punished for this one day can already felt the pain.

Riding back to the packhouse, the car was silent. Would Wesley still protect me? Will he still let me stay, knowing I pose such a threat to everyone else? Trying to hold back the tears, he lifted me to his lap and patted my head with his large hand and held me close. "I'm here for you, I'm never leaving you," he whispered.

I turned my head and looked up at him. He was so tall. I felt so small in his arms, but the best feeling was that I felt safe. His eyes glanced from my eyes to my lips and back to my eyes again. He leaned down halfway, waiting for me to meet the other half. Not hesitating, I lifted my mouth up to his and touched his pouty lips for my very first kiss. Right now, probably wasn't the best time for a kiss but a pull within me wanted it more than anything.

Chapter 17
Charlotte

His lips were soft when they touched me. The little pout he made before he kissed me was the sexiest thing I had ever seen. His lips continued to peck, tasting the last bit of my vanilla lip gloss. He began to lick the bottom of my lip, lingering longer the longer as I waited to respond. His lips parted, and mine followed close behind before he ever so gently inserted his tongue into my mouth.

He tasted like orange creamsicles. So fresh. He caressed my tongue until a slight rumble from his chest was felt through my hands on his chest. My hands continued to stay feeling a satisfying rumble while he teased me with more of his kisses. He trailed his mouth to my cheek, leaving small kisses in its wake. Traced his mouth down to my neck, I let out a small moan I didn't know I was holding. My body heated up the way he could make me feel. Never have I had this feeling before, I didn't know if it was expected, but my body seemed to like it. My hands quickly went around his neck, and I pulled at his low ponytail and let his hair fall around his face. Small tugs made him groan as he kissed a sweet spot between my neck and shoulder. My head couldn't help but fall back to let him get better access.

His grip tightened, pulling me impossibly closer to him. My chest was flushed with his as he pulled me close. With my hand entangled in his hair and his hands around my waist, I felt so content, and it felt so right. I didn't want this moment to end. Falling hard and fast for a man that could have any woman he wanted, and he settled for some broke computer programmer with a horrible past.

The car came to a stop, and he let out a grunt of dissatisfaction. He pulled from our locked lips and gazed into my eyes. His hand came up to my face, and the pad of his thumb danced across my cheek. "Stay with me tonight. Just to sleep, I need to know you are safe," he pleaded in his husky voice. Gazing back into his forest green eyes, I could feel the truth behind them. He wasn't untrustworthy, he was genuinely concerned. He hadn't tried anything before, why would he now?

"Alright," I said with a smile. His grin met both sides of his ears as he gave me another squeeze.

We exited the car, and I went to my room to get dressed for the night. Washing my face for the night, dinner is long forgotten as my body heated thinking about being held in Wesley's arms. He was already undressed, wearing basketball shorts and a white t-shirt. He motioned for me to come to the bed, and I crawled in with him, not hesitating a moment because it just felt right. A man who would fight off any of my demons without question deserved a little reward, even if it was just to cuddle.

I hope Macaroni will be alright with me sleeping in another room.

I snuggled under his neck and felt him draw circles in my back with one hand while he played with my hair in the other. "You know," he began. "You never answered my question," he chuckled.

"What question was that again? It has been quite an evening," I said jokingly.

"I asked if you would be by my side. Will you be mine?" His voice was nervous, and I felt him hold me slightly tighter.

"I thought it was kind of obvious," I laughed. "I don't go around kissing people or sleeping in their beds." He smiled as he looked at me while I looked up at him. "So yes, I'll be yours, as you will be mine, right?"

"Of course. We are each other's," He gave me the biggest grin. His hand went up to my face as we kissed for a second, third, and fourth time before blissfully falling asleep until I heard him mumble, "Mine."

Wesley

As much as I wanted to stay tangled up in my mate's arms, I had to meet Evan and Bruce in my office. My feelings were going wild as Charlotte let me not only kiss her but have her say that she was mine. Not all my secrets have been let out, but I knew she would be able to understand why I kept it from her in time. As long as we share the bond together, I pray she will not be harsh with my reasonings.

Untangling myself from her, making sure the covers stayed around her tightly, I walked down to the office where Evan and Bruce stood. "What the hell happened?" I spoke in a clipped tone.

"We don't know, he came out of nowhere, you know how Vampires are. Tricky little fuckers." Evan crossed his arms as he leaned on the desk. "We just didn't know that Charlotte's foster dad was one of them. That would have been helpful to know." Bruce nodded.

"The security cameras at the restaurant show that he was walking by the restaurant when he spotted her. I don't think he knew she was going to be there; it was an utter coincidence. Bad luck, bad timing," Bruce said solemnly with a shake of his head. He put the pictures of Roman on the table with circles around his face in the crowd. "He was pissed though, when he saw her."

As he looked at Charlotte, Roman's look was pure rage, his jaw was clenched, and his eyes glowed red. The Vampire didn't know how to keep his anger under control in public, something that his coven would be pissed about. Vampires were cold creatures but had set new rules in place almost 50 years ago to protect humans. They stopped their cruel treatments and were only allowed to feed on those willing or drink the blood of animals.

"Why would he care about Charlotte? Why torture her? The practice of messing with humans is outdated," Evan sighed in exhaustion.

"He is probably old, older than we think. Roman may not like the new ways and continues to practice the old. However, it is strange he kept her from a young age and kept her alive all those years. Older vamps would just play with their food for a few months then be done with it. He kept her for years and mutilated her," Bruce spoke.

A growl left my chest, rattling the books on the new desk that was delivered this afternoon. Rubbing my hand through my hair, I tried to think what was it that had Roman so fascinated with her. Was she, his beloved? "What do you guys know about Vampire's beloveds?"

Evan's head shot up. "No, she couldn't be. Why would he mess up her skin like that?" Evan asked in disbelief.

"Vampires are weird," Bruce spoke. "They force their love if that love is not returned. Since Charlotte is human, maybe she didn't feel a bond with him? Or she isn't his beloved after all but decided to take matters in his own hands to control her while she was young, to pressure her into when she became of age to accept a mark." Bruce shrugged. "Then again, I'm no expert on that. We should ask the elders in the morning." I nodded.

"Do we know where he went, at least? Did the trackers find him?" I spoke to both of them.

"He ran out of the state, he was fast and ran through rivers and streams to kill his scent, so he knows we are after him," Evan sputtered.

"Good, we need security up and running at full force. Let everyone know. I'll have the elders check the mark in the morning he'd made on Charlotte. That brand she told us about apparently is fading, and I want to know what it is."

"The hell? The branding he made was some sort of mark, and it's fading?" Evan's eyes turned black. Everyone in the pack had been on edge since the attack only a few hours ago, and now everyone is protective of their Luna from being in any danger. We haven't told anyone about her past, that will be something that she will share on her own time. They do know she has suffered, and someone wants to make her suffer more.

"Yes, I'll have more answers tomorrow." I spoke quickly and exited the room. Charlotte was still sleeping on the bed, curled up into a ball. I slid into the sheets with her, and she immediately grabbed hold of me as her life depended on it. Even though it was the bond keeping her close, I still wanted to keep winning her heart. Just because there is a bond doesn't mean that your mate will love you. Stroking her hair helped calm my beast as we too fell asleep with our mate in our arms.

***

Charlotte sat in office typing away on her computer, creating another program so that I would be alerted anywhere in the world of a breach in our territory. She kept commenting how my phone would have everything I ever needed. My little mate was so bright, coming out with great ideas on how to help the security of her pack. The blue-lensed glasses she wore in the office made me want to bed her even more. Relationships going humanly slow were killing my Wolf, but I wasn't about to ruin all the progress we made.

The thought of her playing sexy teacher or sexy secretary was going to get me into trouble. Quickly adjusting myself before I walked in, she looked up at me and smiled. Our hot make-out session this morning just wasn't enough. Charlotte did do more than I thought she would ever do, though. She put her hands up underneath my shirt and rubbed her hands all over my body which I had to get her to stop by her disappointment. Thank you, mate bond. If we continued any further, I'm sure my Wolf would have marked her then and there.

After checking on her briefly, I headed out to the far south of the territory where most of the elders or the oldest Werewolves lived. They became the historians of the pack, and when we were dealing with a new situation or something that had worked in the past to deal with anything political, I would go to them. Believe it or not, you can learn from your history.

Evan decided to join me, he started to have a real soft spot for Charlotte. After last night's attempted attack and kidnapping, he had taken upon himself to speak with the elders already this morning.

"Greetings, Alpha," Elder Ellery spoke. She was one of the few women that wanted to become a historian. Most would rather sit back and relax, help their children and grandchildren with pups.

"Good morning, Ellery." Her red hair was still fiery even at her ripe old age of 500. That was the best thing about being a Werewolf, in my opinion.

Not aging and immortality had its perks, it just sucks when your loved ones die in battle and having to live without them. Luckily the mate bond helps with that most of the time. You die with the one you love, so you don't ever have to be alone. That is only if love is gained though, bonds don't always bring love if you don't tend to the relationship.

"We had the elders that are particularly well versed in Vampirism come earlier this morning to pull some old files. We have yet to put everything through the computer. We are hoping Luna will be able to help us since she is so capable," Ellery smiled in delight.

"I'm sure she would be very pleased to help once she is aware of our kind," I said solemnly. I didn't like keeping secrets from her, but I just needed more time. I don't think I could handle the rejection if she said she wanted no part of this world. However, I'm afraid she is already in it too deep with Vampires.

Ellery knocked on the door several times to warn the people on the other side of our presence. "Alpha, great to see you this morning," Timothy stood up to shake my hand.

"Good to see you as well, ready to get down to business," I sputtered. The quicker we sorted this out, the better.

Timothy sat down and pulled old parchment papers from the pile. "Evan said that you saw a branding on Luna that was on her chest and there is another one on her back?" I growled when he mentioned her chest, even though it was innocent. "I'm sorry, Alpha, I didn't know how else to describe it."

"It's fine," I waved my hand.

"There was only one thing I found, and it's old, ancient. I'm talking back to the time when the gods had full rule over the mortals." The rest of the people in the room went silent as Timothy continued. "When Vampires were first created, they had almost unlimited power. They were able to conjure things and use witchcraft. Vampires were the ultimate weapon to help destroy or thin out some more evil humans or demi-gods. Once they had done their job, the goddess Hecate revoked most of their powers and created a new being, Witches. She thought that one being having unlimited powers would be cruel. The powers we see today are powers of compulsion, some can even practice opening locks, small levitations, and so forth when they are old enough and begin to tap into their own DNA from their previous ancestors. They have to be around at least 200 years to tap into these powers."

"What does this have to do with the branding, Timothy? I growled. "I'm losing patience here."

"Right, sorry." Timothy looked down. I'm sure all this ties into what we are talking about, but I don't need a boring history lesson when I could be sitting inside with Charlotte. "Does the branding look like this?" Timothy slid an old parchment across the table which had the shape of an infinity symbol with the letters, "Et Ecce Mae" above and below the emblem. I nodded to Timothy, and he rubbed his brow with his index finger. He let out a slight hum and continued.

"Et Ecce Mae, along with the infinity symbol, means 'Mine to behold, forever.' Long ago, before beloveds or mates were explained to Vampires, they would take hold of a human if they had feelings for them or thought to have feelings. Something in their demonic side takes over and becomes possessive over their human. They would keep humans locked up for years if their blood was not ripe enough for the changing of becoming a Vampire. Their inner demon calls out to them to have them checked often, usually by taking a blade and cutting the skin." Timothy dropped his head. "The branding is their pre-claiming. It warns off other Vampires and strengthens the compulsion to the human. Makes them scared to leave, obey them, fear them, and can never tell them lies. It is almost impossible to getaway. How Luna was able to get away, is a miracle."

I stood up quickly, throwing the chair across the room, and pulled at my hair. Growling out, I looked at the rest of the members at the table. Evan and the elders dare not look me in the eye. "What else, what does this mean? It's fading, the Vamp said it was fading."

"Fading?" Ellery questioned. Several other elders stood up to grab other books off the shelves and started flipping pages hastily. Evan shrugged his shoulders at me in question, and I continued to stand. "Does she know that it was a Vampire that did this?"

"Not that I am aware. I guess it is possible."

"Here," Timothy pulled out a witchcraft history book and flipped a few pages on 'bond branding.' "This bond branding hasn't been practiced for quite a while, but it can still be used. Special branding plates have to be made and blessed. How this Roman character got them is beyond me."

"As fascinating as it all is, I still need to know: why is it fading?" I growled.

"The only way a branding bond can be erased is by a true mate's bond. It must be fading because you came into the picture," Timothy said with a smile. "There is hope. I'm guessing you could mark her, and the brand would completely disappear."

"You guess? I need more than just a 'guess' Timothy! I don't want to hurt her!" I spat.

"This is the only information I can give you, Alpha. I'm sorry. I can schedule a trip to visit the Vampire Council of the North America's and see if they could shed some light on the matter." Timothy gulped and rubbed his hands.

"Go. Today preferably. Take three other elders with you. I'll let them know your intention of meeting with them. They know our pack has alliances with them. You shouldn't have any problems," I grunted and started to head to the door when Evan stopped me.

"So, you don't think Charlie has any knowledge of Vampires?" Evan put his hand on my shoulder as we went to the door.

"Right, why?"

"Well, she might know about Werewolves now," he laughed a boisterous noise, and everyone stared at him in annoyance. "Because she just saw a bunch of naked men running around and shifting on the border cameras."

Vera Foxx

Chapter 18

Charlotte

Sleeping in Wesley's room the past two nights has been utter bliss. I haven't slept so well in years. I felt safe, protected, and honestly loved. I don't think anyone has ever made me feel this way. The way he nuzzles into my neck and hair gives me chills every time. I kept trying to sneak my hands under this shirt to feel that purring in his chest I was becoming addicted to. The giggles I kept letting had my mood lightened considerably as his legs continued to wrap around mine.

These heavy feelings I keep feeling with him are so abnormal and not part of who I am. I shy away from people, I am stand-offish, but it isn't like that with him. He took down my walls and he didn't even really understand how much of a big deal that was to me. Now I wasn't as apprehensive about what others thought about us either, all the positive vibes from Ashely and Zachary helped. Heck, Ashley has been squealing every time she walks past the security room while I'm working, making kissy faces. I can't help but smile at her antics. She wanted me to be happy, and I wanted to be happy. What if it doesn't work out, though? I would have to leave and then be all alone running from Roman again.

When we woke up this morning, him nuzzling into my hair, I let out a moan that made him stop. Never having noises leave my mouth like that made me utterly embarrassed. I kept apologizing and he just laughed into my hair, saying it was fine and normal. "I like it when you make sounds like that. It makes me know you like it." He continued to rub his nose up and down my neck, and he began kissing and nipping the skin. If I thought his nose on my neck felt good, lips with little pecks of kisses and sucking were putting me in heaven. I felt something deep within the pit of my stomach I hadn't felt before, a longing, desire, and heat flowed through me. Not knowing these feelings, hoping they were normal, I wanted to explore them more. It must have been the morning haze of not really knowing what you were doing, but I didn't care right then.

His lips traveled up to my mouth and kissed me lightly, like asking for permission. Hastily returning the favor, I kissed him back and nibbled on his bottom lip which made him growl in the back of his throat. His kiss went from light and playful to forceful. Wesley's tongue slid between my lips, rubbing against my now puffy lips. Hands went in his hair, and I pulled him closer as his tongue massaged the inside of my mouth. His muscular hands, at my waist, pulling me closer to him. The warmth of his body only increased the heat between my legs. I swear I needed some sort of friction, but I wasn't ready to venture that far.

As Wesley continued kissing me, his arms wrapped around my back and held my neck in place as he gained better access to my mouth and hovered over my body. My body was encaged with his, the heat of his chest on my body. My hands went lower because I wanted to feel him. I wanted to feel the muscle beneath his shirt. He was nothing but rippling muscles, and I felt electric with delight as I made contact with my fingertips. My fingers traced his pectoral muscles, and he let out a shiver contracting those muscles. I continued my assault on his torso until I reached his abdominal muscles. Taking one finger at a time and tracing each and every square made him quickly grab my hand once I got the bottom abdominal next to his delectable v-line near his hips.

Wesley let out a chuckle and took my hand and kissed it. "I'm sorry, Kitten. As much as I want to continue, and I really do, we should stop." I nodded in embarrassment, and he tilted my chin back to meet his eyes. "Oh, I want to, believe me. I just don't know if you want to tame this beast just yet." I let out a small laugh and tapped his chest.

It had been so hard concentrating this morning. I kept thinking back to that hot make-out session with a little too much touching on my part. I hope he didn't think I was some slut, my body was just having a mind of its own. I sound like some horny teenager.

Tap, tap, tap.

All morning I've tried to keep myself busy to not think about it. I was craving Wesley like he was a drug, and I was an addict. I wanted to get my fix, and I just couldn't right now because I was stuck to this chair, trying to look busy. I can't help that I ran programs and algorithms that I created that look out for all my jobs that I needed to do. Nothing needed to get fixed.

Tap, tap, tap.

106

The new security personnel that watch the camera monitors have been nothing short of being completely silent. They watch those screens like their very lives depended on it, and if their eyes left the screens but a second, the whole world would implode on itself. They never talk, just nod and let me know that they hear me. The complete silence was deafening. Then I heard it, a *ping*.

The ping was for me, something in my software let me know that someone was using high amounts of data usage that could impede the video cameras. The whole security system was on one network, the other community members could not get on this separate internet line, so there was free-flowing data between the cameras and the screen, causing live feed access to the cameras. No delays in the slightest. Someone somewhere had broken into that internet network, or someone with the passcode was using it for another purpose.

Putting my earbuds in to listen to some music and get my head in the game, I started tracing the computer in question. After a few clicks and breaking into the perpetrator's computer, I could see what they were doing. Actually, what they were watching. Oh. My. Lord.

Porn, they were watching porn. My virgin eyes were now tainted with skin slapping, tongue licking, and too many moans and cries for me to comprehend. I started squealing and yelling, "GROSS OH NO, TURN IT OFF! WHO DOES THIS!?" I ripped my earphones off and closed the window with a few clicks and fell back into my chair. The two guards looking at the screen were now staring at me in disbelief and shock as I stood there with utter horror written all over my face. Dear Lord, I hope they didn't think I was watching that.

I started stuttering, "S-someone is u-using t-the internet for s-security to watch...." I paused before I blurted out the word, "PORN!" I squealed. Both of the security guards started laughing while my head was buried in my hands.

"Are you sure that it wasn't you watching it?" One of the guys, named Sven, chuckled while Thomas beside him punched him in the shoulder. "What? Just checking?"

"I would NEVER!" I screamed. "The computer is in the house, someone has the password, the computer belongs to a David Shriver?" I said, shaking from the utter shock. I had never seen a penis, in ready-to-use form, while in usage before.

"That dick," Thomas spoke. "Yeah, he has access to the password, he takes the night shift."

"Well, we are changing passwords, and he no longer has access," I said firmly. "My poor eyes, I've never seen anything like that before." I sighed in exhaustion.

"You've never watched porn? Or seen a dick?" Sven chided.

"No, neither?" I said questioningly. Both of them looked at each other and cursed under their breath.

"Well, damn," Sven said as they both went back to look at the screens. "I'll call Bruce, and he will handle it, Charlotte, don't worry."

I sat back at my desk and realized I needed some coffee. Trudging out of the office and heading to the kitchen, I started the espresso machine to make myself a latte. Putting both hands on the counter and leaning against it, I looked up to see Ashley standing beside me, folding her arms with a smile on her face. "How are you doing, Charlie?"

"Fiiiiine," I said as I picked up my coffee mug. Take a small sip. I sighed and went back to take an even bigger sip.

"Heard you saw your first dick?" As soon as the words left her mouth, I spit my latte all over the kitchen counter. Her laughter was loud as she screamed and squealed. People walking by stared and whispered. Grabbing a towel, I wiped up the mess while Ashley finished her fit of laughter.

"It wasn't trying to go looking for one. It just popped up on my computer because some guy named David used the wrong internet, and I thought someone hacked it," I rolled my eyes and gave an exasperated sigh.

"I know, I know, it is fun to tease," Ashley put her hand on mine. "How's everything going, by the way, with the cameras and security?"

"Great, everything's going well. In fact, I'm pretty bored. I've got programs running to let me know if anything out of the ordinary comes up, so I don't have to stay in the office all day if I didn't want to."

"Aren't you a smart cookie?" She laughed. After a few minutes of meaningless talking, I headed back to the security room with my second cup of latte and sat down at the desk. I looked over at the monitors to not see anyone there. Thomas and Sven were gone, and no one was crewing the station. Since I had nothing better to do, I went to the security cameras and sat down in Thomas's seat.

Clicking the small box at the right-hand corner, I open it up to fill the entire TV. As I'm sipping away, glancing from screen to screen until I see someone moving on the borderlines on one of the cameras. It was Zachary in just a pair of basketball shorts. He was looking around and talking to someone off-screen and put his hands on his hips.

Was everyone in this community so buff? And why is he so far out there? He was at least a few miles away with no shoes and shirt. Before I could ask any more questions, with a quick swipe, he dropped his shorts. Zachary stood there, as naked as the day he was born, walking around. I didn't have to imagine anything—his manhood was there for all to see. Then Zachary and another man walked up to him. They were shoving each other and laughing.

I let out a yell, finally coming out of my shocked state. I had seen way too much of the male genitalia today. I went from never seeing one to seeing three, someone, please help me! Ashley walked in and said, "What? Watching some more porn in here?" She laughed until she froze.

I was still staring at the screen when Zachary got on all fours and began to sprout fur, his arms and legs were bent at odd angles, and his face elongated. Even though I couldn't hear anything, I knew he was making some sort of noise the way his body was bending and contorting into some kind of beast. As quickly as it started, it ended, and I saw a Wolf in his place. He was almost as tall as the man, who was still naked, beside him.

My breath quickened, and the other man transform into the same thing Zachary had transformed into. I turned to Ashley, pointing at the screen. "What the hell is that!? What in the hell is going on?" Waving my hands around going to Ashley, waiting for some kind of explanation.

"I, uh, um…." She held panic in her eyes as they dilated and became glossy. It was like she wasn't even paying attention to me anymore. I turned around, and there were several of them, Wolves. They were all over the screen. My breathing quickened, and I knew I had to slow down, or I was going to pass out.

"Ashley, please talk to me! What just happened? They just turned into Wolves! You saw that, right?" Am I going mad? They really did that, didn't they? Finding a chair, I sat down, my breathing not slowing down and Ashley just staring off into space. This was not happening. What kind of place did I move into?

Before setting my head down on the desk, I felt a warm hand on my back, trying to still myself. Knowing who it was, I looked up at him, Wesley. He found me while my tears were glossy from the threat of tears ready to break through the dam. "I-I s-saw…" before I could speak another word, he picked me up, arm behind my knees and the other arm behind my back. He cradled me to his chest, it was so warm.

"Shh, it's OK," he petted my hair. "What did you see?" he said concern laced in his voice.

I paused, not sure where to start. My morning had been interesting enough and then it threw in some more nakedness and Wolves into the mix. "Naked men, I've seen too many naked men!" I squealed, covering my face with my hands.

"WHAT?" he growled towards Ashley. He growled, it made sense. He was one of them too, they all were! I jumped from his lap, feeling a bit sad about it, but my fear was catching up with me. Ashley stepped back in fear, and I followed. Was he going to change into them too? Right here?

"Wait, Charlotte," Wesley calmed down almost instantly. "I'm sorry, I didn't mean to shout." He held out his hand for me to take. I looked at his hand and then back at his face. He was sorry, his eyes told me, but I was still conflicted.

"Are you, are you one of them too?" I spoke shakily. "The w-Wolves outside…" I pointed to the screen. "Are you all Wolves?" My breathing picked up again, all chance of calming down was ruined. No matter what he said, I was going to pass out.

"Calm down, Kitten," he held his hands up while walking toward me.

"You do NOT tell a woman to calm down! That is the dumbest thing a man could say!" I screeched. Wesley and Ashley looked at each other. "Answer the question, are you?!"

Wesley nodded as well as Ashley. I fell back into the chair behind me and put my hand to my forehead, praying it was a dream. "What are you guys?" I whispered so low; I was surprised they heard it.

"Werewolves," Wesley replied in a hushed tone, and then I fell senseless.

Chapter 19

Wesley

"You are a complete mother fucking idiot!" I screamed at Zachary, who was only in his basketball shorts leaning over a sleeping Charlotte. "What the hell were you thinking? You knew those cameras were out there, and you stepped right in front of one? What the fuck is wrong with you?!"

Zachary held up his hands. "In my defense, she wasn't supposed to be watching them. Where were the guys supposed to be watching the cameras? She told me she never watches because other people are tending to them!"

I growled out at him, and he bared his neck in submission. "This isn't a GAME. I wasn't ready to tell her yet, and you shocked her! Not only that, but she's also been seeing dicks all day," I grumbled while taking my hand and wiping it down my face. Ashley snickered and covered her mouth, and I quickly darted my eyes at her.

"Is there something funny that I am not aware of?"

Ashley stuttered, "N-no, Alpha!" She stood at attention while the rest in the room were cowering in fear. I had Charlotte lying on the desk with her head being cradled by a suit jacket to make it more comfortable. Before I was about to bark out more orders to do damage control, she stirred.

Groaning and rubbing her eyes like a toddler, she sat up. "I had a terrible dream," she said groggily. Blinking a few times, she all looked at us, and her face was crestfallen. "It wasn't a dream, was it?" she whispered to no one in particular. Charlotte's eyes were wide, yet she didn't show fear like she had before.

Charlotte threw her legs over the table and sat up straight while fixing her hair. She glowered at me and pointed her finger. "I want answers. Right now."

111

She didn't seem so scared of me now. I told everyone to leave, but she stopped me. "Nuh-uh, everyone stays. I'm not alone in a room by myself, even if all of you are some sort of wolfy-cult thing," she spat.

Sighing, I let everyone stay while we all sat down in the security room. Once we were all seated, we all looked up at Charlotte. She was sitting on top of the desk, so she was taller than all of us, and that's probably where she needed to be. Feel essential and above us. I'd bow at her feet if she let me.

After she quickly scanned the room, she looked at Ashley. "Why were you in the city working and not here?" Shit, if she answers that, it is going to open a whole can of worms. She was looking for her mate, and when she couldn't find him, I made her come back since Charlotte was her friend—someone that was familiar with her so she wouldn't feel lonely here.

"I was looking for a boyfriend, and once I found him, I brought him back here," she said. Not entirely true, but at least Ashley is trying to help me out. Hell.

Seeming satisfied with that answer, she turned to Zachary. "Do you all walk around naked or something? What is up with that?" Charlotte said in a flat tone.

Zachary stood up, getting ready to explain. "Well, when we shift, we rip our clothes, so a lot of times we just go off naked, there are shorts in different places on the property to change into now that you are here. We didn't want you to catch us naked but… thatwentalltoshitandImsosorry," he babbled. Charlotte sighed and rubbed her eyes again with the palm of her hands.

"OK," she sighed. She was taking this much better than I expected. Still, I could feel the tension and anxiety radiating off of her. At least she wasn't screaming. "Werewolves, how many of these 'communities' are there?" She looked at me for an answer.

"There are at least 100 packs in North America alone. Ours is one of the biggest. These 'communities' are actually called packs, just like what the real Wolves have. We take care of each other and work together as a unit," I paused, waiting to see if she wanted me to go on.

"Tell me more." Her lips were pursed.

"Werewolves have been around for a long time, same as humans. We were created by the gods; many know them as the 'Greek Gods of Olympus.' We were put here to help protect humans. Still, as time went on, we secluded ourselves since humans were seeing us as monsters. With some Wolves, it is the truth, but mostly not, just as there are some bad humans while others aren't." Charlotte nodded her head and crossed her arms.

"Why am I here then? This is a community, I mean a pack of Wolves. I'm human. Why am I here?" That was the loaded question. I had two ways I could answer this. Tell her that she was my mate and that we would forever be soul mates if she would have me. Then again, I could tell her I was just attracted to her and needed her for security purposes. Both have pros and cons, and I don't know how to answer. There was a long pause before she suddenly jumped off the desk.

"Wait, I will tell you, I just don't know how to explain it," I pleaded. I, an Alpha, just pleaded with her. I would do it again in a heartbeat, though. She stopped and turned around with a scornful look on her face. Who am I kidding? She was going to be pissed either way.

"Werewolves have someone called a mate." Ashley looked at me in shock. She knew I wanted to wait to tell her, but I'm ripping it off like a band-aid instead. Charlotte looked at me in confusion while having her arms crossed. "I... we have someone that was especially gifted to us by our goddess. They are made to compliment us, balance our Wolves, and make us happy. They were a gift from her as a thank you to protect those who are less than able to protect themselves." Charlotte continues to look at me, but her eyes seem softer as she lowers her arms. "Most humans call it a soulmate."

Charlotte looks around the room for confirmation of what I just said. Ashley smiles, and her mate, Beau, enters the room with his arm around her waist. Evan, Bruce, and Zachary nod to show that this wasn't a joke. Looking back at me, she spoke again with a soft look and a glassy film over her eyes. "You are my mate, my soulmate," I reached both my hands out to her and took them as I kissed the back of her hands.

"H-how do you know that? I could just be any other person? Why me? Why would you think that?" she started spouting out.

"Your smell," I laughed, "your smell attracts me and drives my beast, my Wolf, insane. That's why I nuzzle into your neck, to get more of your scent." I go to nuzzle her, but she backs away, making my Wolf whimper. The things she has gone through today... I should've realized this was a lot and pushing her this much wasn't good for her.

"What if it is just my shampoo or something," she trailed off, being unsure of herself.

I laughed, "No, Kitten, it isn't your shampoo. Once we locked eyes back at the hotel, I knew that you were my mate. I knew I was supposed to protect you, love you, be beside you and my whole existence was to make you happy."

We both stood there as everyone filtered out of the room, knowing we needed our space. Standing there, almost for a full 5 minutes, she would rock back and forth from foot to foot while I still had both of our hands together. Occasionally, rubbing my thumb over her knuckles. It didn't feel awkward or forced. She was lost in her thoughts, and I just stood there, giving her the time, she needed.

Charlotte looked up at me, to the security cameras, to the chairs where all of us were sitting in and back up to me. She was replaying every piece of information we had given her in such a short amount of time. Eyebrows furrowed and her heart racing, I was ready to hear what she had to say. I prayed we didn't take a step backward, and I would have to try and win her heart all over again if I even had her heart, to begin with, that is.

"Wesley?"

"Yes, Charlotte?"

"This is a lot," she smiled.

"Yes, it is," I gave a short reply.

"I-is that why I feel tingles when you touch me? The feelings of being safe and comforted?"

"Yes, exactly." I smiled at her.

"So, you didn't choose me, someone else did? The goddess?"

"No love, we were made for each other. Two halves that make a whole. Two people coming together to be one person to love and cherish. You weren't raised this way, I understand that, and we will take our time, just like a normal human relationship." I brushed a piece of her strawberry blonde hair out of her face.

"Alright, I'm only doing this because I feel like I can trust you. I don't feel like you are lying, but..." she held up her finger and pointed at me. "You can't hide things from me anymore, I know why you did it with this, but you can't do this anymore. Anything else I need to know?"

I sighed, not wanting this tiny little moment to end. I had to tell her about Roman and him being a Vampire. I could bring up half of it, but then she'll be pissed later. Damn, she makes me have to think.

"I guess I should tell you, there aren't just Werewolves out there. There are other...beings."

"Like what? Vampires? Fairies? Elves?" She laughed jokingly. When I didn't laugh, she stilled.

"They are all actually real and hide just like us." Charlotte's mouth opened and closed for a bit before muttering acknowledgment.

"And, we think Roman, your foster parent, might be a Vampire," I added.

I petted her hair and put her in my arms while I hugged her close. At first, she was hesitant but slowly put her arms around my torso, and I kissed her forehead. "I know this isn't the life you planned for, but I can promise you it's worth it. You don't feel the bond we have as strong as I do because you are human, but I do care for you deeply." Charlotte looked up at me with her doe eyes and stared into mine. There wasn't fear, malice or confusion, she really believed me.

"I just need a little time alone. I'm not mad or upset or anything, I just need some time to process things." I nodded, not wanting to let her go, but she willed herself to leave and head up the stairs. Once she shut the door, Evan walked in with a smirk on his face.

"Well, at least she didn't run?"

"Get Daniel and Zachary in my office," I grunted.

"Aww, are you mad she saw someone else's D before yours?"

"Shut up and do it." I marched up the stairs to my office and slammed the door.

✳✳✳

After chewing out idiot pack members and their insolence, I head back up the stairs to the 3rd floor to check on Charlotte. Looking at my watch, it was past 11:30 p.m. Thinking she must have gone to bed, I put my ear up to the door. I knocked a few times and didn't hear anything. I couldn't hear any breathing or heartbeat. I opened the door quickly to find the bed still made, and a few clothes folded neatly in a pile.

Starting to panic, I ran to my room to see if she had crawled into my bed, a beautiful surprise that would have been, but she wasn't there either. Mind-linking the Wolves in the house, no one seems to know where she is. I didn't want to invade her privacy, but if I can't find her, I'll use my basic instincts of using my nose and smell her out.

She had been to several places in the house, the kitchen, dining room, and living room, but then her smell lingered by the gaming hallway. At the end of the hallway was the pool, the chlorine hit my nose hard as I continued to walk closer. Ripples were coming from the side as I neared the glass door to the entrance.

Charlotte was in a black tank top with a swimsuit underneath and black spandex biking shorts that went down to her mid-thigh. She had goggles on and was taking a dive off the diving board doing laps in the pool. Her fingers danced across the water as she did her freestyle stroke. As she reached the other end of the pool, you could see the tank top really inhibiting her swimming, but I could understand why she was wearing it. She was hiding. Hiding what she had been through.

Finally, having the courage to talk to my mate after our life-altering discussion earlier, I opened the door, and she quickly darted her head to it. She sank down into the water to hide, and I could help but chuckle. "You don't have to hide from me, Kitten." I walked towards her and sat beside her at the end of the pool, not caring if I got my clothes wet.

"I'm not hiding," she said solemnly.

"Really then? Can you stand up?" Knowing she could reach the bottom and come up to her waist, I decided to tease. "So, did you shrink?" She stuck her tongue out at me and stood up. The blacktop hugged her body so I could see her every curve. Charlotte wasn't top-heavy, she was the perfect size for someone who was athletically active. If only I could get a back-side view.

"Why are you wearing a top? You know you don't need to, right?" She didn't speak, she sat there contemplating what I said.

"I... I'm just embarrassed. You are a good-looking guy," she said. "I'm self-conscious about it. I have been for a long time. It isn't something that can be fixed overnight." I nodded my head in understanding.

115

"I just want you to know that I care about you, Charlotte. Scars and all, and I've seen your scars, and you make them out to be this horrible thing about you. You feel ashamed when you shouldn't be. You didn't do this to yourself, it shows how strong you are. I care for you, and no scar would ever turn me away from that." Charlotte looked up with me, tears in her eyes.

"You are just so handsome. You are the first guy I've ever dated, so, of course, I'm going to be self-conscious regardless," she laughed, "but I'm glad you told me that. I believe you." Charlotte smiled at me and put her hand on mine, sitting next to her in the water.

"How about we get you out of there and into bed? Why were you even down here anyway?"

"I couldn't sleep, I think I'm used to sleeping in your bed," she blushed while I smiled. "And Macaroni now spreads out like she owns it so I can't get in without her trying to push me off."

"Well then, let's get you showered so you can come to bed with me," I growled in her ear.

After showering and getting dressed, Charlotte came to my room and hopped into my bed, where I engulfed her in my arms. She nuzzled into the crook of my neck. Our legs wrapped around each other's as we both fell into a deep sleep.

Chapter 20
Charlotte

When Wesley's told me that Roman was a Vampire, my world shut down. I don't think I gave any emotion when he told me. I just looked into his beautiful eyes and counted his eyelashes to keep me from breaking on the outside. On the inside, I was breaking into a thousand pieces. For most of my life, I dealt with creatures that you hear about in nightmares and horror stories. I lived in a horror story for a lot of my childhood.

Wesley's ravishing smile was now painted into a thin line. His lips were no longer pouty and kissable. His whole demeanor sprouted concern. "*As it should be,*" I thought. Getting my world turned upside down, I witnessed my friends become Werewolves, and finding out about other creatures was not part of my schedule for the day. Any average person would be screaming right now, any normal person would be running away. Why wasn't I? Why wasn't I crying and freaking out?

Maybe in my heart, I already knew everything was different.

Roman was a terrible foster parent. In the beginning, he was nice, but once I turned ten, he made my life into a nightmare, and I had no idea why. Now, I knew he wanted to slurp up every bit of me. Why he didn't do it then, I'll never know. Frequently I remember him cutting into me and then licking or taking his finger and dabbing the wound to taste my secretions. "*Not mature yet, my pet. Not just quite yet.*" I hated anything that rhymed after that day.

I was being compared to a banana, bright green bananas tasted terrible, but once they became ripe enough, they were sweet. Unfortunately, looking at a human, he couldn't tell if I was ripe, so he cut me like filet mignon.

Wesley waited for me to gather my thoughts when I told him I needed time alone. The desperation on his face was obvious. I was supposed to be his mate and cling to him and feel protected. Right now, I felt everything but. My body wanted him to feel his warmth and wrap his arms around me, but unfortunately, my mind was taking me to other places. Places I didn't want to talk about, and it was best if I left.

Trudging up the stairs, I opened my bedroom door and sat on the small love seat at the end of my bed. Sighing loudly, I heard a knock at the door. I really couldn't catch a minute to be alone in this house. I still need the lock on my door. "Come in," I whispered. Of course, they heard with their Werewolf hearing and all.

"Hey, Charlie. How are you doing?" Ashley came and laid on the bed behind me and stroked my hair. I sighed and didn't say anything. I didn't know what to think anymore. My friend that I had known for a year, that took so long to open up, had the biggest secret of them all.

"Overwhelmed," was the only word I could reply with.

"Hey, at least you aren't running away screaming. You have that going for ya," Ashley chuckled as she braided a bit of my hair.

"It was probably best to find out this way," I looked down at my hands and played with my fingers. "I had a feeling there might be something more out there, the way that Roman used to taste my blood and all after he would cut me. I just thought he was some sick person, 'How could a human do that,' I always thought." Ashley nodded and put down my hair.

"I know it wasn't something you wanted to hear, but I'm glad you know now. Just know that Wesley and the rest of us here will protect you. You are an important part of the pack now, especially since you are his mate." Ashley smiled.

"I don't know what all that means. I didn't let Wesley go into it because I just shut off after hearing Roman was a Vampire. My body says one thing, my mind another, and then my heart, I don't know what my heart wants." I sniffled, Ashley came and sat beside me on the couch.

"What does your heart say, Charlie?" I looked up at her, seeing the concern and friendliness in her eyes. Even though the past year getting to know her, I knew I could trust her. Even if she was a Werewolf. She never put me in harm's way, always protected me in some sisterly way that I always wanted.

"To trust him, to love him. I've never done any of those things, though, so it is difficult to let myself go like that. My mind wants me to stay guarded." A small tear escaped my eyes as it dropped to the floor. Macaroni came out from under the bed and let out a long meow. Macaroni always knew how to comfort me.

Macaroni jumped and sat on my lap, looking warily at Ashley. She wasn't too keen on being in the house, and I figured out why. Everyone here was a predator to her, and she used to be a top dog—well, cat. "It's OK, Mac and Cheese, they are our friends," I whispered. She let out a giant yawn and settled into my lap while I stroked her to sleep.

"Just know," Ashley began, "that mates are a wonderful gift. Most humans miss out on that. The goddess paired you two for a reason, you both complement each other so well. He's the big Alpha that is dominant and protects his pack. You are his Luna, kind and loving. You give him a reason to have a heart and care for his pack members in ways other than just being protective."

I hummed in response. "Are there others like us? I mean, human and Werewolf pairings?" She giggled. "Yes, actually. She was born human, but her parents were Werewolves. Her name was Clarabelle, and she met Alpha Kane. Now they look over a pack called the Crimson Shadows together." My eyes grew wide. "She's a Werewolf now though, she decided to go through the transformation and become like him."

"Oh, do I have to do that?" I whispered, a bit scared.

"No, you don't. Not unless you really wanted to. You will always be with Wesley, though, once you complete your bond. I'll let him explain that. It is something to be discussed with your mate," Ashley winked. I blushed while stroking Macaroni as she started snoring.

Ashley left shortly after that, and I picked up the sleeping kitty and crawled up onto the bed. I lay there for hours, just thinking about it all. I let it simmer within myself. Placing the pros and cons of staying. Yes, I thought about leaving to forget all of this, but I was kidding myself. I was missing Wesley right now, plus he was a Werewolf, and he felt things more strongly than I did. How cruel could I be?

After lying in bed all day, I couldn't sleep. I didn't want to bother Wesley either. I was sure he was upset with me, so maybe a dip in the pool might help. It was late, hopefully, no one would be down there. Even though many packhouse tenants knew I had scars, I still didn't want to flaunt them.

Shuffling through the closet, I found a black tank top and some spandex biking shorts to put over my bikini. The top covered me nicely, and the bottoms weren't too revealing, but I could still see the purple scars healing. Most of the scars were covered except some around my shoulders and mid-back… This would have to do.

Wrapping myself in a towel, I tiptoed down the stairs until I could smell the heavy chemical smell of chlorine. Diving head-first, I rose to the surface. The cool water made my body calm and relaxed. Taking in a few laps and enjoying the peace of being under the water and not hearing a sound, I heard a door open and close. Putting my hand on the edge of the pool, I saw Wesley. He was still in his dress pants and shirt from earlier this morning.

Wesley was so unbelievably sexy, his blonde hair was a mess, and his white dress shirt had the sleeves rolled up to his forearms. Several rings sat on his hands and his Rolex watch on his left wrist. He looked tired with the bags under his eyes. Wesley quickly had me out of the pool, pulling me back upstairs. Mumbling how I shouldn't be up so late and come sleep in his room.

After I'd showered and gotten dressed, I came to Wesley's room and hopped into bed, where he engulfed me in his arms. "How about we move your clothes in here? I could see this being a permanent thing," he kissed my temple.

"As long as you don't think you will tire of me," I said teasingly. Wesley growled in my ear.

"Don't say such things, you're mine!" He nipped at my ear while sucking on it to relieve the pain. "We will talk more about being mates later, I want to tell you everything. Just know that I'm never leaving you, never." He petted my hair and kissed the temple of my head. "Now that I have you, I can never let you go." I smiled into his chest.

Chapter 21

Charlotte

It was a good thing all of this information overload had happened over the weekend because I was not mentally capable of working on any type of formulas or algorithms for the next few days. During that time, Wesley was always by my side. If I didn't know he was my mate, I would have been overly concerned.

Wesley's constant presence actually soothed me as he began to explain why I wasn't feeling the bond as strongly as I should. He was surprised I could feel it at all, actually. The branding bond was further explained to me after Wesley went back to the elders to work on figuring out how to get rid of it. Day by day, the scar lightened, but it still worried Wesley. He was constantly asking if it hurt or burned. I always told him that I felt absolutely fine, which was true. Each passing night I noticed it was getting lighter. I wouldn't be surprised if in a few weeks it would be gone entirely.

As the week progressed, Wesley had my things moved into his room—I mean, our room. He told me I could change anything I wanted in there since it was mine, and if I ever felt uncomfortable, I could always leave. In fact, he kept my previous room the same and dubbed it "Macaroni's Suite" since she had grown accustomed to having her large bed all to herself.

Even when I brought personal items into Wesley's room, I thought it would get crowded in there. It didn't though, it was almost like I was supposed to live there all along. The clothes that were bought for me took up the vast closet in my old room, but Wesley had another entire wardrobe just for me, along with some fabulous shoes, I might add, in our room. The women that helped around the packhouse were able to help me get my clothes situated, and she kept staring at my neck, and I started to become self-conscious. I knew my scars were beginning to poke through since I did start wearing tops that were looser than normal.

It was later when I found out they were looking for a mating mark, Wesley explained... They wanted to be the first to see Wesley's mark on my shoulder. Once Wesley and I finally decide to 'do the deed.' He will bite me after sex, and that will grant me immortality with him. As exciting as it was, I was scared to death. I still needed time, and he was really OK with it. I would hardly let anyone see my scars, let alone my entire naked body, so of course, it would take time.

Overall, Anna and Alice were very friendly as they helped me unpack. They even brought in magazines and lists of websites where I could redecorate the room as well as the packhouse if I wanted to. I stared at them with wide eyes, not wanting to even touch the rest of the packhouse. With much persistence, I did purchase a new comforter for the bed, sheets, drapes, and towels. They told me I should definitely paint, but I was really enjoying the deeper grey walls.

I put a few of my bras and underwear in one of the drawers that Wesley had opened up for me when I heard a creak from the door opening. Wesley and I hadn't seen each other naked, and I haven't really expressed the want to do that yet, so I was surprised there was no knock. Wesley had always at least knocked a few times before entering, waiting for me to protest.

Unfortunately for me, I didn't see Wesley but a tall, athletic woman with rather large breasts walked into the room. This woman oozed confidence as she held her black Gucci purse in the crook of her arm and her skinny black jeans with carefully placed holes showed off her tanned skin. Her eyebrows were perfectly penciled in, and her dark hair flowed next to her red top just above those large breasts. Did I mention she had large breasts?

Her smile soon faltered when she saw me in the room placing my delicates into the drawer, her hand clenched on the door handle before she slammed it shut. "Excuse me, but what are you doing here?" she spoke with venom.

Now, I have never had a woman speak to me in this way, men maybe when I didn't do the extra work, they wanted me to do at the office. This woman had a different tone. It was of utter disgust. Like I was on her turf. I pushed the drawer in and turned around. Our size difference was astronomical, she had to be close to 6 feet tall with those 4-inch heels she was wearing, and my bare feet barely made me 5'3. "Are you the hired help or something?"

I stepped a few steps closer to her, not keeping my head down like I normally did, and spoke straight to her face. I could be scared of men, but I wasn't going to be afraid of women. "No, I live here. Now may I ask who you are?" I said in a sickly-sweet voice. His scowl only deepened as she began to rummage through her purse. Thinking it would be a phone, she actually pulled out her lipstick and walked to the mirror and caked-on another layer.

"I'm Wesley Hale's..." she paused and looked up in the air before landing her eyes back on me, "woman." She smiled as she dropped her lipstick into her purse. "I suggest you get out of here unless you want a show in a few minutes." This woman started to take off her top and only had a scantily shaped bra that was 3 sizes too small. The boldness she had by just taking it off in front of a complete stranger had me in a huff. Why couldn't I be that confident?

Wait. What?

"I'm sorry, you must have the wrong room. Wesley is my mate. I think *you* need to leave," I said, annoyed. Wesley had a lot of explaining to do. Did he forget to break up with her, or does he have her on the side? I better be getting some answers tonight, or I'll move my flabby butt back over to Macaroni's room.

"A human? Mate? Ha! You would break if he tried to do the things to you that he has done to me." She walked up to me, her breasts jiggling. All the confidence I had to talk to her started to go out the window as she pointed out the flaws I had. Wesley had worked so hard to build me up the past few days, and here I was, crumbling from just the slightest earthquake. "You aren't really serious that he would accept you, right? You lack in all the departments," she pointed to my chest, thighs, and ass. "I suggest drinking some fattening shakes because you are a bit gaunt-looking too. No life in your face at all," she cooed.

It wasn't much, but my wall finally crumbled. To add salt to the wound, she saw a few scars from my shirt that started to hang off my shoulder. "Oh, and you are a bit broken too, it looks like. Who would want to look at that while fucking? It's such a turn-off," she ticked.

I could feel the tickle in my eyes as the water started to cover the surface. Not wanting to cry, I grabbed my phone and headed to the door to open it but was met with an angry-looking Wesley. Once he saw my face, it softened, and he pulled me to his chest. A few sniffles were heard, and the woman behind me started to laugh.

"Delilah," Wesley spoke sternly. "I told you not to come here." Wesley's hold on me gripped only tighter as I took a big breath of his scent. It was the only thing holding me together.

"Now, I know we like to play games. Cat and mouse, predator and prey, I thought it was just a game," her voice was sultry. Delilah's body came closer, and Wesley's body went rigid.

"I've asked you to leave, now get out, or I'll use my Alpha tone on you," Wesley growled. I peeked out of Wesley's shoulder, Delilah flinched, but swiftly composed herself. Quickly, she grabbed her shirt and spouted a few curse words as she threw it on.

"Don't worry, I'll be waiting," Delilah looked at me. "Once you see how terrible her body looks under those clothes, you will come crawling back, especially to play with your favorite things." She grabbed her breasts and squeezed them together to show Wesley as she walked out the door.

Not wanting to cry, I sat up and wiped away the tears and, yes, snot from my face. Wesley hastily got a tissue, got on his knees, and wiped away the rest of the tears that were not listening to me. "Kitten, I'm so sorry," he whispered. Now I knew why he had that hot tub on his balcony, probably to do her in.

I let out a big breath and looked him in the eyes. He was pleading, he was worried, and he looked sorry. I don't know why he looked so vulnerable, but it made my heartache. Was this something I could just let go of? Because my self-confidence just possibly went well below the starting mark from when I arrived. Delilah was beautiful, everything that Wesley was. They would make the cutest couple and the prettiest babies.

Sensing my discomfort Wesley pulled me to his chest. "Kitten, say something. I swear to you, I haven't seen her in months. She texted today wanting to come, and I said I have my mate, and I only wanted my Charlotte. I swear to you, I swear it."

Wesley wrapped his arms around me and put my legs around his waist as he guided us to the bed. He laid down and held me close while I whimpered into him. "I was so stupid, Charlotte, so stupid. We had a fling a long time ago and did some things, but I did it because I was lonely. That's no excuse, I should have waited, but I didn't. I made mistakes, I'm so sorry."

I believed almost every word he said, but I'm not sure I could ever believe it when he told me I was beautiful. The women he must have had, they were beautiful, glamorous, everything I wasn't. I was short, still a bit underweight, and just blah.

Sitting up in the bed, I looked at Wesley. I knew my eyes were watery and red, I looked utterly gross. "I believe you, Wesley. I know you had a past before me. I just wasn't expecting to see her and for her to be so mean," I whispered at the end of my statement.

"She's jealous that I have you. That I love you and want to protect you. That you had become the center of my world when I met you and that you will be my only love. I've never loved anyone before you, Charlotte. Please know this." He petted my hair and nuzzled it into my neck.

"I'm just sorry I'm not pretty enough. I wish I looked like her. Hell, I just wish I didn't have the scars. If I didn't then, maybe I wouldn't feel so self-conscious about it. I'm not as upset as I probably should be because I do feel like you are honest and truthful." I started laughing, and Wesley raised his head up from my neck and looked at me in confusion.

"If you tell me I'm pretty every day, maybe it will become ingrained in me over time..."

"No," he spoke gruffly. "I'm going to tell you, you are gorgeous, every," he kissed my left cheek, "hour," he kissed my right cheek, "of the" he kissed my nose, "day." With one final kiss, he flipped me on my back pushed me to the bed to kiss me. It became heated as his hands wandered my body underneath my clothes. As we intertwined our tongues together, I moaned into his mouth. Wesley's hands pushed up under my shirt, the hot fire touches skimming the bottom wire of my bra.

I let out a small whimper in surprise but groaned as he squeezed my breast. It felt so wonderfully good. I didn't know they could feel like that. He flicked my nipple on the outside of the bra which caused my core to spasm.

Wesley's dick was rigid and was pressed up against my entrance through his joggers. I could feel all of him with only a few bits of clothing between us. The heat from between my legs was driving me crazy, I just wanted some friction. "Wesley," I whispered. My core lined up with his dick, feeling every part of him through my leggings. A growl of a moan left his throat, and he got the idea of what I wanted.

His hips pushed against my pussy, going at a slow rhythmic pace. The fire in me began to build the faster he rubbed himself against the heat of my core. I was so wet, my fingers grabbed his shoulders as his rhythm became faster, hitting the one spot I really liked. His kisses on my mouth stopped as Wesley put his head into my shoulder, smelling, kissing, and tasting me while his hips ground into me harder. My hips tried to join with his as he pushed my core harder into the mattress.

"Oh, Wesley. Oh my, what?" I couldn't finish my sentence. My heart was about to explode as I heard Wesley grunt a few times. "Cum with me, Kitten. Goddess, let it go for me," he growled as he sucked harshly on my shoulder. I let go, and I saw stars in the back of my eye lids. My toes curled as I rode out the most magnificent feeling as we both sunk into the mattress.

Chapter 22

Charlotte

After Wesley went to the security room and chewed everyone out for letting Delilah in, I decided to run some new diagnostics on the security system I had in place for all of Wesley's businesses. Unfortunately, that meant I needed to be in the security room after a brutal verbal beating for the team. I couldn't help but feel awkward about the whole thing, but the three sitting by the monitors gave me a smile and a wave and continued to do their job.

Sitting down and letting out a heavy sigh, I connected the networks, trying not to remember the hot session we just had. My body shivered thinking how wonderful it felt.

Wesley owned so many businesses and tried to keep up with security in each of their buildings, but they were all individually run. He had six different high-profile companies that he owned. Being able to control that, plus running a packhouse, must be tiring.

After merging the security systems, I was able to pick up on a few anomalies that weren't making sense. Wesley told me I didn't have to put any security measures on the accounting department since he had people he trusted. Still, I was bored and did it anyway. He gave me complete access to everything, which I find weird. Being mates must seriously be a big deal.

As I looked at Hale Incorporated, several areas weren't making sense. There were too many withdrawals coming out just before the monthly paychecks were paid to employees. It started seven months ago and has slowly doubled, even tripled. How much money was being withdrawn? To an untrained eye of looking at patterns and rhythms of companies, it would look like it was just paychecks coming out being cashed, but this was different.

Once I added up the numbers, over 1.2 million dollars had gone missing. I'm no accountant, only looking at security and patterns within a company, so I will have to bring this up to Wesley. Clicking a few buttons here and there, I also found that a particular username had been making the withdrawal, which shocked me... it was Evan.

It was Evan's username and password on the screen.

I let out a small gasp, and the others looked over at me. I gave a small smile and told them I lost at a game of Candy Crush. They laughed, and I continued my search. It didn't make sense at all. Why would Evan want to steal money? Trying to cover myself and doing the morally incorrect thing to do, I hacked his computer. I had long come to terms with trusting my gut, and my heart told me this was a setup.

Evan's computer was always on in his room upstairs, which he shared with his mate, so I quickly hacked his laptop with ease. Neither of them were home, so they couldn't see anything I was doing. His computer was clean. Evan usually works here at the packhouse, with Wesley, only going to the city once a month to check on all six businesses. The computer login he used had been traced back to in the town on completely different computers.

This was getting juicy.

Before I could dig anymore, I heard my stomach growl in protest. I went from a pack of ramen a day to gourmet food. The packhouse kitchen had started to spoil me. So many pre-made dinners and lunches from the chefs that I was having three large meals a day. I was finally filling out and not looking as gaunt as I had.

Sliding out of my chair, I headed to the kitchen to see what the chefs had prepared for today's lunch. Grilled chicken parmesan with asparagus tips and linguine. Just smelling it made my mouth water, and I hadn't even popped it in the microwave yet.

No one was around, so taking off my air-pods, I hit play on my phone to listen to some tunes. Since listening to Zachary playing songs from *The Greatest Showman*, I had been hooked. The past few days had been nothing but playing them over and over in my head. Sitting down all day, believe it or not, could be exhausting, but when it came to the song, "This is Me," I wanted to jump, sing and dance. It was such a freeing song that almost captured who I was. I was broken, but this was me. Accept it or not.

As I started jumping around the kitchen, waving a dish towel around, I was abruptly stopped by a large muscular wall. "Umph!"

"Looks like we have a tiny dancer in here, huh?" Zachary looked down at me with his hands on his hips.

"I'm so sorry, Zachary! I wasn't paying attention!" I blushed at just being caught. "I just got too carried away, I guess." I took my phone and turned it off.

"You know," he started, "I want to take you somewhere." Zachary grabbed my hand and led me out of the kitchen. *But my food...*

After going down several halls and a few twists and turns, he led me to a large room with light-colored wood, floors, tall mirrors for walls, and a large sound system in the corner. It was the perfect place for a ballerina or dancer to work out in.

"This place is amazing," I whispered.

"Yeah, Alpha had it installed for the little pups that wanted to start taking dance. Everyone in the pack can use it, though." He looked around the room with pride.

"Do you dance?" I asked.

"I do and quite enjoy it. You have to be pretty strong to lift some of the ladies and gents," he laughed.

I had a feeling that Zachary was gay, but I didn't ask. Whatever he desired was his business, and I would support him in any fashion he wanted. Zachary grabbed a few pairs of clothes and threw them at me.

"And no, I'm not gay," he laughed. I raised my eyebrow. "I know that look, just because I enjoy musicals and dance doesn't make me gay. Straight guys can enjoy them too," he winked. "Here, go change and meet me back in here," he ordered. With lunch forgotten, I grabbed the clothes and headed to the changing room. Zachary gave me a black sports bra, black booty shorts with pale pink leg warmers, and ballet flats. The outfit was so open, and I felt completely naked. I let out a little grunt looking in the mirror. I wasn't pleased about the outfit choice. As if he had heard me from afar, Zachary threw over an oversized black sweater.

"Figured you might want this, but you shouldn't need it. We love you all the same." He blew a kiss and waited for me to come outside. It was an oversized sweater, one that you would see on professional dancers that hung off the side. It would show some of my wrecked body, but not all of it. I threw it on and came out. Zachary had dressed up in a male leotard with tight black shorts and his own flats. His tight top was showing off his muscles as he was drying his hands with a towel. He was handsome but not as handsome as Wesley. Speaking of which...

"Zachary, have you seen Wesley? I actually need to talk to him." Zachary went to the stereo to find a CD to put in and looked back at me, "Oh, he is out on patrol. One male patroller's wife went into labor with their pup. Alpha is filling in until the end of the shift. I nodded my head while watching Zachary.

The song I was blaring in the kitchen came on immediately. My head began to get entrapped by the lyrics.

My thoughts immediately went to hearing Roman hearing those hateful words. *"No one will want you, no one will love you, be ashamed of your scars,"* he would chant in my ear... My breath hitched, and Zachary noticed. Roman was getting inside my head again. Zachary took my hand and led me to the middle of the room. Turning me around, he had me look in the mirror.

"You are not broken, Charlotte. You have a family here that loves you, especially Wesley. You should let your feelings go, do it through dance. That's what I've learned to do." I remember when I first met Zachary, dancing to the exact same song in his room. Zachary had become such a great friend.

So, I did what Zachary told me, I let go. Zachary did his own interpretive dance while I watched how he gracefully danced across the room. He was so elegant, delicate, and refined, not one of his feet made a sound. How could a strong, burly man like him look so graceful? Trying to listen to Zachary's words, I began to move. It was so much easier with the clothes I had changed into.

My movements became more fluid as I continued my assault on the floor. My arms are turning, twisting, and flowing with the beat of the music. My hips gently poured against the rhythm of the of the melody.

The song on repeat, and we continued to dance for a long time. I lost track how much my afternoon was being spent in here, but I never lost energy. We continued beating on both of our bodies as we realized that we may be broken either physically or mentally; we both deserved love and affection. We were meant for something more, and no one or anything should stand in our way for happiness.

Zachary lifted me up in the air like I was a feather and tossed me around a few times. We both laughed and watched our sweat start dampening the floor. The slight wetness of the floor only made me concentrate more on the song as it continued on replay. I had become immersed in the music, starting to believe every word of it as if it was meant for me.

The song was coming to an end for the twentieth time. My mind went to another world. I became more comfortable with who I was as I lifted myself from the muddy ground, I had put myself in. I lifted the heavily drenched sweater and lifted it from my body. Slinging the sweater to the far side of the room, feeling freer than I had ever been. The air flowed across my skin as I continued to twist and contort my body in positions, I never thought possible. My eyes stayed closed, knowing the exact areas of the room to stay clear of.

My heart was light, and for once, it was going to stay that way. I should be proud of who I was and who I had become. I had become stronger, independent and I had finally found love. Yes, as crazy as it sounds, I think I am in love with Wesley Hale, and I shouldn't be afraid.

As the last few notes played, I slowed, placing myself in front of the mirror. Ready to look at my scars, head-on with no longer the crying and fear

I always had looking at myself. Fluttering my eyes open, I then felt a pair of hands on my hips and sparks flying through his fingertips. For the first time, I was looking at my scars without crying, without shame. For once, I opened them to see not just me but Wesley. He held me close to his body, both of us a sweating mess.

Wesley had just come back from patrolling; we were both panting from the running, the dancing. I turned to him and looked up to see his smiling face. He lifted up my chin with his finger and whispered, "I am so very proud of you."

Wesley gave me a slow kiss on my lips. "So beautiful."

Vera Foxx

.

Chapter 23

Wesley

After patrolling for a few hours while another Wolf went to tend to his mate, I walked into the packhouse completely drenched in sweat. I probably stunk too, but I wanted to check on Charlotte to make sure she was doing alright. I felt terrible about Delilah coming to the packhouse unannounced. Anyone with common sense would've thought to contact me before sending the slut in here. We had the cameras, she still had a familiar scent that the pack members knew from coming by six months ago, so they still let her in.

Delilah is from our neighboring pack, I won't lie. We did each other favors while we waited for our mates. I cut it off six months back though because I was fed up with feeling empty. I also knew she wanted to take it to a relationship level, and I couldn't do that. She had to find her mate too. I didn't realize what a complete bitch she really was. How many other women had she been this cruel to? Hell, if Charlotte wasn't there, I would have thrown her ass out myself. After all the work Charlotte and I have completed together was almost thrown out the window. Charlotte has a beautiful spirit and body, I could not have painted a better picture of perfection. I just want her to know that too.

Walking in the packhouse, I could hear music coming from the activities' hallway. Down this hallway were game rooms, movie rooms, the pool, and a small dance studio. I see Zachary half-dressed down the hallway in dancing attire, leaning against the doorway with his arms crossed. He is smiling like a kid on Christmas morning. Putting my hand on his shoulder, I look at him to question him, but he keeps smiling and nods his head into the room.

Charlotte was dancing, her eyes closed, following the beat to the music. Her steps were light and barely touched the floor. Her arms followed her feet traveled across the light-colored floor. The chorus sounded, she took off the oversized sweater, exposing her body to the air in just her dancing sports bra and spandex shorts. Her scars were out, and she was finally letting go of her insecurities and self-doubt. I couldn't help but have a few tears come to my eyes. She has worked so hard while she has been here to get rid of the pain, to feel normal.

The bonding scar looked like it was gone entirely, and the only scar that could really remind her of her past was a carving on the side of her rib cage. His damn name. I'd be sure to carve her name into Roman once I found that bastard.

Her movements slowed as the music came to a close. Charlotte's eyes were tightly shut, ready to see herself as a new person. I walked up to her and put my hands on her hips, and she looked up in the mirror to see me staring back at her. I grinned at her, and she turned around to look at me. "I'm so very proud of you," I whispered as I put my forehead to hers.

Charlotte surprised me again, stood up on her toes, and gave me a beautiful, slow kiss to my lips. "So beautiful," I whispered to her lips. Charlotte blushed and responded with a quiet thank you. She didn't argue, she didn't ask me to stop. She took the compliment as her very first compliment she didn't shy away from. Taking her hands in mine and pulling her close, her sweaty body met my chest while we held each other. She let out a large sigh, I know she'll still hurt and be self-conscious sometimes, but I knew I'd always be there for her.

Then I started to feel a poke in my right pectoral muscle. "Charlotte?" I laughed as she continued to tap me. "What are you doing?"

"How do you get them so hard? Do you work out like… all the time? It's nice." She blushed ferociously. "Wait, I didn't mean to say that part." She covered her face with her hands. I laughed at her, picked her up. She clung to me like a koala. "Woah, you're really tall." This dance has awoken a Charlotte I never knew was there, and I loved every bit of it. I knew she was in here, waiting to come out, and she did it all on her own, the strong future Luna she would be.

Charlotte put one hand on my cheek, leaning into it, I let out a little purr in my chest. Staring at her, I wiped a bit of the sweat from her forehead along with some hair. "Thank you."

"Thank you for what, Kitten?" I rubbed our noses together while kissing her cheeks. "For being so patient. I'm sure it's been hard. I've noticed how mates act around each other, and I know I've probably been more distant than most."

"Kitten," I lifted her chin up to see her beautiful face. "We will go as slow as you want human or not, self-conscious, or not, we only go at our pace, what is perfect for us, alright?" She hummed in agreement and her soft lips against mine again. I tugged on her lip, and she moaned into my mouth, allowing me to slink into her mouth. Walking up to the wall, I pressed her against the mirror and rubbed my growing erection on her core. Letting out a gasp, I to growled while she fisted my shirt to get me closer.

She was panting, so I broke our kiss and leaned my forehead against hers. "We should probably go shower," Charlotte nodded, and I slowly let her down to her feet. Hand in hand, we walked up the stairs together to our room. "How about you go shower first?" I offered, and she looked between the shower and me, the little gears in her head turning. Charlotte's hand didn't leave my hand.

"Or we could shower together," I whispered huskily in her ear. Knowing she has embraced her body, being a bit prouder of what she had accomplished, I just had to ask. I'm a horny bastard of an Alpha, and my mate's arousal from our make-out session was giving me major blue balls. She's just so perfect, and I want to show her how much I care and love her. So, I gave her the best puppy dog eyes I could muster and hoped for a good reaction.

Charlotte smiled and nodded her head. SHE SAID YES! I gave her the best shit-eating grin I could manage and lifted her up and twirled her around like a love-sick puppy I was. Charlotte laughed, asking to be put down.

Charlotte

I couldn't believe I said yes, but those big puppy eyes were killing me. Wesley was so excited that I said I would shower with him. I had been thinking about it for a while. The past few weeks after major make-out sessions and touching all over made me really wonder what it was like under all those clothes. He often would stop me from taking off his shirt, but I think it was because he wanted to see me too.

He let me go first into the bathroom while grabbing some of his clothes and checking his messages. Coming into the bathroom and looking in the mirror made me realize what a hot mess I currently was. Dancing for a few hours really did a number on me. My hair was out of place, and it looked like I was still sweating. My lips, though, were red and pouty from him assaulting them. I couldn't help but grin and replay it all in my head.

Hearing Wesley on the phone reminded me of what I was in here for. Turning on the shower and quickly stripping my clothes, I headed into the steam shower and got the steam really turned up. A little bit of coverage would be nice, and a quick shave. Getting my shave on and finishing quickly, I went ahead and started to wash my hair. Before I could finish washing, I felt Wesley behind me. I was facing the other wall, so he couldn't see the front of me.

Can your entire body blush? Because I'm more than sure that my white butt just did. Feeling the heat from his chest and his friend on my butt, I let out a small gasp. Leaning down, he placed a kiss on my shoulder while he continued to massage my head with soap. His hands worked like magic and could put me to sleep if I wasn't standing. He led me under the water and washed away all the soap, but he turned me around while he did it. Feeling the soap drip down my body, he trailed his hands with it, following the bubbles.

Carefully brushing my nipples with his thumb, I could hear him growl in gratitude. His cock was pressing into my stomach, and I was scared to even look. I kept my eyes on him as he looked at my body. I wasn't afraid anymore, I felt like I was his, and his body was mine as well. My nipples hardened as he leaned down and blew some air on them. They pearled uptight, and he picked me up while my legs wrapped around his torso. Now, he no longer had to lean over to capture them in his mouth.

He lifted me up and then sucked one nipple while massaging the other while I tangled my fingers into his hair keeping my legs tightly around his waist. Small moans left my lips as he continued. His grip became harsh and a little painful, but it only added to the pleasure I was feeling. "I want to taste you," he said huskily. At first, I didn't know what he meant, but he slowly trailed a finger down to my core and slipped a finger inside, all while having his eyes glued to mine.

"Ohh," I moaned at the intrusion of his finger filling me. I felt so complete just with his finger, what would happen if we had sex? Wesley lifted his finger to his lips and put it in his mouth. "So sweet, my little Kitten." His eyes rolled in the back of his head as he sucked all of my juices from his finger. "Let's go to bed." I couldn't speak, I just nodded as he stepped out of the shower with me holding on to him. Not caring if we got the bed wet, he laid me down gently, eyes still glued to mine.

"Tell me when to stop if you want me to stop," he chuckled darkly.

I bit my lip, rolling my tongue over my lip. His mouth was glued to mine in an instant, and his hands felt around my breasts and squeezed them slightly, whimpering at his touch. His kisses went down to my neck, where it met my shoulder.

"One day, I will mark you here." He circled the spot and began sucking it roughly. I cried out as the delight was felt down to my toes.

His mouth and tongue licked every part of me until he arrived between the apex of my thighs. He took deep breaths of my pussy before licking his lips enthusiastically. Taking one gentle swipe at my clit, my hands grabbed his hair as I tried to get him to lick more. This feeling was too great, but I didn't want to let go just yet. He chuckled into my core, and I squealed in pleasure. "Does that feel good, mate? Do you like it when I lick your pussy?" Talking so dirty to me had me begging for more.

"Yes, more, please more, Wesley!" I whispered. His thick tongue hit my bundle of nerves, sucking it with all his might. I threw my head back so hard I could have broken it. I continued to hold onto Wesley's hair and rode his face until I finally came back down from my ecstasy. I was a hot and panting, wiping my forehead with the sweat that didn't work for. Looking down at Wesley, to see that his face was glistening from my pleasure. I wasn't completely sure if it was normal to have so much of me... all over him. He seemed pretty happy with it. Wesley's grin was wolfishly handsome as he licked his lips, ready for another round.

Wesley's hands, still holding my hips while I sat up. Pulling him close to me, I kissed him tasting myself on his tongue. His dick was immense, I could feel it pulsing next to my core. The heat of our skin made it unbearable feeling what we both wanted so badly. It made us both moan while we felt each other's heat. "I want to touch you," I whispered. "I want to make you feel good, but you need to tell me how." Wesley's eyes grew wide, his hands gripping my waist tighter.

"Are you sure? You don't have to. I enjoy just watching you squirm when I give you pleasure." He nipped my lips and rubbed his nose with mine.

"I want to touch you, please." He can't possibly say no to that. I smiled at him, biting my bottom lip. Being able to touch something so forbidden to me was erotic, touching his most private places. He gave me groan, tugging on his dick.

"Only if you want to, Kitten," the rumble in his chest had me tightening my legs. I nodded until he rolled over to his back while I slid on top of him. "I want you to grip it for me, baby, like this." He took my hand, and for the first time, I got to look. It was massive, there was no way that would go in me anytime soon. It was like nothing that I had ever seen, granted I've only ever seen two dicks in my life, but he was huge in comparison. My eyes widened, as my hand gripped around his hot swelling thickness.

"Goddess, Charlotte, that feels so good," Wesley purred. While moving my hand up and down his shaft, I began to kiss his abs, and I went lower as I continued to use my hand to stimulate him. My lip darted from my mouth, thinking about licking the pear of liquid from his dick. I knew women could pleasure a man with their mouth, and I wanted to give him the same feeling he gave me. "Oh, fuck! Charlotte!" He yelled as I plunged my mouth on his dick. I bobbed my head up and down as he continued to convulse, pushing his dick further into my mouth. Wesley's hand went to my neck and try to push me down lower, and I continued to go lower until I felt it touch the back of my throat. I gagged a little, but I kept my composure, adjusting to his length.

"Damn, Charlotte, that feels fantastic," he stutters out, having trouble speaking. "Oh, Kitten, I'm gonna come, get up." Instead of stopping, I sucked and bobbed faster. Wesley growled and released his load into my mouth, and I swallowed it all. It was a spicy and salty all at the same time. I cleaned him up with my tongue, and he continued to groan. Rubbing my head with his hand.

Once I was done, he pulled me on top of him and kissed me tenderly. "Kitten, that was so good. You can be a feisty little kitten, can't you?" Wesley's dirty blonde hair was a mess, hair was in his eyes, across his face, and had of a glowing sheen of sweat to his forehead. "Goddess, you are just so beautiful, how did I get so lucky?" he whispered in my ear as I cuddled closer to him. We were both still panting, both laying there naked as the sun continued to set outside.

It had become quiet, and I thought Wesley might have fallen asleep because his breaths were steady. Without even looking to check to see if he was sleeping, I whispered three words that would forever change us. "I love you, Wesley."

Chapter 24

Charlotte

Wesley's breath hitched. "You, you love me?" Wesley whispered as his hold on me got tighter. He waited for my answer, and as the seconds carried on, his grip only grew a bit heavier. I lifted my head up, and he let go, looking down into my eyes while I stared back up at his.

"I do, I think I really do," I whispered slowly. Wesley's eyebrow raised as to question why I would say, 'think.' I sighed, put the sheet around me to cover my breasts, and sat up to look at him.

"I've never loved anyone, not really," I fiddled with the bedsheets. How could I love someone when no one has ever loved me before?

"You know all my deepest, darkest secrets, the most dreadful secrets. Most that no one ever knows or will know, and yet in the end, you don't think anything less of me. You take care of me," I put my hand on his cheek. "You give me a feeling that makes my toes curl and a force that runs through my veins, causing me to blush at the smallest of things. It makes me want to scream all my worries, my fears away because I know you will replace it with your love for me. Your touch is like small whispers telling me that I will be OK and that you will be with me always with your sweet promises. You make me trust again, you make me feel." A tear dropped down my cheek. "Once I was done dancing today, and I saw you, that was when I thought, 'Ah so this must be love.'"

Wesley sat up and took both of his hands to my cheeks and pulled me close, rubbing his nose to mine like he loves to do. "Is that love Wesley? Because I think I do love you if that's what it feels like."

"My love, the only reason why I know what love is, is because of you. You give me a reason to breathe, a reason for living, and a reason to fight for us. Love doesn't really have a certain definition or meaning, it's a feeling." Wesley pulled me on top of him, so I was straddling him. His mouth lowered, capturing my lips. He tugged at my lip, causing my mouth to open as he entered with his tongue.

We moaned together, touched one another, and made each other fall apart all over again. We touched heaven and fell back down to earth, so many times I lost count. We'd never made love, not yet. But we would be soon, so very soon.

***

The following day I realized I completely forgot to tell Wesley about the strange anomaly from one of his companies. It had million or so dollars missing, and no one had caught up on it. Worst of all, they had used Evan's username and password.

Wesley was still sleeping soundly, we were both up late last night doing things I never even thought was even possible without having sex. My blush instantly appeared as I tried to tap my cheeks to get rid of my flush.

Sensing I was awake, Wesley rolled over and grabbed me, and pulled me close. I started giggling into his chest and feeling the scruff on his face brush the top of my head. "Good morning, beautiful," he said gruffly in his morning voice. That had to be the sexiest sound I have ever heard, and it shot right through my core. Before I could say another word, he laughed deeply in his chest. "Nice to know I have that effect on you, my love." I smiled at his endearment. No matter what he called me, I cherished every moment of it.

"Mmm," I snuggled deeper into his embrace, and he held me tight. "I know you are scared of being marked, but I promise it won't hurt, it would be quite pleasurable, actually. They say it is like an instant orgasm, and we both know how much you like those." I shuttered, hearing him talk so dirty.

"Stop!" I squeaked as he let out a big laugh. Wesley explained that a mark was something so special, better than any vow or marriage a human could have. It was something permanent and intertwined two souls together forever. To think that we would be together forever gives me warm flutters in my heart. He would always be there, scars or not, to be with me to grow old with and have a family. The only problem was the mark itself. I'm scared to death of any more pain, I've endured enough. Was I willing to take the next step for just a pinch of pain followed by pleasure? I think I was.

"I-I do want you to m-mark me," I spoke softly to Wesley as he held me in his arms.

"Are you sure?" his voice was soft, calming, and hesitant. He knew this was a big deal for me. It had been one crazy month-long roller coaster. I went from a loner, a no one, and was scared of letting anyone in to want to be accepted into a pack of Werewolves! My mind must have been completely lost because I was willing to jump in with both feet and not look back.

"Yeah, I'm sure." I traced my finger on the outline of his jaw. His beard tickled my finger as I continued to trace it up to his eyes. Warmth flooded his face, and a small smile graced me. I loved this man, and I wanted nothing more than to make him happy, and I knew that if he was happy, I was over the moon.

"I would do it, right here, right now, but..." he sighed. "I want to make sure it's actually OK. Your branding bond mark is gone, but I want to make sure it is completely gone before I mark you with a true mark. Let me talk to the Elders today." A brief moment rushed through our bodies of disappointment of having to wait but, what was a day or two of waiting?

"That's alright. After a day or two of patience, then we can grow old together," I grinned. Expecting a smile back, I was greeted with another expression. Worry. "What is it? What's wrong?"

"I haven't really told you but, we won't, we won't grow old together." My smile dropped, and panic filled my lungs.

"What do you mean we won't grow old together? What does that mean? Do we die young!?" I asked frantic. Wesley let out a loud laugh and fell back onto the pillows. "I don't see what is so funny, you need to spit out what you want to say!"

"I'm sorry, Kitten, I forgot to tell you. You won't, we won't age. Werewolves stop aging around thirty, we can live a very long time." Staring at him in confusion, I had to think back to everyone at the packhouse. I didn't see any elderly people here. They were all fit and healthy. I tilted my head like a lost puppy. How old was this man?

"Exactly how old are you?"

Wesley chuckled. "145?" He shrugged his shoulders. My mouth was hung open. I was barely 20, and this guy was old. He was robbing the cradle. How was this going to work? He is more educated than I was. I was just me!

"Say something. I know it seems old, but I don't act it now, do I? I mean, look what we did last night," Wesley wiggled his eyebrows. I blushed again and covered my face. "Staaaaaahp! I get it!" I squealed.

"That blush gets me every time," he put a piece of hair behind my ear.

✱✱✱

After showering and getting dressed, I realized I STILL had not told Wesley about the accounting issue. I finally spilled the beans about it all. How they do it during payroll to make sure it doesn't look out of the ordinary, that they are logging on to a specific computer and network and using Evan's password and username when obviously it wasn't him.

Wesley was steaming. His fists gripped the chair, causing the back to crack while I explained. Once I had finished my explanation he buried his nose into my neck, something he enjoyed doing to calm his breathing. The worst part that he was upset about was and none of his accountants had found the error. With a few quick phone calls, the whole department was fired, and raging Wesley went into Alpha mode. I decided to step away from that and go find Ashley and see what she was up to. Ever since I learned about mates and how she found Beau the day I arrived, she and him had been locked up in her room.

It was funny how they were two complete opposites. Beau was stoic and scary, and Ashley just wasn't. She was a little ray of sunshine that had brought me into this crazy world that I have now come to love. I owed her everything, and I honestly could call her my best friend. I'm not sure if I was hers, but I would be Okay with it if I weren't.

Ashley's door was open, and she was sitting at her large desk in the corner of her room. She was deeply immersed in what she was doing. Magazines, scraps of fabric, and her laptop flashing pictures on the screen. The bed was made, and I didn't see Beau anywhere, so greedily, I walked into her room. "Ashley!" Ashley jumped and put her hand over her heart. "Dear goddess, what the hell, Charlie?"

"Did I just spook a Werewolf?" I said, surprised. "Wow, I will take it as a compliment!" Ashley rolled her eyes and continued what she was preparing. "What are you doing that you are concentrating so hard on?"

"I'm planning our Halloween party. Several packs are coming in, and it is a great way to get Wolves to mingle and find mates. It is actually a lot of fun. I'm the party planner, so I'm trying to budget, plan, and get decorations for the event." Ashley was so giddy about doing it she started to show me all the ideas for decorations. Tons of black and red, skeletons, and a dungeon-like atmosphere. It would be a great party, but it reminded me of where I stayed when I was younger, getting cut and beaten to a pulp, but I didn't say anything. I didn't want to be the party pooper. Besides, I was healing from all of that.

"It's only a few weeks away, we should get you a costume. What would you want to be?" Ashley asked while clicking away on the computer. I've never dressed up for Halloween, none of my foster parents took me but they took their own kids. I remember sitting at the window watching all the children go by holding out their bags of candy, going door to door yelling, 'Trick or treat.' I ended up being the kid at home handing out the candy, not receiving it.

"I've never done the whole Halloween thing, but with my new obsession with *The Greatest Showman*, I think I want to be Anne Wheeler, Phillip Carlyle's love interest. I just adore the pink hair," I gushed.

"We should all go as something from the musical! I don't think I can see Alpha Wesley in Phillip's costume, though. He never dresses up!"

"Oh my gosh, he would be so hot in a uniform." I was drooling thinking about it and how nice his muscles would bulge in it. Ashley snorted at me, which knocked me out of my stupor of imagining my mate dressed in red. The few hard knocks at the door had me whipping my head around at the intrusion.

His brows furrowed and his mouth in a line, his hand rested on the door frame as he hung over with Evan and Bruce behind him. "We need to talk, Kitten."

Vera Foxx

Chapter 25
Charlotte

Wesley led all of us to the office. The long walk was quiet and daunting as Wesley held me close to him. Halfway through the walk, he picked me up quickly and welcomed me to his chest as he carried me like a bride through the double doors. I've started to get used to his caveman ways taking me everywhere, and I've really enjoyed it, so I wasn't about to complain. His face instantly went into my neck, smelling my hair and nuzzling me. This only made me worry more since he was doing it while walking. Wesley only did this when he was craving closeness during extreme emotions.

Everyone took a seat on couches and chairs, and Wesley kept me on his lap as we sat down at the large mahogany desk. A large screen pulled down from the bookcase showing an electronic map with several areas circled in red on the far side of the wall.

"What's going on?" Zachary questioned as he walked through the door. Wesley glared at him, and Zachary sat down in the chair and bowed his head in submission. Wesley wasn't playing around; he was in his leadership Alpha mode. It was really hot too.

"Different packs have had breaches in their borders. The problem is, they don't seem to know who is behind them, and they leave as quickly as they come. Most packs don't notice until they have left the territory with a faint lingering scent of smoke and rot in several of the bedrooms of their pack houses." Evan and Bruce looked at each other, probably having a mind-link conversation.

Wesley took out his laser pointer and started circling certain areas on the map, spouting different packs' names and connections with ours. I just continued to stare at the map; it looked like the upper New England area of North America, which was where we were—close to the Canadian border.

"There is a large storm coming in, it is a bit early in the season to be having a major snowstorm, but it will be coming, nonetheless. The Elders have predicted it should be a shut-in; no one will be able to get in and out of the packhouse for days until the snow has been cleared away. Temps should stay well below freezing, so we can't expect any of it to melt."

Ashley set out a low groan, "Aw, what about the Halloween party?" Wesley looked at Ashley and gave an annoyed look. "Out of all the things we should be worrying about, you bring up that damn party?" Ashley bowed her head.

"I was just thinking of Charlie, she's never been to a big party like that. She wanted to dress up and everything!" I smiled sheepishly. Wesley's turned my body to get a better look at me, and the corners of his lips upturned slightly. A grown woman wanting to dress up, he must think I am insane.

"We should still have the party. The storm will be here in 3 days. It will take only two to get rid of most of the snow. However, I've got to leave and come back before the storm sets in." My head turned so fast, my own neck could have broken. "Leave?" I asked.

Wesley's hold around my waist tightened. "Yes, after you told me about the missing money, I fired all the accountants. I need to drive into the city and catch the perpetrator in the act. You narrowed it down to what computer they are using, but there are no cameras in that room. I can't just place it at random, whoever is doing this, they are smart, they would figure it out."

My heart stopped. Wesley will be gone in a few days, and I haven't been without him since I first arrived here almost a month ago. The bond everyone keeps talking about is getting stronger, which I thought was my own insecurities whenever he would leave the room. Since we haven't been mated yet, the feeling of loneliness and abandonment sets in when a mate is gone for too long, or so Ashley says.

"I'm coming with you then, right?" I said, hopeful to Wesley. Wesley smiled down at me and cupped my cheek.

"I can't risk you coming out of the packhouse. There is more protection for you here with all the warriors. Roman is still out there, and he is an older Vampire, and he may have allies helping him." I continued to hold my breath as Wesley spoke. "Kitten breathe, you will be safe here. I don't like it either, and it is killing me to do this, but we need to."

For the first time in a long time, I felt anger. He was willingly leaving me here after he said he would protect me. This bond they talked about always said it was like a knife cutting through to your soul if you left your unmarked mate alone too long. Now here he was going away, willingly even. The emotions were too much, and I didn't know where to put it all. Even though I was human, I felt a pull to him and the disappointment of hurt that he would leave me. Maybe he didn't feel as strong of a force as the rest of the Werewolves talked about.

I grunted in reply, not saying anything.

"The security here is the best in all of North America, thanks to you. No one will get in, you are safe, try and understand," Wesley pleaded. "I'll only be gone 2, maybe 3 days, and I will be back before the storm hits." Wesley tried to kiss me, but I denied him. I was angry at him. After telling him I loved him last night, something in itself was hard for me to do, he was going to leave. I didn't care if it was only a few days. I still felt vulnerable and helpless though my own self-confidence in my looks even though it had increased since arriving.

I felt the eyes of everyone on me as I leaned away from Wesley. I felt his heart sink, and it only made me feel worse. I wanted to turn around and hug him and kiss him, but I held firm to my stubbornness and got up from his lap to leave the room without looking back.

"Charlotte, wait, please." I could hear Wesley's voice fading into the background. Becoming the weak person, I always knew I was, I felt the tears well up in my eyes. I hated feeling this way. I used to be this independent person. I didn't rely on anyone or trust anyone. You didn't get hurt that way, but this stupid thing called a bond was messing me up to pieces. I relied on him too much, and now here I was, upset over a few days of him leaving me.

Maybe it wouldn't have hurt so much if I hadn't told him I loved him. I put my feelings on a silver platter for him to dig into, and now it felt like he snubbed his nose at it. Stomping up the stairs, I went to my old room, greeted by Macaroni and his meowing. I laid on the bed and just cried.

These feelings were just too much, and my heart continued to ache as I knew I would feel lonelier the next few days than I ever felt. These feelings I'm having overshadowed any other sense I have ever had.

The only other time I had felt remotely close to this was when I'd first gotten my period. I was so emotional—crying, thinking I was dying. I went to the free health clinic that had to hand over a pamphlet explaining the birds and the bees. Talk about embarrassing, but it did help me understand more about my body. However, what I was going through now was ten times that, or so it felt that way.

I heard the door whine and saw that Ashley was standing at the door with a frown on her face. She closed the door behind her and joined me on the bed while wrapping her arms around me. "I must look like a spoiled toddler sitting here crying, not getting my way," I sniffed.

"Believe it or not, it is normal. These feelings you have, you've never been prepped for and have they've come on a lot stronger than they normally would have." I lifted my head to the side so I could see her face beside me.

"You've been spending the night with him, cuddling him, holding each other, loving each other it was bound to happen. The only reason you both haven't mated was because of that stupid scarring. It is almost over, and then you both can be at peace. The bond just makes your mind and body go haywire being so close to your soulmate, it just demands it, and you can't have it just yet." Ashley patted my head and gave me a side smile.

"I feel so foolish, I used to be so independent, and now I'm completely relying on him. I'm not sure if I like it. He could crush my heart if he wanted."

"But he won't, and you know that. He has his reasons why he has to go, we may not know what they are, but I do know he doesn't want to leave you." I nodded, still feeling the ache in my bones. "Come on, let's do a movie night with Zachary. Beau is head of the patrol to make sure you are protected while he is gone."

Wesley

"Damn it." I pounded my fist to the desk.

Evan scoffed, "That went well." Bruce held in a chuckle, and Ashley and Zachary had scowls on their faces.

"Really? Do you have to fix the whole money stealing thing right now? When she is at the most vulnerable? She's having to deal with not being fully mated with all these crazy feelings, and on top of it all, she is human! She doesn't grasp the whole concept of a mate, and now you will leave her for a few days. What the hell?" Ashley threw her hands up in frustration.

I rubbed my hands through my messy hair and did a combination of a sigh and growl. I knew she had a point. Bruce squinted his eyes at me in an accusatory manner. "She told you she loved you, didn't she?" Bruce had always had an intuitive nature about him. He was the strong silent type, but he could read people like an open book. Mate bond or not, he could tell when people cared about each other, even with humans. I don't know how often he played matchmaker at the hotels we stayed at between the cleaning ladies and the doormen.

Zachary stood up and came up to the desk. "After all the shit that went down yesterday, after her dancing and being more open with you, she also threw the love card on your deck? Now you are leaving her for a few days?" Zachary was partially correct, I shouldn't be leaving, but I was running out of time.

If I didn't go now, I might not have a chance to catch whoever was stealing money, money that goes to the pack members that really need it. Our pack was strong for a reason all these years, I gave up on a lot to keep us solid and profitable. If I didn't correct it now, what would happen if they did it to my other companies? Charlotte and I are so close to mating, but I'm waiting on the Elders and the Vampire Council.

When the go-ahead is in place, I'm not going to want to let Charlotte go for a few months. It may be hard now for her, but it will only be more challenging once we are mated. Her heat will could come in shortly after, and I was not about to leave her then either. That's why I'm going now because the bond will only get stronger, and it will be harder to let go. Roman is still out there, and I can't risk it while I will be out in the open.

"It has to be done. I have my reasons." I gave my final word as everyone looked at me in disbelief. They can't question their Alpha, I have my reasons, and I'm keeping her physically safe. She has to understand. However, I feel the pain she feels. She's upset, and I can feel her tears dripping down my heart.

"Evan, get the SUV ready. Let's head out now so we can get back quicker." Evan nodded.

"Are you going to at least tell her goodbye?" Ashley asked.

"If I do, I won't want to leave." My eye stung. I couldn't believe I was almost crying. Damn.

"Zachary and I will stay with her then. We will keep her busy." With that said, Ashley walked out of the room to tend to Charlotte.

Vera Foxx

Chapter 26

Wesley

After a few hours, we arrived in the city of New York. I knew this would be hard for both Charlotte and I, but I really had to push through and get this sorted out before some significant life changes were going to happen with Charlotte. If she still accepted me after all of the trauma, I am apparently putting her through, that is.

After a few texts telling her I was sorry and that I would make it up to her and never leave her side again, I was greeted with nothing. I had told her she had to have her phone on her at all times, but I did not want to pull the 'I'm your boss card.' She was my boss now, and the boss had the right to be angry.

After sighing loudly and annoyed, Evan smirked and knew what I was thinking. "Your girl won't text you back, and now you are going to be in a bad mood. I think she has every right to be." I gave Evan a warning glare and continued to stare at the window while the street buildings went by.

Evan may be the annoying brother to everyone in the pack, even the nasty uncle with the dirty jokes, but he has been loyal to me from the beginning. I found him on the outskirts of an abandoned warehouse area where he had lived as a rogue for years. Many people find rogues disgusting and think, more often than not, that they are troublemakers. That was the complete opposite for Evan. When he was 15 years old, his small pack was attacked by Witches and Warlocks fighting for land.

Things in the human world run differently with supernaturals. Annually, all the supernaturals that live here in the Earth realm put in bids for land so they could live peacefully, and everything is charted accordingly. However, when supernaturals started resettling here 300 years ago from the Bergarian realm, they just took things. There were no councils to speak with and divide the lands with the humans. It was a free-for-all. Long story short, Evan's pack was slaughtered, and he only survived because he started his first shift in the middle of it. The Witches and Warlocks thought he was dying and left him there.

While scouting the warehouses with my father, I found Evan roaming around a new textile materials store. We were in the process of building companies from scratch and needed storage. My father offered him a place in our pack, feeling sorry for him, and we ended up growing up together. Evan had it rough. He lived off eating wild animals and had barely any clothing for 20 years. He was almost too wild to talk to, saying he couldn't relate to the humans—he mostly stayed in Wolf form because of it.

My mother and I taught him the ropes and gave him a place in the packhouse. We all got along well, but once he found his mate, he was the one in control. He let his Wolf decide what he should do, and it was a good thing he did. He showered her with gifts, fed her, and loved her fiercely. He listened to his instincts, and many who have Wolves, such as me, have difficulty doing that. Alpha's feel their human side should be mostly in control and decide for the Wolf, not have the Wolf decide in certain situations.

I have that problem. I don't listen to my Wolf as well as I should.

"She needs to hear your voice, not read a damn text. Just give her a call. If she doesn't answer, leave a voicemail and let her know how you feel. I can't believe I have to tell you how to do this; it is the simplest thing," Evan rolled his eyes. "You shouldn't have left in the first place. What did your Wolf say?"

"That I shouldn't go. But hell, I have to get this done before the Storm and the Vampire Council come in. Once I'm given the OK, I will mark her. That way, I can always protect her and know where she is," I sighed exasperatedly.

"*If* she will let you mark her, it sounds like she's pissed," Evan folded his arms and looked out the window. I growled at him, and he didn't flinch. He knew he was right, and I obviously knew I was wrong. We had to get this done fast.

Taking out my phone, I called her. It went straight to voicemail on the second ring, letting me know she ignored me. "Charlotte, I'm so sorry. I just want to tell you that I love you. I'll be back soon." I cut the call and let out another exasperated sigh.

Pulling up to the company, I hopped out quickly, not even waiting for the driver to get the door. The doors were opened entirely, and I stomped up to my private elevator and hit the 42nd floor. Inside, Evan gave me the rundown on who had had access to this specific room with a special key card. It was his name that was swiped in, but Evan had been by my side always. There was a copy of his card floating around somewhere, and I would have to find out where they'd gotten it from.

Calling Bruce back at the packhouse, I had him contact the security team in the building I was in to check the HR department for any duplicate keys.

The room in question appeared in my sight, and I glanced inside the window. There were several computers inside, but the one that caught my eye had a drink next to the mouse. I didn't want to walk in, afraid that if it was a Werewolf, they would be able to smell the remnants of me being there. Alphas tend to have a strong smell that could last for days.

We walked back to my office and decided to wait it out. According to the times Charlotte had sent me before she became angry, it was about 5:30 p.m. when they made the withdrawals. Evan and I sat silently in the office with the lights out, listening for anyone that may come down the hallway. Pulling out my phone, I proceeded to text my mate.

Wesley: Charlotte, I'm so sorry, I miss you. Please talk to me.

I waited 10 minutes before there was a reply. The minutes passed into hours, and I continued to text Charlotte.

Charlotte: You are in big trouble, mister Alpha.

I smiled; I was just happy she had replied to me.

Wesley: Can I make it up to you? What can I do? I'll do anything, Kitten.

Charlotte: Come home. It makes my heart ache with you not here. These are such strong feelings I can't explain. I'm not used to having a longing for someone before. It's so infuriating.

My breath caught. I don't want my baby to be hurt.

Wesley: I will come back soon, baby, I promise. I'm trying to get back as soon as tomorrow.

Charlotte: Not soon enough :(

I was about to give up since it was nearing 7 p.m., and we didn't hear anything, but then I heard a ping on my phone. The app Charlotte gave me alerted me that someone was withdrawing the money right now from the payroll account. Evan and I looked at each other and swiftly ran down the hall. This was terrible, whoever this money embezzler was, would feel my wrath tonight.

There was no noise or clicking of the computer mouse as we drew closer. We burst through the door and found Delilah sitting at the computer. She was wearing all black, and her freshly painted nails were holding a thumb drive into the computer doing all the work for her. Delilah turned around, dropping the thumb drive and raising her hands. "It isn't what it looks like."

"I told you this Witch would cause you nothing but trouble, but no, you never listen to me," Evan mocked while grabbing her by her arm. "Tsk, such a weak Wolf."

Delilah was an average size Wolf but was a on the weaker side. The only thing she had going for her was her looks, and even then, they had their limitations. She wasn't Charlotte.

"What are you doing here, and why the hell are you stealing from me?!" I yelled in rage. I could even feel the veins protruding from my neck as I gripped her throat.

"I, ... I..." Delilah tried to speak, but as my grip tightened and she started to turn blue. Her silent cries only angered me as she gripped my hands, using her fake ass nails to scratch me away. I chuckled, leaning into her, nose to nose.

"Answer. The. Question," I gritted my teeth. Loosening my grip, she fell to the floor, holding her throat and coughing. She laughed mockingly, "You know your choking is still a turn-on, even if you're angry." Evan stepped up and threw her on the chair, handcuffing her to it with a Witch's holding curse on them. She wouldn't be able to shift or get away.

"Speak now, or you will lose your head. I don't care if you are the daughter of an allied pack's Alpha. You stole from another Alpha and his people." I used my Alpha command on her, and she cowered.

"It doesn't really matter now," she rolled her eyes. "I got what I wanted, the question is, are you ready to deal with your actions?" Evan and I looked at each other, cocking our eyebrows. Enough with the games, I was done.

"Is this because I wouldn't take you as my mate and rejected you?" I clashed. She let out a gentle scoff.

"No, absolutely not. I couldn't care less. I can't tell you any more shit," she spat. Evan was about to punch her right in the jaw when I held up my hand to stop him.

"We have a protocol on this since she is an Alpha's daughter. We take her back to the packhouse. I'll get in touch with her father." Evan nodded. He wasn't afraid to hit a woman, especially one that deserved it. As Evan was tying her up, I pulled out my phone to text Charlotte. She would be so excited I would be coming home a whole two days early. I'd felt awful leaving her, but the timing of all this was going to work so well. I'd be home within 24 hours so she wouldn't be as mad.

"Oh, Wesley," Delilah spoke in a whispered voice. "I'm sorry," she muttered.

"Sorry for what?" Thinking she was sorry of just being caught.

"You'll see," she grimaced.

Chapter 27

Charlotte

"You can't hide in here forever, you know," Ashley scolded me as I laid face-first onto the floor. I was dramatic, I knew it, she knew it, heck, even Zachary knew it. Now I was just milking it a bit too much.

"He just left me here, just let me die." I've become dependent on a big strong Alpha man, what have I become? Macaroni looked at me unamused and continued to lick her butt. Thanks, pal. I appreciate the sentiment... as always.

"I know all the emotions and the bond is making you a bit crazy, but we need to keep your mind off of it. So, I have an idea that involves making your Alpha a bit crazy." Ashley smirked while grabbing my phone and flipping the camera on. My head picked up off the fuzzy floor with interest. What did this woman want to do?

The next few hours of ignoring texts from Wesley, Ashley, and Zachary scouted my closet for the sexiest pieces of clothing they could find. It ranged from formal wear, to casual, semi-formal, and even swimming attire. Ashley had done my hair and had it curled to perfection. It cascaded down my back in big, thick ringlets, and the volume was just enough to give me a 'just had sex' as Zachary said. I rolled my eyes and just continued to do what they asked.

I had to give seductive poses, uninterested poses, and even just plain smiles, which was hard to do since my heart was aching the entire time. Ashley and Zachary did their best to keep my mind busy, so the pain in my chest would be distracted. Who was I kidding, though? I was hurting. It was worse than heartburn because there was no way to rectify it. I craved him, his touch, his face, his eyes. When Ashley noticed, I was starting to get into a funk, she would put me in positions that would make a porn star blush.

Zachary found the lingerie that Wesley had apparently bought for me. He had to leave because Ashley said that Zachary might lose his eyes if Wesley found out Zachary saw me in anything this skimpy.

"He's going to love these!" Ashley squealed as I changed back into my skinny jeans and baby pink tee. I rolled my eyes and put my hair back up in a high ponytail.

"I don't know if I want to send him these. It just looks like I'm playing dress-up. I don't look like a model or anything. He will probably just laugh." I threw myself on the bed and let out a sizeable depressing sigh as Zachary walked in.

"How did it go? Do you look as ravishing as Ashley claims?" Zachary took the phone from Ashley and started to scroll through the pictures. His eyes became wide, and he began to smile. "Damn girl, these are nice! Where are the lingerie pictures?" Zachary scrolled down the phone faster until Ashley ripped it out of his hand.

"Those are definitely not for you! This is your future Luna, you do not get the privilege to look at these! Alpha eyes only!" She slapped her ands. I was about to argue about not sending them to Wesley and forget the whole thing until the entire pack house's power went out.

"Well, that is only mildly concerning," Zachary mumbled. I looked around the room, which was almost in complete darkness. Just then, white lights and siren alarms sounded. "Shit! Get Charlotte to the safe room!"

Ashley grabbed my arm and tore through the packhouse. It was utterly dark, and I couldn't see anything in front of my face. Ashley's Werewolf sense have been taking over because I wasn't sure how she saw anything. Instead of going down the usual stairway, we came to a blank wall at the end of the Alpha floor. Thinking we were going to hit the wall at full speed, it opened automatically, and with a few twists and pulls of a rope, we descend past the first floor and into the basement of the packhouse.

"Just do as I say, alright?" Ashley began rushing with her words. "You are to stay down here and not make a sound until Zachary or I come back to get you. Do you understand?" I stood there, staring at her, no comprehending what was going on. Do you understand!?" she yelled while shaking me with her hands on my shoulders. I nodded yes, and she opened a small compartment that I had to crawl into. Shoving me in, I heard a loud click. I was locked in. Now was probably the wrong time to mention I was claustrophobic.

The room was big enough for me to walk around in but was the size of an average bathroom. There was a toilet out in the open, a small mattress with blankets and pillows, and some non-perishable food items and jugs of water. It looked like an underground bunker that could house me for a few days.

Just knowing that I couldn't get out on my own made me panic. Breathing rather harshly, I tried to think of ways to calm down. In and out, I slowed my breathing while holding my hands over my face. This unfortunately reminded me of the days when I was younger, when I'd been locked in the basement at Roman's.

I sat on the mattress and hugged my phone to me that I had amazingly held onto through the giant rush of running. I still had a Wi-Fi signal down here amazingly, but I had no cell service to call anyone.

I laid my head back and banged my head lightly on the wall behind me. It was cold, so I pulled the blanket around me tightly. I didn't know what was going on outside, but I could hear faint sounds of yelling and maybe some growling. Never have I been more thankful to not know what was going on. The thought of hundreds of Werewolves shifting and fighting something, or someone had me scared out of my mind. The one thing that bothered me was why didn't my alarm system go off… and why the power had gone out.

The packhouse was utterly covered with cameras, they still had backup patrollers always lurking. Something must have been working on the inside for it to fail. I set the whole thing up myself and with my very own security software. The only way to switch it off was to cut the power from it was to cut the generator in the basement of the packhouse. I didn't even trust the electricity company to keep us safe. It was overkill but worth it. However, it had clearly failed in the end.

Thinking about how it failed only started to get me flustered. It should not have failed; something was wrong. I tried to lay down and rest, but I was restless. How could I rest when my friends are out there fighting? I stood up to start pacing, but I heard a bang at the door where I'd slid in. No door handle or any other way in or out. It continued to bang louder and louder.

Ashley said not to come near the door unless it was her or Zachary. The bang continued to get louder, and I huddled in the corner on the opposite side. I could hear mumbling people were talking on the other side but not loud enough for me to hear. The sounds of from an electric screwdriver came through the thick metal and then a loud smack. "Stand back!" I heard a deep voice yell. The hair on the back of my neck stood up, I knew that voice.

BANG.

The thunderous sound ripped through the room, smoke trickling in and the door cracked open slightly. I shook and held the blanket around me. *Please don't let it be him. Not him, please.* I begged anyone that would listen. The man bent low with his right foot coming in first and tried to stand up at full height but was unable due to the small size of the room. His back was slightly hunched over, his hair was black as a raven, and his bright red looked straight into my soul. His crooked grin slid up the left side of his face as he saw me.

"Lottie, Lottie, look at you. You are all grown up." My breath hitched, and my heart was thumbing through my chest. Hands shaking, I wrapped the blanket around me tighter, the tears were falling down my cheeks without my permission, and the mascara dripped onto the blanket. "I no longer have to hide what I am from you now, thank the gods, those contacts were infuriating."

"No," I whispered. "Y-you can't be here." My breathing quickened as he took a few steps forward and ended up being just next to me. I leaned my body up against the wall hoping for me to be swallowed up somehow. He hadn't changed, not one bit. Even without the contacts, his eyes were still dangerous, and now his fangs showed past his lips as he continued to look me over.

"I told you, you could never get away from me, Lottie. It took some time, but I found you, my dear," his voice was ominous as he put his hand out for me to take.

I looked at him and back at his hand, *please don't make me take it.*

"N-no, I won't go," I spoke rather confidently. Something stirred in me, I couldn't be the weak person I was before. I had become so much more than what I was. Wesley and everyone here had helped me fight for a better life and people that loved me. Wesley would love me no matter what, he showed me that even with this battered body.

"Excuse me?" Roman sneered. "You belong to me, you will come!" he yelled loudly. His cold hand ripped the blanket from me, and I tried to take it back. Roman gripped his claw-like fingers into my skin of my arm. I screamed in pain, and he only gripped tighter. Warm drops of blood dripped down my arms. Pulling me through the small opening where several other Vampires awaited us.

They started to sniff the air, and their eyes almost glowed. I tried wiggling out of Roman's grip, but it only proved to make him angrier. I wasn't going to give up, no matter how much it hurt, I couldn't go back. The place I constantly dreamed about in my nightmares had to stay in my nightmares. I couldn't make it a reality.

Roman didn't let go, he eventually pulled me over his shoulder, and I hit his back, scratching and clawing him, but he only laughed as I drew blood from his cold, clammy skin. Leading me outside, Wolves fighting off a large number of Vampires and what it looked like Witches throwing balls of fire from their hands. Screaming out for Ashley and Zachary seemed futile since I didn't know what their Wolves looked like. The sounds of snarls, howling and yelling oozed in the air. My minor pleas for help only got lost in the sound.

"Roman has me, tell Wesley, someone tell him. Tell him to find me please!" I screamed and begged. With one last blast from the Witch that seemed to be the most powerful of them all, froze the lot of Werewolves that tried to get to me. With a few laughs from the Vampires and the less powerful Witches, they came closer to us, and a ball of light engulfed us. Many Wolves looked in my direction and watched me disappear.

Vera Foxx

Chapter 28

Charlotte

The light was blinding, and I felt nauseous as the morning departed. Several Vampires, as well as Witches, were transported with us. At first, I didn't realize we were transported, but the dark and dank area we were standing in told me otherwise. No longer was I standing at the front of the packhouse, with the fall leaves drifting around and the young children running and playing in laughter. I was in a nightmare, yet again.

My heart seized. If it could stop independently without the probability of a heart attack, I think mine would have. I was standing in my worst nightmare. I visited the same hell every night for many years and only stopped when Wesley came into my life.

Wesley. Gosh, I missed him. Would he ever find me?

Who knew how long I would be stuck here now in this familiar basement? I could even see the old teddy bear I'd carried around before I left the wretched place. Too scared to grab the one thing left of my childhood when I was finally able to be free from him. That was a day I never wanted to remember either.

"Welcome home Lottie, I kept your room the same." Roman waved his hand around like he was the ringleader at a circus. The chains were still attached to the wall where he would slowly cut me with a rusty knife. How I never got tetanus, I would never know. The small rug on the floor where I slept and healed through the night was still tattered and stained with my blood. He would lick my wounds, and they would somehow heal up within twelve hours, just in time for school the next day.

That tongue, I didn't even want to think what he would do with it now. I was 'of age,' I'm sure. I was considered an adult, and I'm mature. He hadn't seen me since I was fourteen, no longer a child, and he could do what he wanted with me. "I'm not a pedophile," he would say. Like that was any better than what he was. As if he wasn't grooming me. Even then, the branding didn't keep me staying with him though. I learned how to break free, not even being aware he had some sort of branding bond with me. One day, I felt strong enough or fed up enough, one of the two. I decided I wasn't going to listen, and I was done with it and ran. Ran for something better to be a better person even if I knew no one would ever love me.

I would at least be free.

Everyone left the basement except for Roman and the head Witch. These misfits were chatting as they'd just got out of the movies, cutting up and joking with one another as if they didn't just fight and try to kill innocent bystanders. The door slammed, and I winced. The last bit of light that left the floor above me trickled away, and I was trapped. I'm stuck in this horrible basement, never to get out again. He would be more careful this time.

"Let's get this over with," the Witch said, heading over to the corner of the room. The small area looked dedicated to her. It was the only new part of the room. Roman grabbed my upper arm, pulled me to the chair, and sat me down harshly.

"You've been a bad girl, Lottie," Roman said in a sing-song voice. "Do you know what happens when my girl has been bad?" He tied my legs to the chair and kept my upper body free, ripping the shirt from my body, just left in my bra. I gasped, feeling the cold air hitting my skin.

"No," I croaked. "Please don't!" My voice started rising as I continued my pleas. "I'll do anything, please don't touch me!" Tears were already beginning to flood my eyes, my heart rate rising from the panic. Breathing quickened, my eyes dilated, and I could feel it. I could feel the knife, and I hadn't even seen it yet.

Roman chuckled darkly, and the Witch came forward with an iron. A branding iron. I recognized it from the first time he had used it all those years ago. The intricate detail of Latin letters and pictures of evil being with fangs. Now that I know what world I was shielded from all those years, I know what it was. The branding bond that will singe my skin, making me his.

Confusion set in my eyes. He couldn't do this again. Mine just disappeared, it won't stay. I won't let it stay. Starting to fight, trying to untie my rope bonds, and he growled. "Since when did you fight back? Seems you need to learn your place again," he scoffed. As soon as I screamed no, I felt a swift smack across my face. Spots clouded my vision, and I tried to shake them away. I didn't want to pass out; I didn't know what he would do to me.

Shuffling, grunts, and growls filled the room. Once my head shook away the dark spots in my vision, I saw another Vampire. "Alex, you idiot, not the face! I have to look at her while I mate her!"

"Easy there, Vanderveen, it will heal after you mate. It's not like it is gonna scar," Alex taunted.

Hold. The. Phone.

The Vanderveen name, Roman's last name was Vanderveen? That name sounded so familiar; where can I place that last name? I never knew what Roman's last name really was; he always told social services Smith, such a stupid generic name.

And, oh my gosh. Mate. He was going to try and literally mate with me?

Alex whipped his head towards me to get a better look. "She is a pretty little thing, huh? Who knew the pre-pubescent runt would turn into a beautiful little Lottie?" He had pulled my chin up to look me in the eyes. "She will make an excellent chosen beloved for you. I would have done the same if I had known of this face." Roman came over and smacked his hand away from me. My lip was cut, and blood trickled down my chin, the warmth of the blood cooled off as it dripped into my lap.

Roman gave a small smile and dipped his finger to wipe up the blood from my face. "Hmmm," he hummed knowingly. "It really is time, Lottie. Soon you will be mine, and you can't leave ever again after that. You will actually have feelings for only me." I choked back the tears.

"No," I whispered.

His face, Alex. I knew that face. Not just the times I saw him in this same house when I was younger, but another place. Now that I see his red eyes and the evil smirk, he was giving me, I knew I saw him somewhere else, but where?

The Witch brought over a searing hot branding iron that was bright red. "Can we hurry up with this? I've got places to be." Roman smirked and took the iron while Alex held me back to the chair. "Now, read this, and you can repeat this process three times if it doesn't work."

"Doesn't work? What do you mean?" Roman spat as he walked closer to the Witch. She rolled her eyes like it was the most straightforward answer in the world. "She met her mate already, idiot. If the bond is strong, she could fight it. You can try several times to get it to stick. If it doesn't, you could try and force the bond with the bite, but I cannot guarantee she would survive that if her body rejects it. The branding bond helps weaken her so you can bite her and not kill her." The Witch grabbed a piece of paper and slapped Roman's chest. "I'll be back in a few days to get my branding bond iron back."

Alex scoffed as she left. "This is quite a lot for your girl, don't you think? Yeah, she's pretty but damn." Roman read the paper and stuffed it in his pocket and threw a scowl on his face toward Alex. My mind was rushing with different scenarios that could get me out of this situation, but from the looks of things, I was going to get burned, literally.

I had no physical strength to go against two Vampires, heck I was even tied to a chair, and I couldn't break out of the ropes. The only thing I had was my will. My will was to stay as strong as I could until Wesley or any of the pack warriors arrived. The only problem was how long would my will last. If I had to be stuck here and be bonded to this Vampire, I think I might die. I would not submit to him, I couldn't. My heart belonged somewhere else, and I was in pain already.

Roman stepped forward with the iron and began to speak the Latin language. Language was not my strong point in college, so I sat listening to the bitter words. As soon as he spoke the last of the spell, he seared the brand to the upper part of my chest.

Screaming in agony, I tried to move my body to get away from Alex. The band came off of my body, it was black, just like the first time I was branded. There was no blood or blisters. It was dark and singed. He repeated the process on my back, and I didn't even scream. I concentrated on rejecting it. I had no idea how to do it, but I kept thinking of Wesley, the one person who could take this pain from me.

What would Wesley be feeling now? Would he feel this pain I was in? We hadn't mated, he told me we would feel each other once our souls were entangled. Right now, the pain was so much I could only hope he didn't feel what I felt. The pain was unbearable. I didn't feel it in just my chest but all over my body like it was trying to tie down my spirit to an invisible force.

Alex laughed as he let go of my body. I slumped in the chair, burning tears melting my eyes. Everything was blurry. I was still holding on to the picture I had of Wesley I had in my mind, his warm smile, his gentle touches when he would move my hair out of my face. The way he made me feel just by touching me with his hands and the euphoria I felt. How he would just look at me from across the room and instantly feel the warmth from his love for me. I wanted it back. I wanted him. I wouldn't give up, I couldn't.

Before I felt the light go out from me, I remembered the name Vanderveen and Alex's face. Vanderveen, the man's computer trying to infiltrate Hale's network for information, and Alex's face were on the other side of the webcam that I had taken a picture of. They were both after Hale long before me, and I somehow got caught in the middle.

Funny how small the world really is.

Chapter 29
Wesley

Evan and I shoved Delilah in the back of the black SUV. The rest of the remaining, small number of warriors we took crowded the other. I drove while Evan sat in the back with Delilah, still handcuffed with the magic bindings. Delilah kept her mouth shut after telling us she was sorry. We had no idea what she meant with the flash of regret in her eyes.

Delilah doesn't regret anything. She's tough, an Alpha's daughter. Even though she doesn't have the most muscular Wolf, she does excellent with anything mentally tactful, so showing any emotion was troublesome.

The clouds were coming in for the impending storm. They were dark, ominous, almost foreshadowing what I would have to deal with regarding Delilah. I should have never started anything with her, but I was lonely and thought closeness to something would help. She was in the same boat, so for years, we were together, and I wish I could take it all back.

"Storm's coming up, Alpha. Looks like the Elders got the storm prediction right for once." I nodded in agreement. There were sure signs that the elders could predict, mostly being things of nature. The weather was no different, and I could feel the subtle patterns in the weather since they had been around for such a long time. They were just more in tune, and along with the ability to notice patterns, they provide great insight into the history of packs and other supernaturals. I was a bit annoyed they didn't understand branding bonds, but to be completely honest, branding bonds haven't been practiced for thousands of years.

"Hey, have you heard anything from them regarding the branding bond?" I glanced back in the mirror.

"Nah, I can call them real quick. We were supposed to know today. They had an audience with the Vampire Council this morning." Evan got on the phone, and Delilah started sighing loudly, looking out the window. Her leg shook up and down, her eyes glancing from her feet to the passing by of buildings.

"Yes, Donny, this is Beta Evan. Have you... what? Excellent. Right. I'll let him know." Evan was smiling ear to ear after a few moments of nodding on the phone. "Great news, Alpha! Looks like the branding bond won't do anything if you mark her. The branding bond is there to weaken a human's soul so it they can be forcefully marked later. It just suppresses their spirit so the venom can penetrate the body easier. When the spirit is strong, the body will fight the venom and cause them to reject the marking. It shouldn't matter if you are true mates because the soul or spirit is already waiting for you. Since you are true mates, it won't be an issue." Evan smiled.

I blew out a sigh of relief. Mating and marking Charlotte wouldn't be a problem, and when she was ready, I would mark her as mine. Everyone will know that we belong to each other, and once she decides to be a Werewolf, she won't have an issue becoming one if she does want that too.

Being a Luna while a human would be complicated, but I wouldn't mind her staying that way as strong as she is. I would always protect her. With a grin on my face, I gripped the steering wheel while smiling and thinking of sneaky ways to get my Luna to fall in love with me all the more and let me touch her in ways that would make her blush all the way down to...

Ring, Ring, Ring.

Shit, once I start thinking about loving my mate's body, of course, someone would interrupt. "What?" I snapped, not even bothering to look at the caller ID. Once Ashley started talking, my foot became led and pushed the accelerator to the max, and I threw the phone on the floor.

"The hell?" Evan was slung back into his seat, hitting his head. "The fuck is wrong with you what's going on?!"

"The pack has been attacked, Charlotte has been taken." I roared, causing the windows to burst. Glass flew outwards, but many shards landed in our hair as the speed of the vehicle was taken to the max. My knuckles turned white as we hit 120 mph on the speedometer. The fastest we could go. I was going to redline the entire way.

Once back at the packhouse, I burst out of the car like lightning, pushing everyone out of the way. People were trying to speak to me, but I pushed them back if they got too close. My Wolf was on the brink of shifting right then and there. The hair on the back of my head was standing up, and fur was starting to take over my arms. I sniffed and followed her scent.

My claws grew, and I ran through the packhouse, trying to smell honeysuckle and vanilla. Furniture was thrown across the rooms, claws on the walls, and drapes and couches were still on fire. The packhouse was almost in ruins, and I had been too hasty to even look at the territory outside. Charlotte's old room was trashed, and I could smell blood. It wasn't hers. I listened to see if I could hear the breathing of her cat, Macaroni, but there was none. Looking on the other side of the bed, next to the window where Macaroni like to sunbathe laid her cat. The only piece left of any family she had.

On the hardwood floor, written in Macaroni's blood, was one word, "Meow." What a cruel, sadistic fuck. My mate would be heartbroken. A new spark lit within me to continue checking the packhouse. I walked to the end of the hallway and found myself in the panic elevator and jumped the four stories down. Charlotte was scared, I could still smell her fear wafting in the air.

The blanket she had around her still smelled of her. Fear and worry leaked through her scent, she did not feel an ounce of hope while she was down there. She knew whatever was after her was coming.

She was there, she had been in the panic room, but the door had been blown through by something. Following the scent back outside, it stopped on the front lawn of the packhouse. Her smell was gone and vanished. "Explain to me," I yelled, "how the highest security ranked pack infiltrated?! This is unacceptable!" The warriors had lined up in a circle around me. Gripping the closest warrior, I pulled him up by his collar. "SPEAK!"

"A-alpha They cut the power to the generators downstairs as well as the power to the pack. They were never at the borders, they just appeared here!" I dropped the young warrior to the ground, snarling at everyone else that was nodding in agreement.

"Did anyone see where she went?" I snapped. A young pup came up behind its mother and stood forward, trying to be brave. I recognized him as one of the pups Charlotte liked to take to the park when she took a break from her coding.

"I did Alpha, I was hiding under the steps. There was a Vampire, h-he held Luna by the arm, and she w-was bleeding," he stuttered. A growl ripped from my throat, but his mother begged him to continue while he cowered in fear. "The Vampires and Witches all got together, and then a big ball of light came, and then they were gone!" The pup returned to his mother, and she held him close.

Evan stepped up behind me and put his hand on my shoulder to try and calm me. "Did the Vampire look like this?" Evan held up his phone with a picture of Roman on it. The pup looked and nodded vigorously. Marching up to the edge of the forest, I punched the 100-year-old tree in front of me, causing the bark to splinter and fly to the ground.

Many gasped, knowing my great grandfather had helped me build this forest from scratch. Any sort of mistreatment of nature was highly frowned upon in our pack. It takes hundreds of years to make a strong forest, especially one with good strong trees that house enough cover for humans overhead to not be able to see us. My anger got the best of me and taking down a tree was far better than what I wanted to do at the moment. Kill.

"Get the trackers, get Bruce to find Roman's last whereabouts. No one sleeps until my mate is back home!" Never in my life had I felt so much anger. I was considered one of the more level-headed alphas of this generation. The many alphas across the county usually sought out me to help them reason with other alphas during diplomatic disputes. I was considered the calm and rational one.

I no longer felt that. In fact, I felt the complete opposite. My mate was missing, I failed to protect her, and I had no idea how I would get her back. For once, everyone was at a loss of what they should do. We don't usually deal with Witches and Warlocks. They stay to themselves and do not like to intermingle with humans, Werewolves, or other supernaturals of the like.

Growling again in frustration, my Wolf came forward. My Wolf doesn't tend to come forward, unless Charlotte comes around and he wants to play. He's angered and threatened, and our lifeline is no longer here. With a quick rip of my clothes, becoming one with one another, we change into our large blonde Wolf. For once in a long, while we talk to each other, Wolf to human, we would form a plan to get the one person that mattered the most.

The warriors stood at attention, awaiting my order. The rest of the pack tried to put order into the disarray that was caused by the scuffle.

Charlotte

My neck was hurting from my position, it was still hanging over, and my upper torso was finally tied back to the chair. I tried to lift my head, but it felt impossible with the time I had spent in the same position. Letting out a small groan, the doors opened at the top of the stairs. Light trickled in, and large footsteps continued to come down the wooden steps. The ominous whistle began the whistle that haunted my dreams at night before my Wesley came around to protect me.

With a tight grip, Roman grabbed the back of my head, pulling my hair to look into my eyes. "So beautiful," he whispered as he took the other finger and traced it down my jaw. I knew better than to speak, it only makes things worse. When I had a tiny spark in me in my younger years, he punched me so hard in the gut that I had bloody stool for a week. My spark died that day.

Little does he know I have a fire in my bosom now. It burns for Wesley and the love he has given me as well as the pack. They gave me a family and a home. Playing my cards right, I'll get out of here.

My efforts were fruitful since Roman sighed in annoyance once he saw my bare chest, the battered bra covered in dirt and grime still stayed. Still, the emblem of a bond left on my skin was quickly fading. He checked my back to see the other side, and he sighed heavily again. "Believe it or not," he walked to the fire that was still burning near the Witch's work area. "I do care about you...." Roman poked the fire with the iron prod.

"I do these things to make you submit, it is the only way to break your spirit, you see. When I first got you, I really did have good intentions. I lost my beloved a long time ago, and all she wanted was a little girl." I peeked my head up to listen. Roman had never told me why he kept me, why he was nice for so long, and then decided to torment me.

"We weren't fully mated, we just knew we were beloveds. She was unfortunately killed by an evil king that no longer rules, King Darius. My beloved was part of a rebellion 500 years ago to stop him. She and her best friend were killed right in front of me. We were scheduled for our mating ceremony that evening, but Darius had to conquer our village that day." Roman's voice cracked, and a tear fell down his face.

I almost felt sorry for him. The keyword being, almost.

"After centuries of mourning, I finally decided to move on and adopt a little girl in her memory. I was tired of being alone. I wanted to have a family. The one we never had. The first two years with you were incredible. I felt like a father, and it helped me continue her memory. I never want to lose that, sharing ice cream with you, tucking you in at night, helping you with your foolish homework." His eyes looked to the branding iron in the corner of the room.

A few tears dripped down my face. I remember the thought of feeling safe with him. It was so long ago, I had almost forgotten until it was ripped away.

"But then you said something to me that changed everything." Roman's eyes met my terrified ones, and he gave a smirk.

Chapter 31

Under the Moon

Charlotte was coloring while Roman absentmindedly stirred the spaghetti sauce for dinner that night. Roman had been enjoying Charlotte's company for the past two years. Doing something that his mate had wanted to do ever since he met Roman gave warmth to his chest, to have a little girl to take care of. His heart still had not beat since first meeting his mate. Once you meet your mate, your heart begins to beat only for them, however, the untimely murder of his beloved before they were adequately bonded left his heart empty and cold. Only a hard rock of an organ was left.

Charlotte was the only one that made him feel warm on his cold skin. Ever since he had first fostered her, caring for her gave him a whole new meaning to life. After centuries of not having anyone and living alone, having someone to care for was fresh and invigorating.

"Mr. Roman, how much longer?" Charlotte sputtered as she continued to draw a picture of the two. They had been to the zoo that day, looking at the many different animals. Her favorite animals were the Wolves, especially one that looked like an overgrown golden retriever. Her eyes lit up so much when she saw it that he ended up buying her a small stuffed toy that resembled it the most. He chuckled softly as she hugged it to her chest. Even being 10 years old, she was still such a child. Her innocence gave him a spark to please her, take care of her, and keep her from any harm.

"Just a few more minutes Lottie." Roman stirred the pot as he thought of the first time he laid eyes on her at social services. She had been an orphan all her life, never knowing who her parents were. Charlotte bounced from foster care to foster care, and he had no idea why. She was a lovely girl, well-behaved and thankful for whatever she received. Roman could tell she had never been truly loved, people used her for the checks that were supposed to help her grow up, but he knew better. They were all spent on themselves because poor Lottie was in rags.

Roman decided then and there at the social services office that he would take her. She was everything his mate would have wanted. Sweet, kind, gentle, and a child's true innocence. His little Lottie had smiled up at him and asked, "Are you going to take care of me now?" sweetly fluttering her long lashes.

"Of course, little one," he promised, and that was that.

Roman placed the large plate of pasta in front of her, pouring the meaty tomato sauce over the noodles. With garlic bread on the side, she beamed up at him. "Thank you, Mr. Roman!" she squealed. Her appearance was that of an average 10-year-old child. She dressed in the nicest clothes and excelled at her schooling; in fact, she skipped a couple of grades, causing Roman to beam with pride.

Even though Lottie was the perfect child, he could never bring himself to let her call her father or dad. Something was holding him back, and he never knew exactly what.

Lottie continued to scarf down her spaghetti; she often told Roman he made the best which only, in turn, made him smile. Smiling was something he never did until his Lottie came into his life. She gave the spark back to him, his wanting to take care of another overpowered any malice he had left over from losing his mate.

He often thought of her, his mate. Her red ruby eyes and her alabaster skin. Her dark raven hair and her ruby-red lips. Rosie was the complete opposite of her. Rosie had strawberry blonde hair with natural curls. She was short for her age and had a slight tan colored skin. Her attitude was carefree and unaware of the dangers of the world. Roman wanted to keep her in that innocence, but something sparked in him that day with what Lottie had said.

"Mr. Roman?" Lottie looked up at him with her big doe eyes. Roman nodded at her to continue. "Do you get lonely, you know, when I am at school?" Roman didn't know what to say, was he lonely? He had Lottie with him in the evenings and on the weekends, and he realized how much he looked forward to it.

"No, I'm not lonely when I am with you." Roman smoothed the slight cowlick on her head while she ate.

"Hmm," she slurped up a piece of noodle. "But I see a lot of dads and moms together, and you just have me. Don't you want someone?"

Roman paused and looked down at his folded hands, no spaghetti plate near him. Lottie continued to look at him in wonder and complete innocence. "I am not lonely when you are here, Charlotte. You are all I need." His voice was, but a whisper and Lottie smiled as he continued to nod at her to continue eating.

"If I was an adult right now, I would be with you! You are so nice to my friends and me. You make me feel safe. You would make a nice husband." As innocent as those words were, it made Roman's stomach churn. It made him think, think of things he had never felt before. Could Lottie, as innocent as her statement was, be with him later? Her presence always calmed him. She wasn't like other children. Charlotte was ever grateful for whatever was given to her and was never selfish. All and all, the perfect child she would grow up to be the ideal adult.

So many human and Vampire women chased after him. They would throw themselves at him or lust after his money. Women were vile creatures, and he never wanted anything more than to rid them from his presence. Vampires were made for good looks, all the better to make them the apex predators. The humans were good for two things, blood and sex. Lottie wasn't like that though, she cared for him just how he was.

Her features as of now were soft and warm. A few pimples here and there dotted her complexion as she was set to go through puberty in only a few years. She was still short and had a bit of a pudge in the stomach, but that was all due to her baby fat. Her face was adorable, and anyone would be blind to see that she would turn into a beautiful young lady.

"Would I be able to stand a boy coming onto her when she grew older?" he thought. The fact tore him up inside. Not because he was a potential father figure, but because he wanted her to himself. She looked at him no other woman or girl ever had. She adored him and only him right now. Thinking this for only a few minutes, he asked Charlotte, "Would you like that, little Lottie? To be with me when you grow up?"

Charlotte hummed nonchalantly. "Of course, you are so kind and generous and have a heart full of gold. I think you would be a bit old by then, though." Charlotte giggled as she finished her picture. "Here, I made this for you." Charlotte was a talented artist and proudly showed Roman her picture.

It was the both of them, she drew herself as an adult and him the same. They were holding hands, and she was walking into a building. "What building is this, Rosie?" He took the picture from her and traced her figure on the paper. "College! This is you taking me to college and dropping me off." What big dreams Charlotte had, and Roman didn't like it.

"What if I want you to stay with me?" Roman spoke as calmly as he could. "Mr. Roman, you can't stay with me always. I have to grow up so I can take care of you when you get old!" Roman felt a bit of pride in Charlotte wanting to take care of him, but it quickly dissipated when he realized it was because of age.

"I will never get old, I will take care of you," Roman's voice was becoming stiff. Charlotte sensed the uneasiness in his voice. Her childlike mind didn't understand, she wanted Mr. Roman to be happy. "I'm sorry, I didn't mean to make you mad. I just want to make sure I will take care of you as you do with me," she beamed at him. Her voice was soothing, he took his hand and held her cheek in his hand.

"That's sweet of you, but I will always be there for you, I will never grow old, and I can wait for you to become older. We could be together then." Her eyes knitted in confusion. How could they be together when he becomes old? She wanted to take care of Roman, go to college, and have her own family one day. She didn't have romantic feelings towards him. She was his foster dad.

Charlotte didn't want to argue, so she hummed in response, and she continued eating. Roman took this as an agreement in his twisted mind. He began to think of ways to make his desires come true. Tucking Charlotte into bed and giving a swift kiss to her forehead, like always, she drifted off to sleep.

While cleaning up the mess from dinner, the words that escaped Lottie's pretty mouth hurt him. "*Mr. Roman, you can't stay with me always. I have to grow up....*" Growing up for humans meant leaving and taking on new responsibilities, having a job, and building a family. He didn't want Charlotte to leave him, he didn't want to feel the loneliness again. He knew when he decided to foster a child that one day they would go. However, it was becoming far more complicated as the minutes wore on to think Charlotte would gladly leave.

She was her own person, but her presence was something he didn't want to get rid of. The joy he brought him while she was a child would only increase as the years went by. Once becoming a woman, he could only imagine him falling in love with her all the more. Roman's grip tightened, causing the dish to break. He had made his decision. He was going to make Charlotte his chosen beloved when she turned of age.

Without missing a beat, he grabbed his phone to call the one Witch that knew of bonds and magic. "Yes?" The sultry voice on the other end of the phone said.

"Josephine, it is Roman Vanderveen." The phone went silent for a few minutes before he heard her voice again.

"I was wondering when you would call. My speculation was correct about you starting to harbor feelings for a human that is not your own." Roman looked at the phone in confusion. "I'm sorry?" he questioned.

"You forget you specialize in bonds and more so forced bonds. I'm living in the Earth realm now, so I could sense it. You Vampires are like an open book regarding these types of ordeals. It's been that way since the beginning." Roman was done with her riddles; he just wanted her to come and help him.

"Can you come then? I need your assistance." Roman's voice was deep and authoritative. He was an older Vampire, one of the oldest besides the royal bloodlines and those in parliament. "Yes, certainly. I'll be there within the week." With that, she hung up.

Throughout the week, Roman acted as nothing had changed with Charlotte. She went to school, he made her dinner, and helped with homework. If anything, he doted on her more and made sure she was completely taken care of. She would always smile and thank him as he helped pack her school bag every morning.

Josephine finally arrived at the end of the week. Charlotte was sleeping as Roman led Josephine to the door of her upstairs bedroom. Josephine walked in and placed her hand upon Charlotte's sleeping chest to feel her heart. With a slight grimace, she read her soul and realized this would be harder than she thought. Her thoughts returned to the feared day she left Bergarian, the realm she felt was her home. She had done something so unthinkable that she was thrown out of her coven. She had tried to separate a royal bond to that of a warrior and a lost princess that had already mated. Her life had never been the same since.

Anger boiled in Josephine, she didn't want to be a part of this bonding. This would cause trouble here in the Earth realm for her, and the thought of being run out of yet another domain scared her. She would never admit that, though.

"This will be difficult." She turned to Roman. "Her soul belongs to another." Roman's face paled as much as it could for a Vampire. "What do you mean?" he whispered to not waken his future betrothed.

"She can change; her DNA allows her to turn into the supernatural she is promised to. However, she is promised to another, not you. You would have felt the bond right away once you saw her. I do not want to intervene between bonds. If she didn't have a mate, then maybe, but she does so no." Josephine walked past Roman as she went to the stairs.

"No," he whispered to the wind. He followed Josephine and whispered harshly, "name your price, I'll do what you want, she needs to be mine."

"I will not. Last time, this caused me to be in too much trouble. Especially with her being ranked to someone powerful. I have nowhere to go if I get kicked out of this realm. I will not ruin my chances at not surviving." Roman laughed darkly. "You do it, or I'll be sure to tell the Cerulean Moon Kingdom your whereabouts in the Earth realm. Josephine gasped. She knew he would do it, and she didn't specialize in cloaking spells any longer. That was taken from her the day Clarabelle had ripped her spell book to pieces.

"Fine," Josephine huffed, seeing that this was the only way out of this mess. She would make him suffer for it, and it would be delightful to watch.

Chapter 31

Wesley

It had been 6 days since I'd last seen Charlotte. I could feel her pain even though we weren't wholly bonded and mated. It was faint, but it was there. Even through distance, she still held on to me like a lifeline. I tried to fill my heart with my love for her, hoping she could feel something.

He was physically hurting her; I could feel it. I could feel her heart burning and aching, and she was losing her lightfast. He was wearing her down, trying to break her spirit with the branding bonds.

Once I had calmed down enough to talk to the Elders, they had me sit in my office and made me hear them out. They had no idea about branding bonds because it was a practice outlawed thousands of years ago. They were dangerous and often resulted in humans dying. It was dark blood magic that was entirely unfair for humans to deal with. Most didn't have mates, so it was easy to change their hearts for the Vampire into something of love.

Charlotte was different though, it had been fading when I first met her, and that reason was that she was already destined. Part of her soul was intertwined with someone else's... mine. The bond was fading because her soul still yearned for me and didn't even know me yet. My fists pound the table each time the elders pour their compassionate hearts of apologies and pity at me.

Apologies didn't matter, my mate was gone. If I had just bit her, even if she wasn't ready, I would know where she was. That would have been forced, and she would have really hated me. There wasn't anything I could do, this Roman guy had really ruined her, but in the short time she was with me, her own personality started to surface. She trusted me, and she opened up to me, and now she was stuck in the same hell she came from.

My office was a wreck. The computer screens were all trashed, books fell to the floor, and pages ripped out of some of Charlotte's favorites because I couldn't handle looking at them. Liquor bottles leaked onto the floor because not even alcohol would sate me.

The winter storm had rolled in, just like the Elders had predicted. It was a mess of a storm, and the whole village and packhouse were on lockdown while we tried to find other ways to find Roman Vanderveen. Bruce's many connections with the FBI and local police departments had proven helpful. They could put a watch on all credit cards, computers, and other electronic devices such as cell phones. Nothing had moved. Electronically, he was a ghost.

The blizzard let up for some time, and everyone was trying to clear the paths so the cars could let us drive to the first destination, his old home, about 6 hours from the city. My bloodshot eyes were rimmed with red, eyelashes coated in tears, yet I still wouldn't let them fall. If they fell, that meant I gave up.

My hair was greasy, and my beard had grown, I had nothing left to give until I found my Charlotte, my kitten. Evan barged in the door. He had to run the pack in my absence since the storm set in causing us to remain here. There wasn't anything I could do. No tracking or leaving. I had to sit and fester. My own people couldn't come to me because I was an utter mess.

"Get your sorry ass up, Wesley. She wouldn't want to see you like this," Evan reprimanded me. "You need to start thinking of other ways to find her other than computer shit and tracking. What connects her to anyone else?" Evan was fed up with my moping. The truth was my brain was in a haze, my Wolf hadn't talked to me in days, and my body was giving out on me.

I ignored his damn voice and looked out over the snow-covered village. "I've never felt so lost," I whispered. Evan's angered face fell, and soon I saw worry. He has never seen me not know what to do. I frequently had plans A, B, and C, with the occasional D if those plans didn't work out. I had nothing. I had exhausted all my resources to find her. Something that has never happened in my many years of living.

"I know you want to find her. We all miss her, and we know she is hurting. Is there anything else you can think of? Tracking obviously isn't working and using inside intel isn't working either. Are there other Vamps you could talk to?"

"I've tried that Evan," I pulled my shoulder-length hair at the root. "I've contacted the Vampire Counsel, and they haven't been in contact with Roman in over 15 years, they thought he went back to Bergarian. He's an old Vamp that doesn't like the new ways their species has evolved into. He would still drink to kill if it was allowed. He's brutal, animalistic, sadistic." Evan's eyes furrowed, and he walked to the large window I was staring out.

Often, I would sit in my office while Charlotte ran around with the pups with the fall leaves dancing around them. She would help rake up large piles, and even she, herself, would jump in them. Charlotte had become carefree, almost childlike again, making up for all the times she couldn't be.

Evan put his hand on the window, watching the small pups looking lost without Charlotte, who apparently promised to help them build a snowman or snow Wolf. My eyes started to feel glassy again. I wouldn't cry. An Alpha doesn't cry, an Alpha destroys. But there wasn't anything else left to destroy.

Bruce's combat boots could be heard from downstairs. He stomped up the stairs as the snow fell from his boats. His grunting was heard, and other Wolves knew to stay away from him. Bruce was primarily stoic, and hard to read. Even Charlotte had a hard time figuring him out, but he was always kinder to her than others.

Bruce walked in without knocking, us both looking at him in confusion. "Delilah's father has not stopped calling. Now that the snow is letting up, what do you want to do with her? He's driving me mad," Bruce rubbed his bald head with frustration.

Delilah. I perked up at the name. She had told us she was sorry, but the undertones in her voice only meant she was sorry for something else, not for the act of stealing from me. "Shit, get her in the interrogation room NOW! I don't give a fuck what her father wants!" Evan jumped at my voice, and both ran out of the room.

***

Delilah was strapped down to the chair with the cold metal table in front of her. Her eyes were dim, as she had not been fed in a week. Only water was given to her, and she had been stuck in a five by 5 five cell. She had to lay down to get any relief from the small room.

"Took you long enough to come to talk to me," she spat. "Have you finally understood my words just a week ago?"

"You have a lot of spunk for a she-Wolf that is on the other side of the interrogation table."

She scoffed, "My father taught me well. I don't break under pressure."

"What happened, Delilah? You could be a cold woman at times but never like this? Was it the rejection of you not becoming Luna for my pack?"

Delilah closed her eyes and took a deep breath. "There was a time where I thought we could be more, but once you told me your reason, I understood. I needed my mate. I hold no malice towards your decision." Delilah looked back into my eyes. We had grown up together and let out our Wolves on each other when we had sexual frustration, but that is all it was. Just sex. I regretted every minute of it once I found my Charlotte.

"Then why steal from me? I've been missing money for 6 months, well over a million dollars, that help people in my pack and wanderers who need financial help. What the hell were you doing?"

My fist tightened, but I tried to keep composure. She was talking, and I needed her to continue. Evan and Bruce were on the other side of the interrogation room, waiting and watching. More like witnesses, so if her father came in, he could be restrained.

"I didn't know about the previous months. I just did it for the first time when you caught me," she said, shrugging her shoulders. "I can't give you much more information than that." Delilah looked to the side, and a tear ran down her face.

"There is always a choice, Delilah. I will still be the friend you need, but you need to talk to me. I can't hold back my beast much longer, he wants to rip you to pieces because he knows you know something about our mate. All room for kindness is gone." Delilah knew my Wolf, he could be a beast when he wanted to be. Mostly he was calm, and docile but the few times she had seen him fight, she knew he was a ticking time bomb.

"You have to promise me," her tears began to fall. "You have to promise me you will find him," her breathing was heavy. Her lifeless eyes looked into mine.

"Find who? Who do I have to find?" My body was leaning on the edge of the seat.

Delilah took a deep breath and sobbed. "My mate, he, took my mate.

"Who?" I growled.

"Roman Vanderveen."

My Wolf roared. This fucker was getting into all my pockets trying to steal everything from me. My mate, my money, and other people's mates. The hell is wrong with this sick, sadistic fuck!

"I need to know everything, right here, right now. No games, Delilah, none of your Alpha daughter bullshit. I will know when you lie," I pointed at her. "If you lie or leave anything out, you won't get out of here alive, let alone find your mate."

Delilah nodded her head in agreement greedily. She took a deep breath and slowly blew it out.

"It all started two months ago. I had met my mate, Mason. He works as a bartender at a restaurant I was visiting south of here. He was so handsome, and he was actually human." Delilah looked up at me and smiled. "He felt the pull too, and it wasn't long until we were going on dates, kissing, having fun. We were going slow, human pace anyway, and then it came the time to tell him. To tell him what I was and to see if he accepted it." Her lips pursed together, remembering.

"We went to the lake and sat together on a large blanket, just looking up at the stars. No one was around, and I decided to bring it up. At first, he didn't believe me, so I had to show him. He was upset and almost angry after it was all said and done, but he said he still cared for me, in fact, he loved me." A few tears ran down her cheeks as she recalled Mason.

"I told him about mates and the pull, he agreed he felt it too but wanted to meet my family and pack before he made any decision. I agreed, and he said that weekend, we would drive up to my pack, and I would introduce him. I went to his apartment that weekend with the door broken down and blood was everywhere." Delilah's breath hitched. "I didn't know what to think. His body wasn't there, so I decided to track him, and I found him in a suburban residential area. It wasn't rich or poor, just your average size home with a white picket fence. I burst through the door to see him tied up; his nose was bleeding and his body pale. I smelled the faint scent of a Vampire, the rotting dead flesh."

My body stiffened as she continued her story. The only reason a Vampire smells rotten and dead flesh meant they had bad intentions. In reality, Vampires and Werewolves get along much better than humans thought in their own version of the fairy tale world. When a Vampire goes bad, rogue, their scent will change. This guy was bad news if she was smelling the rot.

"The Vampire introduced himself as Roman. He said he had a job for me, and I would never see Mason again until the job was done. I don't even know if he is still alive." Delilah cried her eyes out, and I had Evan bring in tissues and unlock her chains.

"Roman made me go visit several packs to find Charlotte after he saw her at the restaurant with you, he didn't know which pack you were from, he had no picture to give me just the smell of part of her dress. Once I smelled her in your room, and how you defended her, I knew. I had to tell him. I thought my job was done, but he said he had one more job for me, and that was to collect one final payment. Alex, his best friend, is known for his hacking abilities—"

I stopped her. "Yes, I know, he was one of the first hackers back when computers were originally invented. Continue, please." I waved my hand.

"Alex at one point saw Charlotte on the other side of the webcam but didn't recognize her at first. It wasn't until after the restaurant fiasco he realized who she really was and then he knew which pack to head for. Alex was originally doing it for fun to steal from you, but then both of them formed a plan to piss you off more, and that was to steal your money and use it so Roman could pay the Witch helping with the branding. He wanted you to feel like you had paid for her demise."

I stood up in my chair and threw my fist into the silver walls. The burn did not affect me as I continued to punch the wall and throw the table. Glass shattered as the table left the room to hit the double-sided mirror, leaving Evan and Bruce with stern silence. Once I was done, my heavy breathing continued, but Delilah dared to speak.

"They said I was to take the fall. I was to be captured to make it look like I was stealing your money, but really, it was a distraction. To throw you off the trail long enough for them to..." Silence. She spoke no more words. They did all of this, so there was time for them to kidnap her, pay a Witch and keep me distracted. I had been an utter failure of a mate.

Chapter 32

Wesley

After trying to compose myself, I stood up. It was time to finally get to work. We had Delilah, she knew the house her mate had initially been placed in, which could give us a starting point.

Delilah complied entirely with our wishes, and her father was told she was now in good graces and would be returned once my mate was found. I wanted to do more, but political shit and all. After a few hours of gaining more information on Roman and Alex, we had significantly more knowledge than we started with.

"The Witch's name is Josephine, the same Witch that tried to mess up future Queen Clara's bond months ago. Josephine had escaped and no longer resides in Bergarian but now on Earth. Josephine would come by and set up a small workbench area in Roman's basement from time to time. "I've seen her a few times, she seemed, out of practice, to say the least," Delilah shrugged.

"How so?" Evan asked.

"She doesn't look prepared at all, not like the Witches I've come across. She was absent-minded, mumbling under her breath about wanting to be done with this and such. Josephine did not want to be there." Delilah kept shaking her head, showing her confusion about the Witches' state.

"We could use that as an advantage," Bruce crossed his arms with his eyes narrowed at Delilah. "She could be the one to break if they are not still at the same house Roman is at."

Delilah nodded. "I think we should go back to that house, the one you pointed out as one of Roman's-the one six hours from here. It's the same house I found my mate in. Josephine had a lot of her things set up there," she sighed and crossed her arms around her.

"We will find our mates, Delilah. I promise," I patted her shoulder. "Get the cars ready, get 5 units of warriors, and we will head down to the house. They won't be there, but maybe we could catch a scent where they went."

Bruce bowed his head. "Yes, Alpha."

Charlotte

A whole week had gone by, and every day Roman has tried to brand me. It never took, it faded within the hour. Part of me wanted to smirk so he could see that he was truly a failure, but I knew better. I was trying to keep my strength up I was sure Wesley would come for me any day. I still had that hope; I thought I could feel him some nights while I lay in the basement chained to the wall.

I didn't sleep much, but when I dreamed, I dreamed of him. Our lazy mornings as we woke up beside one another, him tickling my arm as he tried to wake me as the sun rose from the horizon. His playful grin when I would swat him away, begging him for just five more minutes. The laughter he radiated was contagious, and my heartfelt so warm. It felt like he was there, I wanted to dream and sleep during the day, so I could be near him and not in this dark, dank basement.

Roman visited me 3 times a day, he would feed me food and put each piece into my mouth. He did it to make me utterly dependent on him and to show me how helpless I was. I wasn't helpless though, I was trying to be innovative. If I went without food, I would become too weak to fight at all.

"I'm glad you are eating, Lottie. It will keep your body strong for tomorrow," he whispered. Continuing to chew the bland chicken and rice, I looked up at him, with a furrowed brow.

"I will brand you one last time, and then I will attempt to change you myself."

I gasped. He was going to bite me when he knew well that it wouldn't work, or was he too far gone to realize? "You will kill me! It won't work, I won't accept it!" I raised my voice for the first time, being trapped in this hell.

"I see that you haven't lost your spunk," he chided. "Do I need to break you, just like I did all those years ago? Just submit Lottie, you once told me you would be with me." Roman gritted his teeth and stood up to put the plate on the table.

"Why would I want to stay? You ruined any chance the first day you hit me!"

"That boy shouldn't have touched you!" He roared while traces of his spit hit my face.

"I was ten years old, and we were crossing the street. What the hell is wrong with you!? I was a child!"

"No one touches what is to be mine, and I beat it into you that no one could touch you but me," he seethed. "I didn't want to do it that way, but it had to be done. You weren't going to listen, you couldn't understand." Roman shook his head.

"I really didn't understand why you would hit me, cut me, I don't understand any of it! If you think I would ever care for you after that, you are dead wrong!" I screamed. I hadn't raised my voice to him the day he bruised me beyond repair. He didn't just beat me physically, but mentally too. It was the day he carved his name into the side of my ribs. Thank God I passed out halfway through, but it still broke me.

Roman got up to walk out of the room, but he paused before going up the stairs. "Once I bite you, you will forget all that. You will be overpowered by the new bond that it won't matter, you will love me," in a flash, he slammed the door, and I choked back a sob.

The psychotic man had officially lost it... well lost it even more than he had before. He wasn't that bad before he started abusing me, in fact he was so nice. He was the perfect foster father before he flipped his switch. Why would he do that? How would that get into his head that beating me would keep me around? I was around. I stayed with him and listened to him like a parent, my guardian.

While I was mulling over my thoughts, a cold shiver went over my body. The basement was damp, daft and the occasional wind would fly through when a door opened, but this chill was different. Looking to the side of the room where the Witch's corner stood, I saw her.

The Witch walked up to me with a tight lip curl. She was in regular street attire with dark jeans and jacket. Overall, she looked human, her face even beautiful with a small beauty mark on just below the left side of her mouth.

"Hmm, you are stronger than I thought. I didn't think you would last through the first branding bond he gave you, but here you are. Brands later and no signs of backing down," she sang.

"Who the hell are you?" my confidence flashed before me, and I immediately regretted it. The Witch bent down and pulled me up by the back of my head, tugging at my hair.

"Watch it," she hissed. "I don't want to be here doing this, but if you die, then my livelihood is at stake, so shut up and listen." I narrowed my eyes at her as she walked back to her workbench and sat down, crossing her legs, picking at her nails.

"Like I said, I don't want to be here. Roman has me like an ant under his shoe, and I really don't appreciate it." I continued to stare at her, waiting for an explanation. "I just wanted to let you know that Roman didn't have to beat you and taste your blood every month for you to mature."

"What?" I let out a breath. She chuckled and swirled some dark potion in her glass chalice. She giggled, "Yes, I told him he had to beat you into submission to break your spirit, but he didn't have to do that. You hadn't met your mate yet, so the branding bond would have remained if he had just been nice to you and treated your fairly."

My mouth dropped open. I suffered all these years because of this wench? "W-why would you do that? I didn't do anything to you! And now you are going to suffer because of some petty pay back?!"

"He threatened me!" She stood up, threw the glass chalice, and took large toward me while I sat still on the floor. "No one threatens me and gets away with it! There was a chance he could have mated with you to make you his but telling him he had to beat you into submission was so much more entertaining. He screwed himself over." She waved her hand like it was nothing. "Now he has threatened to tell the Northern American Witch Coven, which will hunt me out the rest of my days, but you know what?" She giggled darkly, stroking her blackened fingernail over her lips. "It is worth it, to see someone innocent suffering. Must be the maker's sick and twisted personality.

My hands gripped the chair. All the torture was initiated by her. This was all sick and twisted in ways a soap opera couldn't comprehend. Ten-year-old me didn't know what love was, he just took it and ran with it when I told him I would stay with him. I didn't love him like that, I used to see him as a father figure. Used to, not anymore.

I had Wesley was a part of me before we even met, his goddess demanded it. Now that we had met, I knew I had to reject this bite or whatever the hell Roman was going to do to me. I would not succumb to this, I wouldn't have it.

"Um, what is your name?" my voice went quiet. I was still processing the events playing in my mind. She was the one that caused my pain and suffering, yet she was also the one that helped me find Wesley. She wasn't anyone I wanted to associate myself with after this was all over. Still, this woman also helped me find my mate in a sick, evil way.

"Josephine," she said calmly. "I didn't want to help Roman. He forced me into this position," she walked away. "Do you remember the day you escaped?" I remember that day, I couldn't believe my luck when Roman was passed out on the couch, he never slept, especially when I was in the house. I thought he had drunk himself to sleep. He had done that a lot since he'd started hitting, beating, and cutting me.

"He was sleeping…." I started, but Josephine cut me off. "I MADE him sleep for you to be able to escape." She rolled her eyes. "The idiot didn't know what hit him," she tittered. "If he was going to threaten me by exposing my location to the Witches Council, then I was going to make him suffer without him knowing. You know he suffered right? All those years you were gone. I don't know how many bodies he had drained because you were not to sate the demon inside." Josephine ticked as she straightened the collar on her jacket. "I just love watching people squirm, it was the best entertainment with you two, I'll tell you that."

I could feel bile rising in my throat. I had the worst luck on the planet. Being thrown in all these different directions made me want to pull my hair out. "Roman has become so obsessed with you since tasting your blood, that can happen if done so frequently." Josephine pulled out lip gloss to put on her already immaculate lips. "Checking you every month was just icing on the bonding cake." She giggled. "Once you reject his mark, you will die," she whispered. "Then, in turn, I will kill Roman when he is at his weakest."

I let out a sob. "Why, just why?"

"Because bonds are the most idiotic thing ever created."

Chapter 33

Charlotte

Josephine left, I was hoping she would give away my location for Wesley just to further tick off Roman, but she wanted to see me suffer too. This woman was sicker than Roman. She at least didn't lay a hand on me, she just cooed at how she'd used her twisted mind to have other people do her bidding.

I tried to give her the benefit of the doubt, that maybe something happened to her in her past that caused her to be this way. Some man may have beaten her, or her parents were sick people that didn't love her and made her this way. Nature over nurture? The question that plagues every psychologist's mind. The more she talked and taunted me with the things she told Roman to do to me, inwardly made me cringe. There was no hope for her, she made her choice to be this way. I didn't care if she had a horrible past; she was driving someone else to suffer.

After being left alone in my thoughts for too long, I could hear the faint whisperings. For a split second, I thought it was Wesley, but as soon as my hopes were held high, the voice would be gone. Maybe I was indeed losing my mind. I started to call for him, praying his voice would come back to soothe me.

"I still smell her; her scent is strong here." Wesley's voice said mused. He also sounded tired, defeated. I heard it, clear as day as if he was right beside me. *"It is like she is still in the room."* I heard someone agreeing, but I couldn't see anyone there.

"Wesley?" I said aloud. *"Wesley, are you there?"* I shook my head around like I was blind, praying he could hear my pathetic weak voice.

"*Listen!*" Evan barked. Evan was here too. I wouldn't imagine Evan being there too, would I?

"*Wesley! Evan!! Help! Where are you!*" I screamed. I didn't care if Roman heard. My mate was here!!

"*Kitten? Where are you!? Baby!?*" Wesley's voice was pleading.

"Wesley, please, I'm here, chained to the chair!" I started sobbing in relief. I wanted out of this basement and back in his arms. He was so close, and my body knew it too. Hearing shuffling and scuffing of the floors, but nothing moved.

"Please help me!"

"*There must be a protection spell, hiding her or making it so we can't see her,*" Evan said, panicked.

Hearing the door slam open, I heard Roman start to yell. "Stupid, weak ass enchantment." Roman's large feet continued to descend the stairs while my heartbeat quickened. He had fed me only because he would change me, and he needed me physically strong, not so much mentally. I was going to fight through this. Wesley was so close, I had to.

Roman unlocked the chains, and I could hear Wesley screaming, telling me it would be OK. "That's right, Lottie, it will be OK." Roman sniffed up my neck while holding my jaw in his hand. His teeth elongated, getting ready to bite me, and with all the strength I could muster, I tried to pull away. Roman's grip tightened as I shook my head repeatedly. Roman had untied my arms form the chair, trying to wrestle with me as I stood up. My body continued to twist, rolling to get him off of me.

"*Please don't! Don't bite me, no!*" Thrashing, Roman wrestled me to the ground, and several other Vampires came into the room to help him keep me secure. "Get away from me! Don't touch me!"

Wesley's roar could be heard, but so faint you could almost miss it. My heart was beating as fast as a hummingbird. Surely hoping my heart would stop so he would leave me, Roman looked me straight in my eyes. They were bright red, glowing, trying to pierce through my soul with fear. "You will submit to me," he pinned my arms back above my head, and another Vampire turned my head. "Even though this is going faster than I had anticipated, it will have to do."

Roman's fangs descended, the heat of his breath baring down on my flesh. A dark flash behind Roman's head was barely seen. The other Vampires perked up, sensing the change in the atmosphere. Roman paused, looking up, his inner beast realizing they were no longer alone in the room.

Wesley. It was the feeling I always felt when he would come into the room. My breathing stopped, and I felt a warm invisible blanket surround me. It gave me comfort, and my heart calmed. I gently sighed in relief until I heard the deep, throaty growls from both Werewolves and a screech and hissing noise from the Vampires.

One Vampire holding my legs was suddenly missing and the other holding my head fell on top of me. A warm liquid was dripping on my face, Roman snarled. Pulling me up by my arm, he dislocated it in the process, and I squealed in pain, afraid that screaming would draw too much attention for more Vampires to help.

My hair was matted with blood, the scene before me was a massacre. Wolves were jumping across the room, Vampires falling and the Witches that followed Josephine around like puppies were piled on the floor in the corner. I had never seen so much blood that wasn't my own, nor bodies upon bodies lying lifeless on the floor. Wesley's warriors were relentless in the large, concrete basement. Roman continued to look from side to side, looking for an escape. His arm gripped tighter on my dislocated arm, and his claws caused my own blood to stream onto the floor with the rest of the bloody pools.

I heard Wesley yell at Evan, and I finally met my mates' eyes after a long week. My heart jumped, and even with the pain, I tried to pull my arm from Roman. Roman saw the desperation in my face when Wesley and I locked our eyes together. This only infuriated Roman, and he turned me, so my chest was facing him.

"This is for us, only us," Roman whispered, and he plunged his sharp fangs   into   my   neck. I tried to scream, but no sound came out. My mouth was open, trying to let my pain radiate from the pits of my stomach. It wasn't long before he was no longer attached to my neck. My knees gave out, and I felt myself falling, falling until I fell into someone's warm embrace. It wasn't Wesley, but it was something familiar, something safe.

"Charlie, it's gonna be OK. We have to finish watching our movie, remember?" It was Zachary, he continued to stroke my cheek with the back of his hand, wiping the blood that still remained from when I was on the floor.

"You have to stay awake, Charlie. Don't go to sleep on me. things will be fine, ASHLEY!" he screamed. Feeling Ashley's presence, I grabbed onto her arm. I couldn't speak, I tried to say something but the burning in my neck continued to numb my lips. I sounded like I was grunting or gargling.

"Shit," Ashley whispered as she opened a box beside me. Touches of someone's hand on my neck began to wipe the blood away, and I felt the pressure to stop the blood. There was so much pain. No way, it couldn't just be a Vampire bite, it was more painful than that. My neck felt mauled.

"The bastard didn't let go, he ripped into her muscle," Ashley whispered quickly. "We need to get her back to our pack doctor." Zachary put me in his arms, and I groaned. My dislocated arm was lying haphazardly, swinging away from my body. It was then Ashley noticed it was dislocated and cursed under her breath again. Gently laying the arm on my torso, Zachary walked me outside as Ashley held pressure. Zachary tried to get my head to stay in the crook of his neck so it wouldn't flop back and forth as he ran to the car.

"Wes, Wesley?" I moaned. The fighting was still going on, but my eyes kept shutting, trying to keep the grotesque scene away. I could handle my own blood, my own pain, and suffering, but not others. The entire yard was littered with Vampires, when were there so many?

Zachary quickened the pace and put me in the back of one of the packs' large SUVs. The seats were pulled from the back, and they laid me down on a thin mat with IV poles, fluids, and a much larger first aid kit.

"What happened?" The voice was pained as he ripped several plastic bags of needles and gauze.

"She's been bit, one of the warriors ripped the Vampire off of her before Roman could disconnect from her neck."

"Was there venom present?" The doctor threw on some gauze and made Ashley apply pressure. I arched my back in pain, trying to scream, but again, no sound came out. The doctor then took my arm and pushed it hard back into the socket, so it was no longer dislocated. Geez, a little warning?

Ashley furiously shook her head no. "Not that we saw, but we should treat her as such. It all happened really fast, it may not seem so for her, but it was. That is probably why he couldn't disconnect correctly."

My breathing quickened. I took my good arm and reached for someone, anyone. Again, I had trouble breathing and speaking, but one word was all that remained on my tongue.

"W-Wesley." It was hard to talk saying his name was hard, but my soul craved him. My eyes darted back and forth while I felt pricks in my arm, probably an IV for fluids. "He's coming, Charlie," Zachary cooed and patted my head. "He's coming right now." On cue, Wesley opened the back of the SUV and yelled for the driver to get going. Ashley and Zachary left my side and sat up at the front while Wesley grabbed my hand.

"I'm so sorry, Kitten, I'm so sorry I couldn't find you in time." His eyes were watering, blood was thrown across his torso like spattered paint. There were worry lines, and bags under his eyes. I think he may look worse than me. He was not my happy and perky Wesley with a panty-dropping smile.

He had done his best, he looked for me in a place he probably never would have thought of finding. I was proud of him, proud of my future mate.

I continued to speak but had trouble, the muscles near my neck refused to work, causing my jaw to tighten up. There was no slack in it, so I could move my mouth to form my words. I said one word to get through to him, that everything was OK.

"Mate," I breathed. The grim line on his lips softened and turned to a small smile. His hand patted my hair, and instantly, I became drowsy. "Alpha, I'm giving her sedatives to ease the pain, then we can get to work on healing her neck." Wesley nodded and kissed my chapped lips. The comfort flowed

192

through my body as I looked up at his warm eyes. I knew right then, and there I could never be away from this man, I wanted to be beside him forever.

The medication started working, my eyelids tried to fight the gravity, and I fell asleep to get away from the pain.

Chapter 34
Wesley

Every time I hear the heart monitor spike or dip in its rhythmic beeping, my anxiety increases. Which has happened a whole damn lot since we got back. We have been in the medical wing of the packhouse for well over twenty-four hours, and they had just finished getting her settled in a medical bed and tending to her wounds.

Lucky for her, she wasn't malnourished and only had a few superficial scrapes and bruises. Her neck was the worst of it. Roman did a number on her and didn't want to let go. I was grateful that one of the warriors was quick enough to grab her away from him. It was so fast he had just planted his teeth in her pretty little neck, so no venom even seeped through. The only repercussions were hunks of mangled flesh that hung off of her delicate frame.

For a human, this will be painful as shit to recover from.

Charlotte, however, looked so peaceful regardless of her exterior wounds. Once she wakes up, I know she will be in some pain, but I can't help but want to talk to her. I wanted to better explain myself as to why I left. I was doing it because I knew once we mated, I would never leave her side for at least a few months until my Wolf settles. Fuck, I was a damn idiot. Making up for this will be my mission, and I will beg for her mercy and forgiveness.

Tracing my finger on her collar bone on her body's healthy side, you could see small goosebumps form, which only made me smile. Even in a deep sleep, she can still feel me. I hope she will hear me too. I've talked to her about the day, about the sky, the weather and what a terrible mate I had been to her. I would do nothing but listen to her for the rest of our lives.

Hearing a knock at the door, I sat up straight as Ashley walked in and shut the door behind her. "How's Charlie doing?" Her face was solemn, everyone was upset that Charlotte was hurt, and it could have been a lot worse. There was no venom, and hopefully, no physical scars will be with her after she has healed. My own Wolf's saliva has healed her tremendously already. Charlotte being destined to be with an Alpha will only increase the speed at which it will heal up completely in a few days. That was the only comfort I tried to hold on to until it was completely healed.

"She's alright, sleeping." I sighed and folded my arms together. I was never going to leave her alone outside the packhouse ever again. I'd be that annoying mate that makes her sit in my lap constantly, carrying her around like a small puppy. I grinned at the thought.

Ashley took a seat beside me and looked at Charlotte, taking her hand. She traced her wrist with her finger then interlaced her hand with hers. "Now that we know that Charlie is safe, I can show you something if you like to cheer you up. Charlie was super shy at first, but I think her own inner slut came out." Ashley let out a laugh.

I looked at her, curious and my Wolf perked up. Inner slut? Charlotte and slut should not be in the same sentence. What the hell was Ashley talking about?

"Charlie was so upset after you left, Zachary and I decided to doll her up and take some pictures. We were going to send them to you and make you come home," she laughed wickedly. "We made her model a bunch of clothes as well as some lingerie," Ashley wiggled her eyebrows and handed me her phone.

The first few pictures were gorgeous, her in her ball gown and various outfits. She looked so fucking hot. About ten images in, she loosened up and begun to smile. I would give anything to see her smile right now. As the pictures went on, they got more risqué.

Charlotte in some daisy duke shorts and a crop top had my Wolf salivating. The poses had started out innocent, but slowly she came out of her shell and started bending over, showing her ass and tits.

She had a curve to her waist and made her hips look so damn luscious. Perfect for birthing any pups we would have. I couldn't wait to put my hands on Charlotte, feel the apex between her thighs, hell, I'm ready to put tongue there too.

I groaned, trying to hide my raging boner from Ashley.

I took the next swipe on her phone, and she was in a string bikini, dear goddess. It was black, lacy, and it pushed up her ass a bit to show off her glorious globe of an ass. She was in the hot tub on our balcony, bending, overacting like she dropped something. Her cheeks were on full display, and she had her ass to the camera, playfully looking back at the camera. She was laughing and leaning over the railing of our balcony. Her back was arched so beautifully. Fuck, it was glorious.

While staring at her picture, a light bulb went off in my head. Hell, Zachary was there when they were taking pictures. I let out a loud growl that made Ashley jump. "Was Zachary near her during this?!" I stood up over Ashley. Ashley quickly submitted.

"No, no Alpha! During swimsuit and undergarment shots, he left! I swear on it!" My Wolf calmed down as we sat back in the chair. My heart rate slowed as I took a deep breath. Charlotte stirred, her heart rate picking up. "I'll go get the doctor to get her some more pain meds." Ashley excused herself while keeping her head lowered, and I continued to look through the phone.

Damn, I've never been so animalistic until my mate came along. I'm usually pretty laid back, but this bond was really pulling at me. Flipping through more pictures, the more I got turned on. It was painfully hard when I reached the last picture. She was wearing a white laced one-piece suit. She had on white garters, and it went up to her ass and showed every curve. You could tell by the picture it was crotchless, but she had herself carefully situated so the camera wouldn't see.

I growled lowly, and Charlotte's eyelashes twitched. I could smell her arousal, she liked my growling even in her sleep, which made my Wolf puff out his chest with pride. The effect we had on our mate was torture when we could do nothing. *"Only a few more days,"* I whispered to myself, palming my erection.

The doctor strode in, checking the IV fluids and pain medication, while Ashley stood by the door. "Alpha, great news," our pack doctor spoke. He took a needle, tapping it a few times before having the nurse administer more sleep sedatives. "Luna is healing quickly, your venom from your saliva has repaired the tendon and muscles already. In fact, I wouldn't be surprised if she could just take over-the-counter pain killers until it is completely closed." I sighed in relief, happy my mate was going to be fine. "We will get her to sleep another good twelve hours, just so that branding bond is completely gone so she will no longer see it," he winced as he spoke about the brand. "She's a strong one, Alpha."

"Alpha, how about you clean up, and I will watch over her. You can link me if you want to check on her." Ashley took Charlotte's hand again. As much as I wanted to stay, I knew I was dirty. I still had blood, dirt, and sweat built up all along my body, and for almost a week without a shower, I was starting to smell like a damn dog. I thanked Ashley and tried to cover my enormous erection.

I cleared my throat to grab Ashley's attention as I was about out the door, "send those photos to my email," and left as Ashley snickered in the background. Damn.

Once stripping my clothes off in the bathroom and getting in the hot shower, I immediately put my hand on my dick. Fuck I was hard, and I could feel my heart beating inside the head. It was pulsing, ready to be buried balls deep into my mate. The tip of my cock was glistening with precum, and I rubbed it around the head. Letting out a few large breaths, I started stroking. I gripped it tight, knowing my sweet mate would be tight as well. Fucking hell. My Wolf, Remus, growled loudly into the steaming shower.

I felt damn guilty rubbing one out, but fuck, my mate had a body that I wanted to ravage. She was going to be alright, the doctor reassured it, but my Wolf kept scratching in my head to get some sort of release.

She is just so gorgeous, even without a mating bond, I would have wanted her. Precious, innocent, lovely, caring, everything I had ever wanted. To top it off, she was damn sexy, and just a smile could get me hard.

Even with her sitting in the infirmary, sleeping peacefully and pain-free, I felt guilty. I wanted her in so many different ways. I wanted to protect her, love her, shower her with gifts and give her a reason for living. Charlotte had been through so much, and I wanted to keep her safe and help her forget it all.

Taking a few quick pulls of my cock I felt the fire in my balls. They tightened quickly as I thought about those pictures. She was such a tease. I bet she would have sent them to me in a text to try to get me to come home more quickly. So feisty she was, and she didn't know it. My kitten.

Using my hand to squeeze myself, my hips bucked to fist faster, I thought about impaling her, taking her virginity, and making her mine. Her pussy would be so wet from me pleasuring her over and over, swollen from my lips around her clit. Faster, I thrust into my hand, and I let out a large growl streaming rope of my seed on the shower wall. I came more quickly than I thought I would, but when it comes to Charlotte, of course, I won't last. I needed to make sure that when we finally made love, I would last as long as I could and give Charlotte exactly what she wanted. My enormous cock thrusting into that tiny pussy.

Drying myself and putting on some joggers with a tight black t-shirt, I headed back downstairs to relieve Ashley. She sat in the corner, wiping her down, getting rid of the dried blood off her body. Charlotte was naked underneath, but I felt no desire regardless of my thoughts only minutes prior. She was sleeping and trying to recover. I was here to take care of her.

The medical bed was bigger than most. I made medical attendants put a queen bed in here. When the time came when I found my Luna, and she fell pregnant, I could be in bed with her. To hold her and take care of her while she gave birth to our pups. It had always been my dream for the past hundred or years once I realized what a mate bond was. I wanted to experience everything with my mate, and now that Charlotte was here, I would do that. Only when and if she felt like having them.

Curling up next to Charlotte, I pulled her back to my front. She sighed in relief, and I tightened my grip on her. The longer I stayed here, the faster she would heal. Remus came forward in my mind and gave her a few licks on her stitched-up neck. As gross as it sounds, my Wolf's saliva had healing properties that could speed up her recovery process. It already looked so much better than it did before.

Closing my eyes and basking in the bliss of having my mate back in my arms, I thought of the bastard in the prison cells. We'd caught that prick, Roman. My mate would never see him again. She won't know he would be down there as I torture him over the next year then end his pathetic life.

He put up a good fight, I'll give him that. I hadn't had a good brawl in quite a while, and my Wolf was more than ready for his cold ass. As soon as the spell had broken, which we weren't sure how it happened, we all saw those nasty Vamps holding my mate down.

Three damn Vampires against one innocent human. Grinding my teeth, I could feel the blood that spilled as one by one were ripped off her body, besides Roman. It took a few minutes that seemed like hours for the rest of the squad to get there, and then hell broke loose. Vampire after Vampire stormed the basement, keeping me away from Charlotte. The Vamps were easy to throw away from me and crack their necks, but it took time. I was lucky one of the warriors got to her first.

He would be rewarded later, Darrin. He was one of the top warriors and one of the leaders of the top squads we had. Unfortunately, he wasn't aware of how to get a Vampire off its prey without ripping skin. He got Roman off before any venom was introduced to her system, and that was all that mattered.

The whole house was burned to the ground, along with the decapitated Vampires and Witches. Roman was taken to the prison cells, and the weak glamour spell was completely broken once the house caught fire. It wasn't normal for a glamour spell to fail like that. It was to help keep things hidden to Werewolves, humans, and other supernaturals but not other Witches. Witches can see a glamour spell a mile away. However, this spell was even weak for us, and it was breaking and crumbling when we had just entered the basement.

Something wasn't right about it. It had my Wolf pacing, wanting answers.

"*Alpha,*" Evan linked me. "*Alpha, the local Witch coven, Amadaous, is coming in from the north to speak with us about the glamour spell. It is illegal around these parts to use it and want to get some information. The Witch that cast the spell is on the run; looks like she's got a rap sheet all the way to Bergarian.*"

I sighed and pinched the bridge of my nose, "*Are you able to handle the coven? I've already got a few squads out tracking Josephine's scent. Delilah found a few items of Josephine, the witches could use a locator spell on them to find her.*"

199

"Of course, Alpha, take care of your mate. Oh, also, Delilah found her mate. He was upstairs in one of the bedrooms. Other than being severely malnourished and dehydrated, she took him back to her pack. I gave the go-ahead for Delilah's release since that was what each party agreed on."

I nodded even though Evan couldn't see me, *"Great job, Evan. Thank you."*

"How is Luna?" he quickly added.

"Better, with the bond and my Wolf healing her, she should be better in a few days." I stroked her face with the back of my hand.

"Excellent, maybe she will be OK for the Halloween celebration? She has an awesome theme costume going on with Ashley and Zachary."

"Hmm, we will see." I chuckled at the thought of actually dressing up for the cursed danced.

✱✱✱

After twelve hours in the medical unit, the physician gave the go-ahead to move her to our room. Her wound had healed perfectly closed. Even the doctor was even surprised at how fast it had sealed itself. Our bond was strong, and not leaving her side helped considerably.

I laid her on the bed. Charlotte was no longer attached to IV poles or machines, she looked like my own sleeping beauty. She would be weak, the physical and mental trauma on her was significant, and I would stay by her side until she recovered—and long after.

The entire pack was concerned, and the constant pull and tapping into the link was getting annoying. I had to block everyone out and have it redirected to Evan. He wasn't too happy either, but his mate was excited to get him out of their room for a bit.

The pups at the center made beautiful colored pictures and cards and many flowers adorned our room. Everyone loved her so much, and she wasn't even aware of it. Charlotte had only graced us for a little over a month and had captured so many hearts. She would be so excited to see it when she woke up.

Charlotte sighed once again, I prayed to the goddess she would open her eyes with every movement she made. She needed her rest, but I was a selfish bastard. I wanted her eyes to look into mine and tell me she forgives me for leaving. I'll swear to her over and over again that I will never leave her. We would be each other's shadows and travel together as one. That is what mates are all about, though, right?

If she will still have me and be my mate, I'll never leave her. I'll be a possessive cliche bastard of an Alpha Wolf, which I think she likes anyway.

Goddess, wake up, my queen.

Chapter 35
Charlotte

I was in a giant burrito, a lightly heated tortilla, and I couldn't even move, not that I wanted to anyway.

Taking a deep breath, I could smell something masculine with a twist of pine. Letting out a long, loud sigh, I could hear chuckling in front of my face. No longer was I comfortable, but slightly embarrassed.

Looking up, I see the cheesiest grin of a man as intimidating as Wesley could be. His eyes were sparkling, and I couldn't help but smile back. "Wesley!" I screamed and hugged him tightly. I nuzzled my nose in the crook of his neck, and he did the same. His hands wrapped around my torso and brought me close, afraid to let go.

"I missed you so much, Kitten," his voice hitched.

"I missed you too, Wesley, no more leaving me, OK?" I sobbed.

"I swear to you on my life I will never leave you, ever again. You are coming on all my business trips," he kissed my forehead, "every Alpha pack meeting," he kissed my cheek, "every," he kissed my lips, "fucking time I leave the packhouse." His mouth descended to mine one more time, and we tangled our tongues together. He sucked and pulled on my lower lip while I took his upper lip. Both of us moaned into each other until I couldn't breathe.

"Wesley?" I tried to say, but it came out a mumbled mess

"Mhmm?" Wesley wouldn't leave my mouth, and I started laughing.

"What's wrong, Kitten?" he began kissing down my neck and sucking the skin of the opposite side of my wound. I tried to push him away, but he kept coming at me with his mouth and hands.

His hands trailed down my waist, to my lower back, and I kept giggling as he assaulted my body with his large hands. Wesley's kisses turned into smiles and laughter as well. "Okay, I'm done, Kitten. What is it?" He mused, his lips twitching to lean forward back into my neck.

"I need to use the ladies' room. I'm sure my breath is gross," I said shyly.

"No, it doesn't bother me," he pushed me back into the mattress as he hovered over me, kissing down to my chest.

"Wesley! Please!" I whined. "I need to actually use the ladies' room too."

"Ah, I guess you're right," he sighed disappointedly.

"Yup," I said cheerfully. Wesley picked me up, and I grabbed hold of his neck.

"What are you doing?" I huffed.

"You haven't walked in well over a day and a half. I don't want you to fall, Kitten." I laid my head on the side of his chest. I didn't realize just how much I missed this. He was the only reason I was back here with him. I thought of him throughout the past week. If I hadn't, I'm sure I would have submitted just not to be in any more pain. Wesley was worth the pain and all the suffering I had gone through during the years and a week of torture.

"What are you thinking, Kitten?" Wesley set me down on the side of the tub.

"I'm just happy to be back here with you. I didn't think I was going to make it back. I was so scared. I think the only reason I lasted as long as I did was that I thought of you." Wesley kneeled down and put one of his hands on my cheek. "They burned me again, that branding bond thing." I looked down, and I could hear the rumble in Wesley's chest.

"All I thought about was you; Joseline said that they would have to do it a couple of times to make me forget you, to have the pain so bad I would just no longer care and wish for it to be over." I sniffed.

"Kitten, how many times?" His eyes were full of sorrow, those pretty green eyes no longer bright like emeralds. I didn't want to tell him, but I didn't want to lie either.

"I was burned twice a day, every day since I was taken. One for the front, one for the back. He said after a week if it didn't work, he said he would change me. Then he would mark me himself. Josephine said I wouldn't survive both bites, but he didn't care."

Wesley's anger got the better of him and punched a hole through the shower tile. The beautiful, marbled shower would have to be completely redone. "Wesley," I pleaded. I pulled his hand down to see the damage, but his hand was already healing. All that was left was a few drops of blood. I kissed his knuckles gently, and he just pulled me close and hugged me.

"I don't deserve you, Charlotte. You are so damn strong. How could you go through that all week and not break? Hell." His voice was all but a husky whisper. I felt a few drops of tears on the crook of my neck.

"I thought of only you. I know I sound like a love-sick puppy," I chuckled. "I really was, though, every time Roman touched and branded me, I thought of us in bed cuddling in the mornings. Your smile, how you like to fight with Evan over who gets the last piece of bacon, the lovely things you whisper in my ear when no one is listening. That is what got me through it all."

Wesley chest heaved up and down quickly, silent sobs wracked his body, holding me impossibly tighter against his chest. Wesley was my knight, my rock, my ferocious beast. A man of such power, ruling over a pack, strong, resilient, and here he was crumbling at my feet. How could a girl not swoon?

Even if Wesley was late, taking a full week to find me, I persevered. I fought to the very end. For a human, how awesome is that? It was pretty amazing.

"Josephine knew I wouldn't give up being with you. Yet, she still let it happen. She wanted to destroy Roman as much as I did. I don't understand her," I shook my head. "Because she still let an innocent person suffer through it all. I just don't understand that horrible Witch." We both sunk to the cold floor. I laid my head on top of Wesley while he buried his head in my lap while I continued to stroke his hair.

"Charlotte, I love you, with all my being. I am at your feet. Please forgive me for ever leaving." The pajama pants I wore were wet from Wesley's tears. My poor Wesley, poor me. We were delt a nasty hand of cards, but we survived. We both learned from this.

"It wasn't your fault, but I forgive you if it makes you feel better." I whispered.

Wesley continued to rub his head in my lap and on my stomach. His stubbled beard rubbed my lap harder as I felt it tickle my thighs.

"What are you doing!?" I giggled.

"Putting my scent on you. No one touches what is mine." He growled. His voice was dark and heavy, I had a feeling I wasn't talking to Wesley anymore. Never had he sounded like this. Wesley looked up at me. His eyes were black, fangs were sticking out of his mouth.

"Wesley?" I stuttered my words. I was a taken aback, I threw my hands out of his hair and tried to get closer to the wall.

"Not Wesley," the gruff voice said as he lifted me up and buried his head in my neck. I kept quiet and let him do what he wanted. He continued to rub his head and face all over me. I knew I had to stink, I had been lying in a bed for the past day and a half, but I sat there. It wasn't awkward or unsettling, just different. It was like someone else was touching me, but it was still my Wesley. This must have been Wesley's Wolf. He wouldn't hurt me. Would he?

"What's your name then?" I said, finally showing my courage.

He purred as he started licking between my neck and shoulder. It gave me chills, but I tried to restrain a moan I wanted to let out.

"Mmm, Remus." Remus looked up at me, eyes still black. "Scared, mate?"

"No, I don't think I'm scared. I'm...surprised? Wesley hasn't been able to tell me much about you yet."

"Wesley was scared for you. I'm his beast. We do things differently." I nodded my head, daring not question.

"Well, Remus, I need to use the ladies' room, maybe wash up a bit?" I questioned. I wasn't sure if he would let me, his grip was tight as his chest purred into my thigh.

"I stay," he grunted. Reluctantly letting me go, he let me get up to use the toilet. Remus stared at me while I waited for him to turn around.

"Remus, I need you to turn around or go outside the door. I need...privacy," I begged.

"Remus stay." He turned around and sat on the floor with a huff, and folded his arms. I had never used the toilet while someone else was in the room. I was getting peeing anxiety, if that was even a thing. I got up and turned on the faucet so he couldn't hear me go, and he growled in annoyance. Excuse me, Mr. Wolf... sheesh.

After a long shower that involved grunting and pouting, I was allowed a towel, even though he didn't want me to use one. He tried to lick me dry. Ew? "Remus, when will Wesley be back?"

"Mate doesn't like Remus?" His voice went low as his eyes glimmered with sadness. I almost wanted to laugh at how pouty his face got.

"No, no, I love Remus." Remus stomped over to me and picked me up. He made me straddle him while he buried his face into my neck. "Mmm, Remus, love mate." I giggled. "Remus feed mate." I looked at him in question, but there was a big table full of food when I looked up. When did that get there?

With my towel on, he placed me on his lap and began to feed me. It was the juiciest steak, the flavor exploded in my mouth. After a day and half without food, I was starving. The small hum in satisfaction was taken heavier than intended because Remus's hand squeezed tight around my thigh while I squealed in surprise. "I like mate's sounds. It makes Remus hard." I blushed profusely while he chuckled darkly.

"Stooop, Remus!" I whined. The longer he was out, the more comfortable I got. I was really starting to miss Wesley, though. He was so worried and vulnerable when Remus took over. Maybe that was why Remus was able to take hold of his body so quickly.

Remus was about to kiss me until we heard a knock on the door. Remus growled in frustration when the door finally opened. Evan stood there, when Evan saw Wesley's black eyes he stopped in his tracks. "Remus, my man," he said hesitantly. Evan looked at our compromising position Remus realized I was still in just a towel covering my assets, barely.

"What do you want, Beta?"

Evan hesitated. "Alpha, the doctor wanted to give Charlotte a physical now that she is awake. I can bring the doctor in here, or we can have her go to the clinic." Remus looked at me and what I was wearing. I gave him a small smile and patted his cheek so he wouldn't freak out on Evan. Remus's eyes didn't leave mine.

"Mate, what do you want," he purred and put his face into my neck.

"We will go there, Evan. Give me 15 minutes." Evan let out a breath and mouthed a 'Thank you,' and closed the door behind him.

"Remus, we might need Wesley to come back out." I rubbed my hand through his hair. It was getting long, almost to his shoulders. The sides were still shaved, but when it was down, it would tickle my face when he kissed me. Remus whined in protest.

"Need mate," he pulled me closer and buried his face in my chest

"How about tonight, Remus. You can cuddle with me tonight?" His head perked up.

"Kisses tonight?" His eyes were hopeful, playful.

"If you give me Wesley for a little right now." I kissed his nose. In a blink of an eye, I saw Wesley's beautiful green eyes come back to me.

"Fuck, I'm sorry, Charlotte I didn't mean for him to do that," Wesley squeezed me tight.

"It's Okay. I just didn't know you had another big personality in there."

"Yeah, I wasn't ready for you to meet him. He is quite the animal. Since we met you, he's been that way, he is usually pretty chill and only really shows himself during fights. Everyone is scared of Remus when he forces control."

After getting dressed, we both headed down to the clinic to get a check-up. Blood work, blood pressure, checking on the branding bond mark, which had already faded, I was voted a clean bill of health besides a couple deep scratches leftover from Roman's bite.

The whole ordeal seemed like ages ago after sleeping for so long, but I still gave me shivers thinking about it. I was glad I was back and ready to get things back to normal.

Wesley wouldn't let me walk back to his room. He continued to carry me bridal style throughout the house. The constant attention would typically bother me, but I was really enjoying it. I craved his touch more and more, and Wesley said it was because of the bond. We had become so close in just a month and a half by human standards, but I wasn't complaining.

Once we got back to our room, I slid under the covers. Even though I had slept for a long while, I was still exhausted. Wesley went and changed into some joggers and left his shirt off. To say he looked appetizing was an understatement. "Kitten?" he growled lowly.

"Yesss?" I prolonged my words.

"Did you promise Remus he could cuddle you tonight?" Wesley's eyebrow was raised in a questioning manner.

"I'm sorry, babe, he was just all cute and whiny like a little puppy. I couldn't help but promise him," I giggled. Wesley sighed.

"Alright, but I will get you tomorrow all day. We have to put the final touches to the big packs gathering for Halloween in a couple of days."

"Ughhhhh," I groaned. "I'm not sure if I am up to it anymore. I only feel comfortable around Ashley, Zachary, Evan, and you."

I wanted to dress up, but after seeing a bunch of Vampires and Werewolves fighting, I wasn't in the partying mood. I would be happy curling up and watching some kid Halloween movies like Hocus Pocus.

"If you don't want to go, we won't." Wesley rubbed my worried face. "We can stay up here the entire time, and I can think of some fun activities we could do together since you will be better by then," he said, wiggling his eyebrows. I slapped his shoulder.

I had only been awake for a few hours, but I had already felt how much I wanted him. Being away made me realize I wanted to be with Wesley forever. If that meant I had to be bitten, so be it. I've been through a hell of a lot worse and being scared of another sort of bite wasn't going to deter me. The doctor mentioned I should be well enough to complete the mating process in a few days. It's a good thing Wesley left the room for that one. He would be so excited if I said I was ready to his face. I smirked inwardly.

Just then, Wesley's eyes turned black, and it was Remus. "Mate," he breathed. I reached over and put my two hands on either side of his face and kissed him. The kiss went heated really fast as he shoved his tongue down my throat. For a moment, I thought his beast's tongue changed because it was so long. "Mmmhmm, Remus?"

"Mateeeee," he groaned.

"We can't do anything yet, doctor's orders. I said we could cuddle to sleep, puppy."

"Puppy? Remus, not puppy," he pouted.

"You are my puppy! My big, scary puppy!" I giggled. He grunted and pulled me on top of him while he lay on his back. "Sleep, mate." He put my head in the crook of his neck while he wrapped his arms around me, my legs straddling around his waist.

"Night, Puppy."

Chapter 36

Charlotte

After a long, long sleep, I'm talking for twelve hours. Wesley is still next to me but working on his laptop with his computer and his reading glasses. Once I told him it was easier on his eyes to block out any blue light, he started wearing them. Even though Wesley is a Werewolf, it had to help just a little. Maybe he is just humoring me.

Wesley looked delectable with them on. Like a real top-notch CEO that would bend me over his desk. I've never had an eye for a man before, let alone thinking about sex. I was too busy running and thinking they could be nothing but trouble after Roman, which was a shame. Even so, no one looked as scrumptious as Wesley Hale. I don't know how I deserved to be with this hunk of a man.

He hasn't left my side since I came back. I was comforted that he would want to stay with me, but I knew he had to get back to work. When I was gone, he said he stayed in his office and threw stuff, not really working on anything, and poor Evan had been in charge for well over a week and needed a break. My neck had healed up quite a bit last night, just a few scratches that might leave a tiny scar but nothing what I currently had on me.

"Wesley? Why don't you go work in your office for a little? I'm fine, really. I can go find Ashley and help her with the Halloween party." Wesley let out a gruff as he finished his sentence on the keyboard.

"I don't want to leave you," he pouted and began typing again. I sat up on my knees and rubbed his shoulders. He sighed and leaned his head back to give me a kiss. Our little pecks became smiles and nose rubbing.

"I will be on the territory at all times. I'll make sure you know where I am, alright? I'll take the phone. It has a GPS tracker on it. I could even have Ashley bring Beau! I haven't talked to him much."

"Ha, he doesn't talk to anybody but Ashley. He's a grumpy one."

"Is that a, yes?" I drawled out my words. Wesley leaned his head on the back of the headboard. He grunted a few times, probably talking to Remus.

"Tell Remus he can kiss more tonight," I said in a sing-song voice.

"That's not fair. When is my time?" Wesley groaned.

"OK, extra things tonight for you," I wiggled my eyebrows. Wesley gave me that smirk and closed his laptop. He brought me up to straddle his waist, and I ran my fingers through his long hair. His hair was so sexy. I loved it when he wore it down. It made him look so rugged compared to the CEO man bun he sports in Alpha mode. His lips pressed to mine, nipping my bottom lip with his teeth.

I tugged on his scalp a little, and his hands roamed my waist down to my butt. His touches continue to leave fire sparks on my skin, and it makes my breath hitch as I feel it even down to my heat. Wesley growled and pulled me away from the kiss.

"Oh, Kitten, we need to slow down. You are still recovering." His breath was uneven and panting, as was I.

"We can play a little, right?" I played with the button on his collar and gave him some innocent eyes. I felt like a horny teenager which, I kind of missed growing up.

"Yes but... Goddess." He took his hand, threading his fingers through my hair and pushing him harshly to his mouth.

Unbuttoning his shirt while he sucked on my bottom lip, he lifted his oversized shirt that covered my body. His fingers brushed over my bare nipples and moaned at the callouses on his thumbs. My mouth leg his briefly to catch my breath, only for him to flip me over onto the mattress.

Wesley's body pushed me deeper into the mattress, pushing his erection right next to my core. He moved his hips rhythmically brushing up and down the thin material of my panty. His pants were still on, so I began the daunting task to unbuckle his pants. The click of the buckle had my body racing in excitement, hearing it slide through the loopholes had my pussy drenched. Wesley groaned gratefully as the tight zipper was taken down. His faded to black. Remus was trying to come out, and I wasn't sure if I was ready.

"Wesley?" I whispered, looking into his eyes. Wesley blinked a few times, and his green eyes flutter back to me.

"Y-your eyes. I think Remus was trying to come out," I said worriedly. Wesley shook his head a few times.

"I'm sorry, Kitten. I am having a bit of a hard time controlling him." Wesley sat up on the bed and slung his legs over. I quickly got up and threw his shirt back on and sat beside him. He had his head in both of his hands, leaning over.

"Wesley, babe talk to me. What's going on." I rubbed his back and hopped in his lap while he laughed at me, amused.

"He really wants to mark you. He is just really overprotective right now." Wesley pulled a strand of hair from my face. "He-" Wesley tried to talk, but I interrupted him.

"I want you to mark me, Wesley." Wesley opened his eyes several times, his eyes dilating. "I want you to mark me. As soon as the doctor says it's Okay, I want you to. You made me come alive again. In all of this crazy, messed-up world, there is no other heart for me than yours. No love could be comparable to what I have for you." Wesley pulled me closer to his chest, looking into my eyes.

"I will spend an eternity loving you, caring for you, pampering you, and making sweet love to you, baby. I don't deserve you. The Moon Goddess blessed me with the perfect mate." Wesley's nose came down and we rubbed noses. Both of our eyes were closed as we just held each other.

As much as I loved Remus, I knew he would be rough to deal with in bed. I needed Wesley to make love to me the first time. The worry only dwindled as Wesley continued to reassure me that Remus would stay behind once the time came.

After a good hour of cuddling, Wesley agreed to go get some work done. He trailed off to his office, and I went with Ashley. Beau was unavailable, he was patrolling the border. The cameras that had been set up have been ruined by the large blast that some Witch used when they teleported out of the territory when I left. No one wanted to order any more cameras until I came back.

"So, what are we doing?" I asked Ashley. Ashley was pulling boxes and boxes out of the corner of the ballroom.

"We..." she started as she ripped one of them open, "are decorating!" Pack members coming out of the wood works started helping undo boxes and hanging up decorations. Everything had its place, and I wasn't sure if I would be much help, but of course, Ashley gave me something.

"You need to pick out songs for the DJ. Many Wolves here don't get out much, so we need new material."

"Pack DJ? Is that like some special position?" I laughed.

"It should be, but no, it's not. The guy is a total man-whore, Wolf-whore that hasn't found his mate. I swear his dick craves attention 99% of the time," Ashley rolled her eyes. "He can sniff out a woman in heat from almost a mile away because he is always the first to approach." Ashley punched the box to break it down and tossed it aside.

"Heat? What is that?" That was a new term to me. I had no idea what she was talking about, not unless it meant the same thing for animals. Animals... Oh, wait.

"I keep forgetting to tell you this stuff," Ashley mused as she pulled out some fake cobwebs.

I waved my hand around. "What other stuff is there, Ashley? Dang Werewolves, Witches, Vampires, bondings, mates, good gracious, what else is there!?" My voice was becoming louder and louder with each thing I named off, Wolves laughed from the corners of the room.

"Alright, alright, calm down." She put my hands down and sat beside me next to the table. "It is just like for lower animals like wolves, cats, deer that sort of thing. It is when your body is ready to mate and has a high probability of having pups. It happens with she-Wolves a lot. A lot of she-Wolves don't get it until they meet their mate, but a couple of unlucky few get it. We have a shed on the territory that shields smell, and they stay in there up to 5 days trying to keep it at bay. Some, more, contemporary she-Wolves," Ashley laughed, "use a stand-in, and some willing male takes care of them." My eyes grew wide. "Don't look like that. It helps with the heat. It isn't called heat for nothing. It makes your body hot, the only way to calm it down is to orgasm, and it feels so much better when someone else is helping." My face turned the deepest red while I held my hands over my face.

Zachary walked up and tsked. "What did you tell the poor virgin now?" He stuck his hand out on his hip.

"Just about heat." Zachary moved his lips in a big, "O" and chuckled. "I heard it is awesome for the male and almost exhausting," he mused.

"Just kill me, just kill me," I muttered under my breath.

Zachary took a seat beside me and put his arm around me. He was like a big brother. We shared that intimate moment when we first met about our "parents," if you could call them that. Ever since, I have felt such a connection to him.

"Now, I know I shouldn't ask, Charlie," Zachary's brows furrowed, looking down at me with worry. "But I am just looking out for you." Ashley's eyes perked up, and she listened. "Do you know what is involved with mating? Like really know?" My face flushed again with embarrassment. Ashley giggled hysterically while Zachary stared her down. He was serious. If I wasn't so embarrassed, I would have thought it was cute.

"No, I'm serious. I know both of you are close, Charlie, and I'm surprised you haven't yet. I heard Remus came out the other day. Evan pissed himself."

"Yeah, I saw that. Why is that?" Zachary took his arm back around and settled them on the table. He scratched the back of his head watching the other pack members raising the spooky chandelier.

"Remus is usually... usually... pretty tame. When he gets mad or sexually frustrated, which has only happened with you, by the way..." he smiled. "He is unpredictable, like most Alphas. Wesley has been having trouble ever since you went missing. Remus is ready to mark you. I just need you to know what happens. You're like my little sis," Zachary cooed. He rubbed the top of my head with his knuckles. "Owie!"

I nodded, "I know we do… the thing… and then be bites me?" I whispered to him.

"So precious," Ashley whispered and put her hands together like she was praying and laying on them. "Just like a doll." Zachary rolled his eyes his arm gripping me tighter.

"Ashley is no fucking help. Anyway, yes, that will happen. Also, it means that his Wolf and you own each other in the body during mating, and when he bites you, then your souls will be connected." My eyes grew wide.

"It is the most beautiful thing, Charlotte! You can hear each other through the mind-link that you have been interested in, and you will feel each other's emotions so much better. It was the best night of my life!" Ashley swooned and twirled around dramatically and sat in the chair.

"Righttttt." Zachary mocked. "It is supposed to be amazing, it hurts for a few seconds, but that's it. Then you do the 'deed' as you put it, for the rest of the night, just because you can." He laughed.

I put both of my hands to my face and tried to hide from embarrassment.

Chapter 37
Charlotte

Ashley continued to unpack boxes, and I wrote down songs I wanted to play during the big mating Halloween Ball. It was brutal because I don't have a knack for this kind of thing. Sure, I knew what sounded good, but it could be a terrible song to dance to. I went through the '70s and '80s, you can't have a great party without some of the classics, or so I thought. I knew what I liked, so I stuck with that.

Ashley continued joking with Zachary while they hung up the dirty cobwebs in the corners of the massive ballroom. I think they were just trying to keep me resting. Even though it had been two days of being awake, I felt terrific.

For the most part, the ballroom was plain. It was like a giant blank room that could be easily transformed into anything we wanted. Permanent tables laid near the walls that could hold the food with a heating station. A large dance floor was at the center, and many tables for people to sit around and chat. Several bars adorned the room throughout, with the way Werewolves could hold their alcohol, I'm sure they'd have to drink a lot to even get a buzz. The bill must be astronomical.

Most of the room was cream and white; it was an easy pallet to work with. It was three-stories high where people could overlook the crowd below. At the top center was a large double door for anyone that wanted to make a grand entrance. The wrap-around staircase held the stage in the middle, perfect for a DJ. It had a very Cinderella-esk vibe to it before the scary decorations were put up.

Large pseudo-columns adorned several areas of the room that reached the ceiling. They were black and red, of course, and giant skeletons and nasty zombies and ghosts littered the walls. Even a life-sized Werewolf which had to be created by a human who had no idea what they really looked like because it was almost a joke. I started laughing to myself, until I heard a knock on the table to get my attention.

The man wasn't as buff as Wesley, he was tall and somewhat lanky but had a beautiful face. His hair was jet black, slicked back that made it look wet. He had 3 piercings in each ear, one in the eyebrow, and you could see nipple piercings through his meshed black shirt. Dear heavens, that must have hurt. I crossed my arms over my breasts, and he threw his head back, laughing. It was a playful laugh, not menacing at all like his attire. It was primarily black with chains coming from his pockets. I can see how some women in heat would just let him do what he wanted.

"Hello there, I'm Lyle. I heard you were picking out our music list?" I nodded and slid the paper over to him.

"I'm not very good at picking out music. I think Ashley and Zachary gave me this job because these Wolves think I'm fragile or something." I waved my hands off to Ashley and Zachary, who laughed from afar, obviously hearing me.

Lyle only chuckled. "Well, that is understandable and all. You did have some Vamp almost rip your throat out and not to mention the psychological damage you had to face during the week. That is some pretty sick shit." I gave a dark chuckle. "Actually, I'm impressed with what you picked. I haven't heard of all of it before, so I'll have to check them out... Party Rock Anthem, Blurred Lines, Sexy Back, What Makes You Beautiful... great dancing songs, I'm sure." He smirked.

"Pretty sure you are just buttering me up because I basically Googled the best dance songs."

Lyle lifted his eyebrow, "Well, nothing gets past you, Luna." He winked while I rolled my eyes. "I'll be sure to get the best songs for dancing. You are attending, right?"

"Of course, not sure how much dancing, though. Wesley has been pretty adamant that I rest. Something about getting your throat ripped out just a few days ago can wear me out."

"Ha! I bet!" Before I could ask Lyle another question, his eyes turned black. I looked around to see any danger, but Lyle kept looking at me and flared his nostrils.

"Lyle? Is everything alright?" Lyle tilted his head at me and then looked to the right side of the room, where a beautiful she-Wolf was hanging the giant disco ball. He stood up and ran over, his chains dangling and clanging together until he climbed up the later to speak with her. She started laughing when Lyle came up behind her and whispered in her ear. Her face turned beet red, but the sly smile she had told me of a different agenda she might be planning. Lyle slides down the ladder effortlessly while he waited for her, grabbing her hand leading her out the door.

"What the heck was that?" I spoke to no one in particular.

"That," Zachary came up to me, "was Lyle at work. He can tell when a she-Wolf is about to go into heat. It is his specialty. If you can have intercourse before the heat starts, sometimes it lessens the intensity and duration of the heat."

"Oh my gosh, that is so gross. So, she just left with him? And he can just smell that?!"

"Nina has always had trouble with her heat. Her Wolf is a bit of a slut."

"Whoever her mate is, is going to love her a lot, that is for sure. She makes sure that she only does what is necessary though, she really isn't a slut. Sometimes nature takes over, and you can't help it." I nodded, still not knowing how my heat will be one day. I was just glad that I never had to deal with something like that. It sounds so painful and more so embarrassing. I hope I didn't have to beg for it one day.

"And that is Lyle's forte, and why he is one of the head trackers." Zachary continued to laugh while I had a look of horror on my face.

After a few good hours of everyone asking my opinion on where decorations should go, what food we should have, the entertainment, the games, and so forth, I was beat. I sat most of the time, but the constant interaction with people killed my introverted self, and I needed to getaway. My eyes felt droopy, and my butt was completely numb. I thought a hot tub session was in order.

I trudged back up the stairs alone, Ashely and Zachary weren't far behind as I heard them snickering about Nina going into heat. I swear they acted like middle schoolers who giggled when people held hands. My feet stopped moving, glancing back down the stair way. It was a light bulb that went off in my head.

Is Roman gone? I never asked Wesley that. I was so happy to be back in the packhouse to even answer. Was I finally safe from that damn Vampire? Do I even want to know? I shuttered to think that he was still alive and could come back, but Wesley wouldn't let that happen. Gripping the railing, I continued my leg work out going up the stairs.

Wesley would tell me I needed to know. I trust him.

I let out a long, audible sigh as I put on the black bikini that I fell in love with the first day I arrived. Since I've grown into my skin and accepted who I am, I feel confident wearing it. My bum sticks out, so my cheeks show, but nothing a hot tub and bubbles can't hide.

I gently slid the balcony door open and slowly got in. It was early evening, the cold had really seeped in with the storm. It had been warm the past few days and almost all of the first snow had melted. Cranking up the heat, I let my body mold into the hot tub seat. My head laid back on the head rest, feeling the hot water caressing my sore muscles.

Never in my wildest dreams did I think I would be here. Being on the run was my specialty, and here I was, getting ready to let Wesley mark me and become a permanent resident. Was I ready?

Mentally, I think I am. I thought about it while I was in that damp basement. Wesley is the only one that makes me feel safe and cares about what I do. He lets me work, learn and be a part of something bigger, and the best part? He sees me as his equal and not some lowly woman he could just have sex with. He's been extraordinary, slow, caring, and taking care of all my needs. What guy does that? Honestly though?

Getting more comfortable, I felt a warm feeling inside me, and I instantly knew who it was. Opening my eyes, I see Wesley, shirtless in one of those small European swim trunks that were short, showing those fantastic legs. Could thighs be sexy on a man? His definitely were. Heaven's... his muscles went right up to his...

Wesley's deep chuckle had me squeezing my thighs together. He knew he was damn sexy. His blonde hair was down, touching his shoulders, just how I liked it. The sweat was dripping down his shaved torso from the steam the hot tub gave off. He had just a bit of scruff on his face, and he had taken out his small earring. His biceps bulged as he was carrying a tray of strawberries and champagne.

I gave him a big smile and swam close to him, beckoning him to come in with me. He put the tray on the table in the middle of the tub and got in with me without a word. I put my hand on his cheek and pulled him towards me for a kiss.

Definitely not a bad relationship at all. Wesley cares for me in ways they only do in movies. Wesley lifted up my hand and gave a few kisses to my knuckles before saying, "How was your day, Love?" He put his nose up to my neck and kissed my soon-to-be marking spot, and I shivered.

"It was good. I learned a lot about party planning from Ashley and Zachary." I put my hand on his chest and traced the Black Claw Pack emblem on his arm. "Not to sound too cheesy, but I missed you." I smiled sheepishly.

"Well, that's good then because I hardly got anything done because I was thinking of you." He lifted my face to his and kissed my lips. It started light, a few pecks until his tongue was massaging my lips to let him in. Of course, I obliged, and he swiftly put me on his lap. His member was already prominent poking right into my inner thighs. It felt so good against my barely-there swimsuit. He lowered his hands to my butt and felt just how little material covered my bathing suit. He groaned into my mouth and pulled me away. "Oh, goddess Kitten, is this the same suit from your little photoshoot," he groaned with hooded eyes looking at me.

I perked up real quick, and my body went stiff. "M-my p-photos?" I didn't know he was given the pictures yet. How freaking embarrassing! I needed some kind of warning for this! Wesley smiled childishly and rubbed my hips with his thumbs.

"Yes, while you were recovering, Ashley sent them to me. I'm sorry, did you not want me to see them?" Wesley gave me a pouty face and fluttered his lashes that made me laugh out loud.

"Well, no, I just wasn't prepared for you to see those yet. I was going to wait until… well…."

"You were going to send them while I was gone to get me to come back, weren't you?" Wesley chided. He lifted his index finger and waved it in front of me. "You have been naughty, my little Kitten."

Vera Foxx

Chapter 38

Wesley

My little Kitten had been naughty, and it was sexy as hell. She thought she could get away with it after all she had been through, but she was mistaken. I laughed internally as I watched her face glow beet red. The steam that surrounded us had us sweating, glistening in the sun setting just to the west of us.

I had missed her so much in the week she was gone. She suffered so much, and she said the only way she got through was by thinking of us. Goddess, I was more than ready to mark her, to officially make her mine and part of the pack. I wanted it all. I wanted to be a selfish bastard and ignore the doctor's pleas. She had been forcefully marked so many times, even though her body and soul would not accept it, it took a toll on her soul. I was given the word of one week at least. The longer, the better. The doctors knew that any more than that, Remus would retaliate. He loved Charlotte with a fiery passion.

Since she has been back, he has demanded he stays awake to watch her while I sleep Remus is overprotective of her and never wants her out of our sight. I was surprised he allowed us to work with Evan in the office today. We had to settle what we were to do with Roman. Remus's need for revenge must have won out.

Roman was chained up in the cells, no way out and no way in. We have thought of what we could do to make his last year on Earth hell, but I want to eliminate all threats. Remus wants his blood, so he will be killed before the Halloween party tomorrow. Poetic justice, maybe? I laughed internally.

My little Kitten was still blushing as I looked into her eyes. Those innocent eyes that I have slowly tainted. Even though we were in a hot tub, I could almost smell her. Lunas have such a strong scent for their Alphas. I pray no other male ever smells it. It is electrifying what it does to Remus and me. I let out a low growl, and she puts both of her hands up to her face. I give her that smirk she likes so much, and she starts giggling.

"Do you have any idea how incredibly sexy those pictures were, Charlotte?" I whispered huskily into her ear.

"N-no," she barely whispered. "Ashley made me d-do it."

"They made me so incredibly stiff, love. I wanted to fuck you there while you were sleeping." I licked her ear. "The curve of your ass, the way your breasts spilled over your lingerie set was so fetching on you." Charlotte squirmed in my hold while I rubbed her sides up and down with my fingertips. Her heat was grinding on the erection that made me roll my head back. "Kitten, what are you doing to me," I groaned out loud. Looking back into her eyes and stopping her movements, I decided to tease her more.

"I got so painfully hard I had to excuse myself from your room. Otherwise, I didn't know what I would do to you." I tickled below her ear with my nose. "I went back to our room and got in the shower to feel the heat of the water." Charlotte panted, grinding herself into my crotch. Her nails stuck into my shoulders. She wanted some friction, so I would allow it, goddess. It felt so damn good. I grunted in approval as she went pushed harder against me. Untying the top of her suit her breast it fell before me so I could see her tantalizing tits. They were perky and hard despite the warmth that surrounded us.

"I had to take care of myself, thinking of those perky breasts of yours. I had to stroke my cock and think of you." I took one of her breasts into my mouth and to suck and nip. It caused her to moan and push her chest further into my mouth.

"Wesley, please," she whispered. I moved her faster as she ground into me. My hands pulling her up and down my shaft. The water was sloshing in the hot tub, and she grabbed the hair on my head, causing me to groan. Her pussy was so warm, and we still had two layers of clothing between us. I was ready to mark her, Remus wanted it too. Charlotte put her chest on mine and begun to kiss up and down my neck. It gave me shivers as I palmed her ass harder onto me. "Oh, Wesley, Oh, ah!" She whimpered into my chest, and I began to squeeze her ass breasts roughly. Sucking on them, trying to prolong her orgasm. Charlotte leaned her head back in ecstasy when I heard her scream, and it wasn't a good scream.

She quickly covered her breasts and leaned into me to hide. I put my arms around her to hide from what she was scared of and whipped my head around to see what caused her fright.

It was Zachary, her unmated friend.

Remus came forward and let out a roar, and he hugged his mate ferociously. "What the hell are you doing, pup?! Do you want to die today?!" The Alpha aura oozed as Zachary fell to the ground. His forehead touching the floor as he shivered in fear. Remus stood up and wrapped our mate in a towel.

"Have you not heard knocking, you fool?!" Zachary was trying to be swallowed up by the floor beneath him. "What did you see, pup?! Did you see what is mine?!" Remus walked up and pulled Zachary by his neck, having him dangling over a foot off the ground. Remus had been too territorial, and with our mate not marked, it was only getting worse.

Remus was about to snap his neck for his lack of respect for his Luna, and then she walked out. She was dressed in our joggers and an oversized grey t-shirt, her favorite thing to wear when she sleeps with us. "Remus, honey, it's Okay. It was an accident." Charlotte came over and put her hand on our arm. She petted him and kissed him as high as she could reach, which was on our bare chest. "It was just an accident, please don't hurt him, he is my friend. Maybe he has something important to say. Please put him down, love."

Remus wasn't wavering. He was pissed. It was hard to calm him down, and Zachary knew this, hell, everyone in the pack knew this yet he dared to come into my den?

Charlotte came up between us and kissing our chest. Tiny sparks warmed us, and Remus gently put Zachary down. He rubbed his neck to get some circulation back. Remus wrapped around Charlotte and sniffed her neck, nibbling and slightly biting it, leaving bits of blood in its wake. She didn't complain, whatever made him happy. My mate was trying too hard to win Remus over. I could still smell the fear she had when he acted like this.

As she had Remus occupied, she looked over to Zachary. "Now Zachary, what is wrong? Could you not mind-link him? You know his Wolf doesn't like surprises like this." She gave him a pointed look. Everyone in the pack knew to tread lightly right now, and here he was, barging in on an intimate moment, the dumb bastard.

"Evan tried mind-linking, but Alpha blocked us out, and this is important," Zachary breathed quickly. "The Witches, the coven, are here to discuss Josephine and her breaking of their laws." Remus slowly receded. He hated politics. He was all about the physical fight rather than a mental one. I came back to the forefront and kissed Charlotte gently on the lips.

"Thanks, Kitten. I'm alright now. How about you get ready for bed, and I'll take care of them, hmm?"

"You don't need me to help?"

"No love, I want you far away from any Witch, Vampire, or anything else supernatural until you are marked. I'll come to bed soon. I know you are tired." Just then, she let out a loud yawn. "Sleep, kitten. I'll be back." She nodded and went to the shower.

Great, now I have a terrible case of blue balls while I have to meet with some damn Witches.

I quickly changed into my black Armani suit and threw a bit of gel in my hair and combed it back. I'm going to smell like a hot tub, but that is what they get coming a few days early. Taking long strides, I find Evan in the hallway in a suit as well, and we open the double doors together and enter the conference room.

The first to stand is the coven leader, Cyrene, a very old Witch who rarely leaves her fortress' confinement. This had to be serious for her to come. No wonder Evan had Zachary came find me.

"Sorceress Cyrene, it is a pleasure to have you here," I extend my hand, and she takes it gladly.

"Alpha, it has been years. I believe the last I saw you was when your father was still in control of the pack. When did you take over?"

"About 75 years ago," I smiled. She nodded thoughtfully with a thin line across her lips.

"And you just found your Luna, only for her to be taken away. Is she alright? Did the branding bonds fade?" Cyrene grabbed my hand and put the other hand on top of mine. "Mhmm, your bond is powerful. You haven't marked her yet, have you?" Cyrene was talking a mile a minute. She was just as energetic as father had mentioned.

"Yes, she is back now, Sorceress Cyrene, the branding bonds they put on her have faded as well." I gave her a small smile, I wasn't too keen on talking about the matter because I felt I didn't protect my mate as I was meant to. Cyrene had long, straight raven hair. Even though humans think Witches to be ugly, she was far from it. Any supernatural being was beautiful in its own light.

"Well, I wish you had come to me instead of going to those Vampires, they don't know what they are talking about with those stupid branding bonds. Some bad Witches and Warlocks were the ones that first created it. Once Hecate realized what they were doing, she put a stop to it, and it has been an illegal practice for thousands of years."

Cyrene kept waving her hand around and talking in circles as her posse nodded in agreement. Men and women of her coven dressed in regular clothing but had cloaks covering them instead of jackets. Each cloak represented their rank by color. The newest practicing Witches and Warlocks had light grey, and the darker your rank, the heavier practice of the arts. Cyrene was the only one with the blackest cloak, a rank of a sorceress. It held red ribbons that tied around her neck, signifying she was the leader.

"I'm sorry we didn't come to you sooner, we thought since a Vampire was doing it that they were to blame, we weren't sure of the Witch's involvement," I stated.

"Yes, well, it is over now. I'd like to see the girl if possible. I just need her hand and nothing more. No questions, I don't want to cause her to go into a mental shock revealing what happened to her." Cyrene began walking down the hall to our bedroom before I could say anything. Everyone waited in the conference room, and I followed.

"She's sleeping right now..." I started to interject, but Cyrene quickly cut me off. "Just a hand touch, dear, nothing more. She doesn't need to know. She's in a deep sleep right now." I sighed and just let her continue. No use arguing with one of the more powerful Witches of the Earth realm.

As we approached the door, I could hear her soft breaths on the other side of the door, and I gave a faint smile. Cyrene looked up to me with a questioning look. "It isn't just the bond, you do truly love her. I can see it in our eyes," she smiled as she gently opened the door. Charlotte was cuddling up to my large pillow facing my side of the bed. She was taking large breaths into it as she faintly smiled. I touched her forehead and grabbed one of her hands so Cyrene could read her hand.

Cyrene was standing with her, and her eyes were closed. It didn't take long for her to kneel in front of Charlotte. Cyrene's lips pursed together, and her eyes held tight. It isn't often you see a Witch become emotional over someone else's life, but she seemed torn with Charlotte. Evan had his hand on my shoulder. I didn't even notice him come into the room.

Evan had become quite attached to his little Luna, everyone had really. She brought sunshine wherever she went; human or not, she was welcomed with open arms. There are many packs that question humans that come into the fold but not our pack. It was probably because we were so old and so attuned to the goddess' ways.

After a few minutes, Cyrene released Charlotte's hand and placed it gently back on the pine-scented pillow. She snuggled in and let out an audible sigh. We all smiled at how comfortable she looked. "Let's speak outside," Cyrene waved us to the door. I gave a chaste kiss to my mates' forehead and walked out.

The door closed, and Cyrene gave me a grim smile. "She's a strong one, Wesley. I hope you know that." I nodded. "She is the strongest human I've ever met."

"She will make a great Luna," Cyrene wiped a stray tear. "Charlotte's dormant Wolf will be a force to reckon with, that is for sure." Evan and I looked at her in confusion. "Oh yes, the goddess suppressed her wolf birth. Sometimes that happens when the parents are wolves for one reason or another, one cannot know the reasoning of the gods." Cyrene folded her arms across her chest. My shoulder leaned up against the wall, unable to form coherent words.

"What?" Evan finally spoke. "You mean to tell me her parents were Wolves?" Cyrene nodded sorrowfully.

"That they were, I feel it in her aura. In fact," Cyrene giggled to herself, planting her fingertips on her lips, "she is related to someone here in this pack." Cyrene muttered to herself, like talking to another person until she giggled and walked down the hall as if she told us nothing. "Wait," I rushed after her, walking by her side. "What do you mean, she is related to someone here? Are her parents here?" Cyrene stopped dead in her tracks, her head darted to me like I was crazy. "No, her parents truly are dead. This conversation is best with Charlotte here, don't you think?" Not wanting to upset the sorceress, I rubbed my face with my hand in exhaustion.

"It will all come out in time," Cyrene hummed again. "Charlotte will know when she needs to hear it."

Chapter 39
Charlotte

Wesley came to bed at 3am. He isn't the quietest person to climb into bed, which is weird because Werewolves are supposed to be stealthy. I don't know if he meant to wake me up, or he is just so large in stature it makes the mattress move involuntarily. I was so exhausted, that I just cuddled up next to him.

"Wesley," I whined. "You woke me up."

Wesley chucked so hard I felt it vibrate into his chest. "Come here, Kitten." He pulled me up on his chest and tucked my head near his neck. I nuzzled him as he does to me, and he let out a purr.

"I didn't know that Wolves could purr, you sound like a big kitty." Wesley scoffed.

"I do NOT sound like a cat, I'm a ferocious beast that has a soft spot for my sweet mate," he complained. I cuddled deeper into him, and as I was about to fall asleep, I sat up. Wesley looked at me and took his arms to put them around my waist, so I didn't fall off of him.

"What's wrong, Charlotte?"

"Where's Macaroni? I haven't seen her since I've been back?"

Macaroni likes to cuddle with me when I'm sick, I know she doesn't like hanging out with Wesley, but I think she would still come to check on his mama.

"Oh shit, baby." Wesley sat up and rubbed my face with both his hands. He cursed a few times and held me close to his bare chest. "Baby, I'm so sorry, but, Macaroni, during the fighting, she...."

Wesley didn't have to finish. I knew what had happened. Macaroni didn't make it. My cat of nine years was gone, the only family that had been through it all with me. I let out a giant sob, and Wesley pulled me in tighter and dared not to let go.

Wesley continued to pet my hair, and whisper sweet things in my ear, such as she was such a wonderful cat to take care of me, that we were family, and we would hopefully see her again someday with the Moon Goddess.

Selene protects all creatures, especially those close to the Wolves. My tears started to slow while Wesley rocked me in his chest. Wesley was precisely what I needed, my own little comfort pillow. Except he was hard and muscly, and tasty. Was he tasty? Yes, he was, I should just lick, no. I put my nose in Wesley's neck instead, and he chuckled lightly. I should be crying, but my emotions were flashing around like a strobe light. What was wrong with me?

"You know," he started. "If you decide to become a Wolf, you will have the nuzzling thing down pat." I smiled into his skin and gave him a few quick kisses. He let out a satisfied growl and pulled me away. "Don't start stuff you can't finish, baby." We smiled and gave each other another quick kiss.

"I want to be one, Wesley. I want to be like you and the rest of the pack. I can help better that way and help protect myself too, so I'm not some little kitten as you say." I scrunch my nose at the thought.

"You can be whatever you want to be. Human or Wolf, I'll love you the same, but you will always be my feisty little kitten." A few tears slid down my face, and he slid down the bed. "Now, I know you are upset, and I'm so sorry about Macaroni. We can hold a proper service for him after the party tomorrow. Sounds alright?" I nodded and yawned while falling asleep quickly on his chest.

***

The blasting of the alarm woke me up this morning. It was beeping so loud my eardrums were on the verge of exploding. I haphazardly swung my arm around to hit the thing but completely missed and threw myself from the bed. I let out a large groan, and a gust of air was by my side. "I was gone for five minutes, and you are already hurting yourself?" Wesley chuckled as he lifted me back to the bed. I pouted and kept my eyes closed despite my sore bum.

I pointed to the culprit, the stupid alarm clock. "It woke me up!" I whined and covered my head with the blankets. Wesley laughed while he pulled the sheets down and stared into my eyes. "I know you are still a weak baby, you can sleep longer. I just have to go start welcoming the guests for the party tonight. A lot of them traveled far and will be staying here for a few days." I peeked my head up and wiped my eyes.

"Oh, I will come help then." I let out a giant yawn. "Can't let my man do it all on his own, huh?" I gave him a cheesy grin. Wesley gave a quick peck on my forehead. "Go easy today, or we can't party tonight, huh? You also have a check-up at the clinic around 4, so please go to that. I won't be able to attend because of an alpha meeting." I nodded and gave an exaggerated salute. Shaking his head, he left the room.

Walking out of the bedroom, I wore the royal blue dress that Wesley got me on our first date back in town. I left the black cardigan off, no longer afraid of my scars showing, and kept my head held high. I put on light makeup with a bit of a cat-eye that I have come to love doing and some soft pink lip gloss. If I was going to be Wesley's mate and help lead the pack with him, I was going to look the part.

Taking a step at a time, I descended the stairs in the black strappy shoes that Ashley lent me that I never gave back. They made my calves look muscular, and I don't think I would give them back to her. I'm still mad at the waxing just over a month or so ago.

Wesley stood at the door, in his black pinstriped suit with a small royal blue handkerchief sitting just above the breast pocket. He was shaking hands with several Alphas, and I curved my arm around his. He quickly looked down at me and gave me the biggest smile.

"Alpha Rowan and Luna Candice, this is my mate, Charlotte." Both Alpha and Luna bowed their heads slightly, and I did the same. "It is a pleasure to meet you, Charlotte! You have been through so much in such a short amount of time. I'm surprised you are still able to greet everyone," Luna Candice said with kindness.

"To be honest, I think I'm running on the mate bond and adrenaline." I giggled. Wesley pulled me closer and gave me a kiss on the cheek. "We will let you know when the Luna ceremony will take place. We are just trying to let her heal after the whole branding and kidnapping ordeal," Wesley squeezed me tightly.

"Take your time, Alpha Hale. She's a lovely girl that deserves to be courted like a human should be." He gave a smile, and an omega sent them off to their rooms. Three sets of Alpha and Lunas stayed in the packhouse while all the unmated wolves stayed in a dormitory on the territory a mile or so away. They were welcome for breakfast, lunch, and dinner would be served during the Halloween Ball while people searched for mates. Everyone was invited, mated or not, but the main goal was finding mates.

Wesley and I moved outside, along with Evan and Bruce. Wolves were directing cars to the training field so people could park their cars and small buses. This party was going to be huge, and it became overwhelming. Wesley never left my side, his hand always on the small of my back. We had been out for about an hour, and I began to feel hot, even though some snowflakes had started to fall.

"Kitten, are you alright? You feel hot?" Wesley's face was laced with concern, and Evan and Bruce came by to check on me. My body just felt warm, uncomfortably warm when it was so cold out.

"Yes, I'm just a bit hot. I'm exhausted too. Maybe I've just done too much. Do you mind if I rest for a few hours before the party?"

Looking up at Wesley, I saw his face contemplating. "Don't worry, I'm really fine. I think I'm just still recovering, you know?" Wesley nodded, "I'll walk back with you."

Forgetting the doctor's appointment, Wesley started walking me back to our room. Along the way, I got several stares from some visiting wolves. They were looking at me up and down, maybe assessing who I was. They would then look at Wesley and look away. Brushing it off, Wesley opened our bedroom door and led me to the bed. "I'll have Ashley get you ready for the party kitten. Please stay and rest until then. I'll be in several meetings until the party." I nodded and didn't even bother changing my clothes, flopping on the bed in exhaustion.

***

I slept a full 6 hours until Ashley came to get me ready. "Charlotte, are you sure you are alright? You haven't moved a muscle since I checked on you a few hours ago?"

"I'm fine. I was just so tired. I feel a lot better now, though, not as hot as I was." I started stripping not caring if Ashely saw me naked, and headed to the shower. Instead of the nice hot water I usually craved in the steam shower, I turned it cold. Ice cold. It was so soothing on my burning skin. However, the heat on my skin still didn't waver.

Ashley walked in without a care in the world and saw me stark naked on the other side of the glass shower. "Charlotte Crawford, you have been in here 20 minutes, get out or we will be late!" I let out an irritated sigh.

"Don't wanna." I huffed. The cold water felt too good.

"Wesley was right. You have been terribly whiny lately. What is up with you?" She laughed at me. "Do I need to go get Wesley to set you in your place?" My lip wobbled. Why in the heck was I so emotional right now? I might be getting ready to start my period. Great, add another thing to cry over.

"Where is he? He didn't come to check on me all day. He didn't even come to cuddle with me," I stepped out of the shower and wrapped myself with a towel. Ashley came over to put her hand on my shoulder, but I winced as she touched me. "He's been swamped setting up for this ball tonight. You are usually more understanding. Are you sick? Oh gah, are you PMSing right now?"

"I'll get dressed, Ashley. Go be with Beau," I snapped.

"Charlie, what the hell? What is wrong?" Ashley demanded while placing her hands on her hips.

"I don't know. I just need some time alone. Thanks for the outfit. I'll take care of everything Okay? I'm sorry, I'm just not in a social mood right now." I sniffed and sat down on the vanity chair in the bathroom.

"If that is how you feel, I'll leave, Okay? The ball starts at eight." Ashley's voice went quiet, but I just couldn't stand to be around anyone. My body hurt, my head hurt, and I felt hot all over. My emotions and body were all over the place, and it was getting worse by the second. I also wanted Wesley, I wanted him all to myself, but unfortunately, he was busy with everyone else. I folded my arms and put my head on my arms as I cried silently for a few minutes.

Wesley

"So that is all we know? This Josephine? A rogue witch that embraced her dark magic and lost every bit of herself to it? Is that normal?" I asked inquisitively.

"Right, she did lose herself, and it isn't normal. She was a twin. Her twin was born with light magic from a witch, while she took the dark magic of a demon. With either magic, you are expected to conquer it before it conquers you, such as werewolves with their wolves. She decided not to fight it and embraced the dark. I traveled to Bergarian to work with her, but she let the darkness win out in her. There is no hope for her return. She needs to be destroyed. Josephine has caused too many disturbances in both realms." Cyrene rubbed her temples. "I've even prayed to the god Hecate, there is just no hope for her. Hades is prepared to have her locked in a chamber of solitude for the rest of eternity. She has caused too much pain for too many people."

The Alphas in the meeting all nodded in agreement. "We will have to set up something in the future to trap Josephine, get her while she is in her element and is trying to strike a deal. She's living in the human world now, so her powers aren't as strong and needs money to survive. Maybe we need to offer up some money and trick her into coming out. All of Bergarian has a bounty on her head. Now the Earth realm will too." Writing down the plan of action, everyone discussed amongst themselves what they could do to protect their own territories against the witch.

"Alright, tomorrow we will sit down and come up with some ideas, we've run out of time, and I'm sure everyone and their mates are wondering where we are at." Everyone let out a laugh and excited the conference room to look for their mates excitedly.

I swiftly walked to my office to check for messages from the businesses back in the city when I saw 10 missed calls and 5 text messages from Charlotte. My heart sank as I began to read them as I walked to our room. Fuck, she is going to be mad.

Charlotte: Where are you?
Charlotte: I really need you right now.
Charlotte: Something is wrong, and I can't find you.
Charlotte: Babe please answer.

I whispered "fuck," and sprinted down to our room, which she wasn't in. The room smelled completely of her and something else. It smelled ambrosial, sweet, and luscious, a smell I'd never encountered with her before. It was still mixed with her own alluring scent.

"Alpha," Ashley mind-linked me.

"What? Where is Charlotte? I can't find her?"

"Alpha, get to the ballroom quick. I think we have a problem," she rushed her words.

"What the hell is it? I'm coming," I growled in frustration.

"Charlie, I think she is in heat!" Ashley shrieked.

Without another word, I ran down to the ballroom and pushed people aside. A large group of animated wolves were in the middle of the room, with Ashley by Charlotte's side. Ashley was trying to pull her from the group, but the unmated wolves didn't want to leave. Several of them tried to fight while others tried to hold her hand, but she would squeal out in pain as they did so, causing them to coo and offer her drinks or dances.

Her back was to me the entire time, and she was wearing one of Ashley's old costumes since we couldn't get her The Greatest Showman one. It was a black leather dress with a low back and a black tail. She was wearing cat ears, and her hair was curled at the ends. Her arms were also covered in black elbow-high gloves, but even though the gloves, she winced at everyone's touch.

As I came closer, she stilled and turned around to meet my eyes. The look of shock and adoration filled her face. The longing she had as she raced up to me and held onto me gave me the warmth I didn't know was missing. Thank Goddess, she wasn't mad at me for missing those damn calls and texts. Her scent, though, became overpowering. It was intense and enticing. It made me lick my lips, and my dick became hard as steel. Holy shit, that was damn fast. Charlotte's lips were plump, ready for me to suck on, and I swear her breasts grew a size or two. She was ravishing, and everything was enhanced. Charlotte then gazed up into my eyes, and her eyes went from love straight to lust. Her eyes darkened as she grabbed me tighter.

"Wesley, I don't know what is wrong with me. All I know is that I want you, and I feel hot all over. Only your touch is making it better. Please help me," she whispered. "I want you to do ungodly things to me," she put both hands on my face. Oh shit, my day has come to make her mine!

The unmated males trailed closer, and I let out a warning growl. Many cowered away hearing my Alpha voice while some stood still looking at Charlotte.

Charlotte's suppressed wolf, could it be rising? That's unheard of unless it is released by a mates' bite. She couldn't possibly be in heat, but all the signs were there. Hot to the touch, the smell, the want, knowing I'm her mate and my touch only helps her. Shit, how did this happen? I pulled her close to me, and Cyrene tapped me on the shoulder. "You both have waited too long to mate, so now the Goddess put it in her own hands. Better get out of here," she laughed while downing her wine.

I swiftly picked up my mate and nodded to Evan to let him know of our absence. He was now laughing his ass off. "Have fun, Daddy!!!!" He screamed while some of the other Alphas joined in the fun, cheering and clinking their glasses.

Vera Foxx

Chapter 40

Charlotte

Wesley picked me up with one arm under my legs and the other behind my back. I buried my head deep into his chest. I was so embarrassed. If this really is my heat as Ashley had said, everyone could smell me! My face felt hot, my entire body was a furnace, and I could almost feel the sweat dripping down my face. The worst part was the ache between my legs. It was wanting something, needing something to take care of it. I wanted to reach down and relieve it.

Without any hesitation, Wesley locked the door to our room and put me on the bed gently. His eyes were dark, and he recklessly pulled off his suit jacket and shirt, popping buttons and ripping fabric. Damn, that was highly sexy, ripping such an expensive suit for my benefit. My breathing quickened, and I lusted after his body more than I ever had before. His torso was now bare. His abs and his deep V line made me shutter as I watched tattoos disappear into his pants.

I've never thought tattoos to be attractive in the past, but they most certainly were on him. His heavy breathing made his chest muscles rise and fall while he clenched his fists, causing his biceps to bulge. My breathing hitched as we continued to stare at each other.

"What's wrong with me? Why do I feel like this? I-I don't know what to do to make it go away." I whimpered.

"Kitten, you are in heat and…" He crawled up on the bed like a predator. His pants were still on, and I wanted nothing more than for him to take them off.

"But I'm not a Wolf," I argued.

"You are mated to one, love, and we have waited too long for me to mark you," his breath was raspy as he said the word mark. I felt the tingle go all the way to my toes and gave a small moan. "I can make it better, only if you want. It is just our bodies wanting to complete the bond."

I didn't hesitate. "I want to, goddess, please take me, Wesley." Wesley's quick reflexes had his mouth on mine as we sucked and nibbled on each other's lips. His hands roamed my body and ripped the leather dress from me with his extended claws. I fumbled with his belt, and we both took the rest of our clothes off quickly like we lacked the time. We certainly did not.

Wesley went to my breasts that were never held in by a bra and ripped off the nipple pasties I had on. "Damn, wear those more often. That is hot as hell," he rasped. While one nipple in his mouth, the other was in his hand, kneading it, pulling, and flicking. I rubbed my thighs together and received mini orgasm right there. The hotness of my body left me briefly, only to soar again. My hands went through his hair, tugging and pulling his golden locks, and elected a large growl from him. "I need to taste your Kitten. Your arousal is so tempting."

In no time, his face was buried deep in my pussy. His tongue fucked me relentlessly, and I fell apart. Once he started sucking on my clit and finger fucking me with his majestic fingers, I lost my sight. I arched my back and gripped his hair so he wouldn't escape me, not that he would have left my core. I rode his face with a passion as he grabbed my ass and pulled me deeper into his mouth. Letting out a scream of ecstasy, I felt the heat leave my skin for a moment.

Wesley came up from my pussy, glistening in my juices as he licked himself clean. I could have sworn his Wolf's tongue came into play. It made me shiver. His mouth met mine again, tasting myself on his lips. He kissed with love, not lust. I kissed him back sweetly and longingly as our tongues danced together.

The heat and fire in my belly began to ignite again, and I let out a small whimper. "Baby, I'm going to make love to you, if you are Okay with that?" His voice was soft and hopeful. I nodded excitedly and kissed him softly back. "Please," I whispered. "Take me." He kissed my neck and lined himself at my entrance. My legs trembled in anticipation of his shaft finally connecting into my wet cavern, completing us as one.

He inched in, inch by inch, completely filling me until we both felt the barrier. "Kitten, it might hurt," he whispered with a look of concern. "It hurts me more that you aren't moving," I smirked at him while he smashed his lips into mine as he thrust forward. A quick yelp from me and his continuous movements made it all the better. It was a good feeling, warm and thick. I had never felt so full and wanted in my life.

Wesley continued his assault on my pussy. I felt him moving in slightly different positions causing me to moan until he hit a better spot than the rest. "Oh my, Wesley! Right there!" I gripped his biceps, almost drawing blood from how good it felt. He let out a loud growl of satisfaction as he pushed into me harder. I arched my back and threw my legs around his waist, feeling the high I was climbing. Stars erupted in my vision and moaned his name over and over.

"Wesley, oh, that feels amazing." My eyes continued to roll back in my head.

"I'm not done yet, Kitten. Fuck! You keep getting tighter!" I didn't realize I was squeezing so hard. I didn't want to let him go. Wesley pulled out, and I whimpered at the loss of his body. He gave me his signature smirk and flipped me over on my knees with my ass sticking out.

"I've dreamt of this night, Kitten. I've wanted to bend you over with your bewitching ass looking at me as I pound your wet pussy. I want to see my cock disappear." With one quick thrust, I felt complete in other places inside my body. It is in all the right places. I felt every ridge of his giant cock. He hit my cervix with such eagerness it made me scream his name.

"Yes, scream my name, Kitten." His breath became ragged, and his thrusts became erratic. He was getting close, and so was I.

"Ohhhhhh Alpha!" I moaned as I started to reach my high. He gripped my hips harder. I knew he was going to leave marks. "I want you to cum for me, baby, cum all over my cock with your sweetness." I took a slow breath and screamed, "Ahhh!"

Wesley grabbed me and kneaded my breasts as I continued to cum all over his cock. This was animalistic, and I craved every bit of it. My fingers dug into the sheets, pulling them tightly. Wesley grunted several times and pulled out. I whined again, knowing he wasn't finished. "Noo," I complained while he chuckled at me. "I'm not done yet, Kitten." He roughly flipped me back over. How long can this man last? He's flipping me like a pancake.

He thrust into me one more time and pulled my legs over his shoulders. He was relentless. He pounded me harder and harder. The wetness of our skin echoing into the room. Wesley's eyes began to change like dark embers. Remus was present. "Remus mark mate?" he said gruffly.

"Mark me, Remus, make me yours," I moaned as he continued to thrust. Remus growled in appreciation as I turned my head to the side and I took my hand, tickling my marking spot.

"Shit, mate, ugh, I want it," he demanded in my ear. Throwing my legs down and two more thrusts in, I clenched him from the inside as he finally bit down hard on my neck. The pain was intense but quickly turned euphoric. He released inside me at the same time and let out a satisfied sigh. His cum felt so warm as he filled me to the brim.

For the first time, I felt no pain, no hot sensation all over my body. It was cool and refreshing. I tried to stay awake, but my eyelids continued to shut all on their own. Wesley's teeth retracted and licked and sucked my bite. "Sleep, Kitten. The mark will make you tired for now, but your heat won't be over. Sleep while you can, my love." I hummed in acknowledgment closing my eyes.

Wesley

My love was lying in bed, naked against my chest. Her breathing was long and deep while she lay on her side. I had the perfect view of my mark on her porcelain body. Soon it would heal, and the imprints of my teeth would forever keep her safe from any unmated males.

The goddess always has plans that none of us are aware of. With her Wolf deep inside her awaiting for my mark, maybe it had had enough. Whatever it was, I was happy. Happy to have her in my arms, wolf or no wolf.

I loved the neediness she started to have the past few days. That was more of the bond she could feel. Humans can't feel it as much until they are bitten, but our bond was strong even before I bit her. It really must have been her suppressed wolf.

Charlotte's body has started to heat up again, her body has been squirming against my hold. Her heat is already starting to come back. I will never tire of her heat. She is a damn goddess in bed and took me so well for only being a virgin. I'm just glad she expressed her wanting to mate before all of this started. Otherwise, we both would have had a terrible time not doing anything with each other.

"W-Wesley?" She whines as she cuddles closer.

"Yes, kitten, what do you need?

"I really need you," she snuggles in deeper while her hand trails down my naked body. Fuck, I'm already hard and can smell her already.

"Take me please..." she gave me the best pout I had ever seen. Typically, when girls pout, I find it repulsive, but I just want to suck it off her bottom lip sticking out.

I smashed my lips to hers while she fought back. Her hands went through my hair and pulled on them tightly. She pushed me over to where she was on top, which surprised me. My Kitten wasn't the dominant type, maybe this heat was a good thing to experiment with. "I just want you..." she grabbed my angry, throbbing dick and put it at her entrance, "in here." She lowered herself on me and threw her head back, and I gripped her waist. My mate started grinding into me while I yelled a whole new set of curses. Her passage was electrifying, I felt tingles from my cock down to my toes as her body clenched me harder, trying to milk me.

"Do you like that, Puppy?" Charlotte said seductively. Remus forcing to come forward. Though, of course, the bastard managed to push through.

"Remus, not puppy," he growled out as he gripped her hard. "Remus, a beast!" He roared as he flipped us all over mid-air and then had her on all fours. Remus puffed out his chest and rumbled a growl of satisfaction as he pounded into her. She tilted her ass up and gave it a wiggle to entice him more. She began moaning. "Mate is our love toy, right mate?"

"Yes, yours," she whined. "Only Wesley and Remus can have me," she panted. Her breaths were shallow as her cum-drenched our cock, causing it to twitch in excitement.

"Come in me, please. I want to feel more," Charlotte moaned. She really did become my wanting tiny human. Remus had his hold on her. His chest was up to her back, using her breasts as leverage as he continued to force our cock inside. Remus growled, and we finally filled her wet cavern. Remus fell into the back of my mind, and Charlotte was face-first into the pillow. We were soaked in each other's sweat. She was breathing hard and smiling.

"I feel so much better," she said in a whisper.

"I never knew I had such a little minx. Damn." I said, rolling over.

"Come here." Charlotte crawled seductively over to me and laid her head on my chest while tangling our legs together.

"Are all heats like this?" She breathed.

"Oh yes, at least 3 times a year."

"Mmm sounds good to me," she said as she fell asleep for a second time.

Chapter 41

Wesley

After a many more rounds through the night, Charlotte started to stir around 8 a.m. I had a hard time sleeping. I was running on adrenaline, and Remus couldn't get enough of her. He acted like he was more in heat than her. I let him out so he could cuddle and lick and suck her mark as she slept, helping her into a deeper sleep so she could rest. Her body had to be sore from all the sex we had been having. It was her first damn time. I don't know if we could go again until we had both rehydrated.

I mind-linked several omegas to leave a breakfast cart outside our door with plenty of drinks and food. Due to Charlotte's heat, all unmated males had to be escorted out of the house and sleep in dormitories for the guests. From now on, I'll be able to expect her heat that we are officially bonded. I'll be sure to take her on vacation away from the packhouse, so we don't have to disturb the rest of the pack members.

Charlotte stirred again, and I heard the slight knock at the door, letting me know that the cart was there. Untangling myself from her arms was a feat in itself. She craved my warmth to keep her heat at bay. Staying as close to your mate as possible helped ease the pain, even after so much lovemaking.

I pulled the cart in and made Charlotte a plate. She sat up in bed and whined. My tiny mate was so endearing when she wanted me so much. Remus pawed my head to hurry up and take care of our mate. "How are you feeling, kitten?" I put a plate in front of her. Her hair was messy, her lips were swollen, and hickies and love marks were ridden all over her body. It was sexy as hell, and it was taking everything I had not to bend her over now and

239

take her again to leave more. Like I asked myself before, who is really in heat here?

"A bit sore," she said shyly. "But overall, I'm Okay. The heat is still there but not as bad as it was yesterday." She smiled at me and touched her mark that made her shiver. Giving her a quick kiss, I helped feed her breakfast while she sat up in bed.

"It will get better. Last night was the worst, but today and tomorrow won't be as bad. Just know that you can't leave this room. I can't have anyone smelling that intoxicating scent of yours." Charlotte blushed scarlet and looked down at her plate.

"Careful now," I lifted her chin," I might want you before the next wave of heat," I smiled at her. She giggled and swatted my hand.

After breakfast, we put everything back on the cart and set it outside the door. We were both still naked and headed to the shower. I turned it on, letting the steam heat up the shower. "Let's clean up a bit, hum?" She nodded, and her eyes looked me up and down. Even though she hasn't been marked with my venom to turn her into a Wolf yet, I could see the lust in her eyes. "Feeling alright, Kitten?" I taunted her. She hummed a little, and her arms wrapped around my wet torso. The water was falling into our hair. The soap gave our bodies a slippery feel as I felt her breasts rub up and down my torso.

"Babe, you are huge," Charlotte purred as Remus growled and puffed out his chest in my head. He was happy he could please his mate. Charlotte grabbed my dick and rubbed her thumb on top to spread the precum already oozing from me. Groaning, I swiftly picked her up and placed her pussy in front of my face. Her legs were wrapped around my head, and I pushed her body against the wall.

The cold wall startled her as I buried my face into her. Her hands went straight for my long hair and pulled and pushed into it, giving her the pressure she wanted from my lips. "Wesley, oh right there," she moaned. Her hands dropped to my shoulders, gripping them tightly, almost drawing blood. The pain mixed with her pleasure had me fisting my cock with my free hand.

Her back arched as she climaxed on my face, and I swear to Goddess, she squirts into my mouth. It was a fountain of her cum, and I squeezed both sides of her ass as she finished. "Please, Wesley, let me taste you." She didn't have to tell me twice. I lowered her to the ground, and she quickly got on her knees and sucked hard on my balls.

I grabbed the back of her head. "Shit, baby," I rolled my head back, grinding into her mouth. I could see her free hand rubbing her clit, and it started to drive me wild with her pleasuring herself while sucking on me. She moved up to my cock and swirled her tongue around it like a candied sucker and took my whole 9 inches into her mouth. She gagged but fervently tried to stuff it down her throat. Goddess, she took the whole damn thing. Sucking and pulling on it with her mouth, she was trying to milk me dry.

I wanted to let go, but more than anything, I wanted to fuck her against the glass wall of the shower so I could watch from the mirror of her ass smacked up against it. I pulled her from me as she whined and lifted her up. Her legs gripped my waist, and with no warning, I entered her. My head was on her shoulder so I could watch her get fucked in the reflection. Her body was pressed against the class moving up and down, and her skin became red as I forced my cock into her. "Wesley, more." Her nails scratched my back, and her hips began to meet mine as she bucked harder.

I took her out of the shower and had her bend over with her arms on the sink. Her breasts rested on the cold counter, and I started pounding her from behind. I could see her face making the most pleasurable movements as I continued to push into her. My dick would go in her pussy and come out only to excite Remus more. He took over and became rough. His nails clawed one side of her hip with the other squeezing her tits.

Charlotte saw my eyes change and smiled. "Puppy, harder," she smirked. She was taunting my Wolf, and it made me chuckle. My feisty little kitten.

Remus growled at the name and went at Werewolf speed, bucking up against her. He growled as he watched Charlotte fall apart at the pleasurable movements. "Remus, I'm going to..." and she released. She came all over our cock, she was half passed out, but Remus wasn't through. He pulled out and laid her on the bathroom floor on the fluffy carpet. Pulling both legs over his shoulders, he got on his knees and lifted her up. Up and down, side to side, he tried to touch every part of the inside of her body. Her body was shaking, "Remus, I-I-I can't!"

"You will, Remus, not puppy," he growled. With a few more thrusts, we all exploded onto each other. There was so much fluid, it had nowhere to go but out. It was everywhere. Charlotte was panting, almost shaking from the aftershocks of our escapades. Remus gave me control again, and I pulled Charlotte up to rinse her off once more in the shower. Her body was limp in my arms, her head rolling side to side as I held her close.

We both were both wrapped in towels the bed had already been cleaned and made by the female omegas while we were in the shower. Lucky for Werewolves, this was a common occurrence, so there was no shame in any of this. I'm sure Charlotte would have something to say if I told her.

Charlotte held onto me and wouldn't let go. I smiled at her, and we held each other while we still had our towels on our bodies. Her body was still shaking, and she began to cry. "Baby, what's wrong?" I asked worriedly.

"I don't know, I just started crying. I'm not sure?" I buried my nose into her mark.

"It's alright, you just have a lot of emotions going on, and so many orgasms probably have your hormones all over the place. I'm here. I won't leave." She smiled and cuddled up next to me while I pat her hair. "Just sleep or try to. I'm here, and I won't leave. I know this has been intense for you, but you are doing so well." I continued to whisper sweet nothings into her ear as she slowly fell back asleep.

Charlotte

Two more days of hiding out in our room until I finally was over my heat. I needed a vacation from the vacation we had in this room. The room seriously needed some fresh air, so I opened up all the windows and patted down all the pillows and put away our clothes that had been thrown all over the floor. I was not about to have people come in and clean up after us—especially not when everyone knew what had happened.

Wesley finally left to go work in his office, and I told him I would spend time ordering new cameras for the pack territory lines. Now that I know there are Witches, I needed to find cameras with built-in surge protectors or automatic cut-off switches when dealing with extensive power outages. That way, we didn't have to buy new cameras each time some Witch wanted to blow something up.

After walking into the security room, you could feel the staleness in the air. No one had been in there since my kidnapping a few a week ago. All the giant screens were off, and computers were shut down. My goal for today was shopping with a black card that Wesley got me. I didn't feel comfortable using it, but hey, it was for the pack, so I shouldn't feel too terrible.

I was engrossed in this one website with special ops cameras that could slide on a guidewire when I felt something warm fanning my neck. I jumped up in surprise only to see Zachary grinning at me with his fangs hanging out. "ZACHARY!" I squealed.

"Charlotte!" he replied in his best impression of my voice. I chucked a pen at him and laughed.

"So how is the new Luna fairing today? Finally, leave the bedroom?" My cheeks burned red as I smiled.

"Yes, I guess so," I whispered.

"Aw, still so shy," He put his finger under my chin to make me look him in the eye.

"Yes now, leave me alone," I laughed while shoving him away.

"You know, the walls of this place are soundproof, but did you know that the floors aren't?" I pulled my head out of the computer screen and glared at him. Zachary's room was right under Alpha's bedroom. My heart stopped as I came to realize.

"Oh, Alpha! More Alpha!" Zachary mocked as I squealed, holding my ears to my head. "Remus, Puppy!" He let out his high-pitched girly squeal. "I'm not a puppy, I'm a BEAST!" Zachary's low scary voice came in mocking.

He started laughing and was on the floor. His eyes were full of tears as I ran to the couch and started throwing pillows at him.

"I HATE YOU, ZACHARY!" I screamed at him. Ashley ran into the room with her claws out.

"What the hell?" Ashley saw Zachary rolling on the floor, laughing and pointing. She smirked while she walked up to me. She dusted off my shoulder, her lips came close.

"Puppy?" she whispered in my ear, and I tackled her to the ground in an attempt to strangle her. They were both laughing, squealing, and using the words 'Alpha' and 'puppy," and many pack members began looking in from outside the door.

"Kitten? What's wrong?!" I heard a voice in my head. I stopped and looked around and put both my hands on my ears.

"OH MY GOSH, I CAN HEAR THINGS IN MY HEAD!" I screamed, and Zachary and Ashley started laughing more.

"Kitten, it's me. We can mind-link now," Wesley's voice rang through my head.

"I thought that wasn't until I became a Wolf?" I spoke aloud, not knowing how to talk back.

Wesley walked in the door while several pack members were laughing at all of us on the floor. Pillows had been thrown, the cushions on the couch was a mess. Ashley and Zachary were still laughing and snickering while I sat in the middle, hugging a pillow to my chest. Wesley cleared his throat, and everyone stilled. The pack members outside of the door watching started to disperse, and I ran up to Wesley, who engulfed me in a giant hug.

"What's wrong kitten, I could sense your distress through our bond."

"You can?" I looked up at him.

"Yeah, you were embarrassed and upset, and it was strong. What happened." Wesley turned to both Ashley and Zachary, who took a few steps back with smirks on their faces.

"T-they heard us!" I whispered. "Like... through the floor under our room!" My face flushed with embarrassment, and I buried my face more into his dress shirt. Wesley looked up at them and scowled.

"You think it is funny to make fun of your Luna?" he growled. "I know you are all close friends, but there is a point of crossing the line, and you've crossed it. Friends don't do that." Both of them hung their heads. I felt sorry for them, but it was utterly embarrassing. I couldn't help it when I was in heat. Now, I will be all shy again and not have the confidence anymore.

"Stop stressing, love. They were being jerks. They know heat brings out the animal in both of us," he mind-linked me.

"But I'm human, though," I fisted his shirt. "I shouldn't have acted like that."

Wesley's scowl became hard, and he looked at both Zachary and Ashley. "Both of you, triple patrol duty starting now. Get out of my sight and learn

243

how to respect others, especially your Luna. I'm disappointed in your actions towards one of your friends. You know how sensitive she is about this sort of thing. She isn't like other Wolves. That's why I love her. She isn't some slut that enjoys letting people know her sexuality. She's private, and you have ruined her trust in you."

Could I love this man any more than I already did? Probably. He said exactly what I was thinking.

"I think it is the most intoxicating thing when you scream profanities and dirty things to me. I'm already getting hard," Wesley linked me. I blushed more.

Both of them left the room, and I was still in Wesley's arms. "Thank you," I buried my face into his chest. "I know you were trying to stay strong, and you are." He kissed the top of my head. "You are Luna now. You can use your Luna command now, you know?" I looked at him questioningly. *What the heck is a Luna command?*

"This whole bite thing," I waved my hand around to my neck, "you need to explain some stuff because I thought you claimed me not gaining cool telepathic talking powers and yelling at people to listen to me."

Wesley smiled and nuzzled me with his nose. "You know, you are right," I keep forgetting how pure you are and not just wanting a Luna title and just wanting to be with me."

"All I ever wanted was you, Wesley."

Chapter 42

Charlotte

After an eventful morning of Zachary and Ashley getting in trouble, which they deserved! Wesley decided for us to have a late lunch out at the gazebo. It wasn't overly huge, but enough for a round table and several chairs to sit around for a nice women's book club. If Werewolves were in that sort of thing.

The white linens danced in the breeze. Wesley mentioned that the pink lemonade was already set out as our lunch was currently being made, which was a surprise for me. He took my arm in the crook of his and led me out in the slightly chilly air. For an odd reason, the air warmed up after our heavy snow only the week before, and most of it had melted. Ashley liked to call it the "fake winter," before the "maybe real winter," followed by the "yes, this is in fact winter." Wesley noticed my chill and quickly gave me the plaid pullover he had put on previously.

I looked up at him, wondering if he would be cold too, but he just replied, "Werewolf kitten, I don't get cold that easily." He smiled at me and patted my hand. Wesley was such a gentleman I couldn't help but feel the extra flutter in my heart. Wesley let out a chuckle as he pulled my seat out for me so I could sit. "You know I can feel your giddiness when you are around me?" he chided.

"Did the big Alpha say the word, 'giddy,'" I laughed. His boisterous laugh caught the attention of people passing by, and he only smiled and waved while we began to eat our warm pumpkin soup for lunch. We ate in comfortable silence as pack members continued to walk by. The pups were out of school for their fall break and continued to throw leaves at each other.

Once I had my fill, I looked up to see Wesley staring at me with both his elbows on the table and his chin resting on his hands. "What?" I laughed. "Do I have soup on my face?"

"No, my love. I just didn't think it was possible." I tiled my head and looked at him. "Possible for me to fall in love with you more each day." It made me laugh, he was so cheesy, but I liked the extra cheese. His hair swayed in the breeze, and he held out his hand for me to come around the table. He sat me on his lap while I continued to blush into his hair as he smelled my neck. A few giggles and smiles left our lips.

"You know, I think this lunch date was for me to figure out a few things about this love bite you gave me." I traced my nose up his jawline as we rubbed noses together, our favorite thing to do. He sighed. "You're right, but you make it so hard to stay on track."

"What if I reward you?" I traced my finger down his torso, "If you can answer all my questions..." A low growl came from his chest, and I bit my lip and clenched my thighs together tightly.

"Is that a promise?" His voice became dark as I saw his eyes flicker from Remus to Wesley.

"Definitely," I whispered seductively in his ear. Wesley put his hand up to cup my face. "Damn, how did I get so lucky?" He pecked my lips with his, gently massaging them. He parted my lips with his tongue and stroked his with mine. A small moan left me, and I pushed him back while he grunted in disappointment.

Wesley smiled at me and began to tell me what I exactly signed up for without even telling me. Lunas were the Alphas' other halves, they keep the Alpha in line and are very important to the pack. The Alpha holds the pack's strength and keeps Wolves in line and protects the community or pack as a whole. They delegate jobs and train warriors along with their Beta and Gamma. Along with that job, the mate of the Alpha is called the Luna. She can help control the beast or Wolf inside the Alphas. Alphas are known for their brutality when they are not obeyed, and sometimes they can lose control.

With a Luna, the Alpha Wolf can become calmed with even just a touch from their mate. Wesley has been known to be one of the calmer Alphas in the area. He would often go during peace treaty meetings of other packs to become a mediator if a fight broke out. Wesley had a great relationship with his Wolf, Remus; however, the years were starting to wear on him. He was having trouble controlling him, but Wesley said the Moon Goddess put me in his life at the perfect time, even if he had to wait 145 years.

Lunas are motherly and try to take care of everyone's needs, such as helping pregnant women and making sure their mates take care of them. The children are naturally drawn to the Luna as she is a mother figure to the pack. I found myself thinking of the small preschool for the little pups while pack members helped around the pack during daylight hours. My mind often wandered to the little one that cried so much. I wondered how he was doing. They say the poor thing actually was abandoned, and members take turns caring for him. The few times I had free time, I would go and see him, and he would just smile and coo at me. It gave me such a warm feeling, even though I never thought I would have children of my own. That's what happens when you fear for your life every day; you never see a bright future coming out of it.

With the help of a party planner, Lunas help plan mating balls, Alpha meetings, and holiday parties. It was mainly an organizing job because everyone in the pack pitches in to help one another. If only other humans did this. Growing up as one, I noticed how many are more self-absorbed in helping themselves, few helped but not as many and as dedicated as the Werewolf community.

Over the last month and a half, I have learned so much about this pack. Even though the name Black Claw was a bit scary and worrisome at first. It was created so many years ago when it was a small pack of fifty Wolves. They wanted to instill fear so no one would attack while their pack grew.

After hearing a bit of history and all the jobs Luna has to do, I started to get irritated. "So, I am a glorified secretary, huh?" I gave him a disapproving look. We had moved from the gazebo to the swinging bench on the porch. We were both wrapped up in a giant fuzzy blanket, sipping hot cocoa since the air started to turn cool. He wrapped me tighter and started grazing my ear with his nose.

"Well, I could get a secretary if you want, but…."

I thought for a moment of some slutty she-Wolf sitting on his desk with a barely-there skirt and quickly changed my mind. "Nope! Never mind! Only I can be the slutty secretary!"

Wesley wrapped me impossibly tighter in the fuzzy white blanket and kissed me sweetly. Small quick pecks turned into a full-blown make-out session. I pushed back, and he groaned again. "More questions?" he whined. His hand started to roam my body. I'm also beginning to think that a Luna has to please her Alpha's sexual appetite. Not that I really minded, especially since it was Wesley.

"You just assume I know things, I need to know things. I don't want to look like an idiot! I may have graduated early from a university, but they didn't have werewolf classes."

"How did you do that?" Wesley's hand traced my face.

"Do what?" I asked.

"Graduate early, when I did a background check on you there was hardly any information about you. I couldn't even find what high school or college you graduated from," Wesley said exasperated.

"Oh, that was easy. I created an alternate identity on the computer. I graduated high school, college and masters with an alternate name. Getting scholarships would be a bit difficult to receive money to a non-existent person but sending money in wasn't exactly a problem." I laughed. "Now tell me, oh wise Alpha about werewolf stuff."

"Alright, alright. I guess I should tell you that Beta Evan's mate, Jenny, also helps out Luna, she is like your personal secretary. She's been doing most of the Luna duties for a while. Evan likes to keep her locked up though, he wears her out, and he wants her well-rested. She is kind of reclusive anyways.

"Wears her out?" I questioned.

"Yeah, remember back to your first breakfast here with us, and Evan said his favorite thing to do on the property was to fu–" I smacked Wesley before he could say another word.

"Okay! I get it!" I blushed like a candy-red apple. Wesley began laughing and covered us with the blanket. While we were huddled in our little blanket cave, he began kissing my neck. After several attempts to get him to tell me more, I figured I would just wing it and ask Jenny. I can't keep the man's hands off me!

Wesley

I know I was supposed to talk to Charlotte about what it is like to be a Luna, but hell, I didn't want to share her for a couple months. Jenny and Ashley were doing just fine taking care of things, and Charlotte had even helped out with the last event

Right now, being under this blanket, having her wrapped around me, was the hottest position I have ever been in. We were outside, with people walking around nearby, and I touched her in all the right places making her squeal and giggle. "You give me such butterflies," she said in a whisper as she straddled me in my lap. My dick was already painfully hard as we sat there together, wrapped up.

"Hell, forget the butterflies," I said. "I feel the whole damn zoo when I'm with you." Charlotte laughed loudly, and I picked her up, I was going to carry her upstairs.

"What are you doing!? We aren't done with our meeting!" She yipped as I pinched her ass.

"I know, we are just going to finish it upstairs. The thought of me having your legs shaking and having the next pack over knowing my name by you screaming makes Remus a bit irritated." Charlotte gasps and slaps me on the shoulder playfully.

"You have such a dirty mouth!"

"And you are nothing short of insatiable!"

I kept Charlotte wrapped in our fluffy blanket and burst through the kitchen doors, and walked past Ashley and Zachary, who stared at us as they got their bottle of water before their 3rd shift. "Get her done, Alpha!" Zachary howled while Ashley slapped him. Charlotte just laughed as she started to unbuckle my pants under the blanket.

"What are you doing, Luna?" I growled in her ear.

"Just a little misbehaving," she said, like a siren. She kept my pants held up but started to put her hand down to my cock. I grunted at her warm touch.

"If you don't stop, I'll take you on the living room couch." That made her stop for a few minutes, only for me to get up the stairs. Evan was reading a book while he was coming down from the office. He didn't even glance up as he said, "Have fun, kids," and waved his hand and continued down the stairs.

I threw her on the bed with a squeal and jumped after her. "I used to be a modest thing, Alpha." I started taking off her clothes as well as mine, "But you make me want to do such bad things with you."

I almost came right there with the way she said it. My kitten had opened up to me, and now we were experiencing a whole new level of the sexual part of our bond. "I love you, baby," I kissed her neck as she moaned.

"Mmmhmm, I love you too. But, how about you show me how much you love me?" Her eyelids were low while she bit her lip hard, almost drawing blood. I couldn't take it anymore. The touching, the talking, it was all too much. We weren't playing around anymore, so I thrust my cock inside her, she was already incredibly wet. As soon as my face met hers, I buried myself deep inside her, she gasped. That had to be my favorite thing right now, the first gasp of the first thrust I put into her each time we made love. Her eyes looked into me as I slid my cock in and out of her. Her breasts heaved up and down as I palmed one and sucked the other. "Mmm more, Wesley."

I increased my thrusts harder and faster, and she panted my name all the more. I wanted her to scream it. I pulled her closer to me and grabbed her hips. She met my pelvis with hers, and Charlotte came undone so fast I thought she passed out. I followed her quickly as I pinched her clit, and she had another large orgasm after the first one.

"Oh my gosh, what you do to me," she breathed out. "You make me want you all the time, this is insane." Her breath was uneven, and she kept trying to catch her breath.

"Honestly, you have done a wonderful job still being human. I'm surprised you've kept up with my Wolf," I smirked at her.

"So, when I become a Wolf, I'll be able to keep up with you better and not pass out after 3 or 4 orgasms?" She laughed as she laid her head on my chest.

"Yeah, exactly," I cupped her face and kissed her forehead. For a few moments, we laid there in each other's embrace, and I was still buried deep inside her. If I could sleep with my cock suck in her pussy, I would. I'm sure she would find it uncomfortable, or my dick would get hard and start fucking her while she's sleeping. She might like that, though.

"Wesley?"

"Yes, Kitten?"

"Will it hurt worse than a mating bite when I become a Wolf?" I paused. I wasn't expecting her to bring it up so soon, we were still in our honeymoon stage and enjoying each other.

"It will, love. We won't do it for a while, if you want to do it, that is."

"I do," she looked up. "I want to be like the pack, like you." She grinned her pearly whites at me. "I want to be able to protect the little pups who can't help themselves if their mamas aren't around."

My heart swelled listening to her wanting to help protect the pack, especially the little ones. Pups were sacred around pack communities. They were the next generation and that didn't their Wolves yet, so they were vulnerable in our society. Like Charlotte has been most of her life. Cyrene's thoughts ran through my head that Charlotte was born wolfless, and now she was making the decision on her own what she wanted to be.

"Charlotte," I sighed, running my hand through my hair. Her nose came up to me, rubbing it gently. "The Witch, Cyrene came by while you were sleeping. She was able to hold your hand, and see the things you've been through, part of your past." Charlotte's smile faltered, sitting up she tilted her head to the side, waiting. Letting out a shaky breath, I grabbed her hand.

"Now, I don't know everything, but the Sorceress Cyrene said your parents were Werewolves. You were born wolfless, it happens sometimes. You are just a human without one present." Charlotte let out a breath, holding her hands together now.

"Did they not want me, because of how I was born?" Warm tears filled her eyes. Sitting up I engulfed her into a hug. "No, no kitten. Your parents were killed, I just don't know how or why," I tightened my grip on her. Pecking her lips, her eyes dried. "I just wanted you to know, give you a bit of closure if you ever wanted to know what happened to your birth parents." Charlotte sniffled, burring her nose back into my neck.

"Thank you for telling me, it is closure," kissing my chest, she put both hands up to cup my cheeks. I'm glad to know they didn't give me up because they didn't want me. I hope to know someday who they are, maybe I have some family out there." I smiled at her, not wanting to give away one of her family members may be here in the pack. "I still want to change, into the Wolf I should have always been," she smiled.

"When you are ready, we will do it. Let's just enjoy each other for a few weeks, huh? I want to take you on vacation." Charlotte perked her head up.

"Really!? Where!?" All sadness was wiped away as she jumped in my lap.

"It's a surprise," I said with a smirk.

"Maybe I'll ask Remus then." I frowned.

"No, that isn't fair, you can't ask him." Shaking my head.

"Remus loves me, he'll tell me anything I want." She smiled seductively.

"That's cheating he won't tell." I gave a pout.

"Remus, will you tell your mate where we are going?" She bit her bottom lip and gave her big doe eyes a bit of a flutter. Shit, he was going to tell her, I felt him trying to come out.

"Please, Remus, baby. I need to knooooow!" Before I knew it, Remus took control of my body.

Remus

"Mate," I breathed.

"Remus!" Charlotte jumped in surprise and hugged me tightly. Remembering that we were still technically connected from Wesley's early romp in the cave, I held her still.

"Mate sad?" I said, kissing her cheeks.

"Wesley won't tell me where we are going. I said you would tell me because you love me, your mate!" Mate is a little fox.

"What would mate give Remus?" I grinned. Mate smiled at me and licked her lips.

"Mmhmm maybe I could," she lifted her body off of me, and I groaned. Her head went down to my dick. Dear Goddess Mate was going to do it. Mate started sucking on my dick hard. Mate's mouth became a vice, and she massaged my balls with her tiny hands. My hips thrust forward, and Mate gripped me hard. I pulled mate off of me. I wanted to have a mate the way I wanted. Flipping mate over pushing a pillow underneath her stomach, I my cock inside her, and she let out a loud moan. "Remus!!! Ahh!" I pushed her hard and pulled her hips up to meet me. The quick thrusts had mate mewling in pleasure. It didn't take me long. the way Mate seduced me. Mate did things to me, and I liked it.

Mate's breathing was hard as I pulled out of her, and she gripped me tighter. "Remus, I don't think I will be able to walk now," she whispered in my ear. Instantly I was hard again. I had to tell her now, her heat and her husky whispers would make me take her all over again.

"Bergarian, he's taking you to Bergarain!" I shouted.

"To where?!" she squealed, confused.

Vera Foxx

Chapter 43
Wesley

"Bergarian," I sighed in exhaustion. *Damn, note to self, Charlotte can get any secrets out of Remus. Weak pup.*

"*Remus heard that. Mate, too irresistible,*" Remus huffed.

"Where is Bergarian? I've never heard of it." Charlotte gripped my hands, shaking them violently. Can I take her again without having to tell her everything? I smirked at her and she narrowed her eyes at me.

"Don't do that panty dropping smirk, you need to tell me, or I'll get Remus to." She crossed her arms and wiggled her eyebrows.

"Ok, Ok! Damn woman." I rubbed my forehead trying to figure out where to begin. "So, Bergarian is where most of the supernaturals are. There are more than just Werewolves and Vampires. There are Faes, sprites, other shifters like Wolves that turn into different animals, wisps, elves, gnomes, anything you can think of really. They all used to live here on Earth, but humans aren't very accepting and started hunting, killing, and keeping some as pets." Charlotte made a horrified look on her face. "I know, it's terrible." I cupped her cheek and kissed it.

"The gods, who created us, help make a world just for us, Bergarian. It was made so we could get away and live in peace without humans trying to be destructive. There is a portal on the other side of the country where we can enter, and it is basically like another world. We call it a realm." Charlotte's eyes got really big and an enormous smile followed.

"It sounds so magical!"

"It really is. I couldn't explain to you half of the things that are in that realm. There are things there similar like Earth but a lot of the plant life, the way of life is almost unearthly, more heavenly. Right now, there is a span of peace there where there isn't any fighting and people are really changing their ways not hurting one another. There is to be a new king and queen of the shifters soon and it will mark a new era."

"Then why do you stay here? On Earth? Why doesn't everyone live there?"

"Well, some mates live here on Earth. Everyone gets a feeling they should go somewhere, usually the supernaturals. It is like a pull. I've always had a pull to stay here on Earth and look, I've found you." I motioned to her while she smiled at me. I was also born here so I always thought it was because of that but, maybe it really was because of you." I rubbed my nose with hers.

"Many Wolves like Earth, it's more private, less political in terms of supernaturals. Things there are wilder and more primitive. Some Wolves like it that way. It is almost like this is the country compared to the big city of Bergarian with so many different supernatural kingdoms such as Vermillion the Darkened Kingdom, Cerulean Moon Kingdom for the shifters and the Fae Kingdom or 'Golden Light Kingdom,' as they call it. Here we just make our own rules like it is a territory not a country. Charlotte nodded her head in understanding.

"I like it here so much, I couldn't imagine moving somewhere else. I am excited to visit new places though. Why do you want to take me there if you like it here so much?" she wondered.

"My parents retired and decided to settle down in a pack called Blue Waters. It's close to the ocean, really relaxing and a very peaceful pack. They've lived there for a while and enjoy it. I thought I could take you there and surprise them with you." I gave off a big smile, but Charlotte's smile faltered. "What's wrong, kitten?" I grazed her cheek with my thumb.

"What if they don't like me?" Remus growled and made Charlotte jump.

"Werewolves are different, if you are my true mate then they will automatically like you." She gave me a grin and snuggled up in my chest.

Her meeting my parents wasn't the only thing I was taking her there for, but for a whole other reason. She was just marked and went through heat all in the same week. I know she wants to become a Werewolf like me, but I'd never had any first-hand experience with it, I just want her safe. I've already contacted different healers who have had experience in the change it from long ago, before the human ban in Bergarian.

There was a group of human settlers that came through the portal thousands of years ago and many supernaturals captured them and used them as slaves, forced mates, blood bags and sex slaves so after the Shifter War, King Elijah and Queen Eden had all humans removed until they could find a way to have peace with all the kingdoms.

Finding peace was hard, Vermillion decided to have themselves reclusive and rumors of King Darius beating his subjects and killing them on the spot were going around. There was no way of swaying him unless the Cerulean Moon Kingdom had a full out war, which they weren't prepared for after the Shifter War. After many years, the lost princess of the Cerulean Moon Kingdom, Clarabelle, was found and she defeated King Darius all on her own. Making Taliya and her Werewolf mate, Jasper the new rulers. In a span of a month, she had peace treaties. This has made things safter for humans now that kingdoms are willing to protect them and use their armies if they must.

Now I could take Charlotte and see a professional, making this much easier and easier on my worry.

After both of us taking a quick shower and putting on our comfortable clothes, we went downstairs to watch a movie. Correction, we tried to watch a movie. I was laying on the couch and Charlotte was laying on top of me curled up with her new favorite large fluffy blanket. She was fast asleep with her head in the crook of my neck.

I started flipping through the channels and smelled Evan standing in the doorway. "Don't be a fucking creep, come on in." Evan scoffed and sat down while Jenny sat on his lap and cuddled into him.

"You are going to take her to see your parents huh?" Evan gave a smirk. Jenny continued to watch the TV that was currently playing The Godfather.

"Yeah, and I'm taking her to see one of the shifter physicians about her becoming a Wolf. I've never seen a human transform and I'm worried about her." I petted my mate's back while she slept soundlessly.

"Shit, you worry too much. The Moon Goddess wouldn't pair you both up for it to mess up now." Charlotte stirred but I put my hand on her back and rubbed her so she would go back to sleep.

"You are talking damn loud, don't wake her up," I half whispered, half yelled. Jenny smiled, looking on at her Luna lovingly.

"You both are so sweet it almost makes me sick!" she giggled. "I'm so glad you found her, she's so good to you, Alpha. I'll do my best to help her as much as I can." Jenny looked at Charlotte admirably. "I wish she didn't have to go through all what she did, but it did make her strong, didn't it Evan?" Evan nodded and looked up at me while he had his arm around Jenny on the large, cushioned chair they were sitting in.

"Wesley, there is something we need to talk about." I looked at him to continue, I couldn't get up while Charlotte was sleeping, I didn't want my precious mate to be uncomfortable with me moving her. "Josephine is nowhere to be found, Sorceress Cyrene cannot locate her whereabouts. With the bounty on her head, I doubt she went back to Bergarian and she is here somewhere. I don't know if she is going to go after Charlotte or not. With Roman out of the picture, she may just bow out. It seemed like she wanted to punish Roman more by having him unnecessarily hurting Charlie. Then again, no one knows her motives, she is just pure evil," Evan said with disgust.

"She's gone crazy," Jenny spoke up. "When her mate rejected her, she went straight mad. Her twin that she shared a mate with stayed with him. Josephine's sister is Ariande, and she has light magic while Josephine was dark. She couldn't control it and was sometimes mean and cheated on their shared mate who is a warlock. He rejected her because she was causing him too much pain."

"Must have been dropped on her head as a baby or something," Evan choked a laugh. Jenny gave him an evil eye while he slithered back down in his seat. Ha, pussy. "That's what I know, from what my sister in Bergarian said. I can't wait for Hades to deal with her."

Hades deals with the big-time crimes and puts them in a special cell and feeds off their powers to make his power grow. If Hades wants her, it is only a matter of time before he gets her.

"I'll keep that in mind while we are down there. Charlotte will never be alone." I squeezed her tighter to me and subconsciously kissed my neck. I started groaning and Evan and Jenny were holding in their laughter. "Fuck," I whispered.

"Evan, come on before he busts a nut. I can't see my Alpha like that," Jenny pulled on Evan to get up, but he just stayed there.

"Nah, I wanna see what happens," he put both hands behind his head to watch and Charlotte continued to suck then nibble on my neck. Trying to hold it in, I couldn't anymore and sat up with her and trying to hold my boner in.

"What's going on?" Charlotte rubbed her eyes and looked at me. "Oh sorry, I fell asleep," she looked at me sleepily. "Hey guys! What are you guys doing?" Looking around she saw an amused Evan and a worried Jenny.

"Have any good dreams there, Charlie?" he snickered.

"Uh... I guess?" She replied confused, then she looked at my neck and her eyes got large. "What happened to your neck??"

"Uhhhh, shit." I mumbled and Evan laughed loud enough for the whole house to hear.

Charlotte

Jenny and Ashley helped me pack up my bags for Wesley and I's big trip to Bergarian. I was so excited. I had never been on vacation in my entire life and here I was, about to go to a whole new world of things humans never got to see.

"I'm so jealous," Jenny said. "I haven't visited my family in ages. I'd love to go to the Blue Water's pack too. They are near the ocean, and I heard there are actual mermaids or sirens there!"

My eyes grew big. "Really?" I squealed. "I would love to see one! I hope I can take pictures!"

"Oh no, you can't," Ashley said sadly. "Bergarian is a pure place. They have limited technology, well for traveling for sure, there are no cars or gas guzzling machines. You can't take pictures and bring them out of Bergarian. They don't want any chance of exposure. There is Internet of course, that is how most of us communicate now that humans have discovered all that. No more burning letters by some magical fire," Ashley laughed. "Well for some anyway. A lot like the primitive ways."

"Wow, this seems like so much." I said overwhelmed. I knew about Werewolves and Vampires but the whole concept of another world was almost daunting. From what Wesley said there aren't many humans over there right now, will everyone know I am one?

"You are overthinking things, don't worry about it," Ashley patted my back as Jenny slung my suitcase off the bed. "They will love you there, especially since you are a Luna. You will be treated like a princess while in the Blue Water Pack. I think Wesley's dad takes over for the Alpha sometimes when he needs a break. Blue Water's Beta is still learning since he is a bit inexperienced." I nodded, not really understanding anything that was going on.

Zachary came into the room with a black suitcase. "Ready to go?!" he said excitedly.

"You are coming too?!" I jumped up and gave him a hug. "Of course, I can't leave my bestie for too long. Plus, Alpha said he needed a personalized warrior for you, and I was up for the challenge!" Zachary pounded his chest with one hand and looked up at the corner of the room.

"My hero!" I fake swooned as soon as Wesley walked in the room.

"I thought I was your hero," Wesley gave a hurtful look. I ran up to him and jumped in his arms. "You are my Alpha and my prince charming, I think you trump hero by a long shot."

We both heard a bunch of people say 'ewww' and 'gross,' but I didn't care. Zachary looked at the ground and kicked some invisible rocks. "So, being a hero isn't that great huh?" We all started laughing and Wesley and Zachary grabbed our suitcases.

Chapter 44

Charlotte

After a two-hour car ride to the airport, Wesley, Zachary and I got out of the black SUV near the hangers. We weren't flying in just a regular airplane, but a private jet that Wesley personally owns. I stood in front of it in awe as I heard car doors slamming and our luggage being carried to the plane. It was black, sleek, stylish, everything a billionaire CEO needed to travel.

"Do you like it?" I kept my eyes on the plane as I nodded. I've never flown on a plane, I was both excited and a bit scared as I continued to stare at it. I was hoping for something bigger, so if we crashed and burned it would take a while before it took my life. Feeling my stress through the bond, Wesley grabbed my hand and laced his fingers through mine. I glanced down as he took his thumb and rubbed it across my knuckles. "It will be Okay. I'm going to be by your side the entire time, alright?" I continued to keep my mouth shut as my feet mindlessly followed my mate.

Smiling while looking at his hand, I repeated in my mind, "My mate."

Several months ago, I would have never thought I would find peace, especially so quickly. I was scared of people, I was scared of trusting anyone and in these few short months I had come so quickly acquainted with so many people that cared for me like family. Wesley, Ashley, and Zachary had been wonderful friends that got me out of my funk while the rest of the pack protected me, a weakly human. These Werewolves actually searched for me and fought for me to come back to the packhouse and to live among them. They accepted my scars, my timidness, and my past without a second thought. If I had known people like this existed, I would have sought out a mate ages ago.

As we boarded the plane, I was again struck with being mute. The main color scheme was black and tan with Wesley Hale's logo on it. A Wolf with a circle around it howling at the moon. It was simple and kind of cliche' but I still loved it. My man was so smart, I never thought I would see the day I would go from struggling for my next meal to getting a vacation in a land that has never been heard of by humans. A few seats on either side of the plane with several sofas and tables so people could eat or do something business-like stood before me. Two flight attendants would take care of all of our needs such as food and drinks led us to our seats for takeoff.

Wesley sat me down beside him next to the window and automatically buckled me in. Giving him a grin and a silent thank you he kissed my forehead as he pulled out his laptop. "I'm just going to check a few things before we arrive at our destination. We will be gone for a bit, so I want to make sure my junior partners are informed what to do in my absence." I hummed and tried to hide a yawn, but he caught it. "Kitten, lay down," he commanded me. Wesley pressed a few buttons and the seat had been lowered and a leg rest had risen up turning into a small make-shift twin bed. I laughed out loud, and the attendant gave me a pillow and blanket without even having to ask.

"We will be taking off soon, Luna. You can stay laying down though, this plane is well equipped to handle it and you shouldn't feel a thing." The attendant left but my confusion prompted Wesley to comment, "In most planes, you need to be sitting up while taking off, but we have new technology where you won't feel take off as much." He petted my head as I curled up next to him. He was so warm and cuddly even if I was just putting my face next to his thigh.

By the time I had woken up, we had been in the air for two hours. I was wondering how far this portal really was for us having us travel so far. Rubbing my eyes, I saw Wesley to see he had lowered his seat as well and was sleeping curled up next to me. His face was relaxed and all the worry lines he had accumulated with me being kidnapped had almost disappeared. He had barely slept while I was gone and then I turn around go into heat. Which I don't think he really minded.

Running my hands through his hair his face automatically gravitated to my hand. I'll never get used to these sparks. It isn't a prickling feeling but soothing, warm and delicate. Before being marked I didn't feel it as strong but now that I am truly his I feel them so much more. Ashley said once I become a Wolf fully that I will feel it even more. I would feel his feelings, his wants, and desires, everything emotionally is intensified while being a Wolf.

Wesley fluttered his eyes open and stared back at me. "I'm sorry, I didn't mean to wake you," I whispered lowly. Wesley gave me his smirk and pulled me in close giving our noses a good rub. Chuckling he lowered his hand and grabbed my butt and gave it a squeeze. His touches felt so good I gave out a little moan. "Wesley, they will hear."

"They are all in the front of the plane, in the cockpit area. They won't come out unless I tell them to."

"You mean, you are going to tell them not to come back here because you are 'busy' with your mate?"

"Something like that," he huskily whispered in my ear.

Wesley sucked on my earlobe, and I pressed my body against his. My chest heaved at the feeling as he lifted my leg and had me put it over his. His hands tickled the waistband of my black leggings and slid two fingers down to my core. Tickling what was his, it instantly made me wet. "Wesley, Ohh." His smirk turned into a face of lust as he pushes two fingers inside me. I jerked my head back and my breasts came up to show an ample amount of cleavage. My top was low today and Wesley was appreciating it. Lowering his head, he pulled the top even lower and started biting my nipple through my lace bra.

"Damn, you are so sexy," he groaned.

The blanket that covered us began to fall but that didn't stop Wesley from continuing to play. I tensed up and let out a quiet moan as my wetness coated his fingers. Breathing heavily, I watched Wesley pull up his fingers and licked them clean. This only turned me on more and I wanted him, I wanted to suck him dry. While he was cleaning his fingers, I unbuckled his belt and pants and pulled them down enough so his dick could spring to life.

He was large like he always was. Wesley groaned while his cock stood erect for me. I lowered my mouth and licked the top of his cock causing him to hiss. My hand cupped the lower part of his cock and the other cupped his balls. Massaging his balls and licking him up and down he groaned. "Fuck, baby don't tease me," he pleaded. I laughed as I took him in, trying to deep throat him was something I was trying but wasn't really succeeding. I continued to gag but that only seemed to make him harder. "Yes, goddess, yes," he yelped as he guided my head at the speed he wanted. With only a few more bobs of my head, he released his load into my mouth, and I swallowed it all without a second thought. Some leaked down his cock and I continued to clean him with my tongue.

Wesley pulled me up and had me on his chest and kissed me fervently. "Damn, the Moon Goddess blessed me." I nuzzled my head into his neck and sucked on his future marking spot from me. He let out a content sigh and I whispered, "I love you, Wesley. I think the Moon Goddess blessed me more."

Wesley chuckled.

"As much as I want to lay here for the rest of the day, we have to get up."

I groaned.

"We are landing in five minutes and then we have about an hour drive to the portal. It's a long trip love, I'm sorry." I groaned to get up and fixed my hair and clothes, as did Wesley. Zachary and the flight attendants came back to sit down in their seats and Zachary eyed me suspiciously. He stuck his tongue in the side of his cheek, reminding me what I just did. How dare he!! I gave him a glare back and he just laughed as he opened up a magazine to read.

***

We had been in the car for an hour, and we were deep in the woods of the Ever Green Pack, the head pack in charge of the portal and the surrounding land. Alpha Adrien looked in the SUV and gave Wesley a curt nod and motioned him to park the car in a large garage area.

The garage was two stories tall with cars ranging from trucks, SUVs, convertibles and even some junk cars. There were no gas or machines allowed in Bergarian as they wanted to keep their land pure. There was electricity that was powered by wind and the Witches had something to do with that having a constant breeze through the wind fields of the land. I thought it was a great idea to keep the land so pure, if only Earth could do the same

The car was parked, and we exited the vehicle, Alpha Adrian greeted us and gave us both a handshake. "It is great to see you, Alpha Hale, it has been a while."

Wesley nodded. "It has, I wanted to surprise my parents to have them meet my mate. It has been long overdue," Wesley smiled down at me as he pulled me closer to him by waist.

"It is a pleasure, Luna. I assume this is your first time entering Bergarian?"

"Yes, it is. I'm a bit nervous."

"Don't be, it is just like walking through a mist. Just don't go off the path, Wesley will keep you close." Alpha Adrien spoke short and to the point, I'm sure he was tired of having to work so hard. His son was supposed to be taking over the pack soon but wanted to find his own mate first. Wesley said it was stupid that Adrian would even entertain the idea, but he brushed it off as not his problem.

Once you go through the portal, it is as dark as night. They say you can barely see your hand in front of your face. You are just to follow the small grey path that leads to the other side. If you stray off the path you can get lost easily since there is no light. No one has been lost as of yet, but it was a warning of the gods to always stay clear of the darkness. It gave me a shiver that someone would actually get lost in there but it was a protection mechanism so no unauthorized humans could enter.

Our luggage had been taken through the portal and was waiting on the other side. It was just Wesley, Zachary, and I waiting to go through. "Alpha, they are ready for you on the other side. Enjoy your stay," Alpha Adrien gave Wesley a pat on the shoulder.

"Are you ready, Kitten?"

"I hope so," I said with worry laced in my tone.

"You will love it, I promise."

With his fingers laced with mine, we all walked through with Zachary close behind. A slight chill was in the air and no noise or light. You haven't really experienced silence as you do walking through this literal in-between.

Everyone kept silent, it must be an unspoken rule that you don't speak during this trip because we were all quiet as death. The grey pathway continued to guide us and with a quick blink I looked up and we were on the other side. The world was bright, just like Earth can be when humans haven't tarnished the skies. The green was bright and bold and the trees taller than I had ever seen. We had arrived just at the side of a mountain, able to look over for hundreds of miles.

Several dragon-like creatures flew around in the sky, spitting out fire and ice, I couldn't keep my eyes off of them. Wesley stood there and let me take in my surroundings and gave me a gentle squeeze on my hand getting out of my trance. "What do you think?"

My eyes were going in a thousand different directions, I could see animals that were not afraid of us looking at us with curious eyes next to the portal in the forest. They were small Fairies? Sprites? Just small, miniaturized people with beautiful wings. A few of them sat on a large mushroom laughing and giggling to themselves. They were barely clothed, just covering their lower regions. Their squeals of laughter were high pitch and as I tried to get closer, they flew up higher into the trees. I could have sworn they were screaming, "Catch me!"

"Those are woodland sprites," Wesley said, coming up behind me. "They cause mischief, just like every other type of Fae. Fairies belong to the Fae kingdom and there are few races of Faes just like the Sprites."

"They are beautiful, I've never seen some of those colors on their wings," I stood up in awe.

"Mhmm, not as beautiful as you, mate." I turned around only to have Wesley meet my lips with his. "We still have a good hour and half carriage ride, might want to get going, lovebirds." Wesley glared at him while Zachary wiggled his eyebrows.

"Better watch out, Zachary. Wesley is still pretty possessive after marking," I winked.

"Shit, forgot. Sorry, Alpha."

Chapter 45
Wesley

My mate stared out the window in awe as we trotted along the path that led us to the Blue Water pack where my parents now resided. Our whole family decided to move into the Bergarian pack once his Alpha duties were completed to give of a retirement home feel. It was located near the ocean where the salty breeze and the waves were a constant reminder of peace and tranquility.

Charlotte continued to stick her head out the window and watch the wisps that were traveling come up to her. They teased her hair and tapped her nose as their blue hue danced around her face. She continued to laugh and brush them away with her hand, only for them to come in the carriage when she sat back down on my lap.

"Oh shit, you let them in!" Zachary groaned to himself while he took his magazine and begun swatting at them. They quickly went to Zachary and pulled at his hair and unbuttoned his plaid button-up shirt. "No, dammit stop it!" He yelled they tied his shoestrings together. Charlotte let out a loud squeal of laughter which only excited them more and they came back to her and twirled her hair. They let out a quick clicking noise and jetted out of the carriage. Once her giggles died down, I noticed her hair was now curled in a beautiful half updo on her head. She couldn't possibly become any more beautiful, but I have to say the curls certainly suited her.

"Ugh, damn whisps. Always messing shit up." Zachary continued to button up his shirt and fix his hair which was now a full head of unruly curls that looked ridiculous on him. "Aw, you kind of look cute, Zachary,"

Charlotte teased. Look at the both of them as they spoke, I could see the similarities between them. Both had the same-colored hair, the strawberry blonde and the smaller ears with dimples in the ear lobes. Could they? I rubbed my chin in thought.

Remus scratched in my head. I rubbed it annoyingly as he explained he didn't like our mate calling another Wolf cute. Taking over, my body he quickly growled and gripped Charlotte's hips tighter. Charlotte realized her mistake and looked us in the eyes. "I'm just kidding Remus, you are the only puppy for me!" Charlotte giggled again. Her laugh was damn contagious and if it wasn't for the derogatory pet name, she gave us I'd bask in the warm glow she had.

"Remus not puppy," Remus growled at her.

"You are lucky Zachary is in the carriage with us, or you might earn yourself a smack on the ass," I said playfully. Charlotte stopped giggling and had put both hands on her mouth. Giving her the smile, she loves she sat silently on my lap. We both heard a snort and quiet laughter coming from the other side of the carriage.

"Ha, puppy," Zachary whispered, and I gave him a deep scowl.

"No, Zachary! Only I can call him that. He might kill you if you try," she warned. Zachary looked back at me only for him to see Remus's eyes which earned a deep gulp from Zachary's throat.

We continued to travel for another hour until we reached the Blue Waters Pack. It had large white columns at the gates and warrior just outside of the walls. When they saw us, they immediately bowed and welcomed us. "Alpha Hale, welcome." At first, he only saw me until Charlotte popped her head out to see what was going on. She was always a curious thing. My curious little kitten.

The warrior looked in shock at my mate, her blonde curls cascaded out of the carriage, and she smiled at him. "Can we go in now?!" she said quickly. "I'm ready to stretch my legs, I'm going to get a blood clot or something!" Zachary started laughing trying to pull her back in. The warrior continued to stare at her, so I let out a warning growl which snapped him out of his senses.

"My apologies Alpha, I'm terribly sorry." The warrior bowed his head and motioned for them to open up the gates. I pulled Charlotte close to me and held her tightly and it made her squirm in my lap. Unfortunately, it caused something else to stir and she stopped moving immediately. "Sorry, Alpha, I didn't mean to!" she whispered in my ear as she playfully bit it.

"I know you are excited, Kitten, but stay close to me. You aren't a Wolf yet so I'm wondering if my mark isn't emitting enough of my smell. I don't want some damn pup getting near you." Remus snarled in my head thinking of someone wanting to take our mate away.

"I-I won't leave. I don't know this place and I'm a bit nervous anyways." I held her close until the carriage stopped at the front gates. It was the same as I left it twenty years ago the last time I visited. My parents often visited me, so I never had a reason to come back unless there was an influx of unmated she-Wolves looking for their mates. My heart always wanted me to stay near Black Claw and I'm glad I did.

I stepped out and held my hand out for Charlotte who was speechless looking at the three-story mansion, it wasn't as large as the one back home but it was still had the celestial glow as any beach home would have. Light corals, blues and whites adorned the home. Pictures of the ocean, fish, merpeople as well as shells adorned the walls. Charlotte had never been to the coast, and I had every intention of taking her to the beach before her transformation. I wasn't sure how long she would be out and didn't want to return home until she'd seen every inch of it.

I grabbed her by the waist and put my arm around her to keep her close. Many males stared at her, but she never took notice, too busy looking at the crystal chandeliers and the marbled floors. I set glares their way, earning them to bare their necks in submission. My Charlotte was almost too beautiful.

I heard a large howl, and I would recognize that anywhere. My mother came running down the halls with all her might while in her swimsuit and sarong tightly wrapped around her hips. "My Wessie! You are home!!" Damn, forgot about that stupid nickname.

"Mother," I gave a tight-lipped smile as she jumped into my arms. She didn't look a day older than twenty-eight. She had her bright blue eyes set on me and her dirty blonde hair that I inherited from pulled up in a high ponytail. Without skipping a beat, she looked behind me where Charlotte had quickly hid. She fisted my shirt to let me know she wasn't really too keen on the loud obnoxious noises just yet.

"And who is this lovely young lady?" Mother eyed me suspiciously. I'm sure she was wondering if it was some fling like I'd used to bring home.

"Mother," I guided Charlotte around with my hand. "I'd like for you to meet, my mate, Charlotte." I held Charlotte tightly to my body, knowing she was going to hear another squeal. Charlotte nuzzled her head into the side of my body and my mother instantly picked up her shyness.

"Charlotte," my mother breathed breathlessly. Maybe she was in shock that I found her. "It is such a pleasure to meet you and what a beautiful name you have!"

"It's nice to meet you too." Charlotte held out her hand, but my mother dismissed it and pulled her into a light hug. My mother's size over towered Charlotte's but she didn't seem to mind, I even saw a small smile on her lips.

"My goddess you are gorgeous." My Mother's hands cupped Charlotte's face while she gave her a small smile. "You have been through a lot haven't you dear?" Charlotte was trying to hold back tears, so I grabbed her from my mother and nuzzled her neck. Mother noticed the mark. "You've marked her! Oh, this is wonderful! But why can't I smell your scent on her?"

"What?" I growled. "Why can't you smell her?" I pulled Charlotte's shirt to the side showing my mark.

"I don't know, that is so strange. Is it because she is human? We haven't had any human mates run in our family line before? Maybe we should get the pack doctor after she meets your father?" I nodded, still bothered by the fact no one can smell my scent or notice her mark.

I whispered in her ear as we walked to the outdoor patio of the pack house, "From now on, I want you to wear things that show my mark, I don't know why you don't have my smell." Charlotte muttered in understanding.

"Why is that? Is it because I'm human or the bonds that were branded on me?"

"I'm not sure about Kitten, but we are going to find out later. Just stay close to me until we find out."

We walked outside to see a veteran Alpha Werewolves sitting around a fire staring at the beach. The only reason why I knew they were veterans was because they were mated, and all knew my father when he was Alpha back in Night Crawlers.

"Odin, look who came for a surprise visit? He also brought someone special!" My Mother said in a singsong voice. My father was old, old enough for the Viking times of the humans which is where his own parents got his name. They said he looked like a Norse god when he was born, and that he had been the hairiest baby they had ever seen.

Father stood up and took a look at my mate, who again, was behind me fisting my shirt. I smiled and tried to guide her around my she wasn't moving. "Who have you got there son? Better not be some whore." That was my father for you, blunt and to the point. Remus's baritone voice came forward and growled at him.

"Remus' mate not whore. Watch your tongue old Wolf." Everyone sat back in shock. Remus had been making a lot of appearances lately and my own family didn't see him very often.

My father smiled at me and embraced me in an enormous hug with large pats on the back. "Finally! Let me see the little doll, I'm sure she is a beaut! Took ya long enough to find her!" His beard swayed back and forth while the beads on his side braid smacked me in the face. Charlotte made a squeak sound when my father engulfed her in her own large hug, picking her up and nuzzling her cheek, a common occurrence with family Wolves. Charlotte looked taken aback but I couldn't help but laugh and feel proud my father accepted our mate so quickly.

"You are a tiny one arn't ye?" Charlotte nodded quickly and looked at me while he put her down. Grabbing her hand, I held her close. "Did ya mark her yet? I can't smell her."

"Honey, that is a bit much to say right now," my mother tried to calm him. She understood Charlotte was a timid thing.

"Astrid, I was just askin'." He grabbed my mother and gave her a swift kiss. Ignoring my father making out with my mother I butted in.

"To answer your question, yes father, she's marked but no one can smell her. My pack knows not to mess with her but now I'm worried that we are here." Father rubbed his chin to think.

"Let's take her to the pack doctor. It has been a while since a human was a mate around these parts beside the future queen. She's an exception though because her parents were Wolves. I'm sure they can look in them books and figure something out." I nodded as I picked up my mate like a bride she was to the doctor.

"She was born from Wolves as well." I added, but she has been through much in all the years before I met her." Father's fist balled up as I continued to quickly explain my mate's situation.

"Wesley," Charlotte whined as I carried her through the packhouse along with my father. "People are going to stare!"

"Here's the thing, they are already staring at what is mine. I'm just letting them know you are mine and I'm going to rub my scent all over you, so everyone knows. My mark should be doing the job, but it isn't." Charlotte cocked her head to the side.

"Your scent?"

"Yes, Wolves can seep out their scents on their mates before they are marked and mated. I see I'm going to have to keep doing it."

"You mean, you have been putting your scent all over me since you found out about me?" I smiled.

"You were mine from the very first time I saw you, Kitten."

Vera Foxx

Chapter 46
Charlotte

Wesley continued to carry me style through the pack house like I was his prize. There were stares but not of amusement but of pride. A lot of the Wolves must have known Wesley from his parents and how long he has waited for his mate. Some nodded at Wesley, and some gave me a smile and I gave a shy one back. I wasn't really into everyone staring at us so consistently, so I nuzzled into Wesley's chest being the scaredy cat I was. I was going to be a terrible Luna.

I can barely look people in the eye after everything that happened with Roman. I was lucky that I got a job at the real estate office with Ashley. Working on the computers helped me stay away and now I'm being thrust into a high position with Wesley. How am I supposed to help a whole pack when I can barely look his own family in the eye or speak to them? I am hiding behind Wesley like such a child. Squirming a bit, Wesley realized my discomfort.

"What's wrong love?" He looked down at me adoringly as he continued to walk through the long halls of the pack house. Shaking my head, I just held on to him. "Something is wrong, I can feel it." Wesley squeezed me.

"I don't think I will be a good Luna, I'm just too timid to help you with a pack. I can barely stand being around all these people going through the pack house. Are you sure you still want me to help you with the pack?" Wesley stopped in the middle of the hallway and looked down at me. My eyes were glassy, and his eyes furrowed as he grabbed me tightly. Looking to the right he saw an empty guest room and walked in the door. Kicking it open and closed he turned on the light and sat me on the bed. He kneeled and put both hands on either side of my hips looking up at me.

"Why in the world would you think that you wouldn't be a good enough Luna?" His voice was hoarse and gruff. I wasn't sure if he was upset or angry with me.

"I don't know," I looked down with my hands and folded them. "I am just not good around loud and crazy noises, being around new people, large crowds, being around some men. Don't you think someone else would be better? To be able to talk to people better and be more diplomatic and such." A small tear left my eye. I knew so many other women would be better than me. I could just sit in the background and do things that way. Have some other spokeswoman speak for me? It could work, it would be logical.

Wesley both his hands on my face and kissed me. His lips were so soft and delicate. He parted my lips gently with his and his tongue met mine. It was soft, passionate and so loving. Wesley continued to kiss me, just on my lips. It wasn't seductive, it wasn't hungry, it was loving. His hands continued to stroke my face as he kneeled in front of me. Not as a man that wanted a woman's body, but as a man who truly loved his woman, me.

The feeling not just in the kiss but in the bond was overwhelming. My heart felt full and warm, and I could feel how much he was pushing his emotion into me. Feeling the tears well up in my eyes, trying to keep them in, I finally let them out. They fell down my face and it mixed with our mouths, salty tears mixed with our kisses. A sob ripped through me, and we pulled away. Wesley grabbed me as I fell into his arms.

"My little Luna, you are worth everything to me. You are worth being a Luna. Do you not realize how strong you are? How much have you been through how strong it has made you? You may not like being around a lot of people you don't know but when you do know them you care for them. Look back at our home? Everyone loves you at Black Claw and you are not shy around them?"

I nodded as he held me close. I didn't want to let go even though people were waiting. I haven't felt this vulnerable in a long time, and I'm not sure what triggered it all. The day has been overwhelming, I saw some freaking fairies, people shifting into dragons, and so many other mythical things you would have never known to be true. How was I supposed to be a representative from our pack when I was just, me? Sitting up straight I see a worried Wesley. "Kitten, today has been a lot, how about we go to the doctor tomorrow?"

Knowing how much this has upset Wesley about not having his smell on me, I quickly declined. Wiping my tears, I sat up straight in his lap. "I love you, Wesley. I'm sorry, I just want to be the best for you, be a good Luna. Maybe today was a little much and I got overwhelmed. I'm not used to people staring all the time."

"Well, you are gorgeous you know?" Wesley squeezed my hips. "Besides, we make a great power couple, right?" I laughed. "Power couple??" I questioned.

"Yeah, we are both incredibly sexy and have such a powerful aura around us. I can't wait to see what your Wolf will look like." I perked up.

"My Wolf?! Am I going to change here?" I asked excitedly.

"Only if you want to."

"Of course, I do! I want to be strong for the pack," I laughed.

"Listen here, Charlotte. You are strong with or without a Wolf. Do you understand? I don't want you to think that you need a Wolf to be a Luna, you can be a Luna without a Wolf."

"I will try to understand that, I still want to be like you though." Wesley gave me another squeeze on the hips and pulled me up.

"What do you want to do, love? I'll do anything you want." His eyes were pleading, I know he was wanting to know why but took my feelings into consideration. I loved this Wolf with all my being and if it would make him feel better to know what was wrong, then I would find out and put it to rest. We were here to have fun and have me change. It was time to get the hard part over with.

"Let's go to the physician, maybe it is a quick fix?" He grinned, patted my butt and pulled me back into his hold.

"Let's go then," he rubbed his nose into my neck.

The medical ward for this pack house was huge. It was in the south wing of the pack house. Large halls of white and everything was completely sterile. It looked almost like a laboratory with glass rooms and curtains in there for some privacy. I heard one woman groaning and yelling which didn't put me at ease. "Someone is giving birth to twins," Wesley said. "Twins are pretty common in Wolves, the only thing is, if they are identical, they share a mate usually. My eyes grew wide in recognition. "Why is that?"

"Well, it all starts with the one egg before it is fertilized, that is one soul. When they split it occurs a week after the soul has met the egg. Therefore, they share a soul plus a soul mate."

Interesting. "Wouldn't they get jealous of each other sharing a mate? I would be going crazy in jealousy!"

"I can't say from experience," he winked at me. Twins love their mate so much they will do anything to stay together, besides they are siblings no matter what. Hopefully they would want to see their siblings happy too."

"This is Luna's room." A nursed announced waving us into the door. "All Lunas get a little bit better treatment." Wesley sat me on the bed and sat in the rocking chair next to me and held my hand. A few doctors walked in the room with their pristine white doctor coats and stethoscopes around their necks. One of them had jet black hair, bits of white scattered throughout, holding a clipboard. He was much skinnier than the others and had deep grey eyes.

"Good afternoon, Luna, I'm Dr. Prescott, I'm going to be the main physician on your case for you and Alpha Hale. I am understanding we are having some trouble with Alpha Hales smell on you?" I looked at Wesley and he nodded me to continue while he held my hand.

"Um, yes? I've been marked and mated but I guess I don't have a strong smell of his claiming on me." I blushed profusely.

Dr. Prescott chuckled lightly and wrote some notes on the clipboard. "Nothing to be ashamed of Luna, it is completely normal. I know humans have a bit of a different bond understanding. Alpha Hale was there anything you would like to add about the circumstances. Anything unusual about her history before she met you?"

Wesley sat up from his chair and crossed his arms. "Well, yes there is." He used his Alpha voice. "She has gone through a lot of abuse as well as a branding bond that was used to try and force her to become mated to a Vampire." The room was silent, you could feel Wesley's anger through not only the bond but through the room. It always had me in awe how a supernatural being that was so powerful to give off a vibe so strong it could stifle the whole room.

"I-I am so sorry Luna," Dr. Prescott spoke. "I know this may be a difficult topic, but we may need to discuss this a little further and in more detail. Would that be alright with you?" Dr. Prescott's bedside manner was nice, a lot of doctors I met at free clinics were mean and dismissive when I was on my own.

"What would you like to know?"

"Do you know exactly what kind of branding bond they used? There are several different kinds from what I'm told." Wesley pulled out his phone to show him the upper part of my chest. I looked away, not wanting to be reminded of my past and all the scars on it. Dr. Prescott took a picture of it himself for his own files and showed the other doctors in the room. One doctor cleared his throat to speak.

"Hello Alpha, Luna, I'm Dr. Marcio. I am originally from Italy so please pardon my speech. Dr. Marcio really had a thick accent, and it was hard to hear, but we both welcomed what he had to say. "A long time ago, there were these bonding brands they used for Vampires, I'm sure you are aware. There were only a few made because the practice was outlawed shortly after it was created. There is very little information on the after effects on them. However, I know sometimes they would brand humans frequently. May I ask in total, how many times you were branded in pairs, front and back?"

This was the first time someone knew of branding bonds right off the bat, he also knew it had to be done on the back and front of the chest. Wesley gave me a glance to answer him. "Including the time, I was younger and the times a few weeks ago... eight." Again, the room was silent, you could hear a pin drop and possibly the small crying of babies a few levels below our room. "I'm sorry, Luna. Did you say eight?" Dr Marcio spoke in disbelief.

"Uh, yes." I looked down, feeling embarrassed and defeated. Wesley growled and pulled me off the bed and into his arms and pushed my head into his chest. His loud, slow rhythmic heartbeats settled my uneasiness quickly as he gave them hard glances.

"Does she need to answer you again or are you just trying to upset her?" he growled out.

"No, Alpha. I'm sorry, it's just I am speechless. Usually, if the branding bond is rejected, they die after the 2nd try. She managed to survive eight times of these attempts. How did you do it, Luna?"

Wesley gripped me a little harder and I saw the doctors waiting on me to answer them. "I just thought of my mate, Wesley. It was before he marked me, and I was thinking about him and only him. The way we had come to be so close the past month and how much I loved and cared for him. That was what kept me going when I felt them brand me." Wesley gripped me impossibly tighter and shoved his nose into my neck, kissing my mark and causing shivers down my spine. I could feel his regret and remorse for not finding me sooner, but all I felt for him was love.

"I don't deserve you," he mumbled into my neck.

"*We deserve each other, Wesley. I love you.*" I mind linked him.

Dr. Marcio stood up straighter and whispered to the other physicians. "Do you mind if we see your mark that Alpha Hale has put on you?" Wesley growled loudly and hugged me close. "I know this is a lot to ask Alpha, but we must do it to see why other Wolves aren't recognizing the mark." Pushing Wesley, a bit, I patted his hand in reassurance.

"I'll show you," I said. "Just let me stay with him in his arms, if that's alright." They nodded and I pulled my shirt to the side. A few brief moments later Dr. Marcio spoke. "Everything looks in order, it was deep enough, and the scarring is impeccable. You are just missing the smell. Can you mind-link?" I nodded yes and the doctors looked at each other.

"We are going to need some time to look into some textbooks and consult with the elders of this pack. You are fine and healthy but speaking about this bond we may need to speak to those in the Vermillion Kingdom as well." Wesley sighed in frustration and ran his hand through his hair that was tucked away in a bun.

"Just hurry, I don't like my mate being around here with a bunch of unmated Wolves gawking over her." Dr. Prescott hummed and began to head leave. "Wait! Dr Prescott?" I asked.

"When can he change me? So, I can be a Werewolf too?" I asked excitedly. Dr. Prescott smiled at Wesley and back at me. "Overall, you are healthy and fine. I would say it would be fine to go with the change, but I would ask if you did it here in the pack house. It has been many years since anyone in this packhouse has witnessed it. We would like to report your progress as well for future humans that go through the change."

Wesley seemed to like that answer so he nodded the doctors off while they did their research. "Sorry I caused so much trouble, Wesley." I petted his arm as he continued to hold me tight. "I've been in and out of doctor offices with you forever!" I nuzzled into his which he appreciated.

"I like taking care of you and if I have to beat up some doctors to do it, I will."

"You don't need to beat them up, be nice," I chided.

Chapter 47

Charlotte

After the doctor's office, Wesley led me through the sterile halls of the hospital and up to the 3rd floor. There was a wing for visiting Alphas, so of course, our bedroom was immaculate. The room was set toward the back of the house and our room had large windows so you could see the waves roll in on the untouched sand. A small balcony laid in front of us where you could open the sliding windows and walk down to the beach. I continued to stare out the window where the sun was setting and saw colors I had never seen before in a sunset.

Pinks, blues, purples, and even greens were setting, and one very large blue moon was appearing away from the sun. I stared in awe at how big they were to the world. This place was certainly not like Earth. No novel or storybook describe what I saw, it was unearthly, otherworldly really was a place humans could never describe.

Wesley came up behind me and put his hand on the small off my back. "What do you think?" he looked at me, not once taking a glance at the sunset.

"It is all so amazing, I never thought a place like his would ever exist. How is all this possible?"

"The gods blessed us and wanted us to live in peace and harmony. We were created by Ares to protect humans but of course, in time, the humans turned on us. In large numbers they started attacking women and children of our kind, so we were created a safe haven by the gods. A place where supernaturals could embrace what they are and not have to worry about humans. We still honor and protect them by some of the Werewolves staying

277

on Earth, like us. However, there is never true peace here all the time. We are all different with different opinions and ideas." Wesley stared out over the ocean.

"What do the Werewolves protect humans from?"

"The gods themselves, other supernaturals, other humans. We are just supposed to be protectors. I donate money all the time to charities, women's shelters, and children's homes. We also have many Wolves in our pack that are teachers and lookout for signs of abuse in children. We don't go directly to the authorities but conduct our own search of abusers and try to find the proof. Local authorities then take care of it accordingly. "

I wrapped my arms around his waist. He looked down lovingly and squeezed me tightly. "Let's get you to bed, it's been a long day. Maybe the beach tomorrow?" I squealed and ran to get my pajamas. Before I could reach the bathroom Wesley reached for me and wrapped his arms around my waist. Laughing, "what are you doing? You said get ready to bed!"

"I think I owe you a bit of punishment," he said hoarsely. "After everything that you said today." Glancing up at him questioningly he twirled me around to face him. "You doubted your position as Luna, I think that deserves something right?" Before I could argue he picked me up and slammed his mouth to mine. He was needy and hungry, nothing like the kiss he gave me earlier today. He picked me up and made his hands glide up the bottom of my thighs as I wrapped my legs around him. Lifting me effortlessly he laid me on the bed.

My legs were still wrapped around his waist and his large erection had already started to touch my core. There were too many clothes, I wanted him to take off his pants and take me. I moaned, "Wesley, please, oh gosh." He pushed himself near my core and rubbed me with his dick. He was so hard, and I wanted nothing more for him to free himself.

"No, Kitten, I don't think you deserve it. You don't think you are worthy as Luna," he groaned as he continued to rub against me.

"Please, Wesley."

"Are you my perfect Luna?" He continued to grind against me. His kiss went down my neck and to my chest. Gripping my breast with one of his hands over my clothes, I was itching for him to take off my shirt.

"Wesley," I whined. He stopped rubbing against me.

"I asked you, are you my perfect Luna?" Wesley stopped kissing me and looked into my eyes. His hand released my breast. Was he really waiting for an answer? I grunted in defeat.

"Yes."

"Yes, what?" he growled in my ear. I just wanted him so badly.

"I am your perfect Luna," I nipped at his lower lip. He groaned and sat up quickly, stripping his shirt and pants while I tried to take off the sundress

I was wearing, I was taking too long so he pulled it off swiftly with a few claws.

"Stop ripping my clothes!" I squeaked.

"I like doing it," Wesley got on top of me, I felt his erection on my trailing up my inner thigh as he hovered closer. A chill ran through me, and I automatically showed him my mark. It was an odd feeling, my body automatically moved without me thinking about it. Wesley was getting the picture, taking his lips and sucking on my marking spot. Hot tingles ran down to my toes and especially between my legs.

Wesley

My Luna finally admitted that she was perfect, and I was going to take her and take her hard. Even though she had her heat a few weeks ago, I was still gentle with her. I didn't rail her into oblivion, I held back. Right now, I still wanted to punish her, just a bit.

I sucked on her breasts, leaving marks behind. She was writhing beneath me and begging for more by rubbing her thighs together. "No," I growled at her and cupped her pussy. "This is mine, only mine."

"Please," she begged me again. Remus was getting impatient, he wanted me to take her. He had been growling in my head all day, upset that our smell wouldn't stay on her, even with the mark. He wanted to bite her over and over again until it took. He had grown in strength since we had mated with Charlotte, there was no questioning that.

I swiftly rammed my cock inside her without warning, she screamed in shock as I rocked her into the mattress. My weight was on her as my hips thrust forward into her dripping core. Remus had started to come out, but I fought him, I couldn't have him come out now. He would bite too deep, and we haven't talked to her about what the process was for her to turn. I wanted her to relax before we did anything.

As Remus was crawling at the surface we argued. We compromised as our cock slid in and out of her as she continued to raise her hips for me to plummet into her deeper. Grabbing Charlotte's breasts and gripping them tightly she let out a breathy moan as she came undone. "Wesley, mmm." Her whines were so addicting, I loved it when she begged me. She makes me feel so powerful when I can please her, I think that is the only time I ever feel like I have power because she is the only one, I wanted to conquer.

I pushed into her more as my thrust became erratic. Her arms gripped my biceps and scratched me down the length of my arm. Her hand ran to her clit as she massaged it while I pushed right to her womb. "Wesley, cum in me," spoke. Remus gave me a push and I grew my fangs in a fraction of a second, marking her neck again. Crying out and lifting her head she came close to my shoulder and bit down. Even though she wasn't a Wolf, it felt so damn good. My seed filled her cavern and I continued to spurt thick ropes of cum until it was spilling onto the sheets.

Her bite wasn't hard on my shoulder, but it was in the exact spot she would mark me one day. It felt warm, tender, and tingly. It only made me wish she could mark me now with her own bite. She laid back after her orgasm, a little blood was left on her teeth where she bit me. I chuckled softly as I licked it from the side of her mouth.

"I'm sorry," she said breathlessly, "I don't know why I did that, it was almost automatic." I licked her blood clean and laid down beside her.

"I enjoyed it. You can do it anytime you want," I smirked, and she hit my shoulder. I felt it already healing, there was no more blood dripping from her human mark. Charlotte looked at my shoulder.

"Wow, my teeth marks stayed there," she said.

"What?"

"Usually, when you get cut it heals right away and there is no scarring but look at your shoulder." Sitting up quickly, I ran to the mirror. I held my breath as I gazed into the mirror. There was a mark, it was her own bite on my shoulder. Looking at her and back at the mirror my brows furrowed. Could she mark me when she's human?

"That's interesting." I rubbed my shoulder while looking in the mirror. Charlotte stared intently while I looked back at her. "You marked me, Kitten." Her hazel eyes widened and the biggest grin I had ever seen on her face appeared.

"I did!? Really!?" Eyes gleaming, she ran and gave me a hug, while naked and all. We both stood there hugging each other while admiring each other's marks. I guess she really could mark me, and I wonder if this completed mating would also mean our scents were mixed together.

Chapter 48

Charlotte

The next few days flew by after Wesley and I confirmed that the bite I gave him in our intense love making, did in fact, made our mating complete. His smell was all over me is what his mother and father said. I wasn't getting creepy stares from the other Wolves in the pack house and that put Wesley at ease.

Odin and Astrid were really nice Wolves. They had welcomed me with open arms as I got used to this new land. There was talk about us having a mating ceremony, but I quickly declined. My friends back at the Night Crawler's pack would be so upset if they couldn't be a part of it so his parents decided they would come back with us to visit their old pack. I could hear Ashley cursing my name if she wasn't a part of the whole ordeal.

Astrid also told me about the different species that lived here. The different shifters were fascinating, but I was told to stay away until I took a few classes on shifter culture. Dragons had a specific etiquette they followed and if you made one wrong move, they would typically be a bit cranky. They were very prideful creatures. The Fae interested me a lot since they were the first I came in contact with. There were subspecies of Fae, and the small ones were called pixies, there were forest, water, earth and fire pixies that lived all around but took orders from the Fae King Osiris. They had certain powers that all Faes had such as the ability to control certain elements. They do have one special power, those who are higher ranking, but they do not speak what powers they have. I'm guessing they give themselves a powerful edge.

It really was different here than back home with the Black Claw Pack; even the pack house had a different feel to it. The pack house back home was like a fortress, very hard to get into with a large territory to protect. Here, there was a gate and a fence around the territory but not as many patrols. It was the fact that this was a godly world and people knew their place and what species expected of others. For instance, the Wolves liked their territory and for people to stay off of it. Everyone was to respect that and if they didn't, they were given a right to take care of it themselves. No one had done it for over a hundred years, so the pack was a bit of slack protection.

Along with learning more about the Blue Waters pack, Wesley took me to the beach often. I loved feeling the warm water on my toes and the sand under my feet. I don't know how Earth's beaches were but I'm sure I would be disappointed after this beautiful setting. Dolphins and I swear I saw a siren off in the distance, but Wesley said it was almost impossible. They weren't fond of those with feet, something about being jealous they couldn't walk on land like the rest of us. I had to laugh at that.

We also went to the pack village, it had small shops just like ours back home. They had some clothing which was different from the clothes on Earth. Their fashion sense was a bit different. Jeans weren't very popular among shifters, more of linen pants and shirts for the men. A lot of women wore a tighter version of pants, almost like leggings and used a material I was unfamiliar with. It had a slight sparkle to it, and it made the legs look long and lean. I wanted to go and touch the fabric but obviously didn't. Would they want some human rubbing on their leg? Of course not.

Many women also wore dresses if they weren't planning on shifting for more of an elegant affair. There was a baby shower the second day I was here, and you could see the women lining up at a small home near the pack house. They had small corsets with short, puffed sleeves with an A-line skirt. They were beautiful and came in so many different colors.

Wesley mainly kept me in the pack house territory, said it was safer for now and that he would take me out soon. He kept me close with him always as we traveled around, his insecurities of me not having my scent at the beginning of our trip really took a toll on him. Even after my scent had changed, he squeezed me tightly often and glared at anyone that would look our way.

"Wesley, you don't have to scare everyone away, no one will be my friend," I pouted as we entered the private dining room of his parents. This packhouse was so gigantic that each couple that lived there had a small mini suite.

"I just don't want anyone looking at what is mine." His fist tightened around me. Wesley has always been so laid back and very chill, since we have mated, he has been up my butt and around the corner. He was even waiting for me to emerge from the bathroom every morning after my shower. I had to turn the water in the sink and in the shower on to make sure he could hear what I was doing in there. Which ticked him off a bit, but it was getting overwhelming.

Coming to sit down at the table, I bent down only to be dragged over and put on Wesley's lap. His face sternly looked down at our plates. He put his fork into the eggs and put it toward my mouth. Looking around the table I saw several Wolves watching. Wesley told me how important it was for a male to feed his female, so I took a small bite, and everyone looked back down at their plate and resumed their conversation. Wesley took another large fork-full and held it up to me again and I gazed into his eyes.

His eyes were flickering so fast from black to green, I couldn't tell what was happening. Was Remus or Wesley in control? "Wesley? Remus?" I spoke quietly to him. His eyes continued to flick back and forth, and I started to worry, he wasn't responding to me at all. Darting my eyes around the room I see his parents sitting a few seats down. Doing a whisper yell, to gain their attention I asked for help.

Odin quickly wiped his mouth with his napkin and sat up quickly. His eyes were on Wesley the entire time and smiled when he came up to me and put a hand on Wesley's shoulder. Wesley didn't move to look at his father but continued to hold me tightly, still with eggs on his fork.

"What's wrong with him? Why are his eyes doing that, Odin?" The worry in my voice must have caught Astrid's attention and she came to the other side of me.

"Odin, would you stop holding back information and grinning like an idiot? She doesn't know!" Odin let out a laugh again and Astrid hit him in the chest.

"Darling he is fine," Astrid rubbed my shoulder. "He is fighting with his beast, since you marked him a bit late his Wolf is angry and wants to take care of you now. You know a Wolf bringing food to his mate shows he cares for her, and he is also going to have a possession issues for the next few months."

"B-but he was possessive before? Is it going to be worse?"

"Yes, I'm sorry dear. He has done a great job hiding it, but it looks like Remus just wants to take over. Your voice will calm both, just be patient with them." Astrid and Odin went back to sit down, and Remus or Wesley gave me another bite of food. I kept my mouth shut until we were both fed and left the room.

Today, we were going to the pack doctor to get a full work up before I could take the change. As we were walking, I was quickly scooped up before Wesley hit the elevator button. If his eyes were going to be flickering all day, he is going to be getting on my nerves. I need to tone him down.

"Mate," I demanded. His head whipped around facing me. That was the first time he had any reaction to me speaking all morning. I put both my hands on his face and had him look at me. "I love you so much, but you have got to calm down. You are scaring people and making me feel overwhelmed." Werewolves had duct behind us to get away from Wesley, he must be emitting some sort of Alpha testosterone to leave us alone.

His shoulders relaxed and his grip loosened. Giving him a quick kiss, he let me down and I held his hand. "Thank you, love." His hand squeezed mine and got on the elevator. Still not speaking but at least he is hearing me now.

The doctor ran a few tests—blood, vitals as well as a DNA test because he'd mentioned he wanted to see if there was any change to my DNA so if we had children what were the odds of having just were children or humans. The entire time, Wesley held me in his arms as they poked and prodded me. He never spoke but the loud growls that were in the room gave anything away the shaking of the picture frames and the equipment did.

"I'm so glad you both figured out the whole marking smell issue. That one really had us stumped but you both figured it out in a day. I have to ask though, what made you decide to bite him?" Wesley's eyes went black, and Remus spoke harshly. "This is Remus's mate, mate will do as mate pleases." His voice was deep and dark, and I couldn't help but get a little excited, my legs clenched, and my hands pulled down my dress a bit. Remus noticed and buried his nose in my hair.

"I-I am sorry Alpha. I just wanted to know if it was a feeling or desire to bite. Humans don't normally bite during intercourse…" The doctor was clearly uncomfortable so I cut him off before he could say anymore. "Yes, it was a strong urge, like I was supposed to. My body almost acted on its own because I had never thought about doing it before. I do have to say I was born wolfless," the doctors looked at each other. "My parents were wolves, but I never received one."

"Interesting," Dr. Marcio hummed and took the last vile of blood from my arm. "That is something we are going to keep a record of. You have your parents DNA and it's strong even if without a wolf. Maybe you are just a primal human," he chuckled. "Other than that, it looks like we have everything we need. We can start the transformation tomorrow; we can have you stay here in the hospital room or back at your suite-"

"Mate will stay in Remus's room tonight," Remus said blankly. "No one will touch mate while mate sleeps."

"O-Of course, Alpha." Doctor Prescott was shaking. "We will run tests afterwards. We will plan on you biting her tomorrow morning, she needs to have an empty stomach just in case she feels sick during transition."

Remus stood up and without being dismissed carried me out of the room. Letting out a little squeak as he pulled me in the elevator. He set me down and pressed stop for the elevator to hoover between floors. Before I could say a word, he pressed me against the cold walls of the elevator. Eyes black he nipped at my bottom lip before slinking his tongue into my mouth. It was euphoric, each time he kissed me. It was harder this time, possessive as he purred in his chest. Gripping me tightly by the waist, he started to breathe hard and pushed me further into the elevator's wall. His erection was on his stomach, and he felt extremely hard. Letting out a little moan, he stopped.

With his forehead pressed to mine, he breathed in deeply. The green eyes I had come to love so much came back. "I'm sorry, Kitten. I've been fighting with him all day."

"It's alright, I've never seen you guys do that before."

"I've never had it happen before. Remus and I are very possessive of you right now, it is best if you always stay close. I think it is because you are still human, and you are my fragile little doll." He grinned at me and pressed the stop button again to make the elevator move. His hand slid down to mine. "Not much longer," I whispered.

Vera Foxx

Chapter 49

Wesley

Remus was giving me a damn terrible time. He was ravenous for Charlotte, he wanted to fuck her over and over again and let her see his dominance over her. He had always wanted our mate, hell I did too but he was going overboard. We have always made a great team, able to complement each other. Remus, for the most part, stayed quiet unless he really had something to say and it usually was a right decision to listen to him, now I'm not so sure.

Once Charlotte bit us and officially completed the mating he went into overdrive. When we first bit her I knew we weren't as possessive as what some Wolves were, but I figured it was because that was his personality, apparently not. Now the bond was completed, and we claimed each other. He's been hovering over her for the past few days. Hell, she can't even go to the bathroom without Remus sitting outside the damn door. I heard her turning on the showers and sinks so we couldn't hear her. I thought it was adorable, but Remus was pissed as hell. He wanted to know every bit of what she was doing.

After days of fighting, I was getting tired and weak, mentally anyway. Charlotte finally put her foot down after the whole dining room fiasco. People were staring and wondering why we were being possessive suddenly since they knew I already claimed her. Luckily Charlotte has such a strong bond to both of us and didn't kick us out of the bedroom, not that we would leave anyway.

Tomorrow was her big day, as she was going to be bitten and finally turn like she had wanted to for weeks. Part of it I know was for my sake, but another part was to protect herself. She didn't like relying on me and the other pack members for her own safety. She's so strong and understanding I don't know how I got so lucky to be paired with her.

That evening we were getting ready for bed; she has her own little routine she does in the bathroom that I just find adorable. She washes her face, applies moisturizer and cream to help her look, "youthful," she says but she doesn't need any of it. She then pats her face and squints her eyes, like she is telling herself something mentally and points to herself in the mirror. I was leaning up against the bathroom door frame and when she turned around, she didn't even jump.

"Knowing you are always there is great and all, but you need to calm down. I'm only ten feet away from you babe." Charlotte walks up and tugs on my shirt to go to bed. We both climb in the covers, and I feel her warm body up against me. She nuzzles into my chest, and I could hear Remus purring.

"Let's fuck mate now and before the change," he whispered in my mind.

"The hell man, we don't want her exhausted. What is wrong with you?"

"Worried, worried about mate. Don't want mate to sleep for days."

"Charlotte will be fine, they say it is normal she will sleep. That is when the goddess will bless her with her Wolf. Aren't you at least excited about that part?" Remus grumbled and went to the back of my mind complaining.

"How are you babe? You seem upset?" Charlotte looked up at me with her hazel eyes. Always worried about everyone else.

"I'm fine, Remus is worried about you though. He doesn't like not being able to see you for a few days while you sleep."

"Aww isn't he a sweetie," Charlotte chided. I pecked her lips and pulled her on top of me to sleep. I've come quite fond of her sleeping right on top of me. She is like a small little blanket, and I can feel her heartbeat with mine. She let out a sigh and rubbed my arm with her fingertips until we both fell into darkness.

***

The sun had just come over the horizon. In the middle of the night, we switched our sleeping position to the perfect big spoon to little spoon ratio. She stirred and was wiggled her ass right against my groin and it made Remus stir. *"Fuck mate now?"* Remus said, panting. I groaned and Charlotte fluttered her eyes open and smiled. She wiggled her ass a bit more before I put my hands on her hips, unable to control myself.

"Be careful what you start, Kitten. Because Remus has already said he wanted to finish it." Her giggles filled the air.

"Oh really? Puppy wants to come play?" She sang. Remus being the prideful thing he was, came forward like a storm and pushed his dick hard up against her ass. Her groaning only made us harder as he swiveled our hips in a circular motion against her plump ass. "Mmm, Remus." Charlotte didn't even have to look in my eyes to know it was Remus, damn prick. Remus had to bite her, hard and deep, almost to the bone to make the change happen. I had to agree to this because he holds the venom, but I didn't want him to be rough with her, I didn't want her exhausted.

Charlotte

Remus flipped me over, so he was now on top of me, he bent down and started kissing my neck roughly, sucking and nipping and putting his hand underneath my shirt. My skin had chills from his touch and once he started sucking on my breast, I moaned at the feeling. The cool air when his mouth let go of my tit made me let out a breathy moan while gripping his hair.

"Remus not puppy," he nipped at my ear. I loved teasing him, he was so easy. I just had to tell him he was a puppy and then tell him what I wanted, and he would do it to prove he wasn't. Remus continued to growl as he roamed my body with his mouth and hands, I tried to sit up so I could touch his muscles, I was just itching to put my nails in them.

Remus pushed my legs apart, somehow, he had gotten us both naked in record time because I don't remember taking off my clothes. His nose dove between my thighs, licking my clit. My body had trouble adjusting to the sudden intrusion, so my hips squirmed beneath his touch. Taking his massive hands, he pinned my hips in place. His tongue shot in my cavern and made me squeal, "Oh, Remus!"

My hands gripped his long hair, pushing him in deeper as I rode his face.

"Stop moving, Mate."

"But I want to touch you too," I whined feeling the suction on my clit being relieved. He smiled at me and rolled us over, so I was straddling him. I kissed down his neck and had my hands roam down his chest muscles and into the crevices of his abs. I lightly touched his thighs and all around his big friend, but never touched it. It kept twitching and I could see liquid sparkle in the dim room. The chills he was getting were making me laugh internally but he was catching on.

"Mate," he growled and pinched my hips. "Mate–" before he could complain anymore, I took his whole cock in my mouth. He had been waiting for it so long he let out a roar that made me jump in surprise. I started bobbing and moaning into his cock and he gripped me tighter. Massaging his balls caused him to grumble in protest. Remus pulled off and flipped me over. He was definitely a beast since he liked doing it from behind so much.

And maybe me too.

He prodded my entrance and was taking his time, teasing me. Stupid Alpha. I did deserve it.

Vera Foxx

"Puppy," I whined.

That seemed to do the trick, so he pushed himself inside me without a second thought. He pulled my hair and it made me arch my back. I met each thrust with my own leaning back into him. I could feel my own wetness drip out of me. He rammed his dick inside me like there was no tomorrow as I felt my walls clenching him. My breasts were rubbing on the mattress which was making everything feel even better. Remus was being loud, using grunting and growling noises, sometimes yelling a battle cry how much he loved to be buried balls deep inside me. The noises he made turned me on even more and hearing the slapping of our skin was so primal and delicious. I could feel myself climbing.

Being so close almost had me scared, this was it. Once we both reached heaven, he was going to bite me so hard that I really was going to go to sleep and wake up with an entirely different body anatomy.

Sensing my distress, I heard Wesley's gentle voice in my head: *"It is going to be alright, Kitten. We will never leave you while you sleep. I love you."*

"I love you too, both of you. Please keep me safe."

"You can always feel safe in my arms my love, because I will never let you go." I finally let go and fell back from heaven. Remus's teeth bit into the same mark that Wesley had graced me with. There was pleasure but after a few seconds I felt the pain. It must have hit the bone.

I let out an ear-piercing scream as Remus didn't let go. I didn't know if it was normal or not, but I felt him tugging at my shoulder. "Remus, it hurts!" I cried but he still didn't let go. I could feel Wesley panicking and I couldn't feel Remus at all. I was getting tired and fast, my head dropped into the pillow.

Wesley

Shit, shit, shit. Charlotte was screaming for us to stop, and Remus was in beast mode not letting go. I started prodding against him so I could have control again, but he wasn't having any of it. I continued to push until I saw that Charlotte fell asleep. Part of me was relieved she wasn't feeling the pain, but I was pissed as hell against Remus. The hell was he thinking?

Our teeth retracted and he licked Charlotte's wound clean, I continued to try and take back control, but he was still ignoring me, that bastard. He got up from the bed, cleaning her with a towel gently. Putting on a large shirt from my dresser drawer he moved her carefully as he dressed her. Charlotte was laying back on the bed, covers draped over her and Remus was just staring at her rubbing his hands over her arms. I could feel her body against us, she was still breathing but trying to mind link her was impossible. She was out.

290

"You were hurting her, you dick!" I yelled at Remus.

"Mate is fine, it is Okay. Mate is strong." He took a claw and pulled her hair behind her ear, admiring his handy work of a bite. It was red from the venom he inflicted on her, but it was already healing. I could see her eyes twitch; she must have been dreaming.

"You were pulling at her damn shoulder, Remus. What the hell was that?" I said angrily.

"Releasing venom."

"I know you were doing that, idiot, you didn't have to pull on her so damn hard."

"Mate was fighting it, had to make her stop." He shrugged our shoulders and curled up next to her. He wasn't going to let her go tonight, not after what he had to do. I could feel his guilt for hurting her, so I decided to leave it.

"Sleep well, my love," I mind linked her one last time as we stayed close to her.

Chapter 50

Under the Moon

Remus hovered over Charlotte's body the entire day. Her hair was spread across the pillow, sightly breathing with one hand resting on her chest and another around Remus's arm that he particularly placed. He stared at her, memorizing every freckle and eyelash. The way her breathing would sometimes hitch when a cold breeze would go by her face. Her slender neck and all the dips and grooves that go along with it, he loved it. Every part about her body as well as her mind he cherished.

Many, including Wesley, thought he was just a docile Wolf. That he was lazy and only showed himself when he really needed to. Wesley was in control most of the time so naturally, Wesley thought he and his Wolf were perfectly in sync. Part of it was true, they did care for one another but there was another problem Wesley was completely unaware of.

Remus was depressed, even though it wasn't common to find a depressed Wolf but there were some instances. Remus had been with Wesley for many years and as soon as Wesley and Remus were old enough to find a mate his heart soared. Remus wanted his mate badly. The first few years of getting to know Wesley kept him calm, but as time went on and other friends and family gained their mates, he slowly went back into the background. Remus wasn't a puppy, like his mate likes to say, he is an actual beast. When his pack was in danger, he emerged to help Wesley to defend it. Pack members were afraid of Remus because when he did emerge, he was the full definition of a demon Wolf. He was unpredictable and scary and took orders from no one, even Wesley.

Once Remus had found Charlotte, he was elated but still wary. Was this all just a dream? When will he wake up? When he sunk his teeth into Charlotte he woke up. He was still not in his full-blown Alpha possession mode but he was waking up out of his terrible funk. This really is his mate but how long would it last? He had been depressed for at least one hundred some years. Could he come out of it so quickly? He wanted more proof she was there. There was a link and connection, and Wesley could feel it fully, but why couldn't he? He loved her, that was for sure. Everything about her was strong, feminine, funny, innocent, the perfect Luna. Charlotte was his mate, but he wanted more, but what could that be?

It was the damn bite. When her teeth sunk into their skin, a light bulb went off in his head. The full connection between Wesley, Charlotte, and himself took him out of his depression. The new zest for life, the new pull to be with his mate rose and the urge to protect and love his mate fiercely was there. Wesley had been in control for so long, now he wanted some of his time back, especially now that his mate was here.

However, she hadn't moved in an hour or so, she didn't twitch or even blinked. Remus was feeling distressed at his mate's lack of movements and shallow breathing, so he ordered for his parents as well as the pack doctors to come into the room. There was only one problem, he wouldn't let anyone touch his beloved mate.

"You have to let them see her, son," Astrid, his mother pleaded. "It will be best for both of you, it will give you relief as well as check on her well-being. Please, Remus, you don't even have to leave the room.

Remus sat in the bed with Charlotte's limp body in his arms. He had her cradled to his chest now as everyone was staring. Remus was the beast of Wesley, but he had become even more feral now that his mate was going through the change. Several doctors looked at each other back and forth and wrote down the interactions between the two. Wesley's Wolf was in control, and he wasn't going to let go any time soon.

"Remus, please let Wesley come forward. Maybe I could talk to him? We are just trying to help. She needs a washcloth to wipe away the sweat. Could I do it at least?" Remus continued to stare at the doctors and nodded yes for his mother. Astrid quickly ran to the bathroom and ran cool water under the sink. Astrid needed to get Remus to relent or at least step away from Charlotte just for a moment so they could check on her vitals. If her fever got too high, it could cause seizures and ruin the entire process.

Astrid jumped quickly across the room and once he was near Remus, she silently asked permission to put the towel on her. Remus looked down at his sleeping mate, she was beautiful to him, and he promised he would protect her from anything and everyone that might hurt her while she slept. His mate was so nervous, and the pain was a shock for her that it made Remus feel utter guilt. Would she be mad when she woke up?

Wesley continued to nudge Remus, but Remus wasn't going to let him have his way. Remus was her puppy, that's right, her puppy. He finally accepted the terrible nickname because it made her happy. He wiped some of the water that was dripping down her face with the pad of his thumb and smiled at her. Mate was strong and mighty to come up from nothing and now rising above and becoming a leader, a Luna. He smiled at her and all the onlookers watched in awe.

The doctors cleared their throat and Remus gave them a glare. "We are sorry, Alpha Remus. Please let us take her temp and blood pressure. You can still hold her, there will be minimal touching, we swear by it." Each doctor shook in fear, this was a death sentence, and they knew it. "Just think about what Charlotte would want you to do. She trusts us, she said we could take vitals. Can you honor her wishes?" Dr. Prescott said begging. Remus growled at his reasoning because he knew that prick of a doctor was right.

Remus finally nodded but held onto her tight. They took her blood pressure, temperature and were even able to get a vial of blood from her to test the progress. Doctors smiled and bowed to Remus and left the room. Wesley's mother and father continued to stay, he had been beside his mate all day without shower or food. "Son, how about you take a shower, get some food, just a little break. We both can watch her." Astrid looked up at Odin with a large smile as she sat on the bed. Odin was the perfect mate for her, she was compassionate while Odin was the protector. Like how a typical Werewolf couple should be.

Remus moved but still gripped onto Charlotte tightly like she was the most precious gift, just like a mother would hold a baby to her breasts to protect it from all harm. Astrid did a bold move and put her hand on Charlotte, Remus didn't growl, just looked at her hand on his mate. "It is alright dear, both of us will be here. Don't you want to be handsome when she wakes up? You know how she loves it when you wear your hair down." She put her hands on his hair and brushed it out of his face.

Remus thought it over, Charlotte did like his dirty blond locks out of his usual bun he wore. He even started growing a small braid on the back of his head that she loved so much. He laid her on the bed and covered her with blankets, she was a small rag doll he had to place carefully. Kissing her forehead and rubbing her hair he gave her small words of encouragement. "Remus be back mate, sleep."

With that, Remus went to shower and groom himself to make sure he was the most attractive Alpha when she woke.

✳✳✳

Charlotte could feel the wind tickle her nose as she slowly woke. The sun was unbearably bright, it must be noon because it was high in the sky. She rubbed her eyes gently and could feel small tickles across her skin, looking to the left and right of her she saw tall green grass dancing around her. With eyebrows furrowed she sat up and realized she was in the middle of a meadow. Small wildflowers sprung here and there and there was a not-too-distant stream singing across the rocks.

Charlotte thought to herself of how exactly she could arrive at such a place. The last thing she remembered was lying in bed with Wesley or Remus and he… that's right, he'd bitten her. Touching her shoulder, she rubbed it to find no blood, but merely the simple scar that Wesley—and now Remus—had left on her shoulder. Smiling widely, she realized she must be dreaming. Astrid had mentioned that she would dream, where she would meet her Wolf and possibly a goddess. She was very busy though so if you got to see her, you would be lucky.

She never thought she would meet such a person anyway. She was human mated to an actual Werewolf, there wasn't anything too special about her anyway. Standing up she brushed off the dead grass and started walking to the stream. Small little creatures such as chipmunks, sprites and butterflies invaded the stream. Squatting down she put her hand in to feel the coolness of the water. Everything felt so real, that it wasn't really a dream. The colors were vivid, almost more so than Bergarian itself.

After sitting and playing in the water she heard soft steps approaching. It wasn't just one pair of footsteps, but it was a few. Looking over her shoulder she saw a blonde Wolf with green eyes approaching as well as a woman wearing some of the same clothing that other she-Wolves wore in Bergarian. Smiling, she stood up to greet the mystery woman, which she has dubbed the Moon Goddess, because who else could it be? Especially with the moon crescent on her head.

"Hello, Charlotte. Nice to meet you." Her voice was as smooth as the stream itself and she instantly felt comfortable. Not sure what to do, bow, curtsy or even hold out a hand for a handshake she stood there and shyly smiled and held her hands to her chest. Selene laughed and put her arm around Charlotte and pulled her into a hug.

"You always were such a shy one, weren't you? Wesley was the perfect match for you and pulled you out of your shell. Just watch out for Remus, he seems to have snapped out of his funk and you will see him around so much more." Charlotte nodded, not sure what to say to that. She had known that Remus had been possessive but was hoping it wasn't for the long run.

"As you have been told, you get your Wolf today." The Moon Goddess smiled at her. "You were not gifted a wolf at birth because the wolf I wanted to give you was to be special." Charlotte smiled up at the Moon Goddess in understanding. The gods know more than she, and who was she to question it. The path she was led down in life led her to Wesley and that was all that mattered.

"This is Victoria." Charlotte went to step up to her wolf, but it backed up and whimpered. Not wanting to scare her any further Charlotte stepped back and looked up in surprise at Selene.

Selene smiled and took Charlotte's hand in hers and walked her up the stream. "I'm sorry, Victoria is a bit shy, just like yourself. Anytime someone gets their Wolf there is a brief period of adjustment for both Wolf and human. Your mind and your body will have to slowly come together. She will stay in the back of your mind; you can speak with her, but she may not speak back. In a month or so she will start to show herself to you more and the first time you shift, it will be on a full moon."

Charlotte nodded in understanding.

"Born Werewolves don't have to go through this adjustment period because they have already had their wolves." She chuckled as she pulled me into the low-level stream. "But you were born to Werewolf parents, weren't you?" Charlotte gasped at her knowing. Then again, she was a goddess. "They were good Wolves," the Moon Goddess said softly. "They protected you from rogues, keeping you hidden in your car seat. A good human came and found you, took you where all the humans go. If you were born with a Wolf... it would have been disastrous for you." Charlotte's head fell.

If Charlotte had a Wolf then she would have been stronger than most of the children. She would never get sick, run the fastest, and when her wolf finally appeared one day, she wouldn't know what to do. It was as it should be, to not have a Wolf.

"I am very grateful to have Wesley and Remus, I just wanted to say thank you for that." Charlotte quickly changed the subject, not wanting to dwell on the past. That wasn't her life, she couldn't even remember it. She was only grateful her parents had saved her. "They are the best thing that has ever happened to me. I would be utterly lost, probably still alone," a small tear fell from her cheek. The Goddess wiped it away. "He is the most wonderful person, I really don't deserve him or Remus. He made me see who I was really supposed to be." Charlotte sniffed.

"I knew you were going to have a rough life, when your life crossed paths with Roman. I knew you would need something special to help you along the way and save you. I also know you don't want to hear it, but everything happens for a reason. You have become so strong, Charlotte. The trials you have overcome not just physically, but in your mind will give you an excellent position as Luna, never doubt yourself." The Goddess put a hair behind Charlotte's ear lovingly. Several other Wolves trotted up to them and were wagging their tails affectionately. They continued to rub their heads next to The Goddess but still keeping distance from Charlotte.

"Who are they?" Charlotte wondered.

"These are other Wolves waiting for their humans," she petted them affectionately. "There are going to be a lot more humans coming to

Bergarian, and they are already ready for them. It won't be much longer," she winked at Charlotte while she smiled back.

"That's amazing! I'm so glad others get to experience a mate too. Being a human without a mate would be terrible now that I think about it."

"Yes, some humans are deserving of them, and those will get one. You and Clarabelle will be the 'new frontier' of human mates.

"I feel so important," I giggled.

"And you are, especially to your mate, Wesley, and Remus. We must get you home hmm?" I nodded my head excitedly.

"Just remember to take things slowly, pup. Your mate will guide you along the way."

"Thank you, thank you for everything," Charlotte hugged her tightly. As Selene held her tightly the bright sunshine began to fade but even in the darkness, she felt the tight hold on her.

Chapter 51

Charlotte

I could still feel the warmth surrounding me. Even though the bright sun from my supposed dreamland had already set, the darkness did not feel all that cold. In fact, I felt extremely comfortable. Feeling myself nuzzled into a warm, familiar scent I let out a little moan of satisfaction. It feels so familiar, where do I know that scent from? It has intensified so much that it makes my heart skip a beat. It's musky with a hint of sandalwood and coconut. I love it, I want to bathe in it.

A low rumble of a purr goes off in my ear. Fluttering my eyes open I see nothing but a rock-hard wall in my way, yet soft enough to be comfortable. It was skin, beautifully bronzed skin. Looking up through my lashes I see the love of my life staring back at me with the biggest grin on his face, the panty-dropping grin that I love so much.

"Wesley!" I squealed and put my arms around his neck. He chuckles and keeps his arms around me but just squeezed tighter.

"Kitten, goddess, I missed you." His nose goes to my ear and kisses it lightly. "You have no idea how worried everyone has been. You slept for four full days. Remus wouldn't let me have control until you started waking up." His hold tightened and I started nuzzling into his neck, he just smelled so darn good.

"I'm sorry, I came back when the Goddess said I could come back, but why in the world do you smell so good?" Taking another big sniff into his neck he started laughing and peppering me with kisses.

"Your Wolf senses must have picked up." He cupped my face with both of his hands, "that is my smell. I'm your mate so it smells extra good to you, what do I smell like?" Wesley said, full of wonder.

"Sandalwood and coconut, and you have hints of some other smells in there but those stand out the most. I just want to eat you up!" I nipped at his neck, and he growled back playfully. Both of us were a laughing mess, the sheets were falling off the bed and the pillows were now scattered across the floor. There was a knock at the door, but we kept tickling and laughing with each other and didn't notice people had walked in the room. We heard someone clear their throat and both looked up.

Wesley's parents as well as a few doctors came into the room in shock. Wesley only had a pair of boxers on, and I was only in one of his shirts, pretty sure I wasn't wearing any sort of undergarments because I felt a slight breeze. I froze, with a slight yip of a scream and Wesley got in front of me to shield my nakedness. He growled slowly and his claws and teeth come out. His parents and the doctors backed away and close the door. "It's alright, they didn't see me," the obvious blush on my face did nothing to hide my embarrassment.

"They shouldn't have barged in like that, that was ridiculous." Wesley pulled on some pants and a shirt and headed to the door to open it.

"Wesley, wait!" I held my hand to reach him while I was kneeling on the mattress. "I haven't seen you, why don't you come back?" I gave him a pout and he rolled his eyes. That did it, no crabbier Wesley.

"You know how to calm me down don't you?" He hopped on the bed and pulled me to him. "How about, you go shower, get dressed, and then we have the doctors come in to check on you Okay?" I agreed and he picked me up bridal style to the bathroom. "I'll be back, don't leave our bedroom without me, alright?"

✳✳✳

The doctors did their little routine as they had so many times before. Blood pressure, blood tests, temperature, the whole physical. Since Wesley was in control, he was doing well. Remus was a pain from what Astrid said, he wouldn't let anyone near us, and it was all they could do to get a temperature on me. I couldn't help but laugh at the dinner table of all the crazy stuff he did. Wesley kept rolling his eyes yelling at everyone he couldn't control Remus and he wasn't sure what was going on. Remus just overtook his whole body and blocked him in the back of Remus' mind.

"...and then Remus yelled at the warriors outside your door, he said he could smell their pheromones thinking about their Luna as a sex doll!" Zachary roared in laughter while Wesley leaned his head back on the dining room chair. The dining room consisted of large rectangular tables, it was more of the common dining room and not so much as the exquisite one they have for royal guests. A lot of the pack members were there listening in on the stories of the mighty Remus taking care of his mate.

Wesley was over the stories; he gripped my thigh under the table, and I put my hand on top of his. The whole pack house was in an uproar of bragging rights about the first full blooded human being turned in their pack. I got so many congratulations that I couldn't really eat, Wesley was getting agitated because he could hear my stomach growling. Finally, he picked me up and put me on his lap a little harshly. Scowling at him he let out a quiet 'sorry.'

Putting some grilled chicken on a fork, Wesley began to feed me as Remus did earlier in the week. I didn't hesitate, it just came naturally, and I gave him a nod of how good it was. "So, what was it like, Kitten? Meeting the Moon Goddess?" I finished chewing my chicken and pondered for a minute as I swallowed.

"She was, so down to Earth, or down to Bergarian? I don't know. She wasn't intimidating at all, like a motherly figure or a good best friend. I even got a hug." I bragged as I bit into some garlic bread. Wesley chuckled and rubbed his nose along my shoulder. He still smelled divine; it was all I could do not to sniff him.

Astrid came and sat in my seat beside Wesley since it was now vacant. "Tell me, what did she say to you? Everything she says can be interpreted in so many ways, she can be hard to read sometimes," Astrid asked.

"There were a lot of Wolves that came up to her after we talked, they only went to her because they were still shy of me. She said that those Wolves were ready to meet their own humans. I was one of the first full blooded humans to change and it wouldn't end there. So many more humans are going to be coming here and they will gain a mate too, only the ones that are worthy."

Everyone smiled at the table, especially some of the unmated Wolves. "Do you think that means just Wolves or other shapeshifters or supernaturals beings could get a human mate?" Zachary questioned.

"I can't see why other supernatural beings wouldn't get a human mate. I think it is quite plausible," Astrid said. There was silence around our end of the table while the unmated Wolves at the other spoke excitedly. Wolves, just like humans, like to gossip and I'm sure a Bergarian will be ready to make that news spread.

"Your training will start shortly after you gain a good relationship with your Wolf. That will be a few weeks so it will happen when you are back home," Odin spoke as he cleaned his beard from food that dribbled on it. I couldn't get over his size, he wasn't as tall as Wesley, but he was nothing but muscle. His long beard, hair, and braids made him even more intimidating. His sleeveless shirt looked like it was about to rip off of him and Astrid was just a dainty thing like me.

Astrid smacked her mate in the chest. "Don't you be thinking about that. It will be a few weeks. Give her some time to get used to her other features from her Wolf," Astrid gave him a glare and mumbled under her breath. "Damn Alphas can't do anything but have sex and train." I burst out in a fit of laughter while Wesley looked amused. Some of the tables were looking at me but I couldn't help but laugh hearing his own mother.

"You heard that?" Zachary asked.

"As clear as day! Why can't you?" I raised my voice.

"Of course, I can, but humans wouldn't be able to hear it. Looks like the hearing is starting to come in." Zachary gave me a smile and poked his fork into the chicken on his plate and it made a loud, 'tap' sound.

"Ouch, you didn't have to do it so hard!" I rubbed my ears.

"Do *what* so loud?"

I then started hearing the loud clicking and clacking of plates and utensils. I stopped eating and looked around the room, people weren't forcefully putting their forks on their plates, but it sounded unbearable. Closing my eyes, I shook my head and some of the sound went away. Thumping now invaded my ears, loud thumping and heavy breathing. I peeked up at Wesley who was looking at me with concern in his eyes and put his hand on my back. "What's wrong, Kitten?" He wasn't yelling but it rang in my ears. Covering my ears, I pushed the chair away from the table which was insanely loud. It was nails on a chalkboard.

Humming in my head to keep the sound out Wesley seems to know the problem and whisks me away outside. My eyes were open, and he was taking me deep into the forest while I held my ears shut, it wasn't doing much to keep the sound out, but enough to where I wasn't wincing in pain.

"Kitten?" he mind-linked. It was much softer than the noises around me, feeling like the steps of the insects around me gave me an eerie vibe.

"Why is it so loud?" I complained.

"Your senses are coming in, I'm going to help you calm it down, OK?" I nodded, feeling the hairbrush across my ears.

"Concentrate on one noise, listen to my voice, and only my voice when I speak out loud alright?" I nodded again and he spoke softly and tenderly.

"I'm right here, with you now. Concentrate on just my voice. Block out everything else and just look at me, listen to me." Trying to block out the sounds was difficult; I could still hear the stream that was at least one hundred yards away and the stupid pixies that think this is hilarious. They keep shaking their little necklaces and chirping at one another.

"Charlotte, don't worry about those stupid, fucking pixies, concentrate on me." His voice was still soft even after cursing. "I love you so much, Charlotte. I'm so happy you are here with me, giving up a human life to be thrown into something more. Being an Alpha, I'm not supposed to be afraid of anything, however, while you slept to accept not just me but the entire pack, I found that there is one thing I am afraid of. I'm afraid of losing you, Charlotte. Don't ever leave me because I don't know what Remus and I could ever do without you." He was on his knees and his arms were around my waist. My hands slowly came off my ears. Listening to him tell me his undying love, for me, again, was the best feeling. His words helped me learn to concentrate on the one noise and soon all the other noises faded away.

Some noises were still loud but being able to concentrate on one thing at a time will help. Putting my arms on his shoulders I smiled and whispered, "thank you and I love you."

"Soon it will be second nature. For now, we will try to keep loud noises to a minimum. Maybe we should just head to bed." He gave me a wink and wiggled his eyebrows.

"Thinking about ravaging me in bed, Alpha?" I cocked an eyebrow. He grunted in approval and gave me a peck on the lips. The noise had settled down considerably and I was almost feeling normal. What was normal though?

Wesley stood up and tried to grab my hand, but I jumped away smirking at his failed attempt. "Charlotte," he grunted. "What are you doing?" I gave him a little smirk and stepped back a few feet. "Kitten…" he warned as he tried to stalk towards me. I had been reading up on just your average Wolves because Remus was in fact, a Wolf. Reading about their behaviors and possessiveness was quite interesting and I wanted to see if this one theory was true.

"Charlotte, we need to get you back to rest." His voice was deep, deeper than what I was used to and it gave me a chill that went straight to my core. Breathing deep, smelling my arousal, he growled and stalked closer.

Without a second thought, I bolted. I started running as fast as I could, I knew he would catch me, but I was still going to make him work for it. I ran through the trees, each step I made on the forest moss, small little firefly lights came out and zoomed by. I started laughing at the sight, not worrying about if Wesley would find me. The air felt so much cooler than it did earlier in the afternoon. Some forest pixies flew with me and tried to tangle my hair. I just swatted them away and told them to shoo. They would come back and tell me to shoo, thinking my choice of words was funny.

I could hear the stream in the distance, the one that I had heard earlier and thought it would be a good idea to jump over it. I got closer and before I jumped, I whipped my head around to see if Wesley was nearby. The smile on my face faded when I looked back not seeing him behind me, I heard no heartbeat, his heavy breathing, concentrating as hard as I could I listened for him. Nothing.

Surely, I didn't lose him? "Wesley? Wesley, are you there?" Becoming worried, I looked back at the stream and back into the forest. Was I lost? Did I wander off the territory? My heart sped up not knowing where I was, so I headed back in the same direction from where I came. The sun was setting, and the fireflies were more prominent under the moons. The pixies were gone, and it was completely silent. Too quiet. Rubbing my arms up and down to keep warm, I stopped. I could mind-link! Geez.

"Wesley?" I mind-linked him.

Nothing.

"Not funny anymore!"

Nothing.

I was about to scream for help but was tackled gently to the ground in a large patch of the magical moss. It was almost like a forest mattress falling into it. As I fell, I saw the little fireflies fly above me as a rough calloused hand broke my fall behind my back. His warm scent engulfed me as he nuzzled into my neck.

"Gotcha."

Chapter 52

Wesley

Seeing Charlotte this morning waking up was a huge burden lifted from my soul. Remus stayed awake the entire time Charlotte was asleep, I was both grateful and annoyed I didn't get any time to be with her. I had been appalled at some of the things he did while she was sleeping. Not only did he yell at warriors but also demanded all unmated males leave the entire packhouse. We were mated with her so it shouldn't really matter but to Remus it did. Luckily no one listened but it was still embarrassing.

I felt the tension he felt, not knowing how she was doing. He couldn't ask and he couldn't get her to mind-link. This new personality he has shown the past couple of days had been concerning but my mother mentioned that Remus was too calm for an Alpha all this time. Now I will have to relearn to control him as best I can and his possessiveness. Charlotte certainly woke him up from his slumber of whatever he was going through. I'd heard of Wolf's depression but even now I didn't think he would ever admit to it.

While sitting at the dinner table, Charlotte talked about meeting the goddess, she was animated and happy. Her hands would move as she talked, and her smiles were directed to the little pups that gathered around the table.

In the few days we had been here she had won over most of the pups. She talked well with the little ones, and she also did well with the ones without their Wolves yet. Charlotte helped them with their schooling as well as play card games with the older ones. There were many times I had to step in and make sure none of the males touched her. Just because she was marked and mated didn't mean some hormonal teenager might try to touch her.

Many Wolves stood or sat close to her to hear dream but also to congratulate her on the change. I didn't like the fact she was getting all the attention and affection from other Wolves. I was to be her protector and she should only care about me. This newfound possessiveness gave me a nudge and I grabbed her by her hips and put her a little too rough on my lap and I got an accusing stare. Just nuzzling into her made her forgive me but damn people need to leave my things alone.

I'm lucky to have such an affectionate mate.

Charlotte has a long way to go to receive her Wolf in its full form and be able to shift. She will undergo several sensatory changes such as smell, sound, and sight. When she first woke up and commented how good I smelled, it made me feel less creepy now that she understands how I love smelling her. "I can't get over how you smell so GOOD!" she moaned in my ear as she was nuzzling it. Wolves at the table didn't even look up, they knew how good mates smell, this was just our way.

"Keep moaning about how my smell is and I might have to take you under the table," I growled in her ear.

She gasped. "Not in front of your parents," she swatted my chest playfully while I chuckled and put another piece of food in her mouth.

Even with being completely enthralled with Charlotte, I couldn't help but wonder how the pack was doing at home. I quickly mind-linked Evan to get a status update.

"Evan, how is the pack?"

"Great Alpha. Things are running smoothly. New Wolves want to join our pack. I told them they had to wait until your arrival."

"Excellent. We will leave in two days and prepare a Luna and Mating ceremony that will happen in two weeks' time."

"Great idea, I'll let the others know."

Charlotte and I had discussed there are two different ceremonies, and she didn't want to have too many parties. We agreed to combine them all into one sizeable party and she was satisfied. Charlotte never liked the attention on her too much and this was a great compromise. She didn't care for the materialistic things like most she-Wolves did and demanded only one dress instead of two for each ceremony. I couldn't help but laugh at her rant on about wasting money. I'm a fucking billionaire in the human world, does she honestly think we would run out of money?

Charlotte began talking again and when my mother mentioned how alphas only wanted sex and training, which is kind of true, but then I could feel her pain. She was hurting and it was a pain I haven't felt in years.

"Son, her hearing has come in. You know what to do right?" my mother said, concerned. Her hands gripped the table to touch her but even the slightest touch would sound like nails on the chalkboard to Charlotte. Swiftly picking her up I carried her to the woods, the sounds here would be less and there wouldn't be high pitch sounds of utensils hitting plates.

Once controlled, she darted off into the woods. As she continued running and laughing, I went into hunting mode. I slowed my heart, my breathing so she couldn't hear. Her sense of smell would still be there, but I would be downwind of her. There was a perfect spot of Purple Fairy Moss laying on the forest floor. It was thick and soft, perfect for me to pounce on her.

Hearing her footsteps through the woods, she was coming back from where she came from. Feeling the worry and agitation in her voice, I decided to pounce. A soft squeal graced my ear as I pinned her down in the moss and purple lights flew from it.

"Gotcha." I breathed and planted a kiss on her lips. She smiled at me and caressed my face.

"One day, it will be an even fight."

"I am an Alpha, I don't think you could beat me."

"Oh yeah? You just wait," she pointed into my chest. Instead of laughing, I stared into her eyes. The little freckles on her face were still there that I loved so much. I prayed once her Wolf came in it would not erase them. Her skin glowed under the blue moon that was over our heads. Taking my fingertip, I pushed back some hair near her forehead. Her breathing slowed and her hand came up to my face. We just held each other, looked at each other, and studied our faces.

"I love you," she whispered.

"I love you more," I rubbed my nose with hers. Leaning down I held the back of her neck to meet me with her lips. Our kiss was slow, not hungry or lustful like it had been with Remus. Charlotte welcomed it as well as I. Our kiss became more heated, wanting to taste one another. I could smell her arousal and I'm sure she could feel mine.

"Charlotte," I whispered into her neck as I peppered kisses all over her. Breathing was heavy for both of us. Her hands went under my shirt, feeling my body and it gave me a shiver. Her fingers trailed to my v-line next to my boxers.

"Wesley." She pulled my head out of her shoulder and made me look her in the eyes. "Make love to me." I rumbled in my chest of appreciation, it made her hold her thighs together and instantly became harder than I already had. We were both ready, far too ready after our long make-out session and I couldn't hold it in anymore. I unzipped her dress from behind and with one swift pull she was naked in all her glory. She didn't wear any underwear. That little minx.

"Fuck."

She gave me that angelic laugh I loved so much. Her eyes shined and looked at me with such warmth. Damn, I'm lucky.

Her hands trailed up my body as she slowly took off my shirt. Pain painstakingly slow she unbuttoned my pants and I quickly kicked them off and put my body on hers. Kissing her pouty lips, she whined as she moved her hips to touch my enlarged member. "Please, Wesley. I want you closer." Her arms stayed around my neck, and I inched myself into her wet pussy. She moaned as I seeped deeper into her. "You are so big, babe. You fill me up," a deep growl came from my chest as I started to pump into her painstakingly slow. Her hips met mine and helped me plunge deeper into her. The cool air wrapped around us as the night air blew through the trees. We both were a panting mess as my hips thrust into her to fill her needs. The walls were slick, and I knew she was close.

"Wesley!"

"Kitten," I groaned into her mouth as I slammed mine against hers. I wrapped my arms behind her shoulders and with one more quick thrust, we both came undone at the seams. She moaned lightly, so no one would hear the waterfalls of pleasure seeping around our bodies.

Out of all the times, we had made love, this one seemed the most intimate, maybe it was because she now had a Wolf and can feel the same things I could. Her senses were slowly heightening, and the completed bond made it so intense. It also could be the fact we were in nature, where Wolves were supposed to be. We had come into our element and the goddess approved of our love affair under her moon. After panting we both stared into each other's eyes and kissed again. Her tongue intertwined with mine and her arms were around my neck. My hand went down to her lower back as I gently squeezed her plump ass.

"I love you Charlotte," I whispered like it was a secret, when it really isn't.

"And I love you, if I did anything in my life right, it was when I gave you my heart and soul."

My chest swelled with so much emotion, I thought it might explode.

Chapter 53

Charlotte

After spending another day in the Blue Water's pack, it was time to go home. I was relieved to go back because I never felt completely comfortable at Blue Water. Don't get me wrong, they were welcoming and wonderful people, I just missed home. Home was where my close friends were, Ashley, Bruce, and Evan. I was ready to see them. These past two weeks were filled with fun and excitement and a whole new understanding of what Wesley and I have. He knows I still have my insecurities but will always be there for me as I will be for him.

Giving a few hugs to the smaller pups of the pack I waved goodbye, and we climbed into the carriage. Wesley's parents were coming with us, his mother packed several large trunks of clothes, saying she was bringing her old Luna ceremony outfit as well as a few other traditional clothing pieces. I didn't care what I wore, just that I was there with Wesley and the rest of my family.

As Odin sat down in our overly large carriage, I saw Zachary coming out of the house with his suitcase in hand. He had been looking defeated the past few days and his head was down as he helped them load the storage compartment.

"Wesley, what's wrong with Zachary?" I asked

"Zachary has been feeling lonely recently, Kitten. I think it's because the mating ceremony is coming up for you, Ashley finding her mate and not actually finding his mate here, he may feel a loss." Wesley sat up and started talking to his father about some pack business and I watched a defeated

Zachary open the carriage door and sit down beside me. His head leaned over and rested on my shoulder. Something that he enjoyed doing since we were so close, I wish we were brother and sister by blood because he would have been a great big brother.

"No luck, Zach?" Zachary scoffed and sat back up and fixed the collar of his shirt.

"I don't know what you are talking about. I'm just exhausted. All those she-Wolves couldn't get enough of this," he pointed to all of himself, and I burst into laughter.

"Really now?"

"Yeah, I had to pry two chicks that wanted to go at the same time, but I had to tell them I was waiting for my mate. They groaned and thought I was being a prude. The nerve." His eyes rolled in the back of his head. I leaned closer to his ear, knowing well that everyone could hear me anyway.

"She's out there, Zachy. I know she is. She will be the most beautiful she-Wolf and she will bow down to blow you the first time you meet," I started giggling and Zachary looked at me in mock shock. His hand was on his chest and his mouth looked like he was going to inhale a fish.

"What a dirty mouth you have! Do you kiss your Alpha with that mouth?"

"That and more," I elbowed him in the ribs and got a dark glare from Wesley. Oh yeah, he wanted it, I blew a kiss towards him, and he just gave me his smirk.

The journey back was uneventful, the carriage ride along with the airplane ride back was exhausting. The last thing I remember was taking off and when I woke up, I was laying in our own bed. It smelled of Wesley and the entire house had smells I had never smelled before. Ashley smelled of peppermint and lemon, a weird combination but it really suited her. She can be refreshing and sweet while sometimes she could be spicy, especially when she gets mad at Beau.

Evan smelled like old whisky with a hint of bourbon, he really did smell like the fun uncle I used to think of when I first met him. Bruce just smelled like the outdoors, a complete mixture of pine, cedar, and a babbling brook. His smell also made sense since he was outdoors most of the time patrolling.

My hearing would also go in and out but with Astrid and Ashley helping me it had become manageable. Ashley told me how my Wolf would be able to fully control it as soon as she officially came forward. Even though we had been back a few days, Victoria hadn't shown much improvement or willingness to come to the forefront of my mind. If I closed my eyes, I could feel her and almost see her. She just sits back there, sitting and watching what I do with my daily life. Oftentimes at night, when Wesley is sleeping, I will just talk to her, tell her how I feel about all this and how excited I am to finally talk to her and interact with her.

Victoria looks like a timid Wolf, like how I used to be. Sometimes I think she is smiling at me, or she could be making fun of my quirks. I told her about the last pet that I had, Macaroni, and how sad I was. Her eyes looked sorrowful too and she looked like she could feel my pain. Since she was now in my mind, I wondered if she could see all my past?

"Charlotte?"

My memories and struggles, my journey of how I came to finally be with her?

"Charlotte?"

Would she be completely and utterly disgusted?

"Charlotte!"

I shook the thought from my head, we were made for each other, right? Suddenly I am being shaken out of my thoughts by a glare from Ashley and a look of concern from Astrid.

"Goddess child, are you alright?" Astrid grabbed my hand lovingly.

"I'm sorry, I was just thinking," I whispered. Rubbing my eyes, I let out a sigh and flopped back down on the bed.

"I know you have a lot on you dear, but we must finish the Mating and Luna ceremony. It is very hard to condense everything like you wanted," Astrid continued to thumb through magazines picking out decorations. Astrid wasn't happy that I was doing the two ceremonies. She said I deserved to have two parties to make up for all the birthday parties I've missed over the years, to have the spotlight all on me but I couldn't stand it. I wanted to rip it off like a band-aid and have it be over. Wesley was alright with it and that was all that really mattered.

"I know, I don't want to take up any of the pack's time having to do two parties in two days. It would be so exhausting, and I would rather sleep anyway." Ashley laughed.

"You would want to take a nap rather than be social. Silly girl." Ashley held up two swatches of color for me to pick. I had picked winter colors since it would be done in the beginning of December. Light blue, creams and whites were going to be used and I internally wanted some season sprites to come but I knew that was out of the question. It would have been amazing to see them flying around spreading around bits of snow here and there.

Astrid pulled out a dress magazine and started pointing to a few dresses. "Now here me out, I know this will be difficult because human culture has been branded into you, however!" She pointed to a deep red velvet dress. It had a sweetheart neckline, and the fabric came off the shoulders, a perfect way to show a mating mark. Small pearls along the trim of the dress near the chest, it wasn't too much but it was beautiful. The dress was in a mermaid style, very fitted around the waist and thighs until it flared out at the bottom slightly. It was simply beautiful, and it would make my blonde hair really pop in the sea of white pastels we had for the theme. I would literally be the center of attention.

"It's beautiful…" I whispered. I traced the dress with my finger like I could touch it. Ashley looked at Astrid with a knowing look. Astrid nodded and went to her computer, probably to order the dress. "I know it isn't white, for a wedding, but this is for eternity. Red is for love and how passionate you are with Wesley, I think it is the perfect color for you." Astrid's eyes shined brightly at me. She has given me so much love and she barely knows me.

"I do love it, I don't care about it being white. I think he knows I'm not innocent anymore," I chucked like Astrid let out a loud laugh.

"That's the spirit!"

Most of the planning was done, the invitations were sent, and Wesley and Odin finished up the welfare that he was supposed to do before we left. Some Wolves had lost their jobs in the nearby town factory and needed jobs around the pack house until they could get back on their feet for extra money. It was amazing how well the pack worked together. If only humans could work like this, in small communities taking care of one another when something goes wrong instead of relying on complete strangers.

"We are needed downstairs, they have accepted new members into the pack," Ashley spoke from behind the computer. Beau must have mind-linked her.

Skipping downstairs with Astrid we see the new family that will be inducted this evening at dinner. I had read that during induction meetings they have dinner with the Alpha and Luna, and we get to know them better before we show them their home. They also must make a blood oath by drinking the Alpha and Luna's blood to help them with their mind-links to be connected with ours. Officially I haven't been connected with the pack yet so it would just be Wesley's blood they feast on tonight. Gross.

A little girl holding a teddy bear with red hair stood at the bottom of the stairs. She had space buns for her hair style and was shyly hiding behind a tall girl who had a long French braid down her back. There were also two boys, possibly fraternal twins older than the girl. Wesley wasn't in sight yet, but I still wanted to meet them.

"Hello," I said with every ounce of courage I could. "I'm Charlotte, future Luna of the pack." I stuck out my hand ready to shake. The little girl poked her head out behind the girl and gave me a shy smile. I sat down on the floor, and she looked at me questioningly. "And who might you be, big girl?" She gave me a toothless grin and stepped out to take my hand. "I'm Aria, this is my big sister Raina and my brothers Fredrick and Phillip." The siblings looked at each other in shock and back down at their sister Aria.

Raina cleared her throat and stuck out her hand, "Yes, um, I am Raina. I'm sorry, Aria hasn't spoken in a while, we were just shocked she spoke to you." I smiled as Aria took my hand.

"Sometimes kids like me, I'm not sure why," I said gently while looking at Aria.

"I do." Wesley said authoritatively as he walked up behind them along with his father Odin and Evan. "She is your Luna, she is the mother of the pack." Wesley was walking tall and intimidating, more so than the carefree self he usually is. I wanted to question the tension, but I kept it to myself, for now.

Wesley grabbed my hand and helped me off the floor and I picked up Aria. That was when I noticed it, their smell. It smelled wild and musky. It was missing something though; all the Wolves I've smelled between the Blue Water's pack and our pack have a similar underlying smell. They didn't have any. I pulled Aria away a bit and looked at her and then back at Wesley questioning the smell.

"What's that smell?" I mind-link Wesley.

"That smell, my love, means they are rogues."

Vera Foxx

Chapter 54
Charlotte

"R-rogues?" I stuttered. "That can't be right." Most of the literature I had read talked about how beastly and terrible rogues are. Their wolves slowly consume them, and they become wilder as the years progress until finally their wolves take over for lack of companionship. However, these kids seem to be perfectly fine, it must have just happened recently.

"Raina, are you the speaker for this group?" Wesley said sternly.

"Yes, sir," she replied.

"If you could please explain to your Luna why you are here we will then head down to dinner." I put Aria down and Raina took her hand again as Aria went behind her. The twins kept switching their footing back and forth looking at each other.

"Long story short," Raina began, "we lost our pack a month or so ago. Our parents didn't survive the rival pack's attack and we have been in the city using shelters and tried blending into society there, but our wolves couldn't handle it. We couldn't shift like we wanted with so many humans, so we left." Raina held a sad look in her eye as she looked at her siblings. "Then we stayed in the woods for the past week, wandering. We could smell your territory and were hoping if the Alpha was willing, we could start a new life in your pack."

My eyes brimmed with tears listening to their story. Aria held tightly to Raina's hand and the twins continued to stare at the floor. They had lost their parents and have been on their own for weeks. Now paying attention to their clothes, they were dirty and tattered, holes throughout. The one bag they had maybe held another storage of clothes and food. My heart broke hearing their story and immediately went to Raina and hugged her. She was taken aback but put her arms around me.

"How old are you hun?" My face was muffled but she still understood me. Lolli was a good head taller than me, but I couldn't help trying to comfort her.

"I-I just turned 21." Sitting back up keeping both hands on her shoulders I smiled.

"Welcome to the pack, all of you." Glancing at all of them they gave small smiles and we led them to dinner.

They had come from a small pack, Guiding Fire, located in Canada known for their large bonfire parties in the winter. Wesley explained they had only been around for 20 years, one of the newest packs of North America. Their father was the Alpha. "There aren't many of us, just close to a hundred but that was all we needed," Phillip spoke. They were to be the new Alpha's but were still too young to take on the role. They both turned thirteen just a few months prior and the death of their parents, especially their father hit them hard. They had been training to become Alphas when they were ready and now, they were lost and broken, almost no hope for training.

"Dinner was great, thank you Alpha, Luna." Raina spoke again for the group. She was the oldest of the group, taking care of them while they had been wandering the past month. Lolli was definitely a mother figure, she was always checking on Aria and the boys with care, but you could see sadness in her eyes. I knew she didn't have time to grieve, none of them did and it hurt me painfully to see them that way.

Wesley stood up and took a chalice that I had never seen before and cut his palm. The blood slowly dripped into the cup, enough for Raina to drink since she was the only one of age to shift, the boys had three more years. "Raina, I, Alpha Wesley Hale of the Black Claw Pack have inducted you and your family to this pack. You are to honor your Alpha and Luna as well as your superiors. If any of you break the Laws of the Wolf you could be punished, banished or even death. Do you accept these terms for the exchange of safety and family?" Raina took a shaky breath. "Yes, we do." Taking the chalice, she drank down Wesley's blood.

I could hear Wesley include me in the mind-link as he spoke to the whole pack of the new arrivals. I couldn't hear them back because I had yet to go through my Luna ceremony, but Raina had a few tears roll down her cheeks. This had to be hard for her, to join another pack and start all over, the loss of parents and friends. I wanted to help as much as I could and would.

Wesley

"I will offer to train you both to be alphas of a new pack you could create," I spoke to the twins sternly as I folded my hands together and laid them on the desk. Both looked in shock but nodded their heads eagerly. An alpha offering another alpha training was highly unorthodox, but I felt for them, they thought their home pack would be over, but starting over, giving them a fresh start could be good. I'll train them as well as have them travel to other packs to see the different dynamics.

Raina didn't speak much, she gave the exact same description of her and her sibling's time away from their destroyed home. It was an instant red flag how she was able to produce the same words exactly. I felt Charlotte's sorrow for the young children, but something was off, and I wasn't sure if Charlotte could sense it too.

Charlotte had a few new houses built while we were gone, they were easy to put up, she mentioned they are factory-made homes and are done quickly when you don't have any specific specifications to follow such as colors and certain building materials. We didn't deal with the harsh wind, so the idea appealed to me since our pack was growing so rapidly.

Charlotte led us down a newly made path and held the key in her hand, excitement overwhelmed her as she put her arm linked with Raina, she was hoping for friendship with someone her age. I didn't blame her; Ashley was in her forties and Zachary was nearing thirty.

"Here we are!" She sang triumphantly as she unlocked the door. Several omegas oversaw the setting of the house with furniture, linens, and cookware. Charlotte said it was important to have at least a few houses like this so anyone that needed refuge would find it homely, and it was a beautiful home for a fraction of the cost of the others.

The colors were warm, deep reds with pops of yellow and latte-colored tan filled the walls. Warm blankets were spread on the couches and fresh food had already been put in the fridge per my request. The family looked in awe and the little girl giggled and ran to jump up and down on the couch. Charlotte laughed at Aria and Charlotte swung in to catch her before she fell. "Your room is upstairs; do you want to see it?" Aria ran up the stairs. Each new home had a boy and girl rooms with bunk beds plus 2 adult bedrooms. I'm sure the twins could figure out where they wanted to sleep.

Raina began crying and Charlotte immediately went to her and led her to the couch and put a blanket on her shoulders. My Luna was the epitome of perfection. She held her as she cried and patted her head. The boys looked up to me with tears in their own eyes. I'm not much of a hugger but the young boys looked like they needed something. I went up to them to put my hand on their backs for encouragement, but they immediately engulfed me. For young boys, they were strong to be able to have me step back.

"T-thank you so much." Raine cried. Charlotte still had her arms around her.

"It is alright, you are safe here," she cooed. "If there is anything you need. Let me know alright? Several omegas are going to go out and get you all some clothes to last a few days and then I'll take you shopping." Raine let out another sob and Charlotte looked at me with questions.

"*Something is not right.*" Charlotte mind-linked me. "*There is more to their story, I can almost hear it in the undertone of her voice.*" She looked back as Rain, watching her tears fall.

"*There are a lot of red flags, but when there are children involved, I have to be lenient. I'll be having warriors staying close.*" I replied back.

"We are going to leave you guys here to settle in. If you need anything, please come to the packhouse. Dinner is always at seven."

✳✳✳

"What do you think it is?" Charlotte asked as she was doing her bedroom routine. The washcloth was in her hand, and she had a hand on her hip. She was mid-scrub, and her cat eyeliner was about to smudge down her face.

"I don't know," I shook my head. "There is more to their story, I know that. I couldn't reject them, and I couldn't have them live here and leave them in limbo until I figured it out. Pups shouldn't be left out in the cold like that, and I can't have them susceptible to becoming too far gone becoming rogues. It can happen in kids even though their wolves haven't appeared," I said worriedly.

Charlotte sighed and finished washing her face and brushed her teeth. Padding over the bed in a pair of purple satin shorts and tank top she cuddled up next to me. Her mind was wandering, and her heart filled with pity and sorrow. "What are you thinking, Kitten?"

"Do you think their parents are really dead?" I looked at her in shock.

"Of course, they were crying and upset," I said.

"Or, maybe upset because of guilt. You didn't see the others bawling as Raine did," she pointed out.

"The others maybe had time to grieve, and she didn't?" I questioned.

Charlotte blew out some air in frustration. The gears were turning in her head and the scowl on her face was adorable. Kissing her forehead longingly she climbed on top of me to sleep. This position will never get old, being her mattress has become my favorite thing. Her finger tickled my mark and she giggled as goosebumps came on my skin.

Before I could seduce my sweet mate to have me, there was rapid knocking on the door. Charlotte sat up and looked at the door and back at me. "It's late, who is that?"

Zachary didn't wait to be let in, he opened the door. His breathing was rapid, and he looked around the room. Charlotte's eyes met his and he smiled. Running to the bed, Remus let out a loud growl and Zachary fell to his knees.

"Babe, it is just Zachary what are you doing?"

"Mine." Remus broke through. Damnit

Charlotte climbed off and helped Zachary off the floor. "She's here!" he panted, not worried at all that Remus yelled at him.

"Who?" Charlotte cocked her head to the side.

"My mate! I smell her!!" Zachary ranted. Charlotte's eyes grew wide and grabbed both his hands and started jumping up and down and Zachary followed. I realized Charlotte wasn't wearing a bra and her breasts were freely jumping about. Jumping out of bed I grabbed her so Zachary couldn't see, and Charlotte whined.

"Baaaaaabe! You are killing the moment!"

"Your tits were flying about, I don't need him seeing." Charlotte blushed and covered herself with her arms and peeked behind me.

"Well, who is she?"

"I don't know, someone new I think, she didn't have our pack smell. Who visited today? I can't find her! I could smell her all over the private dining room!" Charlotte gasped and then screamed.

"Raine!!!"

Vera Foxx

Chapter 55
Charlotte

"This is so exciting! I need to take her to you right now!" I screamed. Looking at the clock it well past 11 and I pouted. Wesley chuckled in the corner and Zachary's eyes were sparkling with anticipation to see his mate. "Wait," I said. "We should wait until tomorrow." Zachary whined and ran his hands through his hair.

"I can't wait, Charlie, I've waited far too long. She's there, right out there and I need her!" Zachary growled and Wesley pulled me back.

"Watch your growls, pup. Know who you are talking to," Wesley scolded as he held me tightly.

"I'm sorry Alpha," Zachary bowed his head. "I spoke out of turn."

"It's alright Zachary, listen, she has had a rough couple of months. She is probably sleeping right now and barging into her house right now would scare everyone. How about we plan something special and make it romantic?" I internally squealed in excitement. Wesley held onto his chest, probably feeling my overwhelming delight to help Zachary.

"Fine," Zachary pouted. "What should I do? Usually, you just smell your mate and claim her there, this is all new what you are trying to do, let me just grab her." I looked in confusion at Wesley chuckled.

"It's true, we are just a special case, Kitten. Once you find your mate you just automatically accept it and mark each other in a passionate affair."

"Ugh, no fun! Zachary, can you at least bring her flowers when she comes to breakfast then? Something a little romantic?"

"Anything for my mate if you think she would like it. I'm not going to sleep tonight, that is for sure." Zachary pulled at his hair.

"Yay! Thank you! Once you know her story, you will understand. Go to the green house and pick the best roses and be ready at seven for her. I'll be down to watch and be the creepy friend!" I gave him a hug in support, and he pecked the top of my head.

"You have your hands full, Alpha." Zachary shook his head and walked out the door. Wesley lifted me up while I squealed and threw me on the bed. I cuddled closer to him which caused him to let out a yawn.

"You know he is right. I do have my handful with you." He pulled me up to his chest. "I know but you love me anyways," I smiled into his big green eyes.

"That I do."

***

The next morning, I got to witness my very first mate meeting. It didn't really count when Ashley met Beau because I wasn't really paying attention or knew what was going on. Everyone was seated in the main dining room and Zachary had even dressed up in a button-down collared shirt, paired with dark jeans. I've never seen him so dressed up before I almost had to laugh. He was so nervous, he kept picking at one of the roses and he even took off every thorn to make sure his mate didn't prick her finger. Dark circles were under his eyes, I didn't take him seriously when he said he wouldn't sleep.

The new family walked in and Raine immediately had eyes directed to me and smiled. She looked so much more refreshed this morning as well as her siblings. Aria ran to me and engulfed me in a huge hug, "how is my big girl?" Aria snuggled up to me and my heart just about burst.

"I'm fine, we all slept so well. I didn't want to get up!" I laughed and Wesley just looked at the both of us with love. Aria felt like the daughter I could have some day. Looking at Zachary, I gave him a little nod for him to come closer. Raina was sitting across from us when her body stiffened and smelled the air. Her brothers looked at each other and then at Raina, realizing what was going to happen. Turning around, Raine looked up at Zachary who had the biggest grin on his face. He was studying her, looking at every feature her beautiful porcelain skin and red hair had to offer. His eyes full of love as he knelt beside her, the dining room went silent watching the interaction.

Zachary's grip on the bouquet for Raina was evident. He was trying to control himself from taking her into his embrace.

"Mate," he whispered and tucked a strand of hair behind her ear. I could concentrate and hear her heartbeat beating erratically. A few tears left her face as she touched Zachary's cheek. "Mate," she whispered back, and he pulled her from her seat, they were now standing, and his nose was in her neck smelling her scent. A few tears went down my cheek at the sight before me while I held onto Wesley's hand.

Zachary twirled her around and Raina laughed while other Wolves in the room started hooting, hollering and howling. Her siblings were smiling ear to ear while Aria stayed still in my lap. "Look Aria, looks like you have a new person in your family now." Aria smiled and jumped off my lap and ran to her sister who took her in her arms too. Zachary gave a chaste kiss to her forehead and looked back into Raina's eyes.

"Looks like we might need to watch the other kids while they mate huh?" I mentioned Wesley in passing. He groaned and I let out a soft giggle.

"We will get someone to watch them for a few days while they complete their bond, you don't have to do everything, Kitten." His hand went to my thigh. "The only pups I need you to watch are our own." My face blushed as my eyes fell to my lap.

Kids? Pups? I guess I haven't thought of it too much.

As the days progressed, Zachary and Raina became closer, they had yet to mate and mark each other, which Wesley found odd. I didn't think so, why would you drop your pants so quickly and mark each other? Having a spiritual bond would take time and they were with each other constantly. Only a bit more time of courting and I was sure that Zachary and Raina would complete the process. Then again, I don't know all the traditions of Wolves.

I was in my security office, setting up the new camera software with the computers when Zachary walked in. "Zach!" I smiled and gave him a hug. "You remembered me! I've missed you the past week. How are you and Raina doing?" I turned around and sat back at my computer to continue the software update. Zachary scratched behind his head twitching his mouth side to side.

"That's what I wanted to talk to you about actually."

My chair squeaked as I turned around. "Is something wrong?"

Zachary sighed. "I feel like she is keeping something from me but won't tell me what. I don't want to mate with her if she is hiding something. At first, she said she wanted to wait and get to know each other, but now she said she was ready and now I'm not." I patted the seat next to me and he sat down with a solemn look.

"Are you having mating jitters, or do you honestly feel like she is hiding something?"

"There is something," he paused, "*off*. Like when I mention you and how wonderful you are going to be the next Luna and you have really brought life back into the pack. Raine just stares off and doesn't say anything. She also won't talk much in depth about her pack and what happened. Just the same spill over and over and almost word for word." Continuing to listen to him the feeling in my heart worsened. It wasn't just Wesley and I feeling off about Raina, her own mate felt it too.

"Maybe Wesley could talk to the twins. He is out training them today. I'll mind-link for him to ask them. He can tell if they are lying or not better than I can." Zachary sniffed and I rubbed his back. "We are going to figure this out, I promise." His eyes filled with hope and engulfed me in a large hug.

"I just want to love her, trust her."

"You will."

Zachary left and I quickly mind-linked Wesley. *"Hey babe, can I ask you a favor?"*

"Does it have something to do with me tying you to the bed?"

"No, but you can do that too!" I giggled. *"No, I need to see if you can get any info out of the twins, like about their pack and how it was taken down. Raina always speaks about it but not them. Zachary is holding off mating because he feels Raina is hiding something."*

"Ah, so he feels it too. Sure thing, my Luna."

"I love you, be safe."

Feeling a burden lifted from my shoulders I head back to the security software. We also added heat sensing attachments to the cameras just in case any Witches wanted to come by and blast fireballs our way. It would honestly help if I just created our own brand of security cameras with all the add ons I was having to add. Heating sensors, video and what else would I need? Ha, maybe smell so we can tell what kind of Wolf or person was coming into the territory. That would be next to impossible to create.

Switching on one of the cameras I pull it up on the screen. For now, the camera is showing an empty forest spot and seems to be working correctly. Seven more cameras are turned on and I see a few Wolves running the perimeter. Once I hit the 15th camera, I saw something I had wished I never saw. Raina standing on the border with none other than Josephine. She was wearing a cloak to hide herself, but anyone could see that it was her—after all the few days I had to deal with her while she taught Roman the incantation of the branding iron, her face was permanently burned into my brain.

My breath hitched as she stared right into the camera and blasted it with a fireball from her hands. "Oh shit!" I screamed.

Evan strutted in and looked at me weirdly. "Did the Luna just curse? What dimension did I just walk into?" Evan laughed and I gave him daggers with my eyes. "There is a border breach on the Northside, sector 3, it's Josephine and Raina talking. I want Raina alive, but Josephine can be killed on sight." Evan's eyes grew wide, stepping back through the door.

"I'll notify Alpha and let people know to go to the safe rooms. Please head there now, Luna," Evan spoke quickly before heading out the front door. I grabbed my phone so I could still communicate with all the cameras around the territory and yelled for everyone in the house to get to a safe room. It would have been so much easier if I could mind link.

Taking a few steps forward I felt a sharp crack in my leg. Looking down I saw my leg was bent at an odd position and I let out a blood curdling scream. "Dear Goddess, what's wrong?" Astrid jumped from the 3rd floor balcony and landed in the entryway of the pack house. "I don't know," I cried. "I was walking fine and then…" another crack sound came from my forearm. Tears were pooling in my eyes as I started to hyperventilate.

Astrid burst through the front doors. "Shit, you are changing, it isn't a full moon yet! Have you spoken to your Wolf yet Charlotte?" My breathing had become ragged, I had not been told how painful this would be if I was really changing, I guess now I know.

"No, she just comes up to me and lets me pet her in my dreams but that's it!" I screamed again as I heard my lower back break and I fell to the floor. Sweat beaded on my face and my body jerked on its own accord and bent in odd positions. "She's stressed and feels the pack in danger, her Wolf could come to the surface early, just like in normal Werewolves. We need to get her to the safe room now!" Ashely hovered over us, looking for possible threats while Astrid gently picked me up in a place that wasn't broken. Dragging me slowly to a large picture that covered the floor from top to bottom, we heard screams from the outside.

"Shit, take her Astrid, I'll hold her off for as long as I can." Ashley quickly shifted into her red Wolf and headed to the door until they were blown open and she was slung back into our direction. Ashley whimpered but got up quickly and covered both Astrid and I with her body. In defense stance, Ashley growled ferociously and covered my screams of agony. The dark figure walked into the room, a large trench coat with a hood covering the face of the intruder. You could feel the electricity popping in the air as they came in and walked down the few steps into the large foyer, we were now standing in.

The hood dropped with a large gust of wind and Josephine's face appeared. Her eyes were sunken in, red as fire and hair black as night. She had officially become a rogue Witch, in no control of herself or her powers, the demon inside her engulfed every bit of her soul. Raina was standing right behind her with her head down in shame and holding her body tightly. Josephine smirked and held out a light fireball and looked at me directly.

"Hello, Charlotte."

Chapter 56

Charlotte

Another crack of my back and tried to hold in the scream. "Oh, did I cause too much stress for you?" Josephine asks with mock sympathy. Her hand was on her chest as she bent over to get a better look at me. I growled, at her and let out another scream as another bone cracked somewhere on my body.

Josephine cackled while Astrid looked on in horror. "Please, let her be. What do you want?" Raine continued to stand at the entrance of the door, looking behind her. Josephine stood up straight, bouncing the fire like a sphere on her hand. "Just finishing the job, I should have done a long time ago. Roman was so infatuated with her and was willing to do much for her, I just thought I'd kill her off. Hurt him even past death. He's watching you know, that is his punishment. Watching the one he wanted to love. Now that his insanity was cured, he is of sound mind and who knew he actually cared for the girl? Hades is such an evil god," Josephine tisked. "Now I was going to get rid of the evidence of the branding bonds so none of this could come back to me, but it looks like you healed up real nice," Ashley growled, snapping her jaws near her.

"Even though you have healed so nicely I still have to kill you, the dead don't speak you see," Josephine spoke like it was nothing. The fire sphere vanished into thin air and stalked us closer. Her trench coat dusted across the floor, her nails were dark and elongated to talons, not the claws I was used to seeing. Another crack in my body echoed through the foyer and I let out a grunt of pain.

I tried to stand, but the broken bones in my body wouldn't allow me. Going through so much pain in my past, you would think my tolerance for physical abuse would be strengthened but this was another level. A large howl came from me, not a scream, but an actual howl. I was changing, really changing. Astrid's grip on my head as I lay in her lap tightened as Josephine came closer.

"I can't mind-link anyone! No one will answer?!" Astrid screamed in terror and my grip on her hand tightened. Heavy, labored breaths left my lips in fear. We were all going to die. Josephine cackled again as she grabbed my ankle and ripped me from Astrid's embrace. Shrills and howls came from Ashley who was now pinned in her spot, unable to move. "Your pitiful mind-link has been put on suspension," Josephine hissed, "now, what to do with you…." She tisked as she circled me. The breaks of my bones were coming in slower, and I couldn't understand why.

"Have mercy on her, she needs her family to shift!" Astrid screamed who was now pinned to her spot.

"I know she does," Josephine sneered. "I indeed know, Wolves and their need for a pack and family is quite significant for a shift. I was going to just come and kill you, but I like seeing you suffering like this." Josephine's finger waved around in a circular motion as she saw my body contort into a new position. Grunts and short bursts of screams enveloped the room. "I think I want to take you back, see what happens when you are all alone during a shift. No one to guide you through the physical pain that comes along with it. Your past will certainly consume you. It would be amusing for my benefit."

"You can't! It's suicide for a Wolf! Let her go, please! She never did anything to you!"

"That she didn't. I'm just tying up loose ends. No offense," she winked at Astrid. "And to think your poor mate has no idea what's going on." Josephine twirled my hair and my mouth tried to elongate to snap at her. "So feisty," she grinned. "It's settled. I'll take her." Clapping her hands, Raina came forward with her head hung low and tears in her eyes. She was being forced to do this, I couldn't blame her, but I couldn't help but feel betrayal. Mouthing she was sorry, she took a piece of chalk and encircled us. Both Astrid and Ashley were begging for her to let me go but it was no use, within one large flash Raina, Josephine and I vanished into thin air.

Wesley

"That's it, continue to lunge forward when your attacker falters." The twins had been practicing for about a week with me, they had great knowledge in defensive skills, just on target where they were supposed to be.

"AGAIN!" They both grabbed onto each other's shoulders to wrestle their bodies to the ground. Once Phillip was pinned, I yelled for them to stop. "Excellent job Fredrick. I see who the fighter is and who has the brains." Phillip groaned and rolled his eyes he got up.

"I think we both take offence to that," Fredrick said dryly. Lending a hand, he sprung forward and gave a quick nod. "Thank you, Alpha." I laughed as they started shoving each other.

Remembering what Charlotte wanted to ask, I got more serious with the boys. "I know you boys have had it rough the past month, after losing your parents." The twins tensed as I brought up the subject. "I just have a few questions I wanted to ask you, away from your sister. See, things aren't adding up and I need honesty within the pack, you know this." The twins shuffled around and started looking at one another. "You aren't in trouble, but I want you to answer truthfully, you know an Alpha can search out lies." Both nodded as I continued.

I led them to one of the bleachers and waved them over to sit down, giving them some water in the process. They both sat nervously and stared into their drink cups. "I need, in your own words, what happened." The twins again looked at each other and Phillip began to speak. "Alpha, to be honest, we don't know what happened." Looking at them in confusion I nodded for them to go on.

"Our sister came running to us, we were at the pack lake swimming with Aria. Raina came up and she told us to run. She had a bag full of clothes, food and some money and said it was an order. We didn't question it, she was our sister, and she was frantic. So, we ran," Phillip spoke.

"I thought it was strange, we didn't get a mind-link or an order from our father, however, we listened," Fredrick confessed. "After running for a few hours, we stayed at a hotel, away from the pack lands, and she told us what happened. That there was an attack, rogues and destroyed everything and everyone, including our parents." Fredrick started to sniff. I rubbed his back as Phillip continued.

"Raina was beside herself, she didn't cry much but the worry was in her heart, I could feel it through our sibling bond. We trekked on and followed her, she seemed to know what she was doing. We did go to town and then back into the forest, but it didn't seem like a month. Time was short, when she told you and Luna that it had been over a month of traveling, we couldn't believe it. I guess when you are mourning your pack members you lose track of time."

My brows furrowed, this became more and more concerning with every new piece of information. The boys had no idea how long they were without their family, for all we know it could have just been a week. How were their clothes all tattered though?

"Your clothes though, they seemed so worn out? It must have been a while that you were in the wild?" Phillip continued to shake his head. "No, Raina gave them to us. She said it would help us when it came to finding a new pack. We argued about it, saying we shouldn't lie to a new pack like that, but she was insistent. We wanted to use our Alpha command on her but she's our sister," Phillip replied.

"We then thought of Aria, she needed a stable place so we ignored it since it wasn't causing harm," Fredrick said dejectedly.

"Did you feel a break from your family bond? Did you feel your parents die?" Both looked at each other.

"No?" Phillip said, "I didn't know if that was possible. She said they were dead, so we believed her." I brushed my hand through my hair. Something was wrong, really wrong. Even Raina had lied to them. "It isn't as strong as a mate bond-breaking, but it is still there since you are alphas you can faintly feel a gentle break in the bond, you feel their sorrow but you are able to continue on with your life."

I began mind-linking Charlotte, but she wasn't replying, I couldn't even feel her on the property. Panicking I mind-linked Evan who I couldn't contact either, it was static. "Shit, we've got trouble. Come with me, your Alpha training is going to be put to good use now," I growled.

Running through the territory back to the packhouse Wolves seemed confused, they were trying to communicate with one another through links. No one could respond. Many were holding their heads and speaking quickly to find out what happened. On the steps of the packhouse, I find Evan lying face down in the dirt. Rolling him over, he was regaining consciousness but not fast enough for me to find out what happened. I bolted up the stairs to find my mother and Ashley on the floor, unconscious.

"What the hell happened?" I roared, turning around and looking at the twins. Both were confused as I was but that didn't stop Remus from being pissed off. Remus came forward and took control and lifted both boys off the ground by their necks. Their hands scratched and pawed at my grip while anger was radiating off my body.

"Where is my mate, you little bastards?! Took you in, gave you clothes, and you thank me by taking my mate!?" Remus roared. Zachary burst through the door, his hands on his knees, breathing heavily.

"Alpha, I know what happened! Please let the boys go, it isn't their fault!" Gripping the boys tighter we didn't let go, who was he to command us?! The boys' faces were turning blue until my mother came to. Her soft cry made me drop the boys and run to her. "Mother? Are you alright? What happened? Where is Charlotte?" I kneeled to help her up.

"The Witch, a rogue Witch took her," her hand was on her chest, "Charlotte's Wolf is forcing a change!" She screamed at me.

"Fuck!" A forced change is the worst, it is when their Wolves try to come out sooner than they are ready due to stress, it happens especially those in leadership positions. Her Wolf was doing more harm than good and now Charlotte will have the most painful transition because her body isn't ready. The risk of dying from her first shift increased 10-fold and that doesn't include the risks due to no family or me by her side. "Damnit!" I threw my fist into the wall behind my mother. Gasping for breath, Ashley shifted back as she lay naked on the floor. I didn't stare at her body, but I needed answers.

Zachary went to a nearby couch and threw a blanket over her. "Could you not protect her?!" I used my Alpha tone on her. "Could you not maul a silly Witch!?" Ashley cowered in fear and my mother came behind me and put her hand on my shoulder to calm me. It didn't work, only Charlotte could calm down Remus now.

"I-I am sorry Alpha. She used her powers and held me still, I couldn't move! None of us could!" She cried. "I tried! I tried! Charlotte tried to be strong too!" I knew Ashley tried; she was one of her best friends but that doesn't help me now, how in the hell was I going to get her back?

Zachary.

I turned and growled, my claws coming out as I stalked toward Zachary. "How did you know the boys aren't at fault. What information do you have?" Zachary took shaky steps back and reached in his back pocket, his hands trembling as he pulled out a piece of paper that had been read, a few wet spots covered the paper. Tears. His eyes were red as he held out the paper to me and I snatched it quickly.

Looking over the contents of the letter, I realized it wasn't only Charlotte's life in danger but also the entirety of another pack.

Chapter 57

Wesley

Dear Zachary,

If you are reading this, then the truth has come out and my life has taken a turn for the worst. I have agreed to things that I deeply regret, but I hope this letter will give you a better understanding as to why I had to, why I had to betray a future Luna as well as the Alpha of the infamous Black Claw pack....

✳✳✳

Under the Moon

Raine was in the packhouse of the Celestial Moon, their pack was small but thriving, nevertheless. Even though it had only been around for twenty years, they were strong. The warriors were out training as she and her mother was cooking lunch with the few omegas that they had in the packhouse, they were made up of mostly warriors and their lack of omegas could oftentimes make it hard at mealtime.

Her brothers had just come back from basic training with their father, Alpha Emil, and were sweating and tracking mud onto the floors. "Boys!" Their mother, Luna Rachel spoke harshly. "You are tracking mud all over the floor. Why don't you go jump in the lake and wash off before lunch, take your sister Aria with you?" She scolded but held in a large smile as the boys grabbed their sister's hands. The boys were troublemakers and wrestled so harshly in the house that even the indoor furniture saw the brunt of their matches.

Raine continued to stir the deer stew that was to be given to the warriors. Her mother and the three omegas worked their daily routine as Raine began to get lost in thought. Had she made the right decision not to become Alpha? It was proposed to her as a pup, but it never interested her. She had a strong need to take care of those around her but making decisions for the pack regarding warriors, patrols and finance rarely appealed to her. She loved the one-on-one experience and was often found with the doctor tending to pregnant she-Wolves.

Currently, she was studying to be a midwife. That was her calling, but the guilt always slipped in when she saw her brothers training and saw their bruises, she didn't like to see them hurt. Their Wolves had not come yet so their healing abilities were slow. Smiling to herself she could only remember what her mother recently told her: "You are a kind soul Raina, you don't possess the fiery passion of war and battle, your decision is just. Your kind heart deserves to do what it loves and handing the pack to your brothers is a good decision."

Raine glanced at her mother, there was flour on her cheeks as she kneaded the dough for the homemade bread, she had promised her father. Raine continued to chop the vegetables until she got a mind-link from one of the warriors. *"Raine, can you bring more water to fill the water dispenser outside?"*

Raine chuckled, *"Sure thing."*

She decided to do one better and make a large batch of pink lemonade, complete with fresh lemons and ice. The tub was large that she was going to carry, but that didn't seem to matter to her. She was strong, she had Alpha blood in her, so she was stronger than the average Wolf. Gracefully holding the large container, she felt her Wolf stir. Looking around from side to side, she saw nothing that would be harmful but kept alert as she trotted across the pack territory to the training field.

Lurking in the shadows, was none other than Josephine, or it appeared to be. A demon had fully taken control over the once witch, Josephine. Josephine's inability to conquer the darkness inside her let a demon inhabitant take over causing Josephine to be no more. The demon had worked hard on Josephine all these years and finally broke through. Josephine's soul was now fully tucked away in the corner of his mind as she screamed and banged on the edge of the invisible glass that now separated them. The slippery slope of choosing a few wrong choices earlier in her life caused this, she never wanted to be a bad soul but with such a powerful demon twisting in her mind only made her falter.

Josephine had lost her mate, one that she had been meant to share with her twin sister. They were to be mated in a wonderful ceremony in her coven back in Bergarian, but Josephine's cheating ways came through when the demon would randomly take over her body. It wasn't her fault her mind was too feeble to realize what she was doing. Once her mate rejected her and only took her sister, the girl slowly slipped away and had nothing to live for. Now they were rogue, and the she-demon was in charge. Now that she royally messed up in helping Roman, she wasn't just banned from Bergarian; she was also being hunted in the Earth realm. Why not stir up some more trouble before Hades hunted her down?

The young girl, Raina, was carrying a large pitcher of lemonade with a few slices of lemons and sugar in a bag. It looked like she was walking on her toes, happy and pleased with her decision to give the warriors a sweet treat. Josephine snarled at the thought. The warriors deserved nothing. She was able to sneak in past the patrol like it was nothing using minimal scent cloaking magic. She crossed her arms over themselves in her new trench coat. Her head was covered, and she eye-stalked the little Alpha she-Wolf as she smiled and waved goodbye to the warriors.

"Now or never," Josephine squealed to herself. She walked past the trees and toward Raina since she was now out of sight of other Wolves. Raina wasn't paying attention and was easily grabbed by Josephine on her bicep. "Hush now," Josephine covered her mouth as her reeking breath breathed into Raina's ear. "I've got a proposition for you dearie and you are going to want to hear it." Josephine grabbed her and pulled her into the woods and covered them both with a cloaking spell, no one would be able to hear or smell them for the time being.

Raina stepped back, observing the small opaque orb that covered them. Josephine brushed the invisible dirt off her trench coat and smirked. "W-what do you want?" Raina asked. She was docile, not at all Alpha material, it was a good thing she passed the torch to her brothers. "I have a task for you to do," Josephine's voice was sweet. "You are to help me steal the future Luna of the Black Claw Pack not far from here," she said like it was nothing.

Raina looked at her in confusion. "Why would I do that? That is none of my business, let me go! I will not help you!" Raina went to walk out of the orb but was stopped by a sudden zap. The electricity that came from Josephine's fingers flipped Raina around, so she was now facing her enemy again. "I said you will complete the task, and you will do it unless you want you and your entire pack to suffer the consequences."

Looking on in fear, Raina clutched her hands to her chest. Now she used her Alpha abilities to realize that she as well as her family was in danger. She could feel the strong, dark presence of something within this Witch, she was nothing of what she had met before in past greetings of passing covens. Raina had been so obtuse over the years, thinking she lived in such a carefree world, now the real danger had come to find her.

"Do not hurt the pack," Raina said as sternly as she could, which came out more like a kitten's growl. Josephine chuckled at the sudden braveness of the girl. It wouldn't help her, however, in fact, it only made things more interesting.

"Here's the deal," Josephine spoke as she walked toward the redhead. "You help me, and I won't destroy your pack." She gloated. With just the wave of my hand, it would burn with the heat of the 2nd circle of hell and not even charred bones would be left to bury. It would be easy really, you are so small and insignificant, and the council wouldn't even know they were missing a pack," she taunted mockingly. Raina tensed as she felt the truth in her words. "So, this is what you will do…."

Wesley

Zachary,

She told me that she could not access the pack with her magic. A high coven leader and her fellow Witches cast a spell over your territory. No Witch will be able to penetrate it unless they have been invited to join us. Josephine obtained the Amulets of Saron, which let her pass-through strong cloaking spells. I had to carry one amulet over and meet her on our designated day to bring the Amulets together for her to pass over.

I did it to save my pack, my heart hurts every day trying to find another way to get rid of her, but she is powerful. She met me every day to make sure I followed her exact instructions. My brothers and sister were close collateral and constant reminders that if I slipped, one would have an "accidental death."

I didn't mean for us to meet during these circumstances, and I know you would not accept me now for taking your Luna from you. Just know this was a hard decision to make, your Luna is the most beautiful and wonderful person. I do care for you and hope in another life we can meet. Once I know my family and pack are safe, I will leave this world for the guilt I cannot bear.

Your Loving Mate,
Raina

Zachary whimpered as I read the last paragraph. As angry as I was, I couldn't blame her. The Alpha in her wanted to protect her own pack. Remus was seething beneath the surface, we had to think fast before all of our mental capacity for making a plan would be gone. Trying to mind-link Evan, I could feel the strings of the links come back to life, no more static invaded the call I let out to him.

Evan stumbled into the doorway and looked from side to side, trying to figure out what happened. "Evan!" I ordered. He stood at attention and put his arm over his chest.

"Alpha, I'm sorry…"

"No time," I interrupted. Get Sorceress Cyrene on the phone, have them try and do a tracking spell on Josephine again, ready the warriors. As soon as we hear something we leave."

"Bruce," I mind-linked

"Alpha," he replied

"Get a group of trackers to the Celestial Moon pack. They are in imminent danger."

Before I could hear a reply, I cut the link. The women were running frantically trying to grab children and put them in the safe room, most of the women and children would hide until we returned from saving Charlotte and Raina.

My father came in stomping down the hall, his large body having to turn so he could get through the doorways. Even after giving the Alpha title to me, he was still a raging beast.

"What the hell just happened? I was in the training room in the basement and all the damn doors went into safety mode and locked me in. Wesley? What the fuck?" He was fuming.

"Josephine was able to penetrate the border, she's been taken!" I roared. My father let out a menacing growl and ordered omegas to pack bags as well as grab the pack doctor. My mother ran into his arms and started crying silently. "Odin, she started the change, she doesn't have anyone to help her! Her changing slowed down significantly as soon as that Witch took her out of my arms! She is in so much pain, we must find her!" My mother's tears were captured by my father's fingers as he kissed her.

"We will find her love. Get the leftover trackers, even the ones training. This will be a good experience." My father stomped towards the door and shouted more orders as the warriors came up with the SUVs ready to load up medical supplies. My mate was going to be found, it won't take me a week to find her like last time. I've got the Witches council in my back pocket, and I was going to fucking use them.

Zachary looked like a lost sheep staring at the note in his hand. His eyes glanced at the last bit of the paper, where his own mate said she wasn't going to come back. I ran up to him and patted his shoulder. "It won't come to that; we will save her before anything happens. Now suck it up and get into Wolf form." He crumbled the letter and didn't even bother to take off his clothes, he shifted mid-jump off the stairs to the outside of the pack house.

Warriors were in shorts as they stood ready for their orders. This was the second time my mate had been taken for me and it was going to be the last. "Listen up, your Luna has been taken at the worst moment. Her Wolf felt the threat of her pack being in danger and was forcing a shift." Many warriors murmured and the doctor stopped putting medical supplies in the back of the truck. He looked at me in worry. "She had just started her shift; she is in the worst danger she could possibly be in. Her shift has slowed so she is feeling every damn break. It is imperative we find her quickly and get her home. The Witches council will be heading this as well, now, WOLVES SHIFT!"

The tearing of clothing and howls ripped across the lawn. I jumped in the SUV with my phone in hand with Cyrene just on the other line…

Chapter 58

Charlotte

The transportation spell that Josephine used was nauseating. Raina and I were both dry heaving at the quick transport. We appeared in an old cabin that was worse for wear. Cobwebs decorated the corners of the room, the floorboard were littered with holes and dirt. Bugs crawling across the counters. There weren't any electronics in the home and no decorations to be spoken of. It was abandoned and dark as well as the outside, which means we were far from any sort of civilization. My arms and legs were still broken, and my back still contorted to a terrible position, holding in the pain was becoming difficult as I lay on the bare floor.

Raina sat on the floor, her legs held up against her chest as a few tears dripped down her face. The look of terror in her eyes told me she has never dealt with this kind of situation, a situation I was all too familiar with. Pain and lots of it. Being stripped of something happy and then thrown into a dungeon of darkness, never knowing if you will ever emerge or come out. Having this happen to me a third time in my life shows that this might be it.

Josephine skipped across the room and flew herself into the dusty chair while particles of dirt and dust flew through the air. She picked at her nails. "That was truly too easy. I can't believe it worked. You are weaker than I thought, young Alpha Wolf." I looked at Raina who just hung her head lower. Young Alpha?

"You are an Alpha Wolf?" I whispered, feeling the strain in one of my legs as it was about to snap. I grunted and she nodded. "I passed it to my brothers, I knew I wouldn't be strong enough, I never had my heart in it," she said shakily. Even though she brought this Witch on our territory, there had to be a reason as to why she did it. She wouldn't do this out of malice or evil.

"Aren't you going to ask her?" Josephine sat up quickly and patted both of her legs in excitement. "Come on, ask her why she did it!" Her voice was happy, an evil happy that she had just completed the ultimate crime. Being curious myself I looked at Raina and she wouldn't look me in the eyes. Shaking her head, she finally whispered. "She has my pack being held hostage. If I don't listen to her, she will burn them alive. The lives of over a hundred Wolves are in my hands if I didn't take you. I'm sorry, I had no choice." Raine spoke utterly quiet.

My heart instantly softened. Bless her having that on her shoulders. "I forgive you," I smiled back at her softly. Raine looked at me in surprise as Josephine groaned in the background.

"That was utterly boring! No yelling? Screaming? No cursing her? What the hell? This may have been a mistake; I should have killed you back at the back house." Josephine walked to the fridge and pulled out a purple drink and drank it hastily. "I've got things to do. Watch her while I get a few things from the basement. I got to speed this shit up so we can watch her die faster." Josephine stomped off and left me with Raine.

"Don't worry, Wesley will find us and Zachary too." I gripped my leg as it snapped again, I howled in pain. Raine couldn't bear to watch and stayed on the opposite side of the room. I gritted my teeth so I wouldn't scream, and Josephine came back stirring something in a bowl. "Just what I like to hear, more painful screams!" She tutted around the room like she was hosting a tea party, my body shook and as fur was trying to sprout through my body. Small needles pierced through the skin. Holding in my groans, Raine continued to look away.

My suffering was only going to become worse, I still had not heard from my Wolf yet and I had no idea if I was supposed to be concentrating on changing or being a blank slate. Josephine continued to bustle around the room like she was cleaning but stopped and sniffed the air. Walking towards me briskly she got right in my face to study me. I held back the insane feeling to reach out and bite her and looked her in the eyes without fear. Feeling more pain than I was feeling now was highly unlikely. She huffed and sniffed at me again adding, "you are starting to stink," and snapped her fingers and I was instantly transported to a dark room. Groaning at the sudden movement I noticed it was a basement.

Raina was nowhere to be found and my bones ached. Another break in my wrist and yelped at the pain. The breaks had finally gotten to me, there was something protruding from my leg. Getting a good look, I looked down and saw a bone sticking out from my leg. Shaking at the sight of my leg I took my hand to touch the wound only to get a sickly smell of almonds coming from it. If any of my biology reading told me anything, it let me know that I was becoming infected. I was going to get sick of infection before my Wolf could even heal me.

Laying my head down, I felt the hot tears welp in my eyes. Josephine and Raina footsteps could be heard above me and mumbling. I couldn't even concentrate to hear what they were saying, not that it mattered. I was here to die and only then will Raina's pack be out of danger. Maybe my life would save a hundred, but my heart will feel like it was breaking a thousand times over knowing I would never see Wesley again. My heart ached for him, my body ached and not just because of the cracks and constant bones breaking but the thought Wesley might be feeling this too. He didn't deserve any of it, hell I didn't either.

If there is anything I have learned in all my time being in terrible places was not to give up. However, when you are dealing with an agony so painful as your body is trying to turn you into another creature, it's hard to focus.

"Victoria?" I whispered. The only person I could trust now was my Wolf, she had to come forward to help me. I couldn't do this alone, my body and mind needed her too. If I had learned anything from Wesley's mother, it was that I needed to put my faith in my Wolf. "Victoria?" I called out again. Resting my head on the cold ground, I closed my eyes and reached for her, she was sitting in the back of my mind.

"*Victoria,*" I spoke to her internally. "*I need your help, we are alone in this, and we need each other.*" Victoria got up from her sitting position and trotted forwards. My heart skipped a beat as she came closer to me. Holding out my hand to touch her, she didn't move away. I smiled and she gave me a stiff nod. "*Victoria, why are you hiding? I need you, we need to save ourselves, Raina and her pack. We have to keep going.*"

"*There she is.*" Victoria's sweet voice licked at my soul. "*I was wondering when you would call out to me.*"

"*I, I am sorry, I didn't know I needed to?*" I said panicking.

"*No, no, no worries. You didn't know yet. It is quite early. I'm sorry we were forced to change but the threat of the pack made our bodies go into overdrive. You have been through a lot and my instincts just took over.*" Victoria wagged her tail and purred. "*I'm glad you were able to reach out to me, if we were back in our pack, they would be coaching you through this and here you are doing it alone. Mate is going to be so proud of us. I'm so happy to have you Charlotte, you are so strong and together we will be even stronger! You should be dead right now, but all on your own you hung on for your mate and the girl upstairs.*" I laughed as she continued her monologue. "*I will help us the rest of the way alright? Just listen and the Goddess will tell us both what to do, we are far from going to the stars just yet.*"

I let out a relieved sob as Victoria rubbed her head against me mentally. Having a wolf is the best, now we can cheer each other on. My confidence soared as I griped on to the little hope I was holding on to.

"Girl, we got this. You didn't need me to be strong, you got that all on your own. We just need a little wolfy power, right?" I nodded my head in agreement. *"Now, we are going to speed this up. First let's get the infection out of our body and then we can speed up our shift."*

Wesley

Driving into the night, Sorceress Cyrene quickly guided us North. She had a feeling of the area where Josephine had been staying but they weren't sure of the exact location.

"We'll get her back," Evan spoke abruptly. "I know we will." I gripped the wheel. "She's been through a lot of shit but damn she's strong as hell. She technically shouldn't be here after all that's happened to her, she's got a strong spirit." Remus growled at the thought of how much pain she had been in. I let out a sigh, this was getting old. She deserved the world of how much she had been through.

I wiped my hand down my face in frustration that didn't go unnoticed by Evan. Stepping on the gas a little harder, the speedometer reached 100 on the open highway. The trail of cars behind us and the Wolves in the forest around us all kept up the pace.

Evan frantically reached for his pocket and pulled out his cell phone that was put on vibrate. "Evan here." Evan continued to grunt and nod, I tightened my hands on the steering wheel causing it to whine at the pressure. Evan's eyes grew wide as my claws started to come out and quickly put the cell phone on speaker.

"Like I said," Cyrene spoke quickly. "We almost have an exact location, we have asked several covens to assist, even some in Bergarian that will transport here within the next few hours. Hades himself is coming from the Underworld to grab the demon before it escapes her body." Static interrupted her on the line. "There is more to the story, I'm sure, but a rogue demon inhabited Josephine's body at birth knowing she wouldn't be able to handle the dark power inside her."

"Damn, this is ridiculous," Evan growled.

"A fucking shit show this turned out to be," I ran my hand through my hair. I was going to be bald by the time this was over.

"Just keep heading North Alpha, stop in a town called Farheldra. Be ready for snow," and she cut the call. We were 100 miles from the small town as Evan pulled it up on his phone GPS. I stepped the gas even further to get there quicker.

Hang on Charlotte, I'm coming for you.

Chapter 60
Charlotte

"You need to breathe, in and out alright?" Victoria whispered to me as I tried to slow my breathing. She was trying to heal me. It was taking slower than normal she says, saying there was a power hovering over us like a heavy weighted blanket. The hours stretched on as I continued to hear the stomping upstairs, a few times I heard slaps and whimper and a large thump on the floor. Raina was being beaten and I wasn't sure why. Then again, who could really control Josephine? She didn't need a reason to inflict pain.

The smell from the infection finally left and I breathed a sigh of relief. Even though my bones were still broken, Victoria did her best to concentrate on just keeping me comfortable. I only cried silent tears as I waited for the infection to finally clear out.

The basement was cold and damp, just like the previous basement I spent my time in with Roman. I'm guessing it was a running theme of the entire kidnapping and torture. This time I didn't even have a rag on the floor to cover my body, just my jeans with a few holes from the protruding leg or arm bone. If any of this was told to me before I decided to become a Werewolf, I think I would have passed. Then again, I don't do things normally now do I?

I had almost dozed when I heard something being dragged across the floor and whimpers escaping Raina's lips. The basement door was thrown open and Raine was thrown down the stairs landing right on her left shoulder. She groaned and rubbed it gently like a newborn baby. Josephine looked down the stairs in disgust and scowled when she saw me. One or two steps

343

down the stairs she came with a fist balled up, causing blood to trickle down on the wooden steps.

"Still alive? This is taking slower than I thought." Several large steps later she was in front of me while I lay at her feet. Once she squatted down, she pulled my hair with her cold fingers and the other hand and gripped my cheeks tightly. "I don't know what the fuss is about," she scrutinized my appearance, tilting her head side to side. "You aren't even that pretty." Her nose scrunched while she looked down at me. "All these warriors are willing to walk in a lake of fire just to get your pretty ass back to the Alpha. It's pathetic really."

"Warriors?" I croaked.

"Yes, yes, they are all outside. They won't be able to get in though. They've been stripped of their Werewolf senses, they are nothing but pathetic humans now," she scoffed. "My power is too strong for them to see past the glamour I put on this house, they'll never find a way in. Hades will be here before they will get you and the entire house will be put into flames because he will think I'm here. Little do they know I'll be long gone by then. Silly dogs," she cackled. "If only I could hide my damn self for longer, so I don't have to run the rest of my days," she scoffed.

Without another word, she floated up the stairs much more gracefully than when she had previously stomped down. Raine sat up with her back to the wall and winced at the pain in her shoulder. "Raina, are you alright?" She sniffed.

"N-no. What have I done?" Her sobbing made me want to crawl to her, but I couldn't. I was still laying on the floor with no strength to go anywhere. I grunted to try and sit up on my elbow, my left arm was somewhat healed, I mean, I guess it didn't hurt as much.

"Raina…" she continued to sob. "Raina, look at me." Her eyes were red and puffy. Black and blue bruises decorated her face as well as her arms and legs. The clothes she wore were tattered at best, they now looked like rags. One would think she was raped the way she looked. I prayed that wasn't the case. "Raina, this is not your fault. You did what you did to protect your pack. You had no choice. I don't think we are dealing with an ordinary Witch, she has powers that stronger than what an ordinary Witch would have, surely. She mentioned Hades." Raina's ears picked up and panicked.

"H-hades?"

"Yeah, is that the same Greek god in human stories?" I whispered.

"He's worse. Far worse," Raine bowed her head. "If Hades is after Josephine, then she must be wanted for something really wicked. He deals with the worst spirits and chains them and tortures them himself."

"That is why she is wanting to stay longer and escape at the last minute, Hades will burn the house down and make a clean escape thinking her body was destroyed."

A few minutes pass without us saying anything, Victoria constantly reassures me while Raina tries to dry her tears. Over and over, I tell her she is not at fault, that she did what was best for her pack. I would have done the same, no Luna could blame a Wolf for that. She was stuck in a tough place with a Witch breathing down her neck. Letting out a slow sigh I felt a sharp pain in my back.

Bones began cracking at a faster rate than before. Raine came up to me and petted my hair telling me it would be alright. "You need to breathe, Luna. Breathe and listen to your Wolf. She will guide your body, but you can't tense up. Let it go, I know it's hard." My arm sprouted hair quickly and my face turned into a snout. Victoria and Raina continued to coach me through. I'm already tired and weak and trying to let my body go was becoming difficult. I grunted and clutched my stomach as another bone was breaking and slowly my screams didn't sound human anymore, I was howling. My vocal cords didn't work as I tried to speak, it came out a garbled mess. My tears no longer slid down my cheek but fell onto the fur that was coating my face.

Another howl and Victoria continued to push for me. My heart was constricted, and I felt loneliness pull me in. Astrid told me about the extreme emotions that come out during a change and some of your worst fears could come to the surface as your Wolf grasps your body. I felt the loneliness, the hollow pit of my soul that I used to feel every time I went to sleep at night. The cold nights I felt living in fear with no family or friends to call my own. Always running and always fighting. Feeling exhausted I let another howl rip through me, and my heart became warm. The warmth I felt began to grow hotter as my body continued to twist.

"CHARLOTTE!" I heard his mighty baritone voice come from the top of the stairs. Raina stood up to back away as Wesley ran to me. His touch soothed the achiness of my body as he held me close. A few more bones broke and his hand on top of them cleared the pain. I looked at him with my eyes or, Victoria's eyes, and he held nothing but concern. Zachary, Evan, and Ashley stood around and put their hands on my furred body Their hands-on me gave me comfort and I no longer felt alone, I felt like I belonged to a pack. Victoria continued to make the process as quick as possible but only she could do so much with our bodies for the first time for a shift.

"Kitten, it's alright. Relax and let it happen. We are here now," Wesley let a tear run down his face as he gripped my paw. One last reconfiguration of my body and it was over. There was no more pain, suffering, or the feeling of loneliness. I was free from that. I felt warmth, contentment, and love. My family stood above me looking at me in awe. Odin put his hand on his son's shoulder and nodded. While Odin left, he started spouting out orders for the men to be rounded up.

"Do you think you can move, my love?" Wesley's voice cracked. I nudged him with my snout. I whimpered as I slipped. Walking on fours was going to be difficult. Wesley helped me sit up on my hindquarters and smiled. I looked at my paws, they were the golden color I saw in my dream with a hit of gold reflecting off the hairs. I wasn't an ordinary Wolf, I was golden in color and I loved it.

"You are so strong, Kitten. So strong," Wesley hugged me, and I let out a low purr in satisfaction. My eyes closed shut with comfort but slowly I was falling asleep in his arms. Noticing what was happening Ashley spoke to Wesley softly. Whimpering as he shifted me, he carried me in his arms while I was still in Wolf form. Too tired to try and shift back I laid there.

"Good job, Charlotte," Victoria purred. *"We did it."*

"I'm so happy to have you."

"Me too, let's sleep, our body is tired. Mate has us."

Without any protest, I fell asleep in Wesley's arms as he carried me out of the basement.

Wesley

The pain ripped through me once the enchantment was wiped away from the area. It wasn't my own pain, but of my beautiful mate. Remus roared and he rammed forward into my consciousness. "Where is the cabin!? MATE TROUBLE!" The Witches stood back in fear, most of them knew of my calm Alpha tones but Remus was out of control. Cyrene- shocked herself, scrambled to get the covens together to cast the next enchantment.

Remus leaped over the large log and stormed the clearing, waiting for the Witches to lift the next layer of enchantment. Slowly the cabin came into view. First, it was a faint outline but quickly started to appear. The opaqueness of it was enough for me to run forward and find the door. Witches were screaming and warriors were surrounding the cabin. Remus was going to kill this Witch and I could do nothing to stop it.

The cabin was bare, with only a few pieces of furniture littering the area, a small stove with a hot pot of some potion. Blood was on the floor, and it slid to a door that could only mean the basement. Warriors behind me looked through the furniture, doors, closets and the floorboards were ripped to pieces to find the rogue Witch. Following my nose and my ears I hear a blood-curdling scream to hear my mate cry out in pain.

The door was ripped off its hinges as Remus's strength was heightened. Leaping down the stairs, Raina stood over Charlotte's body. Zachary grabbed her and held her close while I touched my mate's skin. She was half-formed. Her skin was littered with patches of golden hair and her fingers were baring claws. Her snout was partially formed and was struggling to speak. Instead of speaking gurgling noises from her maul. She was terrified, in pain, and suffering. Not being able to stand it, I spoke to her and put my hand on her

346

body. It calmed her instantly, her now golden eyes stared back at me. They were beautiful and she was doing this all on her own.

"Charlotte!" I whispered. "I'm here, I'm here," I cooed.

Many more touches and whispers of appreciation, warriors that were close to her touched her. It was common during Wolf shifting for pack members to lend a hand at the shift. It showed respect, support, and love when a new Wolf was coming forth. Her body slacked even more as she felt everyone, even though her body was bare I knew the Wolves that loved her didn't see her that way. Not one ounce of jealousy ran through us as our mate made her change to become a full Wolf.

Her fur was soft, it reminded me of the golden sunrise as the light hit her fur. The pain was over, and she survived. Her pack members and her family were here to see her through just in time. Letting a sigh of relief escape my lips I helped her sit. A wobbly sit but a sit, nonetheless. I pulled her to my chest, she was smaller than a Werewolf but larger than just a full-blooded Wolf. She was light in my arms, and I took note she will now need to eat more than the small portions of food she eats. Her breathing slowed and Ashley whispered that she had fallen asleep.

Hell, of course she would fall asleep. She went through almost twelve hours trying to shift at a painstakingly slow pace. Picking her up and cradling her to my chest she let out a small whimper and nuzzled into my neck. Her nose was cold, letting me know she was going to be alright. Keeping her close to me we headed back up the stairs.

Josephine was nowhere to be found, she had fled from the cabin. I scoffed at the information. Hades was going to have a field day when he got here. Leaving the cabin and taking two steps at a time off the front porch, the Witches had gathered and were talking in hushed voices. My father ran up to me.

"Hades will—" Before my father could finish Hades arrived in a ball of fire and instantly lit the cabin on fire. The fire was so hot you could see blue flames erupting from within. Backing up with Charlotte in my arms we all stood in awe as Hades stepped out of the cabin.

He was wearing a long dark robe, no shirt, and pitch-black linen pants. His hair was a curly bond that reached just below his eyes. The only other thing that was on fire beside the cabin was his eyes. His bare feet stomped the ground and stood before Cyrene, my father, and myself.

"Where the fuck is my demon?!"

Chapter 61
Wesley

Hades' fury was felt around us as the cabin was engulfed in hot flames. The Witches cowered in fear, hell even my warriors took a nervous stance as my father and I stood still, waiting for Hades to release more of his wrath.

"I said, where is my.fucking.demon," he spat. His eyes were on Cyrene as she bowed her head.

"She escaped My Lord. I am truly sorry." Hades glare never faltered as he walked up to her slowly and grasped her neck with his large bare hands. Cyrene gasped and automatically held her hands up to his as he gripped tighter, forcing her up against a tree.

"You are *sorry?*" Hades said slowly. "Sorry won't cut it," he growled. Cyrene's face become purple, so I handed Charlotte's Wolf form to my father. Clearing my throat Hades shot daggers at me as he dropped Cyrene letting her breathe.

"Got something to say, pup?" Remus pulled forward ready to unleash himself, he doesn't like being regarded as a pup, only if our mate says it. Hades was indeed powerful and should be respected, however, respect should be earned not when you are throwing a temper tantrum.

"With all the respect I can give you, Lord Hades," I spoke boldly. "It appears she escaped before we reached the cabin. Her smell was not lingering in the cabin when we entered." Hades tisked and looked back at Cyrene.

The Witches kept bowing and walking backwards to get away from his overwhelming aura. "I have to do everything my damn self," he whispered. Wiping his white, blonde hair back out of his face and letting out a sigh, he looked back to the burning cabin. Breathing was ragged as he thought while we stood silent. We all knew the power that he held. Many used to stay away from him and feared him just because he was the King of the Dead. Who wouldn't be afraid of death? Now people fear him because they have witnessed what his hands could really do.

It all started the day Persephone left him. Selene had just announced that each god would be given a mate as well since it worked so well with the Wolves. Soon the Moon Goddess started pairing up mates for everyone and most were thankful for it, even the god Zeus and he was a complete player among his kind. The day came when Persephone found her mate and it crushed Hades. He had pursued her for a thousand of years but in reality, Persephone never had the same love for Hades as he did for her. There were legends of Persephone crying in the depths of hell near the river of Styx begging for them to let her cross over back to the Earth or Bergarian realm.

Persephone ended up being paired with an angel, Gabriel. Of course, that angel had connections with Zeus and had Persephone pardoned from Hell. Hades was furious and his entire dominion suffered. It has been over a thousand years and his anger has yet to subside. Now with one of his demons on the loose this had only added fuel to the fire.

"The demon's name is Trixen, I had created her for certain purposes but in doing so I gave her too much power since I put too much of my emotion in creating her. Now, all she cares about is ruining the lives of others with a reason or not." Everyone froze at Hades speaking, Charlotte stirred in my father's arms whimpering and I laid my hand on her soft head.

"Since my emotions or essence is in her, she is hard for me to find, I've been searching for years. It seems you coven leaders have done a better job than I expected," he said, strained. Being the King of Hell, he must not be used to handing out compliments. "Is this your mate?" Hades pointed to Charlotte.

"Yes, my Lord." Hades nodded and walked up to her, placing a gentle hand on her head. A look of hurt and regret filled his eyes, possibly sympathy. "She's been through much, I see." His hand retracted and turned to speak to the crowd.

"To end this demon's reign over the Bergarian and Earth realms I am going to need your help from both sides, Witches and Werewolves, you seem capable. Trixen can sense when I am close and continues to run away when I come near, so amongst both of your kind I need you to find and kill her. The poor soul that she has pushed into the back of her mind will not be punished but be reincarnated into another life where she will find happiness. The only way to get Trixen back is to kill the body." The Witches listened on in shock of the mercy Hades was giving. Many whispers scattered across the crowd and Hades grew alight with anger.

"That's enough!" He roared. "Cyrene and Alpha Hale, we'll be in touch." With a blink of an eye, fire engulfed Hades, leaving nothing but ash as the fire dwindled. My warriors let out a sigh of relief knowing the threat was gone. Charlotte began to whimper again, and I grabbed her from my father's arms.

Cyrene bowed, letting me know we would be in touch of what steps to do next. Not only did we get my mate and Luna back but now, we had to help the devil himself capture a rogue demon. I was ready for some peace and quiet, but it seems we would all be far from it.

Mind linking the pack, I let them know we would rest here for the night and head back to the motel. The walk was short, all I did was nuzzle into my mate's head, her fur was soft, and she smelled the same as her human form. My father let us into the dank motel room and closed the door. Laying her on the bed, I covered her with a blanket and held her close to me.

I could have lost her today if we did not arrive at the right time. The emotions you go through during the last stage were rough. Remembering my first shift my greatest fear was not protecting my mate and protecting my pack. So far, I've done a shitty job protecting her. I've said it before but hell, she will never leave my side. My beautiful mate continues to amaze me as she continues to break the odds.

Holding her close to my chest, she let out a large huff. I smiled into her fur, and I could feel Remus getting annoyed.

"Mate, I want mate," he growled. Rolling my eyes, I stripped out of my clothes and shifted, and had Remus lay beside her. Purring and licking her forehead as she slept, he Curled around her.

Charlotte

I groaned as I sat up in bed. The sheets felt cold against my skin but felt soothing at the same time. My eyes opened wide realizing the last thing I remembered was suffering in the basement and Wesley found me. My hands were no longer paws and my skin was clear, touching my face. I also didn't have a long snout or sharp teeth. Sitting up the sheet came off my body and I was completely naked, I squealed when I heard a door open and covered myself quickly.

"Hey gorgeous," Wesley came in and set breakfast beside our nightstand table. *Our nightstand? Are we home? How...?*

"Wesley," I whispered. He held my face with both of his hands as he sat on the edge of the bed and kissed me gently.

"We're home, Kitten. You've been out for a few days." Wesley grabbed some OJ from the table and gave it to me to drink. Keeping the sheet covering my chest and sipping on the cold liquid I sighed. It tasted so good, and I was so hungry. A loud growl came from my stomach, and Wesley laughed, taking the OJ from me.

"Here, let's get you something to eat and I'll answer some questions for you." Taking the plate eagerly I ate the eggs, sausage, and hash browns quickly. I didn't realize I could eat this much and could probably eat more. Wesley, realizing the situation, gave me his plate willingly.

"Now that Victoria is awake, your appetite is going to increase. You have two bodies to take care of." Wesley gave me a kiss on the temple of my head and took off his shirt. His muscles were rippling across his body. He was still tan from our time at the beach, and I wanted nothing more than to claw at his skin and have my way with him.

Looking away quickly, I ate the rest of my food with vigor. I had just woken up after a few days of sleeping and changing into a Wolf. Now I wanted to be satisfied sexually. What the heck was wrong with me? I should at least shower first. I giggled at the thought of taking him into the shower with me, but I pushed it to the side.

Wesley came back and had a new shirt on and sat on the side of the bed and took my plate. "How about a shower, Kitten?" Well, guess he was reading my mind. He handed me a robe, knowing I didn't like walking around naked. Once I entered, I felt the hot steam from the shower as I dropped the towel. Turning around, I glanced up at the mirror to see my naked body.

Every single scar that riddled my body was completely gone. Coving my mouth from the gasp that wanted to escape I touched the side of my rib cage. Roman's name had completely fallen away. "Surprised?" Wesley held the door open, crossing his arms. "Your Wolf has felt the same pain as you, she did her best to clear you of all your scars."

Wesley waited for me as I finished my shower and dressed in a pair of ripped, distressed jeans and a plain black shirt. I brushed my long hair, it had gotten so long since I first arrived here at the pack. It was clear down my back now and had a of a shiny sheen to it since Victoria came into my life.

Coming out he smiled at me and gave me a large hug. "I'm so happy you are safe. You have no idea how worried I was." Nuzzling into his chest, I let out a sigh of contentment and purred. I purred! Looking up at him in shock, he laughed and patted my head. "Yeah, Wolves purr too when they are happy."

"I've got a lot to learn still, huh?" I sighed.

"Yes, but for now, I need to catch you up on some things. There are a few changes in the packhouse I need you to know about." Wesley took me to the balcony where we could look out over the forest. It was mid-morning, and the ground was snow covered. I noticed how I didn't need a jacket and felt perfectly content in what I was wearing. "Yes, you will be warmer now. That doesn't mean I want to hold you every chance I get." Wesley grabbed me and put me in his lap. I squealed, having him cradling me like he used to when we would have late night talks on the balcony. His nose went straight for my neck and inhaled. "Goddess, I love you."

I pulled away and cupped his face, staring into his big, beautiful green eyes', and pecked him on the lips. "And I love you, Alpha." Wesley's grip tightened on me, and I nuzzled into his chest. As I sat there and stroked my arm as we looked out over the territory and watched the pups play outside.

"While you were sleeping," Wesley broke me out of my trance, "Hades appeared after I took you out of the cabin." I stiffened; I remember how Josephine said she would leave before he came. That Lolli and I would burn alive. Shivering at the thought I tried to listen to Wesley. "He burned the cabin down just minutes after we both got you and Raina out. He's hunting Josephine, she has a demon in her and Hades wants her back to punish her."

I sat up, wondering what was going to happen to the real Josephine. "What will happen to the person who originally owned the body?" I whispered. Wesley stroked my hair again and smiled regretfully.

"She will be reincarnated once the body dies to live another life. There isn't really a way to save her."

"So, Josephine's demon is the one that has been causing all the trouble, not the real Josephine?" Wesley nodded. "Things in the supernatural world are complicated." Wesley chuckled.

"Now you see why I stay over here on Earth. A little bit less things to worry about." I smiled and hugged him closer to me. "That being said, things have changed around here with security. You are not to be alone at any time." Sitting up straight, to listen he put his hand on the small of my back.

"The Witches took the protection spell down around the borders, we are waiting for her to return to try and take you again. Three covens are here to stay and mask themselves to smell like Wolves, so Josephine doesn't know their presence. They are going to act like they are here for our mating and Luna ceremony in two days." My eyes widened, I only have two days? How can that be? Wesley smiled and kissed me on the cheek. "Don't worry Kitten, everything is taken care of." Nope, still didn't help my nerves but he continued.

"We don't know when she will come back, if ever but the Witches agreed to stay until she does. This demon likes to cause trouble and a lot of it. The perfect time for her to strike is during the ceremony, some say it is too obvious but hell, she's a demon. Why not do it then?"

"What about the pack? Will they be safe?" I wondered.

"Of course, they will all be safe. The children will be hidden in the panic rooms across the property if the covens feel a new presence. Other packs that are attending have been warned and are still coming to help if there's a problem."

"This is all way too much!" I sighed obnoxiously. "I just want to attend one party where nothing happens!"

"I know, it will be over soon." Wesley picked me up and wrapped my legs around his torso. I started giggling as he peppered kisses all over my face. "How about we go for a run?" Wesley wiggled his eyebrows while Victoria howled in my head.

"Victoria approves!" I fist pumped in the air while he took me down the stairs.

Chapter 62
Charlotte

Hand in hand, Wesley and I walked out of the back of the packhouse. Groups of warriors fought with one another, laughing and playing. One warrior flipped over a younger Wolf who let out a loud yip once he landed on his back. The pups were playing on the new jungle gym I asked Evan to order, of course, they made it higher and more Werewolf worthy, it was towering well over twelve feet off the ground.

The snow had finally come in from the north and a thin blanket settled on the fall leaves last night. Wesley continued taking me on a small path just North of the packhouse, he wanted to show me something on our run and said it was a surprise.

We came to the edge of the forest and Wesley stripped just beyond the tree line. His clothes were now laying on a low limb. He glanced at me and wiggled his eyebrows for the show I was about to put on. Shaking my head, I started stripping. I gently pulled my jeans off my legs and kicked them over to Wesley while he caught them. My shirt slowly pulled off my body as I wiggled out of it. I was left in just my sports bra and underwear, and he bit his bottom lip. Turning to the side I slid my hot pink, lace thong off and kicked it towards him. He caught it and never took his eyes off me. Sliding my sports bra off above my head, my breasts bounced free, and I held a hand over them as I chucked the fabric to him again. I was now completely bare as the day I was born. Wesley growled and I gave him an air kiss back. He gave that glorious laugh that made me feel it all the way to my toes.

"If we weren't going for a run, I'd ravage you now," He growled lowly into my ear. I giggled and stepped up to him and took a nibble on his ear while he held me tight.

"Are you ready?" He held out his hand as I took it.

"No," I whispered. The last time I shifted I thought I was dying, why would I be ready? He tilted his head to the side and kissed my cheek.

"It won't hurt this time, not as bad anyway. I'm sure Victoria has it down, just don't fight it. Concentrate on her and become her." I nodded my head as Wesley let go of my hand and shifted into his Wolf. He was a sandy colored, just like mine except mine had flecks of golden fur. Closing my eyes, I thought of Victoria, and she came forward and jumped into my line of vision. With a sound of a pop, I opened my eyes to see the world differently around me.

I was taller and my vision intensified. I could smell things far away such as a clean stream or squirrels stirring in their nests. My hearing was overwhelming, but Victoria seemed to have toned it down, so it didn't sound like we were walking on cymbals instead of leaves. Looking at Wesley I could see Remus. He was tall, the biggest of the Werewolves I've seen. He had a devilish grin displayed on his lips and gave a lick to Victoria. Victoria walked up to him and started rubbing her fur against him. I didn't hold on to Victoria in my mind, I let her go and she appreciated it.

"Let's let these love birds have some fun," Wesley said in the mind link.

Before I could agree, Victoria yipped and nipped at Remus's ear which earned a low growl in warning, and she took off. Being in the passenger seat was thrilling. She dodged branches, jumped over streams, and even chased squirrels and rabbits. She never held them for long and was always gentle when she would catch them and release them. Often, she would look back at Remus who was always right on her tail.

Remus ran with strength and pride; he was a powerful Wolf. The strides were long, and you could see the muscles in his legs as he trotted and sprinted across the forest. On the constant lookout for the danger, he would stop and listen for anything abnormal. Remus was very protective over Victoria and I since Josephine was still on the loose, but we were grateful.

"Mate loves us so," Victoria purred to me.

"Yes, Remus is just a big puppy." I grinned.

I felt Victoria smirk and she must have used my pet's name because now Remus started nipping at our heels. Both let out loud barks and yips as we came across a large tree in the middle of the forest. There were wooden planks leading up the tree and a large square box resembling a tree house stood tall.

Remus shifted back into Wesley's form, and he pulled some clothes from a trunk at the bottom of the tree. Victoria getting the idea, had me switch back to my skinned form. Wesley handed me a large sweater dress and I took it gladly. After running, flipping, and playing in the snow I did feel the cold.

"Come, this is what I wanted to show you." Wesley had me climb up first to make sure I didn't fall, and I opened the bottom hatch to enter the treehouse. Looking inside I saw old children's drawings with maps of treasure, pictures of other kids that were friends, and a large box nestled in the corner. It was empty here but in its prime, I'm sure it was full of children laughing and playing.

"This was my secret hideout," Wesley spoke as he sat on the floor. I crawled up to him and sat in his lap as he pulled his arms around me. He sighed, feeling content. "When my dad decided to be too rough with me, making me train every day I built this place. There were some nights I would actually sleep in here."

"How old were you when you made this?" I asked.

"Nine. I had some friends help and they were allowed to come here too. Then it ended up being a big party spot as I got older," he chuckled. I haven't been here since I became Alpha at 25." I stared up at him in awe.

"Wow, and it's still standing? This place has to be close to 100 years old then," I smiled. "You were an excellent builder back then. Maybe you should build our own house," I giggled at him. Wesley pushed back a piece of my hair and lifted my chin up to look into his eyes.

"That's what I wanted to talk to you about actually...." Wesley made me straddle his waist and put his hands on my hips. I blushed at the position. "It has always been a dream of mine to build my mate our own home. I didn't want to make it before I knew you because I wanted it to be exactly how you wanted it." I smiled as my face lit up. "Would it be alright, once all this demon mess is over with, if we built our home? I know you like the packhouse but——"

I cut him off. "I would love, more than anything, for you to build us a home." I cupped his cheeks. "It will be our home with a few kids running around and not worrying about people barging into our room all the time," I giggled while he squeezed my waist. "But really, anywhere you are, is home to me. I'll go where you go, I will follow you. A home built by you will be amazing."

"You want to have pups?" His eyes grew twice the size and a large smile plastered on his face.

"Out of all that you pay attention to the baby part?" I poked his chest.

"Of course, because I'll have fun makin' 'em all!" He tickled me until I was crying, and I finally had to throw out my surrender.

"Please, I'm done! I'm going to pee!!"

We finally stopped laughing and he pecked me on the lips which, turned out to be a make-out session. I'd never tire of his kisses, the way he makes me melt with a single touch. His tongue exploring my mouth makes it feel like the very first time. I moaned into the kiss, and he began chuckling. Reluctantly we both pulled away and I set my hands on his chest.

"We should head back," I whispered. Wesley looked out of the treehouse window and saw the sun was setting.

"We should. I don't need a demon trying to take you from me in the dark." With another peck, we climbed down the tree house and landed lightly on the ground. Taking both of our clothing off and stuffing them in the box, we shifted and raced back towards the house.

Once we arrived and were clothed, we reached the backyard. A large fire sat in the middle. The elders were howling, and the children followed along blindly, holding tree sticks and glow sticks. Many elders were in headdresses and traditional clothing I had never seen before. They shouted in a language that was unfamiliar to me and I looked to Wesley for answers.

He had a small smile on his face as we continued to approach the bonfire that engulfed most of the backyard. "They are blessing us, there are rituals our ancestors used to bless a new Luna and for the lineage of my Alpha line." I blushed thinking about them dancing to my fertility, Goddess helps me. "They are also dancing for protection against the demon." His face went hard and squeezed my hand tighter. I patted his hand and gave it a quick kiss.

"Everything will work out. We have so many people working with us, I just know it." Wesley's eyes softened as he looked at me.

"You know how to soften me up, Kitten." He rubbed our noses together while Astrid and Ashley came running up.

"Charlotte! Come quick!" Astrid grabbed one hand and Ashley grabbed the other. Looking in confusion, Wesley laughed and let me go.

"Where are you taking me!?" I gasped at them pulling me to the fire. The women quickly put on a large fur on my shoulders as well as a headdress of a Wolf. I looked at them in confusion and the elders quickly grabbed my hand and took me to the fire.

"Repeat after me," the elder spoke. Looking at Wesley for confirmation he smiled waving his hand that it was safe.

I repeated the unfamiliar language and as I finished, the elder threw a powder into the fire. The fire rose ten feet higher turning blue and purple. They all started shouting around the fire saying the request would be fulfilled. Astrid and Ashley laughed and continued to dance around to the tune in their own heads. Pups pulled me along to join them, so I did. We danced and the pups sang songs of strong alphas beating evil rogues and demons.

Looking back at Wesley, he had his arms crossed over his chest, smiling at me as I played with all the children around the fire, oblivious of what I just asked the goddess to do for me.

Chapter 63

Wesley

Charlotte danced around the fire with the pack. Her blonde hair swayed as the hood of the traditional cape of our pack fell to her shoulders. She was laughing and holding hands with the pups as they danced around her. She was the mother of this pack; her tender heart had captured the pack in ways I couldn't understand. Even though she had gone through many hardships before she met me, she was still able to shine through and conquer not only the demons in her head but the enemies of this world.

Charlotte keeps glancing at me as she comes around one side of the large bonfire that took up most of the yard. It took the pack all day to gather enough wood to make a fire of this size. Many men stood around in pride at the size. It was to represent a new life, a new beginning, and protection among our large territory. With Charlotte's new security measures more Wolves could spend time with their mates and still be able to protect all of us from harm.

She stopped dancing and gently swatted a pup on its rear to make them leave. Charlotte stared at me and pulled her hand up and beckoned me to join her. The little smirk playing on her lips made my heart jump on the inside of my body. Only she can make me feel this way and to know she only has eyes and heart for me makes me feel a puff up with pride. Her smirk becomes a smile and then a giggle the closer I get. She skips over to me and jumps into my arms and wraps her legs around me. "There is the mighty Alpha!" she whispered furiously in my ear. I squeezed her ass in recognition and gave her a kiss.

"Dance with me," she demanded and let her legs go from my waist. The pups were being led home by their parents and the elders threw one last powder into the fire as it started to slowly burn out. My parents gave me a wave while Ashley turned on music more appropriate for me to dance with my lovely mate. I held her close and put nose to ear, tickling her which caused her to giggle and kiss my cheek.

As the song began to play, I could sense the large smile on Charlotte's face. Pulling back, she looked at me and her face shone like the moon. Her smile was bright and immediately stole my breath. "I love this song," she looked at me dreamily at some '90's song.

Smiling at her I pulled her back to me and kissed the top of her head as we listened. The past few days had been rough, and I never wanted to let her go. I wanted to keep her all to myself and never let her leave our room. To bask in each other's presence, but that isn't who she is. She is a light at the end of the tunnel, she is the moon of the pack, she is the light that will continue to shine for me. Without her, knowing who she is and what she does to me I know I can't live without her.

At the last line of the song, I picked her up by her thighs and wrapped them around me. She holds my face in the palm of her hands. "I love you," she whispered and tickled my lips. The sparks flew across my lips, and I instantly connected mine to hers without hesitation. Moaning into my mouth I started walking back to the packhouse. The door was unlocked, and the lights were off.

Going from memory, I walked up the stairs, not missing a step in the dark, not taking my lips from hers. Opening the door with one hand and the other firmly cupping her ass, I held her tighter and kicked the door closed.

Gently laying her on the bed, we continued to massage each other's tongues. Whimpers came from her as I growled as she nipped at my lower lip. Her hooded eyes looked into me, and I saw nothing but passion, desire, and love. Remus rumbled my chest with a purr as she moved my hair over my ear. Leaning into her touch she smiled at me. "How did I get so lucky?" she whispered. "To have this life with you?" I smirked at her and gave a low chuckle to which she responded by rubbing her thighs together.

"I think Kitten, that I am the lucky one," I said with my raspy voice. My lips crashed onto hers, hungry to fulfill her need, her want, hell, mine too. My hands trailed her body, pulling off her clothes and she did mine. Hearing small rips of our clothing I could hear her giggles fill the air which only added to my playfulness. I nipped at her ear, tickling her with my tongue as I trailed down her neck. A small gasp left her lips, and I took shock as an opportunity to pull her top over her head. Her head playfully bounced on the bed and her legs wrapped around my bare body.

Our playfulness soon subsided as we touched each other. Her hands touched every part of my chest, my stomach, and thighs. She sighed lovingly as she felt the sparks go through her fingers. My body ached where her fingertips brushed against my skin, wanting to feel more of her touch. I rolled onto my back, having her straddle me. Charlotte sat up and gave me her beautiful white smile before putting her lips on my neck. Trailing my neck to her mark she started sensually sucking the skin, giving me shivers down my spine, letting out a groan. I felt my cock become wickedly hard, wanting to feel a release.

Charlotte

I felt so empowered and in charge as I sat on my mate. His thighs were large, and it was hard to keep straddled around him with my smaller frame. He looked so delicious, I just wanted to eat him up and that is what I was going to do.

I kissed his mark and it caused him to groan, he tightened his hands on my hips and bucked wanting some friction. I smiled as I let go of his mark with a pop. Kissing down each peck and down to his abdomen, I kissed each ab down his v-line. Wesley let go of my hips, letting me travel closer to where I wanted to be. Kissing each side of his thigh, I grabbed his large member. Feeling his heartbeat inside, I knew he was wanting his cock sucked.

Licking the tip, Wesley grabbed my hair on my head and pushed me down. I bobbed him up and down his shaft as he spat out curses. "Fuck, Charlotte!" His grip became tighter as he pushed me down deeper. His cock hit the back of my throat. "Goddess, just like that, just like that," he praised me. "Such a good Kitten, fuck yes!"

He was trying to push me off of him, but I wanted to taste him and have him finish inside my mouth. I wanted to show him how much I loved him, how much I cared about his pleasure because he was always the one trying to cause mine. Wesley wasn't having any of it as he pulled me from his cock and had me get on my knees, having my butt facing him. I growled at the sudden loss of him in my mouth but before I could say a word of protest, he lined himself up and plunged into me. Letting out a squeak feeling how full I was he continued to push deeper inside me. Thrust after thrust, it wasn't aggressive, it wasn't animalistic, it was another level I couldn't speak of. He hunched over, pushing into me and grabbing my breasts below me, massaging them and tweaking my nipples that only added to my pleasure. Meeting him thrust for thrust, feeling his desire I moaned for him in a whimpering mess.

"Wesley, yes, please," I begged.

"You feel so damn good, Charlotte. Every bit of you," he panted. "Goddess, I love you." His thrusts became erratic, and the arch of my back become painful. Noticing my discomfort, he rolled me to my side and had me on my back without breaking our connection. The love in his eyes as he looked into my soul was breathtaking. Each time we made love it felt like it was new all over again.

The sweat on our bodies mixed, his pants became closer as we both reached heaven now falling back down to Earth. He fell to the side of me and pulled me close. I nuzzled into his embrace as he held me. We didn't have to say anything at all, the bond proved that. I could feel his love for me and my love for him.

✳✳✳

"Hurry up, Charlotte! Get your lazy ass out of bed!" My eyes flew open at the sudden intrusion of the door being flung open. Rubbing my eyes, I gave Ashley a glare. What the heck did she want? "Your dress fitting is in fifteen minutes! Hurry up! Looking over to Wesley's side of the bed it was empty. His side was cold, so he had been gone a while.

"Wesley?" I mind linked.

"My kitten is awake," he laughed.

"She is, now where are you?"

"At the training fields with my father, I'm going to get fat and lazy if I don't start working out."

"Pretty sure you can't get fat with all the love making we do," I could almost see the grin on his face.

"That is true. You better hurry up, Ashley is trying to yell at me to get you going. Your dress came today, and they need to put the finishing touches on it. Get going and remember to stay in the house unless you have a warrior with you."

"Yeah, yeah," I waved him off.

"I mean it, Charlotte."

I cut him off and padded over to the shower. Even though I only had 15 minutes to get ready for the day, I was going to spend most of it in the shower. No point of doing hair and makeup because Ashley was going to strip it down to nothing and turn me into a "doll," she would say. I took my time, shaving every inch of my body so she didn't have a chance to rip it out with her foul waxing stuff she likes to do once a month. "Not this time!" I sang to myself in the shower.

Once I was done, I wrapped a big fluffy towel around my body. My hair was soaked and looked almost brown in color when wet. Taking my hand I wiped the mirror, expecting to see myself reflecting back at me. Only it wasn't my face. The face of the most frightening creature I've ever seen stared back at me.

Her eyes were sunken in, looking into the hollow pits you couldn't even her eyes. Black spider-like veins were crawling out of her black orbs. His skin was deep red with black hair protruding out of her head like silk. Her hand was touching my shoulder, nails black and talon like, you could hear the shuffling of her feet making clunking noises on the tile floor. Looking down, there were cloven hooves. The horns elongated from the top of her head that looked like rams. Fear had struck me to the core, even Roman couldn't invoke this sort of pit in my stomach.

Turning around from the mirror, I only see Josephine. Looking back at the mirror, the demon. It was then I realized that Hades' rogue demon had come early and undetected.

"Hello, dearie."

Chapter 64
Charlotte

My breath hitched as I saw, in slow motion, Trixen pushing me to the tiled floor. With my new senses, I wondered how no one else could feel her presence. I couldn't even sense she was behind me let alone in the same room.

Flipping over quickly, the towel now pooled around my back and my breaths were light and erratic. The tapping of her cloven hooves as she came closer made my heart clench in fear. Training with Wesley had never crossed my mind yet, and now I'm really regretting my decision. Reaching for Victoria I couldn't hear anything, there was a wall I couldn't break. Sensing my distress, the female demon, Trixen, chuckled darkly as the sounds of Josephine's voice and her own mixed together.

"You can't run now, pretty Luna." The clacking of her hooves stopped in front of me. Her hand came down to grip my throat, but I quickly darted away and grabbed the towel rack for support. "I don't have time for this. You can't link your pack and you can't access your Wolf, so I suggest you give up quietly and it won't be as painful." Trixen's forked tongue slid from her lips and swiped across her chapped skin.

Trying to think, I darted from the bathroom only to be slung by an invisible force, face first, on the bedroom floor. My forehead bounced on the fuzzy shag carpet. Picking myself with my forearms I saw her strolling quickly towards me. My instincts say to run but my gut tells me to stay and fight. Maybe Victoria was still in there after all. Jumping to my feet I grabbed the drawer of the nightstand and pulled it out. Books, letter openers and pens fell out quickly and with one giant swing I aimed the corner to the side of the demon's head. Not expecting the impact, it hit her on the left side of her temple causing her to jerk her head backwards and drop to the floor.

Looking down at the drawer, I saw blood splattered across the corner. It wasn't just a little either. Trixen held the side of her head and groaned as she shook her head back and forth to regain her balance. Even though she was a demon, and a powerful one at that, she was in pain and taking a few minutes to recover. She can get hurt in her human body.

The newfound thought gave me a jolt of energy as I took the drawer and slammed it back into her head. She screeched something inhuman as blood pooled on the back of her head. The wound on her temple began to heal but at a slower rate. My mind had a large film of static come through as I heard faint voices of Wesley trying to reach me.

"Op... en.. Do," was all I could make out. The static subsided and I could hear pounding on the master bedroom doors. Dropping the drawer, I took two large steps forward only to be grabbed by my ankle and pulled harshly down. Her body might be able to break but her strength was still there. I yelped in pain and felt her claws dig into my ankle drawing blood, a loud yelp left my lips as I could now hear people on the other side of the door, mainly Wesley.

"Open the fucking door!" The banging on the large mahogany double doors rattled but to no avail would they move. Why would they? There was a mental block on their Wolves and the strength we draw from them. Wesley roared on the other side while you could hear Odin, Zachary, Evan and Bruce arguing. Not able to pay attention, my vision diverted back to Trixen.

"Can't run now!" she cackled. "Do you hear that, you pathetic Wolves? You. Are. Useless!" The blood that was dripping from her wound was now healed and I had to start all over in trying to subdue her so I could open the door. Her hands began pulling me as she stood up, dragging me to the open balcony door. Reaching out, trying to find anything on the floor as she drug me, I found a letter opener and grabbed it. With one movement of my arm, I sat up, digging it into her upper thigh. She grunted in pain, but it wasn't enough to stop her.

Again and again, I took the letter opener, forcing it into her leg until she finally gave out, with as many open wounds she had, maybe it could stall her. I stood up, getting ready to sprint to the door again but she pulled me back with the invisible force she had used to push me earlier. The letter opener was still sticking out of her thigh as the force drug me to her. My nails scratched the wood as I panicked at the sudden realization that I may not leave this room, alive anyway. I concentrated with all my might to grab ahold of something, but the slick floor was all I could find, her chuckles were dark, and her fanged teeth were now on display. It had to be the most horrifying thing I had ever seen. Her forked tongue slithered in and out of her teeth, smelling my fear.

"Why are you doing this?" I screamed. There had to be a reason and if I was going to die, I wanted to know the biggest question of them all from her, "Why!"

The tail I failed to notice came around and wrapped around my neck and sat me up. My hands instantly went up to try and pull the tail from my neck. Trixen leaned in, I could smell the rancid rotting meat of her teeth.

"You want to know why?" She whispered and licked my cheek. I nodded quickly to hear her answer, still hearing the banging on the door I tried to gain some sort of courage, which there was none.

"I was created by Hades himself, the god who lost his love Persephone to her true mate," her tongue danced on my lips, and I shivered in disgust. "When he creates a demon, he puts a drop of his blood into them so he would always have control. He can command, order, kill and even save his demons but he did something different with me. Hades gave me a bit of his essence." I scrunch my face in confusion.

"Silly little Wolf, it means he wanted me to be his soulmate. Without his blood, I had the agency to do as I will. I gained some of his power with the essence and left the Underworld and entered another body. Josephine was weak so it was quite easy." Her voice became sickly sweet and trailed her claw down my chin and to my chest. "Soulmates only make gods weak; it has made Hades weak for even desiring such a thing, let alone indulging in it," she spat. "See how desperate he was to create a creature like me? Again, soulmates make you weak and create rash choices all in the name of love. Now I have no ties to Hades, and he cannot command me. I do as I please, even if that means hunting, stalking, devouring souls like Josephine's and yours."

As she monologued, her power had dwindled. I could feel Victoria clawing out of the wall she had been captured in. Her howling in my head let me know she was coming but I didn't know if she would be too late.

"And souls like yours, the innocent and meek are insanely sweet." Trixen opened her mouth wide and was going to devour my neck until I grabbed on to the bloody letter opener, she had left in her thigh carelessly. Once her eyes were set on my neck and her teeth grazed my skin I thrust forward into her bare chest.

Her tail loosened around my neck, and I pulled the letter opener from her. Sitting back, she looked at me in shock as she grabbed her chest. As soon as she fell back on the ground with a thud, Victoria howled at me to finish the job. My right hand-formed into our mighty claws and I clawed through her chest. I was relentless, I continued to pull at her, ripping meat from the bone and pulling out her heart and throwing it across the room. Bloodstained my hands as I looked at it in disbelief.

Still naked, blood dripping from my body, I had never witnessed or done anything close to this. Tears flooded my eyes. Flashbacks of my childhood began to surface.

The branding she had done to my chest to force a bond, to force me to love someone that shouldn't have been mine. The scars that Roman had inflicted on me all because Josephine had told him I should have been beaten into submission. The sleepless nights on a cold basement floor, the rats scurrying across my body, looking for food, and oftentimes nipping at my toes.

It all came back like a real nightmare. My eyes started to see spots, my hearing became tunneled and the last thing I saw before I slumped to the floor was Trixen's heart laying across the room.

Wesley

"Someone get this damn door open! Get a fucking ax or something?" I screamed. Remus couldn't be felt, as well as for the others and their Wolves.

I had felt immense pain while I was training with my father and instantly knew it wasn't that of my own. Sprinting across the field, Witches were congregating around the packhouse, talking amongst themselves in hushed tones. "What is the meaning of this, what is going on?"

"There is a disturbance, but it is so faint we can barely feel it," Cyrene spoke. Without another word I raced up the stairs to hear a struggle in my room when I put my ear next to the door. This was a fucking bad time for having soundproof rooms. Trying to open the door, it was locked so I screamed for her.

"Charlotte!! Open the door!" A muffled scream was heard and I knew that bitch of a demon was there. Cyrene put her hand on my shoulder. "She's here."

"No, shit, get me in there," I yelled.

"All of our powers are weak, the demon is suppressing the power around the other supernaturals. It is part of his essence," Cyrene said hurriedly.

"Contact Hades, the bitch is here, now go if you can't help." Cyrene ran off and the rest of the Witches were making a pentagram on the floor of the foyer several stories down.

My father came running up to the door and we immediately started running into the door with our bodies, trying to shake something loose. "Damn doors!" my father roared. "An ax! Get an ax!" Evan and Bruce came running up the stairs, starting to argue with my father how an ax wouldn't work on the reinforced mahogany doors. Trying to think quickly, I thought of the window but even that would be a steep climb and without our Wolves and strength it would be worthless.

The Witches downstairs were still conjuring an old way to summon Hades and with a few more poundings of the door I felt the static in my head. Remus pounced forward, "NOW!" he roared as he burst through the barricade in my head and the doors flung open with a loud bang. Scanning the room, I see nothing but blood. Remus begins to whimper while everyone behind me stills.

That is where we see Josephine's body, now of the looks of a demon, Trixen laying dead on the floor. Her chest was ripped open, parts of her were slung onto the bed, the walls, the plush white carpet that Charlotte loves so much. It was a gruesome sight even for my father who inhaled deeply and let a soft, "holy shit," from his lips.

The bond pulled me to the corner of the room. My small, bloody and naked mate laid slumped against the wall. Growling at others to leave as I raced towards her, I grabbed her and cradled her in my arms. Her hands still had her claws, wet tears still trailing down her face. My ear went straight to her chest, just to be sure her heart was the one I could hear beating. It was there, it really was. Her wounds had already healed, she was safe. Safe and in my arms.

Vera Foxx

Chapter 65
Wesley

I took Charlotte's bloodied body from the floor. Our closest friends and my parents stood at the door, waiting to see what I would do next. Cradling her in my arms, I grabbed a blanket that was still splattered with blood, I covered her so no wandering eyes could lay on her. Walking out the door silently, everyone parted in the hallway as I walked down to her old room, the room she only spent a few days in before the bond finally took over and she started to trust me.

Walls were still painted the light grey that she loved, the room had been kept exactly how she decorated it the first few nights here. Her small plants sat by the window, the cat bed for her departed cat, and the few old pieces of clothing from her old life still hung in the closet. Looking down at her unconscious state, I sighed heavily.

Feeling the eyes on my back as I stepped further into the room, you could hear whispers of what they should do. To leave Charlotte and I alone together after almost having a near death experience twice since the short time I've known her, or to stay to make sure we both would be Okay. Remus urged me that Victoria was healing her, that she would be alright physically, but no one was sure how she would be mentally. She had witnessed and acted in something no human and hardly any supernatural ever had to overcome and that was fight a demon and just in her frail human body.

Looking to my left and giving a quick side-eye to my audience, I growled. "Leave us," and headed to her ensuite bathroom. Avoiding the bath, since once she would be placed in it, she would be bathing in a pool of blood, I decided the shower was the best. Turning it on, adjusting the temperature so it was just right, I peeled the blanket off her body and stepped in with my clothes on, not wanting to put her down.

I let the warm water run, just over our bodies as the double headed shower rained down on us. The blood slipped from her body and stained the floor. I gently held her in my arms as I used the soap to wash her hair, condition it and then spread body wash over her. This act alone I felt was more intimate than the times we had made love. I wanted to take care of her body, mind, body and soul.

A few whimpers left her mouth, and I quickly kissed her cheek, cooing at her. "It's alright now, Kitten. I've got you. I'm not going anywhere." Her head fell back into my chest as I turned off the water. Taking a towel, I wrapped her gently, drying her face, arms, and legs. My clothes, still drenched in water, I made my way to the bed and carefully laid her down, still wrapped. Not caring if I ruined the room in my wet clothes, I stripped entirely and dried myself.

Pulling the bed sheets back I picked up my still naked mate and put her under the covers along with myself. Immediately, she curled into my body, and I held her tightly. Petting her hair, whispering how much I cared for her, sweet nothings in her ear that she craves, I did it. I stayed with her; I didn't care that Hades was on his way to take care of the body. I was going to stay here with my mate until she awoke. I would be the first person she saw.

***

A few hours had passed, and Charlotte was starting to stir in her sleep. Little moans and whimpers left her mouth as she nuzzled into my neck. I chuckled because her eyelashes were tickling in that one spot I liked. Charlotte's eyes fluttered open, and her eyebrows furrowed in confusion.

"Am I dreaming? Is it over?" Her eyes brimming with glassy tears broke my heart. Both of our hands found each other's faces and touched them as if we were both going to fade away.

"It's over, no it isn't a dream," I said huskily.

"Thank goddess!" Her grip became unbearably tighter. It was hard to still fathom my weak little mate before the change now, her strength almost matched my own at times.

"Do you remember what happened, Kitten?" I asked, concerned, pushing her hair out of her face.

"I-I killed her. Blood, so much blood," she whispered and gripped me tighter. I hold on, not letting her go.

"Yes, it's over. You did it, and almost without your Wolf, Love. You are so strong, so strong." After a few minutes of her regaining herself, processing what had happened she let out a long sigh. I kissed her forehead and rubbed my nose with hers in which she started to giggle. My mate was finally coming back to me.

"I don't want to do that ever again," she chuckled.

"I don't want you to either," I laughed.

"Oh! How long did I sleep!? The Mating and Luna ceremony! Did we miss it!?" Charlotte jumped up, not realizing she was completely naked, and her chest was now in my face. I groaned, trying to hold myself back. I can't do this now, shit.

"Kitten, you have only slept a few hours, in fact, dinner will be soon. You didn't miss anything," she sighed and snuggled next to me.

"Good, I didn't want all that food to go to waste, you should see the cake. It is like 5 tiers high, and it has ice cream in it!" I threw my head back and laughed. Only my mate would be talking about food right now.

"Alright, since you are feeling better," I kissed her lips. "Let's get dressed. We have an important guest with us at dinner." Charlotte made a face and looked at the corner of her eyes, thinking.

"Really? Who?"

"Hades."

Charlotte

Wesley snuck me back to our room, the room was almost completely bare. Furniture, rugs, carpets, doors and even my favorite fluffy rug was missing. The doors to our room had been taken down and the smell of bleach was in the air. I plugged my nose with my fingers, Victoria had not controlled my smelling ability yet, so it was burning my nose.

"Go get dressed kitten, something semi-formal." I looked in confusion and he patted my butt to get me moving. He had draped me in the large comforter as we had walked down the hall, so I kept it around me as I walked to the closet. If I didn't have to think about what happened earlier today, I wasn't going to. I was going to mentally block it out the rest of my life.

Heading to the closet, I picked out a royal blue tea-length dress that flowed effortlessly outwards at the bottom. The top had thin, jeweled silver straps. Putting on my undergarments and then the dress itself, I stood myself in front of the mirror. It was beautiful, something I would have never picked out for myself when shopping. It sat out in the front of the closet begging for someone to wear it though. Continuing to look at the mirror, I laid my eyes on the far-right corner of the room. The large piece of carpet missing was beckoning me to look. Closing my eyes, I held in my breath and turned. Slowly letting out an unsteady breath I look at *the spot*. The hardwood floor was staring at me in the face, no longer covered with the white frilly carpet. There were no signs of blood and no dead body to be seen.

This exact spot was where I had ripped the demon's heart from her body. I didn't notice the few tears trickling down my face until Astrid walked in along with Ashley. I didn't even have to look to see if they were there, I could smell them. Both pulled me into a hug that I never returned. I was going to remember this day for the rest of my life. I was able to beat a demon, but the morbid way I did it will always haunt me.

I had put all my fears into that fight, I fought for my ability to look past all the pain I had in my life. I took every breath, swipe, and claw and dove it into that terrible demon that only killed for fun. Astrid sat up straight after hugging my short stature and gave a small smile. "Let's do your hair and make-up, huh? As much as you don't want to, we need to let Hades know what happened." Nodding reluctantly, they continued with their artistic hands curling, powdering, and painting my lips in the bathroom, the one place where no blood had touched.

Once I finished getting ready, my dashing Wesley stood in the doorway. Black slacks and tie with a white dress shirt. Looking deliciously handsome, he gave me a smirk and held out his hand. Taking it gladly, we walked down the stairs to meet a brooding Lord of the Underworld.

Hades was nothing of what I pictured. He was wearing a three-piece suit, fitted to mold his body. His white-blonde hair was hanging over his eyes as he looked down at his hands. Rings adorned his fingers as he played with them while he waited for us to join him. We were to have a private dinner in the East wing dining room, meant for exclusive Alpha meetings.

Sorceress Cyrene was also there, donned in her formal witching attire, all black with her intricately tied corset. Wesley pulled out a chair for me and I sat down. Hades did the same and pulled a chair out for himself at the round table and put his elbows down and held his head in one of his hands. Blowing a piece of hair out of his eyes, looking bored he took this time to speak.

"So, this is the little she-Wolf that defeated a demon?" I was silent as he spoke, such dominance he held in the room. Never in my wildest dreams, I would be faced with such a person, a god I mean. They were supposed to be Greek tales but obviously, that wasn't the case.

"Yes, Lord Hades, she..." before Cyrene could continue, with a wave of Hades' hand she stopped speaking. My eyes never left him, and he never left mine. I could feel Wesley squeezing my hand. "You mean to tell me, a young she-Wolf, just turned, beat a class five-level demon? I find that hard to believe," he scoffed. Everyone remained silent and I turned my head to Wesley, not knowing what to do. He wasn't mind-linking me so maybe I wasn't supposed to.

"That's right, you can't mind link because I know what you are thinking," he hummed and picked up the ice-cold glass of amber liquid. He let it touch his lips for a moment before he drank it all down in one gulp. Dramatically putting it back on the table and catching my gaze he smiled.

"I'm impressed." Cyrene let out a large breath and Wesley gave me a reassuring squeeze. "However, there are a few missing pieces to her story that she told you. Trixen said she wanted to kill and since I failed to give her a drop of my blood when I created her. So, I couldn't find her or control her. My own men couldn't get close to her because they held my blood and she could detect that small anomaly," Hades' voice grew sad as he continued.

"I created her because I am angry with the goddess Selene for taking Persephone from me. I've been given powers to help create things so why not create someone to be a companion, on my rules? Selene took one thing away from me that I cared for, so I don't trust her to give me what I supposedly need." Hades gritted his teeth in anger and slammed his fist on the table, causing the dishes to rattle. "Taking things into my own hands I tried to create a demon that would be with me. She still needed a choice, so I denied my blood as to give her choices and I didn't control her. Once she was created, she was everything I had wanted. The first few days she was like a newborn calf learning to walk and talk, understanding who I was and why she was created. Her powers then started to come in, that is where the problem started." Hades looked out the to the snow that was falling out the window.

"Trixen realized she had great power because I leaked some of my essence in her so her soul could connect with mine. Little did I know when I did this, my anger for mates also poured through, thus giving her a vendetta against all who had mates." Cyrene's eyes widened at the sudden realization. My eyes softened and I put my hand on Lord Hades' hand. Wesley and Cyrene tensed as I did so and Hades' facial features were no longer stern and stoic but hurt.

"She's out there you know, your mate," I rubbed my thumb across his knuckles. It must feel intimate for him, but at this point, I didn't care, I wanted him to know there are people that care about his wellbeing too. "I don't know your whole story, and I don't know what happened to your last love, but I promise you, when Selene pairs you with your mate it will be the best thing. It will make all the terrible past times not seem as harsh once she comes into your life. It will be like a clean slate. She will love you for you and no one else and never leave." Wesley squeezed my hand again and I let go of Hades. Hades' gaze continued to look at his hand while he cleared his throat.

"Well, my visit here is done. Thank you for both of your help. I'll be sure to have Hecate bless the covens and packhouses." Before we could object, Hades was gone in the blink of an eye.

Chapter 66
Charlotte

Once Hades left, we took our food to eat in the main dining room. Wesley sat at the head of the table and quickly grabbed my waist and sat me on his lap. Giggling at him he squeezed me a bit tighter and kissed my cheek. I got so darn lucky!

"Don't leave us in such suspense, Wesley, what the hell did Hades say?" Everyone at the table was staring at us waiting for us to speak while we were having our little moment. I blushed at the attention and Wesley chuckled in my ear. Wesley sighed and started to speak. "Long story short-" Wesley began but I squeezed his arm. We didn't need to tell Hades' story. That was his own personal problem that the world didn't need to know.

"Just an out-of-control demon with a vendetta against people with bonds. Just an insufferable thing that wished the worst in everyone. Hades was grateful to the covens and our pack for being able to help," I spoke for Wesley. Evan hummed as well as the others and we began to eat our food.

Zachary was sitting beside Raina, her wounds had healed well, and Zachary sat awfully close to her. Their eyes twinkled at each other as they looked longingly. Their hands were intertwined, and they continued to whisper to each other. Their problems seemed to have vanished and a new blossoming relationship was on the horizon.

"Raina? How is your pack, is everything alright?" Raina perked up and wiped her mouth with her napkin.

"Yes!" she chirped. As soon as the demon was killed the spell was broken and they were able to roam freely around the pack. It was almost like a forcefield," Raina animatedly waved her hands around while Zachary smiled fondly at her. "Once it was lifted, I was able to mind-link my parents and tell them what happened. They are so grateful to you and Alpha; they are on their way for the ceremony tomorrow!" She smiled. Aria and the twins continued to eat their food as Raina explained. The boys would be able to go back and train with their father then.

"I'm so glad to hear that, Lolli."

"Everything alright now, Zachary?" I linked him. *"She didn't mean for any of this to happen, she really had no choice."*

"I know, Charlotte. I could never be mad at her for that—never. Thank you for being so kind and fond of her. It means a lot to me, to us."

"I for one, am glad I came home. Looks like you need me here Wesley, you have gone all soft on the pack," Odin burst in the conversation. "Maybe we need to get back to the basics with you." He waved his fork around while Astrid slapped him in the chest.

"His mate is here, dear, don't try to cut him down in front of her!" Astrid growled at him.

Odin looked back flabbergasted, "I'm just saying, the warriors are relying on too much of this tech that Charlotte has put together, and look, she got kidnapped twice and she is the only one that can run it. She can't be scouting the territory, be a Luna and take care of pups!" Astrid glared at Odin and in return looked at me. My face grew red. Pups? Already?

"Only when you are ready, Charlotte. There is no rush. We didn't have Wesley until we had been mated for well over one hundred years. Odin just needed so much of my attention for a while after mating," she chuckled while pulling his long hair back with her fingertips.

"Yeah, Wesley still takes all the attention away from others," Odin joked while I laughed.

"There's nothing wrong with being an only child, I'm sure you had fun grabbing your mother's attention while your father became flustered," I joked.

"Now, I have you to give all my attention to," he growled lowly in my ear and goosebumps trailed my skin.

"He won't be an only child for long," Astrid said offhandedly as she blew on her soup to cool. Forks dropped, Wesley and Odin stared at their mother in disbelief. "What?" I whispered.

"That's right, Odin, we are going to have another baby." Astrid's eyes glistened in happiness as she put her hands together and Odin gave an enormous smile. His beard shook as his mouth hung open.

"*Again*? Really? It happened so fast!" He boomed. "I'm the manliest Alpha out there!" Odin stood up from his seat as the chair flew to the floor. Pounding his chest like a wild beast he began yelling. "You hear that! I'm going to be a father again and I only had to pound her once we decided!"

Odin let out a warrior cry and everyone at the table was laughing and cheering while Wesley sat there silently.

"Aw, is my puppy upset he isn't the only child anymore? You have to share your mommy and daddy?" I cooed. He laughed, "no, I'm just shocked. It's just, wow. I'm going to be a big brother." Giggling at him, I pecked him on the lips as we watched Odin's father jump around the room as the warriors dodged his hugs and victory punches.

After dinner I headed back up to my old room, the baby pink and the frilly white comforter was still there like the last time we left it. It was only a queen bed, but I didn't mind. More cuddling for us.

Wesley went to his office, saying he had some papers and emails to look over from his companies that he had to take care of before the ceremony. He hadn't been back to the city in a while and there were major decisions that were going to have to be made and the steady cash flow that helped our pack thrive was something he was not willing to part with.

Stripping down and taking a quick shower, I rubbed the vanilla body wash all over me. The events of today had me exhausted but Victoria kept pacing around my mind.

"Victoria, you are making me all anxious."

"We should go to mate, he is stressed." I hummed in response. Maybe we could help him with some work I proposed to myself, but of course Victoria heard.

"I think, we should help him de-stress," Victoria licked her lips. *"Didn't you see how sexy he looked at dinner?"*

"We had a near death experience today, and you are wanting to jump his bones right now?"

"Yeeeees," she sang.

I rolled my eyes and walked back to our closet back in our room. There were drawers filled with different pieces of lingerie that I haven't even tried. Wesley usually pounces on me, and clothes don't really stay on anyway. I never tried to even dress up for him. Starting to hum as I thumbed through the drawers, I noticed a little number that I fell in love with.

It was black, not my normal color for my undergarments. Baby pink and whites were my go-to, this was sultry and sexy and super lacy. It was a one piece that had a massive push up bra to cup my breasts, so they were almost spilling out. Squealing in excitement and jumping up and down how pretty it was I accidentally knocked over the black stilettos I was going to put on. Bending over I noticed a drawer at the very bottom that I haven't opened labeled, garters. The gears in my brain started turning and got an even better idea.

I completed the look, the one-piece lingerie bodice, the tights and the garters that hooked onto it as well as my stilettos. Do I want to walk in with a robe on? Gasping at my newest idea I looked for a short pencil skirt and tight black blouse. Throwing my hair in a bun, I then took my thick rimmed black glasses and put them on. Smiling at myself, I turned in every direction admiring my work, and Victoria agreed, we would bring him to his knees.

Wesley

Shit, could today be any more of an information overload? Trixen was gone at the expense of my mate, Hades' mate trouble confessions, the mating and Luna ceremony was tomorrow evening, Alphas and Lunas from around the country were slowly trickling into the dormitories, my parents announcing their second pregnancy that will give me a new sibling plus the pack businesses have been waiting on my approval on some new projects. I'm fucking spent.

How Charlotte has been able to keep up with it all is a miracle. If I were her, I would have run away with all the shit that has gone down with her being here for a few months. Kidnapped, fucking twice. I let out a growl that shook the desk. She fought for her life, takes care of members of the pack all while smiling and making sure I'm alright after finding out I was no longer going to be an only child, hell she is fucking fantastic.

Throwing down the computer glasses and rubbing my eyes while I leaned back in the chair, I heard a squeak at the door. Charlotte was dressed in a tan, tight pencil skirt with a black blouse and high heels. Her hair is in a bun and her thick-rimmed glasses were on. Holy hell, things just got hotter here. My dream has come true and has walked through the damn door.

"Shit," I muttered

"Hello, Alpha. I was wondering if you needed some help. You look," she paused and licked her beautiful red lips, "stressed." Damn, I'd love those red lips somewhere other than my mouth. Her slow walk around the desk had me in a trance, drool was pooling in my mouth as she approached me and went behind my chair. Her hands went straight for my shoulders and began to knead them. Goddess, it felt good. I let out a low groan that only made her chuckle.

Charlotte leaned over my shoulder and loosened my tie and unbuttoned the top two buttons. Her massage went down to the front of my chest as she caressed it. Closing my eyes, I felt her touch all over me, before I knew it, she had my entire chest and stomach bear with her rubbing her hands all over me. "What can I do to make you feel better, Alpha?" she whispered in my ear while gently tugging it with her teeth. Walking to the front of me, admiring her work her finger trailed down the middle of my chest.

Charlotte straddled me in the chair and placed small kisses down my neck, leaving little love bites. My hands instantly go to cup her ass and give her a gentle squeeze only urging her to continue. As her kisses fueled my fire, she unbuckled my pants and pulled the belt out of the loops quickly causing it to snap loudly. "Do you need a release?" Her hands go up to her hair and let down her long flowy locks. Remus howled in my head as her sultry eyes looked down at my crotch. She kneeled in front of the desk and pulled my cock out. Licking and sucking the tip. Red lipstick stains that had trailed down my chest now stained my cock. "Kitten, fuck me, please," I begged her. Hell yeah, I was begging, this was the hottest thing I've ever experienced.

As she lowered her mouth onto my cock there was a knock at the door. Instead of stopping she started vigorously sucking me and not letting go. I threw my white shirt over my torso, trying to button it back up. Charlotte's mouth was like a damn vice holding me in place. Before I could object, the door opened wide, and in walked my mother.

I started cringing internally because hell, I'm not going to be able to keep a straight face with her. Charlotte is continuing to deep throat me while I try to keep my composure. "Wesley, I just wanted to talk to you for a second. She sits down in the chair, letting me know she is going to be a minute. Fuck, fuck, fuck. Charlotte grabs my balls and starts to massage them, and I hold my hands together on my desk with a strained face.

"Wesley? Are you alright?" My mother asks.

"Yes," I said weakly.

"Oh honey, I know today was hard, you should cry and let it out. I won't tell your father." She consoled me. I wanted to cry, but in frustration for her to fucking leave!

"Mom, can we talk about this tomorrow?" I strained. "I just need to be a-alone." My knuckles turned white as Charlotte took a break from my cock and licked balls, it felt so damn good.

"Alright, but we do need to talk. I know the whole new sibling thing must have hit you hard, and just wanted to talk about it."

"Thanks, mom, I'm fine r-really though," I gritted. She was back to deep throating me again. Beads of sweat formed on my forehead as I was trying to hold on longer. With one last backward glance from my mother, she told me goodnight. Once the door was closed, I pulled back from my chair quickly picking Charlotte up plopping her sweet ass back on the desk.

"You naughty little minx," I whisper yelled.

"Something wrong Alpha?" she giggled. Damn that giggle.

"That was the hottest damn thing you've ever done but next time let's make sure it isn't my mother in the room," I said lowly. My pants had dropped to the floor, and I took my shirt off. One button at a time, Charlotte revealed a one-piece bodice that had her breasts overflowing. They were perky and just for me. I ripped the skirt off, not being able to take it any longer and she surprised me again. Fucking. Garter. Belt. Holy hell it was a sight.

"I'm going to ravage you, Kitten."

"Meow," she giggled in reply.

Vera Foxx

Chapter 67

Charlotte

"Did you invade my dreams to find out my fantasy?" He grabbed my hips and smashed his lips to mine. I instantly moaned and wrapped my legs around him. The belt was digging into my thighs as he kissed and sucked at my breasts. There wasn't going to be much foreplay, I already knew that. His dick was throbbing when I had him in my mouth earlier. I internally praised myself for that.

"I'm going to fuck you right here, on my desk. You are going to take it long and hard; do you understand Kitten?" He bit my neck and I let out a small cry. "Yes, Alpha!" I hissed. Wesley unbuttoned my one piece at the bottom, not even bothering to take the entire one piece off. Without warning he forced his cock into my dripping core. I yelped in surprise, grabbing ahold of his biceps as he pushed his cock harder and deeper inside of me.

My back was rubbing against the desk and a few of my garter straps popped from the strain, causing a loud smack against my thighs. "Holy shit," he growled as he pulled me impossibly closer. He was standing up by the desk while I laid there and took his beatings in my pussy. I was a moaning mess and several times I could feel my wetness soak down my thigh. "You are always so fucking tight, Kitten. Always so ready for me hm?" I groaned as he went unbelievably harder.

"Do you like it, Kitten? When your Alpha pounds you on his desk?" I grumbled incoherently and he took his mouth to harshly bite my nipple. "Answer me, do you like it?" Both his hands gripped the side of my thighs and stopped. "Answer me," he growled out.

"Yes, Alpha! I like it!"

"What do you like, Kitten?"

"When you fuck me on the desk," I said breathlessly. Flipping me over with ease, Wesley had my ass in the air and me leaning on the desk. Completely turned on, juices flowing out of me, and his angry head of his cock was pulsing, it looked furious that he hasn't had his release. Parting my lower lips, he entered me, the slapping of our skin was loud in the empty room. His grunts became quicker, faster and erratic. My high was coming, I could feel him dig into my thighs, one hand came up to cup my breast squeezed harshly.

"Ahh, ahh!" I moaned and he continued to growl in my ear fiercely every time the hilt of his dick hit my ass. "Come with me, Kitten," he finally whispered. With one last thrust we were over the edge, screaming each other's names as he laid his chest on my back. His hands intertwined with mine as his large body encompassed me.

Clothes laid scattered on the floor, most of which I would not be able to wear to go back to our room. The desk was covered in sweat from our romp on the desk. A few pants later, Wesley got up. His body was glistening, I wanted to lick ever bit of that salty sweetness off his abs. Pulling me up and holding me close we both laid naked on the couch.

"Fuck, Charlotte. I feel better." He laid me on top of his body, both of us a mess but didn't really care. My ass was in the air, praying no one would walk in. "You can come help me with business work anytime you want." Wesley kissed me on the forehead while I giggled at him.

"You don't think your mom knew I was in here, do you?" Looking up at him between my lashes.

"If she knew, then she hid it well. Usually, Wolves can smell arousal, but your mouth never left my dick, so who knows," he shrugged.

"Just know, I will get you back," he winked. I giggled and pecked his lips.

✳✳✳

The next morning was chaotic. Ashley and Astrid were banging on our door at 6 a.m. telling me I needed to get up and kicked poor Wesley out of bed. His scowl at his mother was priceless.

"You can see her tonight when she walks down the aisle," Astrid chastised him, waving him out the door. He ran back in quickly and gave me a kiss before leaving.

"Damn, he's got it bad!" Ashley laughed.

The rest of the morning, I was pampered. I've never really been pampered before, but it was a full-on spa in my room. There was a masseuse table brought in and my body was completely putty by the end of the 2 hours session. Even though I had shaved the day before, Ashley insisted she wax me because it would be great for exfoliation and Astrid agreed. Let's just say screaming, hair pulling of other people besides me, and cursing was involved. Ashley and Astrid couldn't believe I could even say some of those words but after all the pain I had been through in life, waxing was probably the worst.

Okay, not really but whatever.

Evan would often come up to check on me, my old room was completely a mess with fabrics, clothes for Astrid and Ashley, my dress, and of course the "after mating ceremony attire," which I didn't think about. Wesley is going to rip it off anyway, right?

"Damn, ladies, what the hell happened here?" Evan picked up a piece of wax paper with hair on it. "What the fuck is this?"

"Um, that is my hair they ripped out?" I replied embarrassingly.

"EW SHIT!" He tried to throw it away, but it stuck to his fingers, so he started screaming. "The hell! Get it off!" Everyone watched him dance around the room until it floated to the floor, and he ran out. "Just was checking on you since Wesley is being a prick about not seeing you. See you in an hour!"

Once the mask was completed, my makeup and hair were applied. "Just something natural, nothing all out," I looked at Ashley.

"Of course not. We would never do anything you didn't like," she winked.

Astrid brought in the dress, and it looked better in person than it did on the computer. It was elegant, sophisticated, and sexy all at the same time. Red velvet went straight to the floor with a small train. The pearls outlined the top of the bodice and pinched my waist giving me an hourglass figure. It was surprisingly comfortable until I saw the back.

The website hadn't shown the back of the dress, and I should have thought of it, but I was too busy ogling the front. The back went straight down to my lower back. It was utterly sexy.

"Wesley is so lucky to have you dear. "Now, don't cry, you will ruin your makeup. I know we went extra dark on the eyes, but you needed a little bit of sultry with this dress." I nodded in agreement; it did look amazing. I felt amazing.

"We have to go now," Ashley stood at the door. She was wearing a simple white gown that came to her knees with a beautiful shawl. Astrid was also wearing something similar. The women were to wear white, while the men could wear black pants and a white button-up shirt. Astrid said it was going to look beautiful during the ceremony and I was excited to see it.

They both left the room, and I heard the click of the door. Looking back in the mirror, I took another glance. I had gained such a wonderful family. Growing up without one made me appreciate every detail they did for me. This entire pack was going to be my family and I was going to help them along the way. My own children will know the love and support this pack gives to one another.

"Charlotte, it's time," I heard Ashley peek through the door. Taking a large breath and looking back at Macaroni's bed, I gave it a small wave. "I wish you were here too, Mac and Cheese," I sniffed.

I gently shut the door and being careful to walk in my black stilettos from last night's romp in the boss's office, I went down the stairs. It was eerily quiet as I walked across the foyer and to the back of the house. The ceremony was to be held outside, even though it was cold, Werewolves could withstand it for a few hours. My bare shoulders and back would feel a nip in the air of it since I was still getting used to Victoria taking care of me, but for a beautiful ceremony, I'll endure.

Zachary stood in his dark slacks, looking to the open doors. His hands were placed behind his back as his dirty blonde hair waved in the gentle cold breeze. Pulling out his hand as soon as I stepped beside him, I grasped it. His eyes didn't look at me, but the warmth in his eyes told me he had something important to say. "What is it, Zachary?" He hummed, brushing away a tear.

"You know how I've always felt comfortable around you?" he whispered. "How I always thought of you as a sister? I swore it was the Luna in you, but I just found out an important piece between us that connected us together." His voice cracked as he squeezed my hand again. His tall stature bent lower to meet me almost nose to nose. "You are my mother's sister's daughter." Zachary snorted. "You are my cousin, Lottie." I gasped, putting my arms around his neck.

"Cousins? That's basically brother and sister," I joked while he sniffed into my shoulder. "Yeah, basically the same thing." Standing up to his full height, he wiped his tears. Cyrene told me, we can talk about it another time but, I was hoping to walk you down the aisle, it's tradition to have a blood-related member walk you to your mate." I giggled, taking his arm. "I'd love that."

The door was open to the patio and two large warriors stood on either side. They both smiled and bowed slightly and moved to let us through. It was snowing, small flakes flurried around me and beckoned me to continue. Upon looking closer, I see they weren't just snowflakes in all the snow, but small little winter pixies giggling and tinkling in their talk. I smiled widely as they continued to push us down the aisle.

Everyone was wearing white, almost like no one was there, but looking down the snow-covered carpet, I saw Wesley. Wearing his black tux. Against the snow he was regal, proud and majestic. He gave me the same smirk he always does, the same one that caught my heart. Tears brimmed his eyes. The big Alpha was crying in front of his pack for me. I looked down, almost embarrassed.

"Don't look down Kitten, look at me," Wesley mind linked.

My eyes shot up to him and only him. Once I arrived, he held out his hand and I took it gladly. Zachary gave a gentle squeeze to let me go. My red dress made me stand out like a sore thumb, all eyes on us as we played through the double ceremony I had them create just for me.

Sorceress Cyrene stood at the front, also in a white dress with a red ribbon around her neck that held a medallion showing her power over the services.

"It has come to my attention that our dear, sweet Luna, wanted a double ceremony to not impose on others for coming to visit twice. A true Luna she really is." I smiled at her and Wesley squeezed my hand. "Let us begin."

Wesley got on one knee, which surprised me as he held my hand. "I vow to express my love for you as often as I breathe each breath, nothing will divide us because I know that with your love, I will always have strength. I promise to never lose our spark and to always do the little things to make you happy. I will honor you, cherish you and give you everything you so desire my, Kitten. You are my life and I give my life to you." He kissed my hands and stood back up.

Cyrene motioned for me to say my vows and Wesley pulled me close, so I was chest to chest with him. He winked at me, and I said my vows to him from the heart. "I promise to always make you laugh and to laugh together, that we will be a family forever, that we will face each adventure and conquer it all. As long as the sun shines in the day and the moon and stars shine at night, our love will always be alive." Wesley pulled me into a sweet kiss, that quickly became a bit more. Wesley tried to pry my mouth open for him to deepen the kiss, but Cyrene intervened with a throat clearing, a few chuckles from the crowd had me blushing.

"This now concludes our mating ceremony portion. The vows to each mate have been said and they have already mated, so we can skip the whole howl-…" Before Cyrene could finish the statement, warriors and guests howled in happiness at our mating completion. We had vowed to be with one another in front of the entire pack, sealing the deal so to speak.

Once the howls calmed down and Wesley's peppering of kisses up and down my neck Cyrene continued with the Luna Ceremony. Wesley stepped to the side and Cyrene stood beside me and we faced each other.

"My dear, Charlotte Hale, with the power invested in Selene which has also been granted in Alpha Wesley Hale, I give to you, his blood. With this blood that you will drink, you will become one with the pack. You will be able to mind-link others and command when you see fit. Your Alpha will never be able to command you because you are his equal. Do you promise to love your pack, to take care of the weak and to empower the strong? Do you promise to fight evil from those who cause a threat to the Black Claw pack, to protect them with your life?" Several people started chuckling and laughing.

"Well, she already proved that right?" Evan yelled from the back. Astrid gave him a stern look while Odin rubbed Astrid's stomach lovingly.

"Yes, I promise all these things," I spoke confidently. Taking the cup, more like a chalice, it had running Wolves surrounding the lip of where I would drink. Looking inside, it wasn't much, but enough to make me feel sick. To think that I was covered in blood yesterday and now I am going to drink some didn't settle with me. My head started to feel dizzy, and Wesley came up to steady me.

"It's alright," he cooed. "It's just mine. It won't hurt you, if you don't want to do this, you don't have to." Wesley rubbed my arms to comfort me, and I shook my head. Not looking, I took the large mouthful and swallowed it whole. Cyrene grabbed the chalice from me, and Wesley held me up as I began to hear howls and talking in my mind. There were so many voices, it was giving me a headache.

"Easy everyone," Wesley spoke through the mind-link. "You can personally congratulate her later, let's give her some space." Wesley steadied me as I sat back up. He gave me a quick peck on the lips and Cyrene gave me some water to chase the metallic taste from my mouth.

"Ladies and gentlemen, I give you Wesley Hale and Charlotte Hale the Goddess's mated pair and your new Luna!" More cheers came from the crowd, and I gripped onto Wesley's arm to hide my face. My social meter had officially gone through the roof, but Wesley didn't seem to mind. Once the crowd died down, he walked me back down the aisle. Both of us stood out in his black tux and my blood red velvet dress.

"Let's go party," he whispered in my ear as I heard the music began playing in the house.

Chapter 68

Charlotte

As we entered the packhouse, we walked down the long hallway to the ballroom. The snow was coming down in heavy blankets so the decision to have it moved inside was a no-brainer. As much as I enjoyed the snow and the beautiful flakes of dusting during the ceremony, I knew we would be soaked by the end of the dance.

Lyle was in charge of music per usual for parties. Young pups were already dancing on the floor, and I was immediately pulled from Wesley to head to the floor. Various songs such as The Macarena, Chicken Dance, and the Hokey Pokey were played, and I happily agreed to play with the kids. After the third song, Wesley quickly pulled me to his chest by my waist and whispered, "You are mine now, no more sharing." He nipped at my ear, and I quickly agreed. He took me by the hand and led me to our table.

There was already a plate of food lying before me, obviously done by Wesley because it was overflowing with my favorites. Lasagna, steak, southern-style green beans, and collards. An interesting mix but I was going to enjoy it anyway. I wiggled in my seat in excitement as I put a large fork full in my mouth. Wesley smiled and wiped my mouth like I was a messy child.

Ashley and Astrid really did make this party shine. The white theme is still applied in the large room. Lights that cast a light blue, winter glow on the walls, and small blue lights danced on the floor. The light was dimmed to give everyone a welcome, romantic feel. Many Alphas and their Lunas took it as the opportunity to cozy up in each other's laps while the pups ran around giggling at the snow pixies that decided to stay.

Every time a pixie would fly across the room, small puffs of snowflakes followed, and I acted like a crazy child wanting to follow. Wesley grabbed me, knowing I was getting ready to take off, and sat me on his lap. His warm hand was on my lower back, exactly where there was no fabric. My face heated at the warmth. His other hand came up to my inner thigh and started to rub in between my legs. I put my head on Wesley's neck. "Babe, what are you doing?" I whispered.

"I think it is time for payback, Kitten," he growled in my ear. "I think I'm going to finger fuck you right in front of everyone." My eyes grew wide, and I tried to wiggle out of his grip. "Now, now don't make a scene or I'll fuck you on this table." His heart rate didn't change, was he serious right now? The tablecloth was the only thing covering his dirty deed. His eyes were clouded with lust as he went to the slit of my dress to get better access to my drenched self. Little did he know, I wasn't wearing any panties.

My face flushed as couples came up to greet us and Wesley's hand was touching my freshly waxed pussy. *"Oh, my Goddess,"* I mind-linked. *"You are insane."* Wesley smiled and nuzzled me lovingly like he wasn't going to guide two fingers into my extremely wet cavern.

"Oh, but I am serious." He bit his bottom lip and started rubbing circles on my clit. I jerked at the sudden touch but quickly tried to control the situation with a laugh as the couple were talking to us. What were they talking about? I didn't know, heck I don't know if Wesley knew.

"When can we expect some pups?" Alpha Samanos asked Wesley. "We are going to take it slow, we have plenty of time," Wesley said while scratching his eyebrow with his other hand. "What do you think, Kitten? When do you want kids?" His finger was slowly entering my core and I squeezed and grabbed onto his thighs, surely, I've ripped a hole in his pants with my claws.

"O-oh, u-um I haven't really t-thought about it. We've been b-busy a b-bit," I giggled.

"Are you alright dear?" Luna Laura asked, "You look so flushed," her hand went to her chest in concern. Wesley sped up and my clit was quivering as he stuck two fingers into me. My nipples were pebbling, wanting more friction in my upper and lower body.

"Y-yes! I'm a bit tired! Not used to such a large crowd too." I closed my eyes and put my hand over my eyes. Alpha Samanos winked at Wesley and took his concerned wife away. Oh gosh, he knew!

"Kitten, let me take you out for a bit, if you'd excuse us." Wesley pulled down my dress and pulled me out the door.

Wesley led me to the kitchen and locked the door. "You are so mean," I let out a small growl, more like a kitten growl. Wesley smiled mischievously and made me wrap my legs around him as he picked me up. Having a slit close to the front of the dress came in handy. "That was payback, now I'm going to fuck you against the fridge. Are you going to be good, Kitten?" I nodded quickly and he unbuckled his pants. The clinking sounds of this belt made my pussy throb in anticipation.

Pulling his pants down just enough to pull his massive cock out of his pants and pulled the slit of my dress over the front of my bare self. "You were a naughty kitten huh?" He picked me up and pushed me back to the fridge. The coolness of it made me shiver and my nipples hardened. "You didn't wear any panties, did you?" I groaned as he lined up his dick to my core. "Maybe, I should punish you and not let you cum." Huh?

Wesley pushed his cock into me, as I whimpered into his neck. His thrusts were hard and deep. I could feel his back and ass tighten as he pushed deeper. My breasts rubbed against the fabric of the dress, Wesley could feel my frustration as he pulled down each side of the dress, so my breasts burst out. Wesley sucked greedily as he continued to take his thick cock spreading my folds. My breaths were light and airy as Wesley's were deep and throaty. I could feel his hands grip my ass tightly, knowing it was going to leave marks. "Fucking hell," he groaned.

"Remus, wants control, Kitten," his eyes were turning gold and I agreed for him to let go. Remus came forward and his claws broke the skin around my ass. It was a little painful, but it was a good pain with the pleasure mixing together. "Ahhh! Remus," I whined. Feeling a strong slap on my ass, I shut my mouth.

"Mate don't talk, only Remus talk." Remus pulled out of me, and I kept my moans to myself, I was throbbing, still not getting any release yet. He pushed me to the small eat-in kitchen table and pushed my chest down to it. My nipples felt the cold and I whined again which earned me another slap. A large growl came from Remus, and I looked behind me. His canines were out and if I never thought possible, I could have more juices come out of me. Dripping down my thigh, Remus leaned over and smelled my core. He buried his face in my pussy and began licking up the slick. I groaned, feeling him tasting and licking in all the places that wasn't my core.

A little nip caused me to jump, and he growled in satisfaction as I kept my mouth quiet. Putting my hand over my mouth to keep my cries to a minimum. His tongue circled my clit as I held in my cries. My high was coming fast and I wanted to jump off the cliff as soon as I could. "Remus, please can I cum?" I begged. I hadn't forgotten Wesley's warning about not wanting me to come, so I will beg for anything. Remus will give it to me, he's, my puppy.

Remus growled into my pussy, and I swear I heard a yes from him. Finally, letting go, I flew off the cliff and landed in the warm water below, and let it engulf me. Liquid streamed down my leg and into Remus's mouth as he greedily lapped it up. "Mate, tastes delicious," he growled. He stood up and he kept his hand on my back so I couldn't get up. "Remus is going to fuck mate, and mate will take Remus's seed."

His naughty words made me want to cum all over again. "Yes, mate," I whispered which earned me a satisfied groan and Remus slammed into me. He was rougher than Wesley, his throatier groans and growls made his entire body shake. It was animalistic, it was powerful, and I was so turned on I didn't even know what day it was anymore. I needed him to fill me with whatever had.

His claws dug into my hips and together we felt our release coming. "Come, Mate." That was it, I let it all go as he did, and he bit back into my mark was a fury. The pain mixed with the pleasure made the orgasm so intense I saw stars, or maybe a few slutty pixies came in to watch. I didn't know and didn't really care.

We were both a sweaty mess as he helped me to a padded chair. Remus grabbed a towel and cleaned me up as he peppered kisses on my face. My palm reached his cheek as I gave him a sweet kiss on the lips. "Thank you, puppy," I giggled. He huffed and let Wesley come back to the front. Remus wasn't much for a crowd anyway.

"Holy shit love, that was amazing," he was still panting as he kissed the shell of my ear.

"You both make a great team you know," I laughed at him as he pulled me to a standing position. We both looked decent, but my nicely curled hair was now a mess. All of the adults will know what happened just because now I am sporting a fresh mark on my shoulder. Those need time to heal sometimes.

"Don't worry, they won't think anything of it, in fact, I'm pretty sure a couple is doing it in the broom closet outside." My face turned red as I started laughing again and he led me back into the ballroom. We really are all just a bunch of horny Wolves.

Wesley didn't falter, he led me to the dance floor and pulled me close to him. His hair was a little messy, but I liked it that way. He was still sporting a bit of stubble which I had grown to love. It felt great between... some places.

One hand was in mine and the other around my waist as we danced our slow song, many joined us on the floor as the pups sat in the corner of the room, pouting that there wasn't something 'fun' to do.

As we danced, my mind wandered to when I first met my big Alpha. The hotel, the sparks between us as we touched. My finger trailed up the lapel of his jacket until I reached his beautiful locks of hair. Twirling it with my finger, a thought came to me. "Was it you?" I gave him no context. His head tilted to the side in wonder as I giggled. "The man at the club that danced with me, was it you?" Wesley chuckled, pulling my waist closer to his body. "It was." I hummed, laying my head on his chest. Of course, it was Wesley, who else would I have felt those sparks. Before getting comfortable, my mind began to wander again.

"Wesley, when do you want to have pups?" I lifted my head to meet his green eyes. With his next sibling on the way, he may want some time to enjoy his little brother or sister.

"Honestly?" he questioned, and I nodded and laid my head on his chest. The music was smooth and relaxing as I cuddled him closer. We were now only swaying back and forth, as well as most couples on the floor.

"We have forever, my love. I'd be happy with or without children, as long as I have you, I would be the happiest man alive. It's like we are a painting, both of us are within it. The scenery is beautiful, we have each other. The painting is complete," Wesley lifted my head by tilting my chin to look at him. "If a few more mini-Wesleys and Charlottes seem to pop up in there, I'd be alright with that too." His thumb rubbed my cheek. "I'll love them as much as I love you and you already know that means 'a hell of a lot.'"

Smiling at Wesley, I stepped up on my tippy toes to meet his lips with a soft, warm kiss. "I love you, Wesley. Thanks for rescuing me."

"Oh, Kitten. You are the one that saved me."

Chapter 69
Epilogue

Charlotte was straightening a picture over her headboard of their bed in their brand-new home. The Southern-plantation style home was considerably smaller than the large packhouse that was just over a mile away, but it was hers and Wesley's, nonetheless. It had five bedrooms, all of those were vacant besides their large master bedroom on the second floor.

The bottom floor was an open-concept style with all the latest furnishings. Whites, light greys, and creams covered the area. Small plants that Charlotte had always loved such as succulents, dragon trees, and parlor palms. The cream-colored leather couches had brightly colored pillows that complement each piece of the room. Large bookshelves donned her favorite novels as well as Wesley's who also had his business textbooks. It was purposefully dressed that way. Growing up in dark basements and living in small dull apartments for the first twenty years of her life was enough. Wesley humored her and let her do whatever she wanted with the house as long as he had his 'Wolf den,' in the basement.

It was completely decked out in large flat-screen TVs, video game consoles, pool tables, and poker tables. It was the hotspot for the mated warriors while the packhouse housed more of the unmated few.

Wesley had a small office at the front of the home, so pack members could come by in the evening for any urgent matters to take care of, which was usually just a bunch of Elders that didn't know how to schedule a meeting properly.

"Kitten, you shouldn't be up there!" Wesley took long strides into their light blue bedroom with a creamed-colored comforter. Charlotte was balancing on the bed, trying to straighten their Mating and Luna ceremony photo. The red dress hung around her tiny waist and Charlotte could only sigh as Wesley lifted her back into his arms, carrying her bridal style back to set her on the floor. "Do you think I'll ever get my body back?" Charlotte rubbed her abnormally large belly as she looked at their picture.

"Kitten, you are a Werewolf, of course, you'll get your body back. Even if you didn't, I'd still ravage you every night, as I do now," he growled playfully in her ear. Charlotte giggled and wrapped her arms around his neck.

"I love you, babe," she nuzzled into his neck.

"And I love-" before another word could be spoken, a shrill of a scream came bouncing into the room.

"Charlotte!" The boy screamed in excitement and ran to her arms. With a loud thud, Erik fell to the floor at Charlotte's feet. "What did I say about running in the house?" Charlotte laughed while picking the 5-year-old up. "To not to," he sniffed and rubbed his knee.

"What would your Mumma say? Running in here like some crazed rogue Wolf?" Erik gasped and heard a light tapping of the floor behind him. "There you are, I said you could go visit after your lunch." Astrid strolled up to Charlotte and pried the boy off of her. Before she could, Erik nuzzled Charlotte's cheek and finally let go.

"I'm your brother but you talk to your sister-in-law like she is your real sister!" Wesley whined playfully. "Charlotte is nice, she lays in bed with me to help me sweep. Charlotte keeps the demon monsters away! She killed one Wessie!" Wesley groaned at the nickname. He hated that nickname, almost as much as Remus hated it when Charlotte called him, puppy. Remus snickered inside his head causing him to huff.

"Yes, she did," Wesley grabbed him from his mother's arms. "She's the strongest Luna in all of the Earth Realm." Erik gave Wesley a final hug before being brought back to Astrid.

"Sorry to bother you both, Erik wouldn't lay down for a nap until he saw the both of you. I swear you guys are more of his parents than your father and I." Astrid bounced Erik, lulling him to sleep.

The home was complete three years, Wesley had gotten to work on the nice-sized house for Charlotte shortly after their ceremony. She threw up some plans in no time, saying she always loved watching Gone with the Wind on old library computers when she spent her time there. Charlotte definitely scaled down the house to a moderate size but still had the southern charm she had loved.

"I just hope he takes well to having a new playmate. They might as well grow up as siblings," Charlotte spoke. "I've been thinking of changing one of the guest rooms into a place Erik could stay if they want to have sleepovers."

True to Odin's word, Astrid and Odin decided to stay back in the home pack of the Black Claw. Odin wasn't kidding when he said his son had become too soft on the warriors and the security of the boundaries, even though they were just fine. Odin just needed an excuse to stay and watch his family grow.

"I think he would love that," Astrid began stroking Erik's head as his eyes fluttered shut. "Here, lay him here and we can go downstairs." Charlotte pulled the blanket up on Erik who nuzzled into her own pillow. Sensing he wasn't going to wake, they all walked down the stairs to see Raina and Zachary eating the leftover pizza from the fridge.

"When we moved into our own house, I thought we would get a bit of privacy," Wesley groaned while he held a tight hold on Charlotte's waist.

"Nope!" Zachary popped the p. Being neighbors was the best idea ever!" Raina giggled at Zachary while she patted her small belly. She was newly pregnant and craved anything that Charlotte was craving. That's what happens when you spend every day together. Ashley wasn't any different, she was also sporting a slightly larger bump and was due next month.

Charlotte smiled at the group. "I don't think I could possibly be any happier. I've got the family I've always dreamed of right here. You can invade our home anytime you like. Just you guys though, I don't need the whole pack in here," she chuckled. They all agreed as many reached for a slice of the leftover pizza.

Charlotte felt a slight pain in her lower belly. She was accustomed to pain; the round ligament and the sciatic nerve gave her the worst of it. There were some nights when Wesley would rub her lower belly and massage her rear end to give her some relief. It was all he could do to hold back from taking her. Her plump ass was just like a ripe peach, ready for him to sink his teeth into. The past few days though, she said things were off-limits, saying there wasn't enough room for his large cock and a baby. He chuckled at that thought—even though it was probably true. Even when in enormous amounts of pain, she would always boost his ego with her words. It was almost as good as taking her to the kitchen counter. Almost.

Charlotte grabbed her lower abdomen and felt the pain radiate from her lower belly but started to encompass her entire stomach. "Ahh!" she felt a sharp pop and a trickle-down her legs. Feeling completely embarrassed she tried back away from the kitchen table. "Kitten, what's wrong?" Wesley's senses went into overdrive and could instantly smell something sweet with a hint of metallic. "Your water broke!" He exclaimed excitedly.

Wesley had been hovering over her since day one. He tended to her every need and touched her growing belly constantly, wanting to be part of every moment with their pup growing inside of her. "Mom, please go get our bag upstairs, I'm going to take her to the packhouse." The pack doctor was linked immediately and said she would be there as soon as they arrived.

Meanwhile, Charlotte was in an enormous amount of pain. The contractions were coming in quickly and lasting for long periods of time. In all the pregnancy books she had read, she knew the first baby should take some time, but this one was hell-bent on coming out. Wesley held out his hand to help her walk but stopped immediately holding her stomach. "I-I c-can't," she cried. Wesley patiently waited until her contraction had passed and picked her up bridal style to the car.

Evan was outside, chopping wood, he and his mate had decided to move on the same street as the Alpha. His mate was nursing their twin children to sleep at the moment inside their nursery. "Evan, drive us to the packhouse, Charlotte is going to have the baby!" Evan threw down his ax, sweat still dripping from his brow, and bolted to his truck. Charlotte was nestled close to Wesley and whimpering while she held onto his hand, squeezing. Evan swore he could hear a few bones breaking. Wesley didn't let his stoic face show any emotion. He was concentrating on Charlotte.

The pain in her belly extended all over her body, the sweat was now pooling around her. The contractions were coming hard and fast, she didn't think she would make the drive to the packhouse that was only a mile away. "Hang on, sweetheart. Everything is going to be alright," Wesley tried to soothe his mate. "Concentrate on your breathing."

"Concentrate on your breathing, you are breathing down my neck is making me hot!" Charlotte screamed as another contraction ripped through her. Wesley sat back and continued to pull her hair out of her face. He knew she was in pain, so he didn't let it bother him. Evan held in a chuckle as they pulled up.

Without waiting for the engine to be turned off, Wesley gripped Charlotte tightly who let out a groan of pain. The clinic doors opened abruptly for Alpha and Luna to enter. "In here, Alpha!" one of the nurses called and they were led to the birthing room.

"It's here! I feel it!" Charlotte was hastily put on the table and Wesley cradled her head while they lifted half the bed so gravity would help the baby to descend. It was easy for the nurses to pull up her dress and address the situation. The doctor had just entered the room, fully dressed and ready to deliver. The nurses gasped and quickly got the supplies from the side of the room.

"What's wrong!?" Wesley demanded, the nurses continued to shuffle across the room, gathering the supplies. The doctor looked at Wesley and down back at Charlotte. "The head is out, but the cord is tripled wrapped around the head. Luna, I'm going to need you to push."

Wesley's face grew worried as he looked at Charlotte, her face filled with sweat and pain. He had never wanted to see her in pain, ever since the time he picked her up from facing a demon all on her own. "Come on Kitten, push for me. Get our baby out." Charlotte took all the strength she had and let out one long, final push.

Both had decided against finding out the gender of the baby and doing ultrasounds, wanting to make sure it was a complete surprise. The thought that the nameless baby might be in trouble stirred something in her and with a mighty push, the baby was released. The cord was unwrapped, and a large gasp came from the baby. Strong, mighty cries escaped from its lips. "A girl!" The doctor cried and Wesley, along with Charlotte's face, beamed with excitement. Charlotte grabbed Wesley's arm as he came down and kissed her sweetly.

The baby was wrapped and brought to Charlotte's chest which she quickly found her breast and she began to feed her. "She's so beautiful, Kitten, just like you." Wesley took his large hand and gently stroked the baby's head which caused it to let out a small whine. Once the baby was finished, it tried with all her might to open her little eyes.

Wesley took the baby from Charlotte as they began to clean her from her afterbirth, Wesley held her close to his bare chest to give it warmth. The baby snuggled into him deeply, inhaling his scent. A small smile graced his lips as the baby fell asleep. Charlotte looked longingly at her mate, how proud she was to have him, to have him as a person. None of this was ever possible if it weren't without him.

"What should we name her?" Charlotte whispered. Wesley sat next to Charlotte on the bed and draped his arm across her back so she could confide in his warmth. "I'm not sure, what do you think?" Charlotte hummed while nuzzling up to Wesley.

"How about, Ember?" Wesley raised his eyebrows at the name, it was different. "It's beautiful, where did you hear such a name, Kitten?"

"It came to me," she whispered while Ember slept. "I think she will do great things in the future." Ember started to grunt and snuggle closer to her mother's voice. "I think you are right, Kitten. Any of our children you bear will hold great importance."

Erik came running into the hospital room as quietly as he could. He popped his little three-year-old head up and stared at the baby before him. "Is this Niece? Niece is pwetty!" Astrid and Odin walked into the room; the now large room seemed a bit smaller as the whole family surrounded the bed. All eyes were on Charlotte and baby Ember.

"She is the sweetest thing. This is the first girl in many generations for Wesley's side of the family," Astrid cooed. "Yes, this will go down as a great mark in history for the Hales." He smiled with pride.

"Great job son," Odin slapped him on the back which earned a small growl. "Charlotte did the work; I just had the fun." All of them began to laugh as they all took turns holding baby Ember.

"Niece sweeps awot." Erik complained.

"You did too, Erik. It was rather boring the first month." Charlotte jokes. "And her name is Ember, not niece. She is your niece but that isn't her name."

"I like Niece," Erik pouted.

"Alright, time for the new mom and dad to get some rest," Odin laughed as he picked up Erik and sat him on top of his shoulders. Sleep well, you two. The fun is just starting."

Wesley and Charlotte basked in the darkness as Ember continued to sleep. Their little family felt complete, but Wesley often commented how he wouldn't mind a few more pups in the future. "Hold on there, I just popped out one, give me a break. How about one hundred years huh? Just like your parents?" Wesley scoffed.

"No, I want our children to grow up together, it was lonely sometimes." Charlotte nodded and let out a giggle. *"This picture-perfect family couldn't get any more perfect,"* she thought.

Printed in Great Britain
by Amazon

79538512R00234